Glossary

Ajanta – group of caves sculptured in erotic figures.

Aré – Hindi for 'What do you want?' or other challenging question.

babu – businessman, dealer, entrepreneur; often, a money-lender.

baksheesh – handout to a beggar; now also a bribe or payoff.

bahot theek hai – Hindi for 'Everything is all right.'

Chandni Chowk – a main thoroughfare of Old Delhi.

charpoy – a low bed; usually on four short legs with a strung-rope mattress.

chowkidar – a night watchman.

chuprassi – a porter or messenger.

crore – ten million rupees.

desi – Hindi term of scorn for the uneducated.

dhoti – wrapping worn by Indian male.

ghat – Hindu funeral pyre.

Gandhijikijai – Hindi for 'My heart is for Gandhi' or 'I serve Gandhi'; slogan of the Gandhi movement.

godown – warehouse.

Grant Road – red-light district of Bombay.

Harijan – Hindi for Untouchables.

havildar – an armed forces rank; Sergeant.

ji – Hindi diminutive denoting respect and affection.

Jumna – one of India's great rivers, rising in the foothills of the Himalayas and skirting both Old and New Delhi. It is known for its treacherous currents.

khitmatgar – houseman or butler.

lakh – one hundred thousand rupees.

lathis – private 'law enforcement' groups for hire; usually, service pensioners.

Lok Sabha – lower house of Parliament; from *lok*, 'the people', and *sabha*, 'house or chamber'.

maidan – communal land; pasture.

namaste – traditional Indian greeting, palms together, hands to forehead.

pagri – turban-like headdress.

For SuSu

My wife, all-pervasive peacemaker,
calmant extraordinary, cordon bleu
manqué, and the best reason for
writing this, her book.

R.L.L.

Chapter 1

Prem Naran knew himself to be lucky, because the Guru had told him so, that Saturday. In strict terms, if you are told, quietly, by that authority, you are a lucky one, and nothing will get in your way that you cannot smash, or dissolve, or otherwise dispose of, should you argue or make a question?

You are looking at your Guru, your master of the past ten years. His eyes still seem as if he bathed them in strong tea, and the iris is one circle after another of blue rings, pale blue out, deep blue inside, but you could look only at one at a time, and if you tried to look at both in a slide of the eyes, they seemed to change colour, to green, even to red, and you are feeling great fright.

'Yes,' the Guru said. 'No question, you are a lucky one. Sometimes in the stars there are peculiar combinations. Or in the stored riches of men and women. As they live. We can never be certain if this child is to be a Gandhi, or a sweeper. Gandhi was a fool. He was shot as a fool. He brought the people to his own furious level. What was it? Ridiculous. What has happened since? Confusion. Nothing. Money is everything. Without it? Nothing. Gandhijikijai!'

Prem held up the right hand.

'Guruji,' he said. 'The four personalities? Can I make?'

'Three, yes,' the Guru said, quietly. 'The fourth needs far more reading. When did you think of the fourth one? The moment of his birth is important. Of course. As important as the rest. He could destroy all of them. And you. Did you think of that?'

Without answering, recognising the truth, he counted out

7

the money, added two thousand rupees, and bowed, hands to forehead, went out, pulled the bicycle from the hedge, and bumped down the Chandni Chowk to Lok Sabha, a long noisy way, but he had so much to think. Noise was friendly companion. He put the bicycle behind the office, and took the steps up to the corridor, and went in the big office on the left.

'Mr Vishnai is looking for you,' Mawri, assistant messenger, shouted over typewriter clack. 'It's important!'

Prem half-ran down the corridor's circle to Archives, and Mr Vishnai's office. From here came all the orders from the Prime Minister and most of the Cabinet. He knocked, and waited.

Baljit, Mr Vishnai's secretary, opened the door, and Mr Vishnai saw him from the further office.

'Come here, my good fellow, quickly!' he called, and held up a long envelope. 'Find the Minister as soon as possible. He is to digest this report and be at the Prime Minister's residence at nine o'clock tonight with his observations. *Don't* say you can't find him. There seems to be a good deal of colour coming out of this. It looks to me like blood. Corruption in the police? Who could believe it?'

He crowed as a bantam cock, and Baljit laughed, going to the door, giving him the heavy messenger's leather wallet with the brass insignia.

'We telephoned everywhere,' she said. 'Those we could get. No use. He could be at a club, or with friends, or in a bar. Who is to tell? But find him!'

'Yes,' Vishnai said. 'His hands *only*. No delivery by another. You personally. Understand?'

Prem raised his right hand in salute, and trotted back to the office.

'Out the rest of the night,' he told Mawri. 'Got to find this one. His hand, *only*. Don't forget to pick up the mail, and don't leave till you hear from me!'

'Suppose you aren't getting through?' Mawri shouted behind.

'Eight-thirty you can go,' Prem said, into the roof, and ran for the bicycle, and a short ride over to the Secretariat.

The head doorman showed in the register that the Minister had left an hour before. The suite was shut. The secretaries had been gone some time, by the side door.

'He's driving his own car, so he'll probably come back

later, if you want to wait,' the doorman said. 'A day and night worker, him.'

Prem tapped the heavy leather wallet.

'I'll be back in an hour,' he said. 'He's wanted by the Prime Minister.'

'No rest for the sinful,' the doorman said, and tucked in a loose whisker. 'If I see him, I'll tell. He should write where he is going to be. The driver always does.'

'Then he didn't want anybody to know, eh?' Prem said. 'One of the embassies?'

'There are more than a hundred,' the doorman said, turning the sad Sikh eyes. 'If you get more than five telephone numbers in the next two hours, I will pay gold from my own sadly scraped savings!'

'Which way did the old monkey go?' Prem asked.

The doorman pointed down the Mall.

'Right,' he said. 'Into the city. An official car would be noticed, hm?'

Prem looked down the long width.

'I will have to get my brains busy,' he told the air, and the Sikh nodded. 'Where would he go? In his own car? Not an embassy. A club? Too early. A bar? For an unofficial meeting? It's often done. But a private car has no authority, or promise of ministerial favour It has the taste of dim values, and back streets, no favours, and also, even the underhand. The Minister is not in office long, and not much known about him, no time for any staff gossip. No rumours. His home state has pinned him as one to go his own way without by-your-leaves. Everyone knows he was expert at sacking half a department. That's been done!'

The Sikh nodded the khaki turban in agreement.

Prem knew too well if that envelope was not in those hands only, and long before nine o'clock, his future was holding more than a vestige of doubt.

'Where, first?' the Sikh asked. 'You got great choice!'

Prem thought of the Guru, and the nature of luck. He tried to recall those tea-stained eyes, and sent a thought, and tried to hold it all the way down, but often he was remembering something else and it seemed impossible to control what he wanted to think, and he supposed that only saintly ones, living apart in ashes, and wearing ash-smears to proclaim poverty, yes, only they had the right to make their minds do as they wished. But then, was the mind a sort of tool, to be

9

used apart, as a hammer, or a kind of key? What used it? Who? Was he two people? Or, as he wanted to be, four? But if he was pushed in the use of one mind and that one his own, how would he use four more? Perhaps that was what the Guru meant. He had to go back and ask the proper questions. With the right amount of money. Prem Naran, a messenger, supposedly, had small wages to draw, even after twenty-two years of service. But then, nobody knew what else he did, even the Guru. *He* only knew that one, Prem Naran, wished to become four other men, all different, and he was giving lovely and wise advice about three of them, and jibbing only a little about the fourth.

But only Prem Naran knew that he had been three other men, and himself, for almost sixteen years. Nobody else had a small notion.

He turned the roundabout, cursing a scooter-cab that almost hit him, and woke to find himself near the Mashoba Hotel, and turned in, taking the wallet off his shoulder. It was a passport anywhere, and he was known. The doorman saluted.

'I have to find this one,' Prem said, holding up the envelope.

The doorman shook his head, looking away.

'Not here,' he said. 'Not the past week!'

He was lying. He had been bought. Prem knew it in a heartburst.

The eyes of the Guru seemed to light the garden.

But he nodded, and turned back for the cab rank.

He strolled through the waiting cars, swinging the wallet, nodding to the drivers he knew from seeing them so many times at the House. At the end of the line, he saw Kulwant Singh, a driver of long years, cleaning the car.

'Seen this one?' he asked, showing the envelope.

'He's new?' Kulwant Singh said, and nodded. 'Drives an Aston-Martin? Blue? He was at the Janpath not long ago. But he took a cab to Maiden's, then to American Express in Connaught Place. From the back door, then a cab here. To the side door. Yes!'

Memory gave the doorman's lying eyes, two dead coins on a dirty plate.

He gave Kulwant the note, enough to buy many other favours, and walked through to the reception desk. He wasted time. He knew them all and all of them had the eyes of a secret withheld, and words would never pry it loose. Money had been there.

'I know you are all busy,' he said, to the girl receptionist, a pretty one, in a green sari. 'Two of our members stayed here, and they lost shirts at the laundry. They are enquiring, and I've got the job. As if I didn't have enough to do!'

'Poor man,' she said, smiling. 'Go up to the housekeeper. Down there. Anybody will tell you where it is. No satisfaction, come back here!'

That was all he wanted. A reason for being in the hotel. The Minister clearly had a lot of them in his hand, and everybody had to be careful of a Minister.

And so, he reminded himself, had Prem Naran.

He found a nice girl assistant housekeeper, and told the story of the shirts.

'Always they are losing shirts!' she said. 'Always, always they are losing. Shirts. Handkerchiefs. Everything. Thieves!'

He wrote the names off the top of his neck, and she copied them into a book.

'If they are there, they will be found, or payment in satisfaction,' she said. 'Anything more?'

In a quick movement he held up the envelope, with a forefinger on the seal.

'You see,' he said. 'This man *must* have this. You see where it comes from? Where is he?'

Her eyes looked, her cheeks crinkled fat, her mouth went in a wide slit, and she held up her hands to the shoulders, open fingered.

'How shall I say?' she whispered.

'If you want the police here, very well,' he said. 'I must deliver these orders. If not, it becomes your responsibility!'

'No!' she almost shrieked. 'I can't lose my place, you know it?'

'Why should you?' he said. 'Tell me where he is. You stay here. Nobody will know. Even me. Tear up the piece of paper I have written. Who will know I was here? Who will know you spoke to me? Or I to you? What's the number?'

She wrote on a laundry tag.

'You can't say I told you,' she said, almost crying. 'Along here, and to the left. Watch the floor men. Sweepers, valets. They might be something more!'

'So might I,' he said, and gave her two notes. 'Here. Forget we have a face. Till next time. Is there a woman in this?'

She smiled down at the notes, and nodded, and he tenderly patted a quivering backside and knew he had her whenever he wanted, and went down the corridor, so quiet in green carpet, and along to the room. Three men squatted in the corridor, pretending not to see him. But when he stopped at the door, they all got up. They were in hotel uniform. The DO NOT DISTURB light shone orange.

'Aré?' one of them questioned.

'Keep your distance,' he said loudly, and thumped the door, and pressed the button. 'I want the Minister!'

They stood back, uncertain.

He fisted the door to rattle, and pressed the button a long thumb-thrust.

There was a move on the other side. The lock snapped.

He waited. The men went back, a step at a time.

The door opened.

An old woman, with long white plaits, looked out.

'The Minister, only,' he said, holding out the envelope. 'Prime Minister's orders!'

She nodded, no alarm, and shut the door.

Moments, and the door opened, and she nodded him in, and shut and locked, and went to sit on a carpet.

'Well?' the voice said, behind.

The Minister, in a long white gown, looking angry.

'The Prime Minister's office,' Prem said, a little lost, and held out the envelope, with a slip to sign, and a pencil.

'How did you find me?' the Minister said, signing, and in no good mood.

'Luck,' Prem said, a flash, daring. 'Only luck. The Prime Minister's house, tonight, nine o'clock –'

'I can read,' the Minister said, reading. 'Be at my office tomorrow, ten o'clock. Here. You did well!'

A bundle of notes. Not good manners to count. Good enough.

He saw the handbag, black crocodile, three big gold initials, E.E.D.

Ha?

Edila Emi Dowl.

Principal private secretary. Top rank. United Nations. Moscow. London. Translator. Everything. And beautiful. Anglo-Indian? Who is caring? Seven languages. Cash. Jewels. Gifts. A woman.

He looked on the floor.

12

The Minister held out the receipt.

'My office, ten o'clock,' he said. 'No argument. *Be* there. Go!'

The tone, the contempt for underlings, for Harijan, Prem knew well, but both could be put to good, sensible use. A little time, the opportunity, and the profit would be sweet.

He could wait.

He put hands to forehead, and the old woman opened the door. The men were still there, pretending not to see him, and he went down the corridor to the stair taking his time. He waited a few minutes to see the Minister leave the lift, and hurry down to the side door, and out, and took the lift, still sweet with the Minister's cologne, and went up to the fourth floor. The men had gone. He knocked, and rang. There was space of time. He knocked.

The door opened, and white plaits looked up at him.

'Nobody,' she said. 'Everybody gone!'

The bag was still there.

'I need the address of the Minister,' he said. 'It is important. There is no time or place on this receipt!'

He said it loudly, so that waiting ears might fill.

'Let him in, Vutthi,' a woman's voice, soft with despair, from the other room.

He went in, she shut the door, gathered the sari between her legs, and sat.

E.E.D. came in, brushing gold hair to the waist, wearing a long pale-glow of raw blue silk. Beauty. Fragrance. Fierce grey eyes glistening. Angry? Half-swallowed sex?

'How dare you come here?' she whispered, still brushing, and about the same sound. 'I shall talk to the Minister!'

'I am on Prime Minister's orders,' he said, and held up the receipt. 'I must go back to the House, and present this receipt to the Chief of Archives. Therefore, where is the address of the Minister's house? I will never find by telephone. He *must* sign!'

'And if I refuse, you will speak of this,' she said, still brushing.

'I never speak,' he said. 'I am many years not speaking. I have no mouth!'

'I wish I could believe it,' she said, and put down the brush. 'I'll give you the address.'

He gave her the pencil, and she wrote, and held out the slip.

13

'There,' she said. 'Is that all?'

'Except that I wish to see you,' he said. 'I mean, *see* you. Nothing else. Just look at you. How many times do I find such a woman? You are a delight of Krishna. May I not share manly visions? Not touch. Never. I don't like another man's woman. But I love her beauty. It fills me!'

The eyes were grey, alight, truly fierce.

'I can make your life such a filthy misery!' she said, and turned her back. 'You'll lose everything, job, pension, character, nothing will be left except suicide!'

He waited.

'I don't know why such bastards as you are born!' she whispered. 'You make a disgust of everything. Anything beautiful becomes a heaping of cowdung!'

'I only want to *see* you,' he said. 'Nothing else. I have *told* you. *See*. Not touch!'

She raised her arms in a wide what-can-I-do? at the picture of something Western on the wall above the bed, and pulled apart the belt.

'If you so much as come one inch nearer, I'll scream the place down, and I don't care what happens!' she whispered. 'I don't *care*. Here!'

The robe slipped down.

She breathed the dreams of another life. Only a Minister could afford her. She held the marvels of Ajanta. But white, white as buffalo cream in early morning, almost with the fresh of steam warmth. He made a circular turn of a forefinger, and she turned towards him, slowly, in a dancer's wave of the arms and hands, and her eyes, looking at him over her shoulder, told him that she was not so angry as she might have wanted to sound.

'You are the most wonderful woman I have ever seen!' he said. 'It's enough. Thank you!'

'Enough?' she said, and turned full, and he saw that her love-moss was not gold, but black, and long, and braided in little plaits, tied with black velvet ribbon in small bows, of a secret beauty that sent his head in a silly spin.

'Enough for this time,' he said. 'Always two or three times a month. Yes, I shall keep you in a secret temple of my mind. Always filled with lotus and other lovely flowers. You will be a Shiva. Who can touch Shiva? Only worship, nothing else. Two or three times a month. Or more. As you wish. But you will call *me*. I shall never call you!'

'Call you?' she whispered, in a brilliant, smiling, angry, haughty frown. 'Call *you*? I?'

'Yes,' he said, nodding at white plaits, still squatting beside the door. 'She can always find me. Without a telephone. Or notes. Remember. I have *the* one, you see?'

He held up the address.

'The Minister's address in your handwriting,' he said. 'And many witnesses, here, in the hotel. Two or three times a month I will worship Shiva. I sprinkle blossom!'

He went to the door, and silver plaits opened for him, holding a white length.

'You will always find me,' he told her, and she nodded, and he went out.

He knew she was Harijan.

Untouchable.

She also knew he was Harijan.

The link was strong.

It could never be broken.

Both, he knew, were eternally sure.

Shiva danced in her temple, white, with braided black love-moss.

He knew many thousands more Harijan, and they, many thousands also.

Among many thousands is help for many more thousands of thousands.

Walking down the corridor, he almost sang.

But at the office, a shock.

'Be careful,' Mawri said, showing a sheet of orders. 'That one, in this Ministry, is perhaps going? You know which one?'

Prem saw in the head of the paper.

'Make a new list of all Ministries,' he said. 'Ministers and secretaries. One and one. Or else we will have confusion of papers. Who is to get what. More important, we have the names of the secretaries. We make no mistakes. This is not the place to make mistakes. We have to be right. Make the list. I want it tomorrow. How can we work not knowing who is who?'

'It will be done, Premji!'

'Also, complete description of secretaries. Who, families, school, how introduced. Who put them in position. Why is this Minister going? To another Ministry?'

Mawri pulled down his mouth.

15

'Perhaps he can do better? Or if he does worse, it will be easier to throw him out? And throw mud on his party? Who knows about politics? They are all the same. What is in your pocket will soon be in mine. Isn't it so?'

'It is true. Make that list. I want it tomorrow. I want to know if his secretary is going with him. Or where she is going. Which department. I want to know!'

Mawri nodded.

'Very well, Premji,' he said. 'I will find!'

Chapter 2

At the office of Vishnai, Baljit's delighted 'O, you *found* him!' more than repaid the long ride back, but there was better reason in Mawri's message, propped on the lunch box, 'Go quick, the Disco. Urgent ! ! !'

He ran down the dark corridor, checked mail-boxes, made sure doors were locked, and out, to the end of the car park, snapping finger-and-thumb at Bedwa, lying in the old blue truck piled high with the day's thrown-out paper and envelopes taken from the waste-baskets of both Houses. Putting them into a tank with Malwan Khan's liquid from the chemist shop behind the Chowk took all the writing off them, and Riba stripped them carefully, and laid them to dry flat, and packed them in twenty-five sheets, or twelve envelopes, and sold them for a third of the ordinary price to schoolies, and businessmen, and letter writers. Nobody could tell they had been used, and if pages were embossed or printed in difficult inks, they could be cut off on the guillotine he bought for three packets of cigarettes from Hari Chand when he sold the camera shop because he was a fool to drop bad heroin to tourists for big prices, and the police picked him up at a time when he had no money for the special reason he had to pay thousands for his daughter's marriage to a graduate of Lucknow University, such a catch, eight years out of work, and asthma.

Riba was still packing pages when they turned into the yard. She wanted to run to make tea but he waved her down. More than an hour unloaded the truck, and he counted the previous day's work in packets of pages and envelopes, and took the money, and paid out their share, and they bowed, hands to forehead, in respect of a benefactor, and he knew he was, because all the salesmen made a good living, and Bedwa and Riba made far more than they could have done as sweepers, if they had been lucky enough to have the job, but they would never have had enough money to buy the official. As themselves, among their own, they were rich people, and they had high standing, only because of Prem Naran, and the truck.

'Now you will take me to the Disco,' he told Bedwa. 'Wait in the usual place. There may be trouble. I am not sure. In any case, there is no trouble for you. Eyes open!'

Bedwa put hands to forehead, and went out to the truck, and he followed all along the way, looking at the noisy night scene, sad that he had not had a bath. Without water, life had no wonder, and a body had no juice.

The place was in full jam with tourists and golden people with only enjoyment to do. Slop Disco took the froth from the beer glasses. Champagne was rare, except at the back in the Sludge. Beer, yes, it was not, out front. It was never Coke, only what Malwan Khan made in that long shed behind the Chowk, that he sold in big jars as Oky-Coky, at a small price, and Prem sold it by the thousand dozens to more than five hundred outlets every day. Others had tried to break in, but he had teams of pensioner lathis always spoiling to break a head or burn a place down, and it was well known, though nobody opened a mouth. It could be shut.

Zona stood at the office door. She missed nothing. In a raised chin she called him, and went inside. He had to climb about chairs, almost over people, and the music never stopped and the drums could dizzy the head. There happened only quiet when she shut the heavy door, and slipped the lever.

'Look at that, will you, there?' she said, in the Goanese English. 'The load of yesterday. Gone more than half, and paper instead. Does he think I am mad, that Padchand?'

Prem sorted out a few cigarette cartons, pulling at the stuffing, slapping it flat. They were all notices printed in Hindi giving festival dates, and the closing of departments on certain days.

'How many in all?' he asked. 'What sort of cigarettes?'

'American, of course, and fifty-two cartons, and a few

more packets,' she said, and shook her bangles in a wriggle of fingers. 'All these years, the first case of thieving. I thought you are blaming me. I had to call, mh?'

'No blame,' he said, and put some of the papers in his pocket, taking out the notes, counting. 'We are straight, and fifty-two more cartons tomorrow. Open and make sure we are straight. Not the value of one packet comes between us. Yes?'

He felt the small hand pressing along his thigh, and gently bent away.

'Not now,' he said, looking at the cartons. 'I have a call. Lessons must be impressed, I have no doubt, with a modicum of suffering?'

He liked saying it. Mr Raybould always said it at school when the boys were hoisted on the porter's back to have the cane across the rump. It could have been this morning. The sting was still burning.

He saw fright in her eyes, and she shuddered, because she knew.

The back way was easiest, and he half ran to find the truck. Bedwa put on the lights, and started.

'Get the lathis,' he said. 'Meet me at the house of Padchand. Soon!'

He went out in the road and found a motor-scooter, sitting back, feeling hungry, but most, wanting a bath. Padchand's house had been jerry-built inside the Fort, against the west wall, in warrens of stalls. He wondered when he saw the dark windows. In the cloth shop next door, the owner measured sari lengths looking green in strip-lights.

'Padchand? O, yes!' he said. 'He is transferred. A fine job in Bombay. A higher appointment. The wife and children are staying in Patna till he finds a house. An important man. I am missing a good friend. But if we are serious, we must always go up, no? Of course. Of *course*!'

Prem waited for the truck. He bought a betel chew from a hawker and leaned in shadow against the wall, enjoying the plump taste. Evidently the money he had paid to Padchand for the cigarettes, and the stolen cigarettes sold to somebody else, a nice sum, would pay for out-of-pocket for the move. But dear friend Padchand, colleague of so many years, and willing provider of sales from bonded stores and every sort of contraband against ready money down, whether in Delhi or Bombay, there is always a lesson to be learned that is never wasted. In your first-class air-conditioned coach, and about now, after your dinner, also air-conditioned, and enjoying your toothpick, make ready for the destroyer's rage, for Kali's vengeance. Dear sir, prepare your head.

The truck came to the paving. He took out notes and gave them to the lathi squad, two each, and three to Bedwa.

'No work tonight,' he said. 'Take me to Malwan Khan!'

The lathi squad got out, ten of them, and hands to forehead, went into the bazaar lights, gone.

Malwan Khan's sheds were still in clatter of work. Everything was made there, complexion creams, shampoos, soaps, aphrodisiacs, nerve pills, vitamins, Oky-Coky, and, of course, rotgut, and a promising line in animal fattener. Malwan pointed to the big machine and signed he had to watch, and Prem went into the main office, and to another, and a long corridor, and at the end, a small place with a desk and chair, and no paper anywhere, but three telephones. They were all connected with the main switchboard, one for Delhi calls, one Delhi to Bombay, and the other to Calcutta, and if there was delay it was weather, or fools trying to bring down the social order with bombs. He had only spit and contempt for such. There had to be a social order strictly kept. Only with that, people could have a living, and work, and pay each other.

He got on to Das in Bombay, and waited, listening to the sound of voices going all that way in bubbles, and then a shout.

'Das?' he said. 'Prem!'

'O, Prem. I am here. Tell me!'

'Listen carefully to me. A *bisth* cobra is coming, first-class, air-conditioned. The name is Padchand. You can call down the line, and get his carriage and compartment. He travelled yesterday, first-class, air-conditioned because Government. He is transfer from Delhi to Bombay. Higher office. In cigarettes and alcohol, and French perfume, and radios, cassettes, is there more need?'

'None. Padchand? You know the trains are several hours slow. Thousands are sitting on the tracks. They are hungry, and no money. The trains will be late, you know?'

'I hear. There will be more time to assemble your delegation of welcome!'

'Ha!'

'You will not allow him from the station until he has paid

you, cash, for five hundred cartons of American cigarettes
he stole from me – '

'Ha!'

'Ha. If he has not the cash, tip him, strip him, break one
leg only, and lovingly and carefully take him to the hospital,
and leave him on the steps. Let him enjoy his medical benefits. He is a senior servant, of course?'

'Of course. It will cost him nothing!'

'You will then visit, with suitable flowers, to ask for the
money. You will be a son. Only a soft voice and sweet, sonly
smile. It is all. You want the money.'

'It is all?'

'No. It is not all. Why should you be put to trouble, and
all your good boys? Are you to have nothing from this vulture? Stealing from me, and me having to appeal to my
friends? Is this a friend? Tell me what is just in this?'

'Nothing just. Nothing!'

'You see? We agree. When you have got my cigarette
money, and sent it to me, without service or rebate, then you
will visit again, with flowers, as a dear son, and you ask for
a sum commensurate with your services, and his position. If
he feigns any ignorance, you should mention, with such delicacy, that he has another leg, and again he can enjoy his
Government medical benefits. Nothing it costs him. He
should also be reminded that he has a twelve-year-old, and a
ten-year-old daughter on the tip, the very edge, of good
marriages. He could find them on the other side of the bars
in Grant Road in a few months. At ten rupees a time, they
could find many clients – '

'I would be first!'

'Simply say. We want no importunities. If you have to
strip him, and take his luggage, send all the paper here. All
sums, fifty-fifty. As always?'

'Always. It's all?'

'It is it. Good-night?'

Malwan Khan came in, wiping his hands, and sat down,
taking a cigarette, and lighting, in a deep breath, and blowing. Watching other people smoke, Prem often felt he should
not. They looked, and sounded, so disgusting.

'We are ready to market G, H, I and J,' Malwan Khan
said, coughing in a deep lungful. 'I have got five thousand
ready of each. Where, first?'

'South,' Prem said. 'We shall know the result. If it is bad, it won't harm here. If it is good, we have word-of-mouth praise. Of course. Quarter pages in the newspapers. If good. If not, no. But it's time for rhinoceros horn?'

'Time, but too little,' Malwan said, and pulled the little beard. 'I must have more!'

'I shall find it,' Prem said. 'Does it help?'

'If you think so, of course,' Malwan said. 'If you have a worn-out cock, how will rhinoceros horn, or anything else, help you? If you have got a cock, you have got a cock, man. If you have not, try a bloody splint. Just as good!'

'Why doesn't a girl buy rhinoceros horn?' Prem asked. 'Don't they feel they need anything?'

Malwan coughed, opening his arms.

'Such a question?' he said. 'They have got a hole. Put something in. Have they got anything to raise? Except price? Who knows the difference between one hole and another? But I have got some ginseng for you. It is secret. You can sell for thousands. Try it?'

'I am not a needer,' Prem said. 'When I am, I shall run to you. Now, let me make sure. There are no drugs of any sort here? Liquid or powder?'

'None. I will not *have*. Didn't I tell you?'

Prem got up, stretching.

'There will be big police raids soon,' he said. 'They are being investigated for selling drugs. Themselves. From stocks they captured. You are bound to be among the first. Clean up everywhere. Warn your people. My name will not be mentioned. Where did you put it?'

'In the laundry place at the Lady Weddesley's School. It is safe!'

Prem nodded at the bare light. He saw, and heard, other things.

'Good,' he said. 'Well, now I'm off for a bath. At last!'

'Ha!' Malwan said. 'To New Place? How fortunate you are to live in blessed luxuriance. I am only a scientist and chemist. I cannot aspire to such hedonism. I am enslaved by a poverty I am only struggling against. There is no hope of success!'

Prem turned his back.

'Except in the first months we worked, have you had less than two lakhs on every last day, and often five and seven?' Prem asked. 'You are less than satisfied? Shall I leave you?

Will you try to bring your own salesmen? You would lose my outlets, transport – '

Malwan got up, and laughing, bending over his shoulder as if scorning.

'Ah, Prem!' he said, pulling a last lungful, and coughing. 'Of course not. It is true I have had the lakhs. But how could I bank? I could be instantly taxed a fortune. Why should I be taken in foolishness?'

'But you could buy a house?'

'The building inspector would be there with continually open hands. I will live in humble poverty in my dark little house, never less than thanking you for such wonderful and wholesale co-operation in my business of such wretchedness!'

'A bath, and my wife will massage my feet,' Prem said. 'And listen to me. No business is wretched that brings two partners minimum four lakhs a month, and more. Equally divided. To the rupee. Think, and remember!'

He shut the door, and only pretended to stroll down the corridor, through the sheds, and over the yard to Bedwa.

'Go to the Lady Weddesley's School,' he said. 'Hide the truck. See who is there. Go to the laundry place. See if you can find our blue box. Take it home. Hide it. If not, come to New Place. *With* the lathis!'

He saw Bedwa go, and took a scootercab among the stench of traffic, across the city to New Place.

Once it had been new, one of the residential palaces begun by the Raj, but never finished because of Independence, and still a skeleton except on the ground floor, lived in by hundreds of Harijan families until the monsoon rained them out. Prem's three rooms on the ground floor were kept for himself and his wife, married at the age of five, and still with him, a songbird even though his children had died at birth. After the sixth, the American woman doctor had told him, 'Now just you listen here. She's torn to bits. Leave her alone, will you? Lay off!' And the anger in the strong voice was like ice in a drink, and he left her alone, and Prahash said nothing, then or after.

The scootercab bounced over the wide space in front, tipped side to side by cracks in the concrete, and mounds of human and cattle dung, and he could smell it burning in the heaps beyond the house, and in between the puff-cheek blow of the night wind, there was smell from the ghats, not far

23

away, and the corpses burning, and a whiff of sandalwood, and a cloy of joss, and cooking aroma, a mix of tumeric and cumin, and sometimes the smite of a family currybowl, all taken immediately in the long blow of the warm night wind. But then the winking stink of the ghats came again, sly, with a digging finger, to remind that one day somebody would smell the burning meat and bones of the body he thought of as his. It was a question he had never been able to puzzle. Such good feelings, and firm warmth, frying on logs? It made fools of priests and philosophers, but of the Guru, he was not sure.

He went into the small place built of cinderblocks, finding his front door across a floor heaped with human ordure, and reached, to knock on the glass. His wife was there, blurred in the opaque, and she opened, and he stepped over the mounds, toed off his shoes, and went in. She knelt, and began to undress him, and he took off his shirt.

It was always the same, night after night. Undress, bath, while she ran gentle hands with soap, the shower, a pat of hot towels, the rose oil, and clean clothes, a seat on the mattress, and the plates of food. The cook on the Howrah Express had sold him two fat peahens, young, for a carton of cigarettes, and she nursed them into a dish for a maharaj. While he took the crumbs of the jalabi from his fingers, he smiled to hear the trucks bumping over the cracks outside.

'Go into your room and shut the door,' he said. 'This is the police. Have no fear. They will have nothing!'

Boots kicked the door, and Prem walked to open it. but slowly.

Inspector Ram smiled, brows up, a why-am-I-here? parody.

'Routine inquiry,' he said. 'I only want to see that you have nothing on the premises. Information was laid, you understand?'

'Please,' Prem said, with an open hand. 'My wife is next door.'

'We shall disturb her for only moments. I have a warrant.'

'I shall report to the Minister tomorrow,' Prem said, sitting on a chair in the corner, because they would certainly search the mattress. 'What is the allegation, or suspicion?'

'Contraband, drugs, theft, receiver of stolen goods, hawker of false passports, dealings in illicit currency, and crime against the State, too many to tell!' the Inspector laughed and turned to the squad. 'It is a clean house. Take your boots off. Search!'

Prem felt the veins in his face pulled down as stretched gut, watching a trained team – not ordinary constables – turning over every piece, passing a loop of buzzing metal over the floors and walls, opening the mattress, tapping the legs of the tables, turning the photographs and pictures, going to the bathroom to pry up the floor, emptying the water tanks, bringing Prahash from the bedroom, taking it all to pieces, and going out in teams to search the rest of the building. All the families were outside, still, in deepening darkness, with always a stink-fat reminder of the ghat, and the drums thudding, one now, and another more.

Inspector Ram came in and slapped a long leg with a cane.

'Nothing,' he said, still smiling. 'I am glad. We have been to your office. Nothing. Prem, for a man in your position, with such a reputation, you are too pure. It is suspicious!'

'What is the suspicion?'

'That you deal in many ways. Of course? A living must be earned. What is living without profit? Where were you going to find it? Except from others wanting profit?'

He heard the truck squeaking over the concrete.

He seemed to take his face between both hands, and smother.

Bedwa knocked, stepped over the mounds, and stood in the doorway.

'Sahabji,' he whispered, looking first at the Inspector, and then at his feet. 'I have got the laundry. But it is damp.'

'Search!' the Inspector shouted outside. 'What is in there, I want to know!'

A lot of movement outside, lights, and the Inspector pulled Bedwa into a corner, and pointed a finger to keep him there. A sergeant came to the door with a package, torn open, with shirttails hanging down.

'Nothing, sir,' the sergeant said. 'We let out the tyres. Nothing, anywhere!'

'Too smart!' the Inspector said, laughing. 'Good. But we shall keep an eye on you. And our foot on you. I hope you are careful!'

Prem turned his back, and heard them go, and picked up the torn parcel.

'Only three in the laundry,' Bedwa said. 'Not yours!'

'Take it back,' Prem said. 'You did well. Let us go to

25

Malwan. You go to the school and put back this laundry. Not mine. Bring the lathis to Malwan. Unless you see me, don't go in!'

Bedwa went away, and Prahash put her head dearly on his shoulder.

'No harm,' she whispered. 'Please, no harm?'

'For you, none,' he said. 'Sleep with music!'

He went out to the back for a shovel, and scraped a path through the ordure, and put on his shoes, and walked out to the boy in the scootercab.

'You have been patient, and hungry,' he said. 'You will feel reward in the palm of your hand. Go to Malwan Khan. I am not here. You are not. You know nothing of Malwan Khan. You have an old scootercab. You would like one new? Did you ever see me?'

The boy smiled, shaking his head.

'Thousands I am seeing every day,' he said. 'Why am I seeing you? When shall the new one come?'

'Be at Lok Sabha tomorrow afternoon,' Prem said. 'Main entrance. Three o'clock. What did I say?'

'I heard only the drums,' the boy said, and kicked the starter, waiting, and turning out, to the stinkcrash of motors and the ratscreech of brakes on the roundabouts, and the graceful insults in girls' voices of drivers saying out loud what only the thought would make dirty.

'Dirt is always in the mind,' the Guru said. 'Cleanse yourself. You have a brass pot to wash your body of interior dirt? Keep another for your mind. Use it!'

He saw the eyes, rings of pale and dark blue, changing to the advertising sign, and touched the boy to slow down, keep out of direct lights, find a way through small lanes of stalls, to the other side of Malwan Khan's sheds. Shadows still moved at work. He tapped the seat to stop, and got out, and the boy shut the motor. The blue truck was not there, or hiding. Just then Bedwa came, no higher than a child, from behind a cloth stall, and turned his head, and went back towards the shed's greenish light, and the lathis followed, and became part of the dark.

Prem went into the shed's space, puddled with fat scourings from the complexion cream mixers, and looked for the sad, sullen face of Ghal, always tired, always in half a yawn, always pointing to somebody else, or running to a machine, any excuse not to talk, not to say he was Malwan's only assistant, a graduate in chemistry, but earning no more than Malwan would pay, about a twentieth of his worth in wages alone, but at least five times more than he would earn outside as a Harijin.

'Ghal,' he shouted, in the stink of boiling fat. 'Where are you?'

He came from the room piled to the roof with cream jars, and tubes, and packaging, and stood, staring, tired, not part, not wanting.

'Listen, now,' Prem said. 'There will be changes from to-night. Can you take charge here? All departments? Without advice or supervision? Of any kind?'

Ghal nodded. Nothing changed in his eyes.

'I am in charge now,' he said, and swallowed a yawn. 'What difference?'

'You will be responsible. To me. Your salary is ten times. From tonight. All profits, monthly, split half, to the rupee. We speak between four eyes. Remember. I also have other friends!'

He looked towards the tall line of lathis in shadow beyond the doorway.

'I have no mouth,' Ghal said, in light, as though other thoughts burned.

'Work tonight and tomorrow as if no change was, except that all the people here will earn five times more,' Prem said. 'Have you seen me?'

'I have never seen you!'

'Did you hear words?'

'I hear the machines!'

They put hands together, and bowed, hands to forehead, and Prem went out, with Bedwa, and the lathis behind.

'Malwan Khan's house,' he said. 'Ten times ordinary rate for the lathis. He will go in the Jumna. Look for buried money. Do not touch his woman and children. Let them take all they want, and burn the house. But save the paper. For me!'

Chapter 3

'Prem, we have spoken for almost thirty minutes and you have told me nothing, and I want to know *why*!' the Minister said, from the window, back to the room. 'You understand me? I want to *know*!'

Prem bowed low, hands to forehead.

'If I knew what the Ministerji wanted to know, I would tell,' he said, above a whisper. 'So far, questions about the police. In my lowly place I know them. By their names. But talking, or going home, or any small friendship? Impossible, as I have said. How possible?'

'It could be flogged out of you?'

'If it is not in my mouth, how is it in my body?'

'A flogging is not pleasant!'

'I would find it in my lowly duty to accept to be flogged, if it would assure the Ministerji that I am Prem Naran, humble and faithful and smallest and most devoted servant!'

'I could take away your position?'

'To crush the ant from its way? What is any ant?'

'You don't speak as a messenger, or a porter,' the Minister said, pushing the curtain aside. 'Are you a member of a political party?'

'I have no party, Ministerji. I shall never have. I know politicians. I have no vote. I have no wish. Why should I?'

The Minister looked at the file on the desk.

'You were pupil of the Lord Reading School for three years,' he said. 'After, at the Normal in Lucknow. Then the Rajagopalachari at Vaipur. Why all the chopping and changing?'

'I was an orphan. My father – I called him – Mr Raybould. Where he went to teach, I went to learn. He put me in here as a runner. He died. I became junior messenger. I earned promotion. I have always served. Truly. As he taught. He was a wonderful man. To me. To everybody. If I meet a Raybould boy now, we think of him. O, yes, we cry!'

'He was against Independence?'

'He was persecuted because he *supported* the Gandhi–Nehru–Maulvi Pasha movement. How many times he was in prison? How many English wore the Gandhi cap? How many wove their own? He did. I did. And how many wear them today? Or weave their own?'

'No necessity,' the Minister said. 'What we wanted, we were given. How many railway officials do you know?'

'We send many consignments to Government Offices and State Legislature,' Prem said, keeping heat from his voice. 'I know them all. All transport. All lines. All timetables. All officials. Railways. Roads. Air. Everybody. Anywhere. I don't need a book. Why should I? For these years, I am here. Every day I hear the times, when, how, what, how much. Should I neglect my job?'

'You are well taught,' the Minister said, looking at a corner of the desk.

'I was first always in English. Then mathematics, and bookkeeping. Then business, and organisation.'

'You were very young,' the Minister said, looking in the other room, at E.E.D., in a black sari, a marvel of quiet.

'If the tree has sap it will rise. Make sure of the sap. It is the juice!'

'It seems to me that you could be useful,' the Minister said. 'I could crush you in a moment. Remember that. I shall think. There may be small jobs you can perform. I shall consider. Where is the Mashoba?'

'I have heard of it from others, Ministerji. I have never been there. It is far beyond my small place. I have said I have no mouth?'

'Go,' the Minister said, and fell, not sat, in his big black leather chair. 'I shall call you!'

Prem went out, low from the waist, both hands to forehead, though in reaching the far door, he passed close to E.E.D.'s desk, and he took the small, warm, sandalled foot, and pressed, and it stayed in his hand, and he exulted, and opened the door, and stood in the corridor, and breathed hard, thinking of the Guru, and Mr Raybould, and himself, but there seemed no real link.

He cycled back to the office, and made short work of mail collections, and filling members' boxes with letters and notices, and then watching the sweeper empty the waste baskets ready for Bedwa. The Houses were in recess, but the staff were still busy, and the drafting clerks worked almost day and night, trying to build paragraphs in English, and then Hindi, and every word an argument of shaken fists, a cat-fight in each comma, riots over a full stop.

He wanted to push them all out and do both by himself, without one single bead on the brow. They were all lawyers or failed B.A.s and they haggled for the sake, only to prove how profound their knowledge of legalities, what scholarship in languages, how many saints on a pin's head, what number of tones in the length of the sitar. The foolishness, Mr Raybould often said, of urbs. Every second they are having to make sure they are themselves by knowing. They know, therefore they are. They do not know, they are not. They are burning constantly on the ghats of fear, leaping in their frightfat, spitting sour little globs of tension, and covering with courteous behaviour, a skin that an argument will tear, provoking screams, pouts, refusals to speak, and then flowers, and exaggerations of sorrow. But still the ghats burn.

At ten to three the gate havildar called to report a waiting scootercab. Prem collected mail and registered packets, and got in, and the boy started, and stopped at the main mail office. Prem got receipts for the packages, dropped the mail, and walked out.

'Such a small time for such a lot!' the boy said.

'They know who I am. I don't have any queuing to do!'

'My sister has to wait for many hours every day. To weigh the letters. Then to buy the stamps. Then to make sure the weight and the stamps are both correct. Hours she is waiting. She could burn everything. But what can she do? Where would she find another job?'

'She speaks English?'

'Who gets work without English?'

'What does she do? How old?'

'Twenty-four. A secretary. Firebird Insurance.'

'What tribe or sect is your father?'

'Of the tribe of tyre repairers. Of the sect of the hungry.

30

It is what my sister says. Who speaks of this? We say we are Maronites. She went to school with them. What other way?'

From the boy's back, he saw, and heard.

They were of the Great Family.

'How much do you pay for this scooter per day or week?' Prem asked, and pointed to the turn. 'Here. Go to Dal's.'

'I pay for petrol, and I give my father half of the fares,' the boy said. 'I give my mother one half of mine. My father got it in a traffic wreck. His friends in the market repaired it. We all stole pieces –'

'Where did you get the licence?'

The boy laughed.

'I have not got one,' he said. 'If I am stopped, I pay. What can I do?'

'You must have one. How can you drive decently if you are stopped by any policeman? I shall get it.'

'You are son of Krishna?'

'We are brothers. Enough. Wait here. Keep a look for me, steady!'

He went in the wide doors of the showroom, and Dal saw him through the plate glass of his office, and swung bare feet high off the desk, and came, fat, big, laughing, black.

'O, Prem, my both eyes and ears!' he shouted, and threw out his arms to embrace, but the turning police trucks outside brought a dance out of the way.

'Bedwa brought the box?' he whispered.

Dal nodded, staring, aware.

'Where is it?'

'In a tool chest in the garage outside. Why?'

'Get it for me. No time. Go!'

Dal turned on heelless slippers, heavy, ponderous, and the mauve underlip quivered in a thickness like liver, but he moved swift as a scorpion, out to the big garage at the back. Prem made a movement of the hand on the window to catch the boy's eye, and pointed to the back. The scootercab started, and he ran to the garage in time to see Dal lift the blue box out in a clatter of tools.

'Give it to the boy!' he whispered. 'Tell him to hide it and come back here. Quick!'

He pointed to Dal, and signed the boy to take the box, and go, and waved again to come back.

He ran into the showroom, and lounged against the door

of Dal's office, watching the police trucks stop on the driveway. Inspector Ram got out, stretching, tapping the cane in the other hand, smiling the up-brows-why-am-I-here? parody.

'Well, Prem?' he said, a nice fellow. 'What are you doing here?'

'I am waiting to go to Wenger's for a cup of coffee with my friend, Mr Dal,' Prem said. 'Please join us!'

'Ah, but there is duty, you see?' Inspector Ram said, a serious man. 'We were late in the traffic. The scootercab is very useful for dodging. What did you bring?'

'Myself, only!'

'Why did you come?'

'For a coffee, as I have said, and to collect forms, for licences.'

'Nothing else?'

'Nothing.'

Inspector Ram turned, and nodded, and the police ran, six to each new car, and took them to pieces, down to the wheels, but Dal had come back, smoking a little cigar in a smile, and sat on a small table. As fast as the police finished, his own men ran and put the cars together, so that when the police went in the garage, all the cars were as they had been, and the big showroom settled almost in a sigh with the silence of wealth.

'I want to search the office,' Inspector Ram said. 'Especially the safe!'

Dal threw the keys on the table.

'I shall want to see your warrant,' he said. 'Many ministers use the garage. We are all free men. This is not a police state!'

Inspector Ram drew a long orange sheet from a side pocket.

'Read it,' he said.

'I'll keep it,' Dal said. 'I have many friends among the magistrates!'

'I *want* that!' Inspector Ram said, holding out a hand.

Dal took the telephone, and dialled.

'I am calling my lawyer,' he said, laughing the fat smile, full of goodwill. 'He will put a mongoose up your arse, my friend!'

Inspector Ram gave the keys to somebody in a shirt and shorts.

'Open up,' he said. 'Everything!'

'Hullo?' Dal said, all lilt and light. 'Is the chief magistrate there? O, yes. Please say Chan Dal, the enfranchised agent for most American, British and European cars would like to speak in legal terms. I have a police enquiry here. There is a question. You will send? Ah, I shall wait!'

'Please take your time until the lawyer is here,' he told the Inspector. 'We shall find out which country we are in. Yours, or mine!'

'Is there a difference?' the Inspector said, turning to watch the safe opened, and not caring. 'We shall hear what the lawyer has to say!'

The safe door opened, and the two men pulled out papers, and rattled out drawers, and another took the box with the metal loop that buzzed, and went over the walls.

Nothing.

They turned to the Inspector and looked their blankness.

He slapped the cane on his leg, and stood, jerked his head, and they all went out.

'You are not staying?' Dal called.

'What, me?' the Inspector said, without turning. 'Why should I waste my time? But you should be warned!'

'You see?' Dal said, watching them climb in the trucks. 'If there is a military takeover here, look for me against the wall!'

'It can happen?' Prem asked, jolted.

The fat underlipping shook side to side as a water buffalo's dewlaps.

'Look at outside,' Dal said, waving a large, dimpled hand. 'Look at the papers. You have the right job. You hear nothing?'

'I have no ears,' Prem said.

'Let us all be as wise. Here is your boy. Where did he put the box?'

'Wherever it is safe. How much?'

'Let us meet in the Sludge,' Dal said. 'Have you a figure?'

'It is pure. No adulterate. Not less than two crores. Shall we speak, or shall I listen to other offers?'

'Now, Prem. You have *no* other offers!'

'Then I shall accept the offer of three crores? Any hesitation I construe as refusal. I shall offer you the next batch!'

'Ah, Prem, but you are unjust!'

'I am a man of business, dear Dal. Because we were in school, does it mean I have your feet to lick when you are wanting? No. I take the offer of three crores. The next time,

3   33

the same quantity is five crores. Finish. Where is the scooter-cab?'

Dal raised his chin to a corner of the showroom. He showed himself in a bad mood.

'It is the only one. I will sell it to you if the package comes to me!'

'Five crores!'

'I will sell that model only for *two* crores. There is only one of its kind. If you want it!'

'And so I have three crores for the package, cash, *and* the scootercab? *Done!*'

Dal put his chin in his hands, and closed his eyes.

'Always you win,' he said, in mud.

'If I had told the Inspector to look behind for the second safe, would I be a friend?'

'How do you know there is a second?' Dal said, upright, in a startle. 'You know?'

'We've had one in the office for the past ten years,' Prem said, in pretended disgust. 'Go back to sleep. You only worry little girls. Where is the scootercab?'

Dal led into the showroom, left, to an alcove, and waved a hand.

The beautiful new thing gleamed, a glory of matte black, with a shining engine of silver, and a lovely black hood, and a cab in black leather, and all with a new smell, seeming to say I am Power. I am Ganesh. I am Maharaj of Elephant Strength.

'It is something quite new,' Dal said. 'It is my idea. You like?'

'Let me see what the boy says,' Prem said. 'He will know. Call him!'

A man shouted, and the boy padded in a run, stopping in the arch, thready blue shirt, dhoti not clean, dusty feet in wrinkled plastic slippers, swinging the crash helmet, looking about as in a strange temple of many new terrors.

He turned to Prem, and his eyes bloomed upon the scooter-cab, and the helmet stopped swinging.

With a downward motion of the hand, Prem waved him nearer.

'Very well,' he said, loud in a silence of glass walls. 'Do you think you could ride it? Try!'

The boy slipped off the sandals and went, slowly, a sleep-walker, to the platform, and stood, as in worship, and a hand

34

went out to the pillion, and another to the handlebars, in caress, and he stepped up, and got on the saddle, sitting, staring at the wall, a small one, in presence of all hope.

'You are comfortable?' Prem asked.

The boy nodded.

'You could drive it?'

Nod.

'Remembering I have first call,' Prem said. 'As I promised, it is yours. Come. Let us get the licences. Over here!'

'Off the platform and in the garage,' Dal told his men. 'Fill, check the oil, start his book. Only here he will deal. Petrol, oil, spares, maintenance, only here!'

The boy came through the men slowly, and in a step of Prem, dropped the helmet, and knelt, and crawled to kiss his feet, and the tears broke sharp, spotting the floor, and Prem caught the shoulders, and pulled the boy up, shaking him, trying to look him in the eye.

'I promised,' he said, quietly. 'Why is it something for tears?'

'You *are* the son of Krishna,' the boy choked. 'I will serve you beyond death. Only call!'

'Fill out the forms on Mr Dal's desk,' Prem said, turning the shaken shoulders towards the office. 'Every detail, *truthfully*. One hesitation, one less than fact, only *one* untruth, and you are the dust of the streets as you were before. Understand?'

The boy nodded, wiped tears with thumbs, and went in the office, and Dal's clerk gave him a pen.

'You must be *mad*!' Dal whispered. 'You are giving such an *urchin* this?'

'*Giving*?' Prem said. 'If we think to Mr Raybould, what are *we*? Only urchins?'

Dal looked away, at traffic beyond the windows, no sound.

'We made our way,' he said. 'As he told. Put *yourself* in a *position*. No?'

'Of course,' Prem said. 'Be very tranquil. Through this boy, in three months, I will control all traffic, and not only in Delhi. I will give this boy his head. You see?'

'What's his name?' Dal asked. 'Who has heard of him?'

'I don't know his name, and nobody has heard of him,' Prem said. 'Who *heard* of us? Who knew *our* names? Before we took the names from Mr Raybould? This boy is with *us*. Of the Great Family!'

Dal groaned in depth of closed eyes. His shirt had opened. In that black balloon, a teapot could have nestled in the yawning navel.

'I'm hungry,' he said. 'I shall cook something. If I have such shocks, always I am hungry. I am like a baby for the teat. I have got a fat kid. I will cook him. For us?'

'Not for me,' Prem said. 'First I must go to the Licence Office. Then back to work. The boy will not take the machine until he has the licence in his name. We are co-guarantors. No argument. You owe me three crores. Cash, the day after tomorrow. Another consignment on Saturday. It is almost forty kilos. In the streets worth fifty million dollars, pure. How they sell, adulterated, two hundred and more millions.'

'You should go to New York,' Dal said.

'Everlastingly, no,' Prem said, everlastingly sure. 'Here, I know my source. Source is my only strength. Here, I control. There, I am at mercy. Of every dirty twister. Dirty twisters are here, yes? But I can cure.'

'I hear Malwan Khan had some unexpected luck,' Dal said.

'We should all expect the unexpected if we try to make ridiculous people of our friends,' Prem said. 'Malwan made a great deal. He was a dirty old miser. Not even a decent *babu*. At least they provide money. Stiff interest? Well? But people can live, deal, sell, buy. Malwan held his money. Starved his family. His *family*. Think!'

'An unhappy one,' Dal said. 'Before I forget. I spoke of the Sludge? Why don't you *do* something?'

'Something, what?'

'Talk to Zona, of course? The girls in there are not what is expected. With champagne? Such a cost? At least, let us be provided with the best. At those prices. Why not? I could bring my own girls, so much better!'

'If you have got girls, why go to the Sludge?'

'It has a pull. After all, girls, yes, six or eight, but forty, fifty, sixty? Tell her quality has fallen off!'

'Off?'

'Do you expect to deceive me in the matter of girls? Why did we all go to the Sludge? Girls, of course. They were the queens of their kind. Marvellous. Every kind. Today? Bengalis. Starvers. Anything from the farms. Their fathers can't make a living? Send the girls to make money. But in the Sludge? At such prices? Who wants the rake from Muzar-

36

fanagar? A ribrack from Jhansi? How do we know they are clean? There's cholera everywhere.'

'Wait,' Prem said. 'I will see to it. How long has it been?'

'Two months,' Dal said. 'I think. The last time it was like crawling through a lot of broompoles and sweeper's brushes. After all, we are looking for the beauty of woman, aren't we? Hiding ourselves in the flesh? Do we require bones? There used to be Europeans and Somalis and Ethiopians, and tall girls, and Americans, and Turks and Greeks. Now? Straw. At those prices, straw? Who pays willingly for champagne and straw?'

Prem widened nostrils in a breath.

'I shall see to it,' he said. 'What is your information?'

'Somebody interferes,' Dal said. 'I think you should put your finger between Zona's eyes. She knows who is worrying her. Who is threatening?'

Prem looked at traffic silent through the windows.

'I shall find out,' he said. 'Have no doubt. The day after tomorrow, cash?'

'I have not got the box. When?'

'Now!'

The boy came, with the forms, held between two fingers at the top, two at the foot, proudly, as a charter.

'Good,' Prem said. 'Your name is Gond? Very well. Mr Dal will sign. I will sign. Then we will go to the Licensing Office, and they will seal. You will have a licence for the new scootercab, and one for the old. You will be free. Who will work the old?'

'My younger brother,' Gond said. 'Shall I pay my father?'

'Not one paisa. He let you go without a licence, and took your money? Nothing. Pay your mother. Your brother will also pay her. Nothing to your father. You have ears?'

'They hear. When shall I come here to sit in my own place?'

'When the licence is sealed. Leave the old scootercab here. Let them look it over. Give it a coat. It will come out new for your younger brother. For two days you are on your feet. Go to the Disco. And the Sludge. Watch both the back doors, you and your brother. Never leave until Zona locks up. If she does not, who does? Follow her, follow him. Come to me at One-One. Yes?'

Both hands to forehead, Gond bowed low.

'Good!' Prem said. 'Come. The Licensing Office!'

37

Chapter 4

Prem cycled at lunch time over to the tyre market, a place of stalls and ragged canvas and thousands living and working in dust, to re-cap tyres for sale at a tenth of the original price. Only the best workmen made a fat living and stayed in work, because if truckers bought sets of re-capped tyres, and they stripped in the road, the buyers went back to break heads and burn. Gond's father had a big place, with the equipment behind, and many men to help. A lot of work went on, thirty-eight tyres he counted while he waited, but he could hear the tools beyond, and a good generator fed the power, so the old one was not of the impoverished, and lying in the small tent on a red charpoy he looked to be a raj on his own. And drunk, and taking a gulp from the gourd on the floor, no deception, because a bottle tells, though a good gourd does not, but a man's eyes tell quicker than all.

He knew he had nothing to do or say, and he cycled back to the Disco, and went downstairs in the empty, humid space, smelling of dust after the sweepers had raised the rolling clouds, and lifted a hand to the barmen cleaning glasses, and tapped on the door.

Zona opened, and shut behind, and sat against the desk. Mujid, the accountant, went on adding the book and his spectacles sparked as diamonds, and the junior barman filled a basket with the night's stock, and the air conditioner hummed its raga.

'What is wrong?' he asked.

'Let us go to Wenger's for coffee,' she said, and took the handbag. He followed her into the darkness, and heat, up the

38

stairs to fresh heat of sunshine, and along the circle to Wenger's, shaking his head at boys trying to sell dried cobra, and flawed silk squares, and trays of other rubbish.

'The police have been twice,' she said, looking ahead. 'They are not being paid?'

'Of course,' he said. 'Always. Who told you?'

'Mujid. He was in early. Then they came while I was taking stock. The Inspector said there was something with the licence. Oh, a lot of things. Mujid wants to leave. He said it is unsafe. The barmen want to go. The business is going to fall in wreck!'

'Why?'

'Somebody is not liking?'

'Who?'

She shrugged in the doorway.

'You know how many would like that business? You know how much they see falling in the bank?'

'Who is it?'

She sat down, drying her underlids on a tissue.

'Many. But I think the top is Rada. He is always complaining. The air condition isn't right. The loudspeakers don't work. His music is made to sound out of tune. He is the star of broadcasting, but he is made to howl like somebody only this moment from Muttra? I asked him why he doesn't bring his own electricians. He said I could be found on the roadside. Without a tooth!'

'Witness? Somebody heard him?'

'No. It was in the bar. With all the noise!'

Her shoulders were up and down, and she felt for the handkerchief.

'I'm frightened!' she whispered. 'He has so many friends. Police, everybody. He will break me like a peanut shell. Shall I cover my teeth? Two boots, he said. How shall I find myself?'

Prem ordered the coffee.

'I want you to go back and take charge in the same way. No difference. Except that tonight the new band will come at seven o'clock instead of eight. You will pay them the same. They are as good. If Rada makes a noise, there will be help. We are both hearing?'

'Hearing. But I don't want to lose Mujid. He is a strong one!'

'He will stay. Well, Barud?'

The assistant barman came from the waist.

'The police are there,' he whispered, over the chair. 'They want the licences, accounts, customer dockets. Everything!'

'Give them all they want,' he told Zona. 'To the last piece of paper. It is only honest. Everything paid, to the paisa. Play their own game!'

She got up to go, and turned.

'And my teeth?' she said.

'I will take the best care,' he said. 'The *very* best!'

He sat for a few minutes. A threat to a man was nothing. He could take his chance, or go. But to a girl, so helpless physically, no, and to threaten her teeth with a couple of boots, no.

It was a cold *no*. Apart from that, she worked for him. She would be difficult to replace. But how to defend her, that was a true puzzle. And how to defend Disco? And the Sludge? They were naked, and Mujid was right. The place was unsafe. A petrol bomb, a chemical bomb, a few sticks of something, all easy to get, or make. A police raid, court appearance, remands, inquiries, weeks, months, difficult.

He cycled down to Dal's, and found Gond on the concrete of the garage, looking up at Ganesh, ready, except for plates and the licence. His other machine was stripped for painting, and new upholstery.

'You know the musician, Rada?' he asked, looking down the avenue.

Gond nodded in a sideways turn of the head.

'You know where he lives?'

Slight sideways turn of the head.

'I would like you to take your scooterboy friends there. Take all the musical instruments. It is supposed to be the finest collection in India. Take the gold. Jade, ivory, carpets. Everything except the furniture. Except. If there are thrones. Or charpoys in lacquer. Everything out. How?'

'My father's friend has a quiet truck,' Gond said. 'Rada's place is quiet at the back.'

'I will have the lathis there.'

'No lathis. They have big feet. What else?'

'Where will you put everything?'

'I will tell you. It will never be found!'

'And payment?'

'I will come to you and tell you. Tonight?'

40

'As soon as you can. Tomorrow you come with me for the licence in your name, and your brother's, and the plates!'

Gond slid his fingers over Prem's ankles, a kiss of devotion, and Prem went out to the cycle.

But he still had to make sure of Zona's teeth. He left the cycle in the usual place, and told Darva, the head sweeper, to warn Bedwa he wanted to talk.

The office was at peace. Never mind what the papers said, the office was always at peace. Nothing happened in the office. Everything happened in the country. In the office, nothing. It was always quiet, beautiful, as if lotus stuffed the air. He went out to collect the mail, and in the Assistant Secretary's office, Baljit sent him in to the big desk.

'Well, Prem, good fellow,' Vishnaiji said, blotting another signature. 'We are hearing some pretty news. You are going up. You will be giddy with promotion. The Minister must have taken a tall fancy. What is this? How did you do it? Such a short space? Have you given him a potion?'

'I am the lowest,' Prem said. 'Why should I have promotion at this time? Where could I be promoted?'

'Well, to ministerial thingamagig and factotum,' the Assistant Secretary said. 'Where the Ministers could deal with you direct instead of down here. You would deal only with me. Of course, consultatively. Always. You would therefore consider a gift? I, cigars. My secretary, perfume. Baljit is a girl, of course. And you have Office Number Eleven. You know it? *Eleven?*'

'Number Nineteen, Chanel!' Baljit called, from next door. 'But a *big* bottle!'

'Let me hear,' Prem said. 'They will be on the desk. But I have heard nothing!'

'Wait for tomorrow!' Vishnaiji shouted, in a laugh. 'It is also back-dated!'

Prem walked out almost drunk, pretending the lurch due to the weight of the mailbag. But he knew that in the small office, around the circular corridor, unused for many years, there hummed the hot breath of power, real power, not of ministers and signatures and rubber stamps shaking the panes, but of people, a hub, humming, wanting and getting.

A word in that office, and it was done. His word, and any service was possible.

But he knew he must sell the Disco and the Sludge and all the other, lesser byblows. They must go because they

41

were a weakness, open to Inspector Ram and his kind. Not that there was anything criminal. All the papers were in order. No debts sullied the books. Presents were given on time, down to the last Customs agent and control clerk. But he could not deliver himself to the Inspector Rams by being blind or greedy. If pressure went on, in the new position, he was only a squirrel to be shot at. At the moment, he was a senior messenger and the various businesses might be looked on as highly commendable essays in initiative by a lowly one.

In that new, unlikely, most wished-for office, he was no longer lowly, and the daily inflow of unseen money would be many times the takings of his businesses even over weeks. It was idle and senseless to burden himself with what might destroy. One minor conviction in any court, and he was useless to the Ministers, and finished elsewhere, even, he knew, where he was, as senior messenger.

He took the cycle from behind the office, and went over to Dal's, walked in to the office, tore a small piece of paper from the salespad, and wrote a figure, keeping the chit in his palm. Dal was used to it. He said no word, mumbled a little, spat, folded a betel and chewed, and went deeper in the chair. But all the time the eyes were aware, dark, almost in shining mudpats.

'I am told I am going to other places,' Prem said. 'No longer messenger. My own office, A clearing house. For many ministers. You follow?'

'Follow!'

'I want to sell Disco and the Sludge. I can still handle alcohol and cigarettes. Although, they are always available. I am always able to supervise and guarantee supplies. With nothing to do in the daily running. I am not there. I am unknown.'

A motor outside on the bench *spat!* and stopped, started, and *spat!* and stopped.

A fly sang his small song, and got caught in the fan, *plup!*-ting! a nice sound for death.

'How much, everything?' Dal asked, without moving.

Prem showed the paper in his palm.

'Reasonable,' he said.

Dal put his jowl in his hand and looked away.

'You take nothing out,' he said, to the traffic. 'That price is both places, stores, behind locked doors, all in? And you guarantee supplies? How?'

Prem smiled.

'I have got the right desk,' he said. 'The *only* desk!'

Dal got up, and took the paper, looked at it, and tore it up.

'I will take,' he said, 'Cash?'

'Of course. Why not?'

'Where do you put it? Which bank?'

'My bank? Am I such a fool to open an account for more than my wages?'

Dal laughed with his belly. It jumped up and down.

'I don't want your people,' he said. 'I put in mine.'

'Good,' Prem said. 'Tonight we are closed. Tomorrow if you wish. You are the owner. You are the one to say. The cash, when?'

'Tomorrow, this time, with the three crores. I will have here three big cartons. They will smell only soap. How will you take it away? It could be stolen?'

'Not my way,' Prem said. 'Tomorrow, this time?'

He went to the Disco, and left the bicycle outside the bank, and went downstairs, but the door was locked, and no rattling brought it open. He ran up, and round the back, but both doors were shut, and the garbage had gone, with all the bottles. Both doors stared, shut, yellow-flaked, mute.

Something was wrong. He felt it between his legs.

He went to the bank, but both the tellers shook their heads. Zona had not paid in. The account stood at the total of the day before.

He strolled out in Connaught Place, looking across the green, listening to the noise. He could go to Zona's house or to Mujid's, but that would be giving any watcher a link.

The boy selling dried snakes came nearer.

'Gond told me to stay here,' he said, to nobody. 'If I saw you, to say Wenger's!'

Prem gave him a note.

'Stay here,' he said. 'Eyes open. We help each other. Who else helps?'

He strolled along to Wenger's, into the pastry shop, and downstairs, and sat at a table in half darkness. Many were there. He knew none. A waiter took his order for coffee.

Zona, from nowhere, sat opposite.

'A terrible time,' she whispered. 'Rada has gone mad. He is in hospital. All his instruments are stolen. Everything. He has nothing. He came down here. A lunatic. But even the instruments at the Sludge? Gone. All stolen. Poor man. Poor,

43

poor boy. What a horror. So the police came in to look, but there was nothing. Mujid said it would be wise to lock up. So I did. Was I right? Do you blame me?'

'Nothing else to do,' he said. 'You still have your teeth?'

She put a hand over her mouth. Her eyes seemed to see another world.

She sat back, gathered the handbag in her lap, and smiled, nodding.

'I think I know,' she said.

'Good. Tonight we don't open. Tomorrow I am no longer the owner. You will work for me. Not in my name. You don't know me. You will take a small office. Modern. I will meet you here, tomorrow, three o'clock. We will settle details then. You work for me. Find the office. Let me know tomorrow?'

'I have nothing to do with the Disco or the Sludge?'

'Nothing. Give the keys to Mr Dal at the Dal Showroom. You work for me. Enough?'

'Enough. I'm so happy. For my teeth!'

He waited until she had gone, and cycled back to the office, and sighed, to know the peace. Everything was in order. Nothing was going to hell. All was in tight control. It was a nice feeling. He took Mawri with him to slot the members' mail and newsprint. All the boxes were jammed full, and many they took out, and put back in better order. There seemed a sterner idea of service.

'They have so much to do,' Prem said. 'Not like us. Do they stuff boxes with mail? Who are we? Do these waste a thought on such nonsense? It is why we must serve them. You see?'

'They could pay us more,' Mawri said. 'Everybody is growling!'

'Let them,' Prem said, and stopped to look at him. 'For everyone in a job here, there are ten times ten thousand waiting outside to step in and work for even less. You know that?'

'Of course!'

'Of course? Then how can you listen to nonsense? It is low level foolishness. Never allow it to be said near you. Don't forget those words can be made to fit your mouth. How long would you be here?'

Mawri frowned in positive terror.

'O, but no, I didn't say it. They said to me!'

44

'You listen to brush-gossip? Sweeper's chat? What is your position, here? Have you no sense of who you are? What is your dignity? Be careful you are not picked out as a trouble-maker. You will be thrown to the hyaenas! You know there are informers everywhere. Where is your common sense?'

Mawri put an index across his throat.

'Silence is golden!' he whispered, eyes up. 'If anyone comes near, I will kick!'

Bedwa raised dust outside, waiting with two parcels, and just beyond, Vutthi's white braids shone in half dark. He took the two parcels, and went across to Vutthi.

'A quarter to eight, here, back entrance,' she whispered, giving him a paper. 'I will meet!'

He nodded, and she went through the bushes.

'Gond is waiting at the truck,' Bedwa said. 'Not good!'

He went over where the sweepers were stacking papers. Gond came from the darkness.

'Inspector was two times at Dal's,' he said. 'The first time asking what he knew of you, and he said only he knew you at school. The second time he asked about the Disco. Dal said he knew nothing. Then the robbery at Rada's place, and Dal got angry and telephoned his lawyer. Inspector told his men outside he would throw both of you in chains one day!'

'Let us see,' Prem said. 'Be at Dal's tomorrow with another boy. Take old scootercab. Three-thirty. Seripur. You know it?'

A sideways nod.

'I will give you the address. The day after, be here nine o'clock. I will get the licences and plates. I would like to know about the Inspector. He is an enemy. Where does he live? Who are his women?'

A sideways nod, a white, quiet laugh of teeth, and gone.

He went in, and along to the Assistant Secretary's office, and knocked.

Baljit opened the door, and he gave her the parcels, and smiled in a low head, and went back to the office to finish work.

He wrote in the register, and tallied postal totals, and checked receipts, and while he reached for the messenger's file, the light went on overhead, and the bell *clashed!* and the Assistant Secretary was calling him, and he ran.

'You made the jump!' Vishnaiji said, waving sheets of paper. 'From nothing and nowhere to Grade Two. You see?

45

A little while, nothing in our lives, you will be Grade One. It could *not* have been done without a big shoulder on the ministerial level. And a little help here, perhaps? Your cigars were superlative. The perfume was a royal remuneration. Please sign here, twice, and as last act of your office, take them to Personnel. Tomorrow you have your own office. You know it? Take the keys from Security. They expect you. I look forward to a long, happy, and remunerative association. To say the least!'

He went out feeling drunk, and Baljit pinched his arm and his waist when she opened the door. He turned to her, and gently pinched the right breast, at any other time not in realm of thought, but she smiled and stayed there, and he knew, and shut the door.

He took the short way to Security, and the havildar gave him the two small keys, one for the door, and one for the safe, and he signed the book, and ran down, and stood outside the door many long moments of fragrance, thinking of all the kindly people, and all their smiles that had brought him there, and he knew he must repay.

He opened and walked in, switched on the light, and blessed the head sweeper for being busy.

Years before he had looked into the office. One light showed several broken chairs thrown in a corner, some bottles, a heap of paper, a broken waste basket, and dust.

Speckless, that, in all fact, was what he saw.

Shining with polish. The walls had been washed clean, not a spot. Two bluish strip lights shone, and he knew that behind that desk he would appear as a blue god. He knew that the days of half-sleeve shirts and any old trousers were past. A black suit, good white shirts, black or grey ties, and shining black shoes, yes. Wearing a Nehru frock might seem to copy the ministers. He intended to start quietly, in order.

First the head sweeper would have a robust gift.

He tried the telephone on the floor. It was live. He dialled Gobind's, the outfitters and bespoke tailor, and asked for Gobind, himself. He supplied uniforms for the Disco and the Sludge.

'I shall be with you in thirty minutes,' he said. 'I want four good suits for myself, to measure, and a dozen white shirts, to measure, and six pairs of black shoes, to measure, and I want the first suit and shirt and pair of shoes to-morrow. I have a new position. Possible?'

46

'We shall be waiting, Premji. We have always known you would rise!'

Premji!

He felt drunk.

But drunkards must be careful. He unlocked the safe. It was an empty green box.

He locked the door and looked at the polished wood, with a round, not square top, that made it the only door of its kind in the building.

He thought of the Guru, and sent love, and spread love all about, on both sides of the door, with especial provision for all inside. Slowly he walked back to his old desk, that was only part of the long general counter.

Everybody had gone.

It was better.

They had feared him always. He had known from the first day. He was put in by favour. Nobody knew whose favour. Therefore they had to be careful, and the days, weeks, months passed, and still nobody knew which hand rested on his head, and slowly, he made his way through their fear until they knew he was one of them. The night of the famous staff meeting had set seal. They were all ready to strike, or carry the black flags.

'We are paid less than the porters of third class hotels,' he told the Minister, in the empty place of silence, down there, where thousands squatted. 'Are we servants of less than third class? Are the members of both Houses less than third class? Do we give members the used towels of the one next door? Do they sleep in the sheets of the couple of three nights ago? Two nights ago? Last night? Do they sleep in the eggs of the careless? Are these, the representatives of our nation, to be treated with such abandon of disgust? Do we, respectable men, loyal men, devoted men, tolerate such insult? We wish, we want, we *will* be paid at a rate which raises us from whoreshops –'

The minutes-long shout was still in his ears, and the stiff pay increase in all grades followed.

Everybody knew.

He tidied his part of the desk for the last time, and made it a cruise of love. For all those years he had been there, building, always, building, but something interfered with thought.

Bedwa scratched on the window.

He put out all the lights except the night watchman's, and found the head sweeper sitting on the steps.

'I want a good rug in that office,' he said, passing a note. 'I want the floor always polished. Many Ministers are not coming back. Take a good red rug out of any office. It won't be missed. Tomorrow I will have new furniture. *Polish.* There is no window? Wash the walls. I leave it to you!'

He got in the truck and told Bedwa to go to Gobind's, and after, to the address Vutthi gave him.

'I think you need the lathis there,' Bedwa said, looking at the road. 'It is known she is under strong guard. She is woman of the Minister?'

'Stop!' he said. 'Very well. I will go to Gobind's, and then to New Place in scootercab. You take a few lathis to that address and find out what you can. See me at One-One tomorrow. Noon. Ask for me in Number Eleven. It is the most pleasantly important in the entire building. The whole nonsense. And here is a present for you. And ask Vutthi what she is doing, sucking me into ruin. Is that what she wants? What have I done to her?'

'I will have a strict answer,' Bedwa said. 'Here is a scootercab. Good-night, Premji!'

Chapter 5

In the new black Gobind suit, and the white Gobind shirt, and the grey tie, and the black shoes, he went to the office before six o'clock next morning, and found the head sweeper surpassing any furthest wish. A fine red rug spread on the polished floor, and somebody had lost a wonderful desk, and a high, leather chair like the Minister's. Gold-framed pictures of Mahatma Gandhi behind the desk, Pandit Nehru on the right, and Rajagopalachari on the left, were squared with a smiling photograph of Mrs Indira Gandhi over the door. A new leather chair for a visitor, a table for papers, and a large glass ashtray, and the office was already humming, in fact, to his ears, roaring.

He stood in the doorway, and thought of the Guru, and breathed in every scrap of air, and all that came into his eyes. He breathed with his ears. He heard what was going to be said. He saw what was going to be done.

This little hub had always been a clearing house for ministerial paper. Whatever the Ministers wanted was got. What they did not want got expunged. If they wanted appointments, they were made. Others wanting appointments with them were served, at a price. Everything had a price. Nobody enquired. Whatever favour was got had a price. After all, if a man goes out of his way, there is a price. A favour is a favour, and they have a price, ranging from a favour in exchange for a favour, down to goods and chattels, or hard cash. But hard cash has to go through channels so that somebody is lost at one end, and nobody is seen at the other. There can be no trace. It is anonymous.

4

This office was the house of anonymity. No names were known. No single person was established, or recognised, or identified. Everything was paper, and if paper offended, it was destroyed, and so the head sweeper became an integral part of the staff. He was never far away. Called, he was in, out, and the offence was burned, never to be seen again, or witnessed, far less to be sworn to.

The telephone rang and petrified him. He took seconds to know that his – *his* – telephone was calling him in his own office.

But this was honour.

He leapt, gathered the receiver as a lost child.

'Prem Naran,' he whispered.

'Ah, I'm so glad!' A woman. 'I came in early especially. Come over now, will you? I have tea ready.'

E.E.D.

'Yes,' he said. 'Certainly. Of course. Office Two-Two-One, yes?'

'Which other?' she said, and put down.

He knew, then, that he must have Gond and Ganesh there all day, and every day. Cycling was over. Gobind suits and cycling, no. Office Number Eleven, and cycling, less.

He called Central, and asked for a taxi. Lucky. One was at the Secretariat on radio net. He had to be careful. They were also on the police net.

The cab was there before he knew, but he had time to slip a note to the head sweeper and see his serious, shut-eyed pleasure, and he was off. But he knew that Gond and Ganesh were the answer.

The doorman saluted him as a Minister, the security guards clipped heels, the head porter bowed him to the lift, and he was taken to the first floor by a havildar, and left, as the door opened, with a salute.

E.E.D., in a blue sari, could have come from a temple, a white fragrance.

'Well!' she said, clasping hands. 'What a swell we are!'

'I hoped you would like,' he said.

'Like?' she said, frowning, head forward. 'But you show the best possible judgement. Exactly what the Minister hoped. You are dressing the part without advice. It shows other facets of intelligence. They will all be needed. Is your telephoned tapped?'

'Possible?'

'Is this?'

'Possible. But after today, not. This, or mine!'

'Guarantee?'

'Take an oath!'

She smiled down on a red leather folder.

'The Minister was right,' she said. 'An unusual one. You *are*. I think so. Where were you last night?'

'I was warned there were some looking for me!'

She slipped her eyes to him.

'Who?' she whispered, worried.

'Police?'

'*Police?*'

'Or is the Minister worried?'

She laughed up, in silence.

'Perhaps,' she said, and gave him the red folder. 'Your first job. First test. It's dreadfully difficult. I told him I thought it unfair. But he insists either you are first class, first day, or nothing from then on. There is no learning in this business. That's what he says!'

'I am at one,' Prem said. 'Make a mess the first moment, make a bigger mess from then on!'

She tapped the folder with a beautiful finger and a shining pink nail.

'There are two beauties in there,' she said. 'Let me see how you deal with *them*, never mind the others!'

'I will deal,' he said, and stood. 'When shall I come to you without nonsense?'

'Resolve those two,' she said, looking at the folder. 'To-night, eight o'clock!'

She pulled the sari aside, and showed the breast.

'We are sealed,' she said. 'I like showing myself. Only if you solve those two!'

'I shall solve,' he said. 'If you show the rest that I worship!'

'I shouldn't,' she said, and stood, and threw off the sari in two wonderful movements, and she was Shiva, naked except for the bodice, and he looked, and head low, opened the door, and went out.

Downstairs, a police officer pointed to a seat in the jeep, and took him over to the office. He hurried through, seeing nothing, knowing that everybody saw him, and opened the door of Number Eleven as another warm home.

The two problems were money, of two ministers wanting

to borrow and not wanting anyone to know. They were nothing. Others were a little more troublesome only in a minor way. A son of one Minister and the daughter of another had failed examinations, and so forfeited rights to foreign scholarships. He settled both in two telephone calls with money to be delivered within twenty-four hours. The other matters were dust, and brushed aside.

He called in the communications chief, a small man, of long experience. At other times he might have knelt to such authority.

'This telephone is tapped,' he said, jabbing it with a pen. 'Take it off, or I will deal with you. You have two sons and a daughter at school? Be careful they stay there. Room Two-Two-One, across the road, is also tapped? Take it off. It is your only warning. Report to me before noon. We understand? Remember, I have ways of finding out!'

He slid across the desk the envelope which showed the edges of notes.

'Let me know,' he said. 'That's all!'

Just after eleven o'clock, a voice said there was no tap on the line, or on Two-Two-One.

He called E.E.D.'s number, and heard her voice in a rumble of the belly.

'There is reason I should see the Minister,' he said.

'He is waiting. Come, now?'

He went over in a car with somebody thinking him a ministerial personage, and hurried in to salutes, and somebody in the lift to take him up, and salute at the door.

'Well,' the Minister said. 'What have you to report?'

'Everything is done,' he said. 'There are no gross tieups. I find nothing here difficult!'

'The money,' the Minister said. 'Settled?'

'Settled. All that has to be done is sign the paper, place and date, verify the interest rate, date of repayment, capital and interest, and they receive the money. Or else they may dispose of favours. In which case, all debts are forgotten!'

'I knew I had chosen the right man,' the Minister said, looking through the folder. 'You restore my faith in human nature. You have the brains. And obviously, the ability. I want this money this afternoon!'

'At three o'clock, it will be here, Ministerji!'

'Where does it come from?'

'If you do not know, how can you say?'

'Reliable source?'

'My life is on it!'

'Very well. I think we are very happily met.'

He took a long envelope from the middle drawer and unfolded clipped pages.

'These are railway stations,' he said, pointing. 'Each one has a code name. I want you to learn the code names. All of these by heart. Only here, in this office. When you know them, this list will be destroyed. Miss Dowl will examine you when I have gone. Let us say three-fifteen, after I have the money? What is the code word for Jabalpur?'

Prem looked at the list.

'Ghanj,' he said. 'And our main is Bhoon, but the local is Vala!'

'You've got it,' the Minister said, 'I didn't know I had such luck. It depends on your memory. There are ninety-two stations. Can you get them all in your mind? Is your head so good?'

'By five o'clock I am code-perfect, Ministerji!'

'Miss Dowl will examine. You hear, Miss Dowl?'

'I hear, sir!'

The walk back in strong sun seemed to do him good, but his head was alive in wonder that such a good life had come to him really without asking. He went around the yard until he found the truck. Bedwa came from shelter in the bushes, with Gond behind.

'Go to Seripur,' he told Bedwa. 'Give Babuji this paper. Bring back money, well-wrapped cartons. Three only. As soon as possible. Say I shall be there about six this evening. With much more!'

Bedwa went off in the high salute, and Gond put both hands to forehead.

'You have the scootercab?'

A sideways nod to the back of the bushes.

'Ten minutes, we go to the licence office. Bring me back to Dal's. Put on the plates, and bring me here in Ganesh. You will be here all day from now. I will have my own transport and chauffeur, and I shall pay you weekly. Good?'

Gond raised a hand and eyes above.

'Ah, Premji, I shall serve so much!'

Two letters waited in the box, both from ministers, both wishing to see him privately and immediately. He called the secretaries, and set a time, and took Gond to the first.

'The Minister will see you,' the tall Anglo-Indian girl said. 'Please be as quick as possible. He's awfully busy!'

'If he is quicker, I shall be quickest,' he said. 'Am I told to tell the Minister to be quick?'

'You know what I mean!' she said, in a pout. 'Don't chatter on, that's all!'

'Come down to my office, and I will show *you* how to be quick,' he said, and went to the door, and knocked.

'Prem Naran, sir!'

The Minister, in white homespun, looked up from a pile of paper, and put down a gold pen.

'Ah, yes!' he said. 'I shall be obliged if you can relieve this department of an embarrassment. We have somehow become saddled with a lot of confiscated property. Various merchandise. We can't turn it over to anybody else. New laws have been passed. They prohibit sale by auction, or any other method. The matter cannot be publicised. You see the problem? By one means or another I want it sold, and the cash returned here, less, let us say, twenty per cent?'

'I shall do my best, Ministerji. How much is it worth?'

'The accountant seemed to think about ten crores, knock-down prices. But there must be no names. No publicity. I shall deny any connection!'

'Where is the consignment?'

'It is all lodged in a departmental godown at Bombay. Miss Turlo, outside, will give you a discreet letter to identify you, and permit you access. You will then decide what should be done, but without further reference here. My colleagues seem to have great confidence in you. Let us see if I can support those opinions. That is all!'

Miss Turlo's red dress showed her thinness and small teats.

'Here's the letter, and here's the return airline ticket,' she said, in a high nose. 'This is petty cash for expenses. I shall want an account!'

'You shall have,' he said. 'Please get me on a flight to-morrow afternoon, and book me at the Taj Mahal, three nights.'

'You can do all that in three days?' she said, real surprise. 'This is the only list we have. Keep it!'

She gave him a thick wad of stencils, closely typed. Front pages had been worn off. Only the items were listed. On the first page he saw two hundred Chrysler engines, and stopped reading.

'I have to go to another Ministry,' he said, and put the wad under his arm. 'Please send the ticket to my office. Number Eleven!'

He went in the lift, and came to Gond, and back to the welcome of his office, and put the wad in the middle of the desk, almost tasting the pleasure of reading it.

Out again, with Gond, to the other Ministry, P.

'Oh, yes!' the secretary said, quite an old woman. 'You will have to deal with the new assistant, Mr Bhatt, from tomorrow. The Minister is now waiting!'

The Minister was short and fond of the table, in a black Nehru and white jodhpurs.

'Please take a chair,' he said, and leaned back, clasping his hands. 'This is a business of immense delicacy. I must impress that upon you without a moment's delay. It is also a highly personal matter. If I had not been assured of your capacity to – ah – restrict curiosity from any quarter, I would not have asked you here, you see?'

'I have no mouth!'

'Very well. Some ten years before I came into politics, I bought a piece of land, and formed a company to promote an industrial complex. It is now built. At the same time, a foreign country made a loan, and machinery was bought. Output was good from the start. We had no worries. A further loan was made, you may as well say, to me, personally. When I took part in politics, you understand, I had to give up the private sector. But that property was still mine, although, naturally, I put it in the name of someone else. My son-in-law. Without ornament, a scoundrel in every way. He now says I made it over to him. He takes all benefits. He had thrown aside my daughter. He now tells me I am responsible for paying the loans. He is a billionaire on my charity. How do I deal with him without ruining myself?'

Prem listened to the fat voice, and sniffed danger, remembering whispers of a scandal, and newspaper stories that stopped when the editor was removed. He could almost feel his fingers caught in that machinery.

'If you could give me details, Ministerji, I could perhaps go and talk to somebody,' he said. 'Your son-in-law, for one. Have you an address?'

'My secretary will give it to you. But you have no idea for dealing with this beyond *talking* to somebody?'

'I must first find out what I am talking *about*. What do you think your son-in-law owes you?'

'First, some millions of dollars, and then Swiss francs. And property. A great deal. If you help me, remember you shall have a generous reward. My secretary has the details. I shall hope to have news conducive to your reputation!'

The secretary gave him four large folders, two of them thick, one bulky, and one thin.

'If you need clarification, call me,' she said, softly chatty. 'But I'm leaving this week-end, and somebody else is coming here. I've already warned him this is not something to tamper with. It's well outside official business!'

He looked into her brown eyes, so full of pity.

'I tell you now, I see no way to work,' he said. 'For the moment. There was a measure of dishonesty?'

'*Dishonesty?*' she said, and laughed beautiful teeth with gold pieces. 'Oh, *no*. Dacoits? Thugs? Banditry? *Yes!*'

'Our side, or theirs?'

'Ours!'

'Then why are you here?'

'This is a Ministry. I am employed. You see?'

'I do,' he said. 'I am in Office Eleven. What is the new man's name?'

'Bhatt. Mohan Bhatt. Young. Ambitious!'

'I will do my best!'

He went down to the comfort of the little room, and sat in the chair, feeling the best of his place, and setting his mind against all that could take him out, any failure, or any apparent failing. He saw in the four packets a threat. If he was unable to do anything, it would be a black mark. It would be known. The Minister involved would heel his name underfoot if it came up, and others would hesitate, or refuse to use him. His office would come down to nothing, a place for paper, routine nonsense, and people would soon know, and smile in that way, and pass him by, and neither would there be salutes, and the head sweeper might even turn his head, and Gond would go without pride.

He opened the packets as if they held the plague.

But as he read, he saw that the Minister had whitewashed his part, and there was no covering it. The financial details held no interest because he knew nothing about the figures, who supplied them or who vouched for them. No accountants were mentioned, or banks. Lists of amounts, in millions, and blocks of type explaining only that somebody was trying to paint himself as less than a swindler, and in every paragraph pointing the finger.

He took the packets, and went out to Gond, and showed him the way to Finance.

Sen he had known from the school in Lucknow. He would never go far because of sect, but he was safe because he knew accounts, and he was trusted by his Superintendent. He sat in the shadowy office, filled with paper curled in the corners, and wrote in a ledger with beautiful script, in English, and with another pen, made the same entry in Hindi, equally beautiful.

'I wish you would look at this and give me an opinion,' he said. 'I will pay for your time. I think it is plain work, but I have been asked to see if I can solve anything. I have got to be in Bombay for a few days. I'll come over when I get back. All right? But nobody else can see it. Or hear about it!'

'You have gone up, my God, look at you!' Sen said, in the well worn shirt and old trousers, and hair anyhow, and wanting a shave, but still gentle as he had been as a boy. 'What, exactly, are you supposed to do?'

'See if there is any chance of getting some money!'

'Isn't it something for a lawyer?'

'If we can find anything. Remember, you are on ten per cent of my share. Do you know a lawyer?'

'The best. But he is like me. Yes. Stuck. Except you. How did you break?'

'I don't know, I'm not sure. But I did. Here's some money to carry on. Four days, I'm here. Crack your brains!'

He went out to Gond, and they turned for the Licence Office. Two moments, and the signed and stamped papers were his, and he went around the back for the licence plates, three sets, and gave them to Gond, and followed his dance, holding the plates to the sky, to the cab, and out, to Dal's.

Two boys polished Ganesh on the concrete apron. He shone as a god.

'Wait, Premji!' Gond said. 'Only two moments, I'm back!'

A mechanic screwed on the plates. They were white, with black figures, and they gave Ganesh a final wonder. The two boys sat on the apron, looking at him without looking.

'I suppose you two would like one,' he said, not to them. He saw the sideways nods, still not looking.

57

'Be of help to Gond,' he said. 'You have no idea what is in his sky!'

He went in to the office. Dal stood in the showroom, selling a car to a somebody, but left it to a salesman and came over.

'How would you like to buy two hundred Chrysler motors, not out of packing cases?' he asked the calendar. 'How much, cash, new?'

'Car, or truck?'

'Truck. Three-quarter ton.'

'I might go three hundred.'

'American dollars?'

Nod.

'There are other things. Spares. Electric goods. Interested?'

Nod.

'I am in Bombay for the next three or four days. They will have to be brought here. Who is your haulage company?'

Dal opened the drawer, and took out a card.

'See him,' he said. 'It's my company. Send everything here. Give me a call from Bombay. It's my town.'

Gond stood in the doorway. He wore a new black driving suit, trousers, jacket, and half wellington boots, and a black crash helmet with a plastic visor. He looked fit to drive Ganesh.

'He's a good boy,' Dal said. 'He's got good boys with him. They've surprised me, how they work!'

'I think we shall need twenty more like this model,' Prem said. 'Cash. Will you order?'

'Certainly,' Dal said. 'Your money for the Disco and other things, the stocks, and further items, is in those cartons, over there. Will you take them?'

'Gond!' Prem called. 'Load these cartons. We will go to Miss Zona, and then to Seripur!'

Chapter 6

Seripur had been chiefly important in his life. Mr Raybould
had brought him there the first time, from the north, never
remembered. He had no memory of years before. He must
have been five or six. The banyan tree seemed just the same,
tall to the sky, wide in the arms, black in shadows, always
wearing a finery of coloured rags and paper, little cutout
windmills and tin shapes to blink in the sun. The little house
Mr Raybould had built hid in the garden he had planted,
and in time, land had been bought on every side to make a
large green place, and after he died, if Prem bought land on
the east, he bought equally north, west and south, and the
square grew larger, and the houses, exactly like Mr Raybould's, were built along the borderlines, so now there were
four streets of houses all round, with garden and swimming pool in the middle, and the school and children's play-
ground on another piece of land outside. Young men could
build a house with a loan from Babuji, cross-legged under his
little desk beneath the banyan, and fathers could borrow for
a daughter's marriage. Interest was only two per cent per
annum instead of twenty per cent per month, and because
Babuji knew everybody there were never bad debts.

The money had first been Mr Raybould's, and after, Prem's.
Slowly the bank account had grown. But when the first hundred houses were paying interest and capital, a steady rise of
money warned that use would have to be made of it, and
with Babuji's help, he had bought into surrounding farmland,
and let out lots of families for cultivation and guaranteed a
price for the product. Three years of drought could have

brought disaster, but he told Babuji to lend without interest, and use extra money for the people to buy food, and fodder for the animals, and the village went without hardship, or any death from hunger, and everybody knew why, and they said nothing, only with their eyes, but eyes are not mouths, and Prem did not want it known that he owned the bank and the village and the land outside, or that he bought the harvest, or supplied the machinery or paid the schoolteachers and the two nurses of the first aid room.

Nobody knew him, or of him. His name was never said. But they spoke of him without mouths, and always he was in their eyes, and the flowers in their prayers were for him, and he knew it as strength, and the children ran to have his hand on their heads, and their mothers smiled.

He went in on the back road, and took Gond to Babuji, with the three cartons of cash.

'This is Gond, my own driver,' he said, after the hand-to-forehead greeting. 'He will be my messenger from this day. Bedwa will come when there is anything heavy. Now, please, you will count, and I will come back and look at the books. How is the month?'

'The best of all, and better next,' Babuji said, and showed a betel smile, so quiet and kind. 'I feel I should have an assistant. So much pen and ink!'

'I think I have an answer, Babuji,' he said, sitting with a hand on Babuji's feet, as he had done as a child. 'We are too big for a pen. A typewriter and calculator must come. Have you anybody?'

Babuji looked over small gold spectacles, in an age of grey knowledge, at the village street, at a couple of men cycling, four water buffalo, and a pair of dogs lying in a puddle, and children playing ball outside houses of mud walls.

'No,' he said, in truth. 'Many young men I know. But they would come here only to make money. Only those giving them money would be allowed to talk to me. This has never been. It will not be while I love this tree!'

'Good,' Prem said. 'Let us go to the bank!'

A little way from the tree, among the open-front shops, a flat wall of cement blocks painted blue held a sign in English and Hindi SERIPUR TRADING CO. A dark-blue iron door bought by Mr Raybould from a railway siding opened in rusty clicks of Babuji's key, but it took three other men to push it open.

'Oil,' Prem told Gond, and he ran back to Ganesh and pushed the crowd of children away to unstrap the tool kit, and bring back the oil can, with the long brass beak that bled drips, and the door opened and closed as any other, in a woman's kiss.

Inside, one long room, stacked with Pears' Soap more than fifty years old, and Simon Artz and Jean de Reszke cigarettes, and Cuban cigars, by the thousand, and cherry toothpaste, and Parker pens, and Coats' cotton reels, and hundreds of lengths of raw silk, and linen, and cotton, leading into another, longer, room, stacked with spare parts for motors, and another room full of electric spares, out, to the office, at the end, a bare place, with only a table, a chair, and a charpoy for the night watchman, and his brazier.

'This must be decorated,' Prem said. 'I will send someone. We need a decent office. I will build on another for me, and one for you, Babuji.'

'The tree is my place,' Babuji said. 'When I am tired, there is rest in the ghat!'

Prem left him to count, sent Gond to look after Ganesh, and took his keys outside to Mr Raybould's house, hidden under flowers, and opened up, and remembered the first days.

Nothing had changed. Everything stood where he remembered. Under the polishing hands of Halima, everything shone, floors, panelling, furniture, as it had, as Mr Raybould had always insisted. All his books racked the walls, with all the others bought since. His clothing was still in the wardrobes and drawers. His pipes and pens were still on the desk. Fresh flowers were still every day in the vases. Flowers grew in pots on the window sills and on the verandas, and every night, joss burned to keep mosquitoes and flies away, and there was still a nest of cobra in the roof.

As it was, as it had always been, all those happy years.

He went to the end cupboard, and put a key in the electronic lock, and the cupboard swung open, and he went down the stairs, to a lift, and pressed the button to shut the cupboard above, and send the lift down to the ground floor.

The glass door slid, and he stood in curious light. The long, wide room, furnished in maroon leather furniture, teakwood, libraried on all four walls, gleamed as a host of friends.

Here, he was at home, as himself, in his own time.

The ceiling was the glass bottom of the swimming pool in

61

the middle of the green space. Swimmers made beautiful shadows.

'My son,' Mr Raybould had said, 'When you want to hear me, when your head feels like a squeezed lemon, when you're tired in every muscle and sleep isn't your friend, you'll find me in Haydn. He's a prince of vigour and delicacy, and a man's sweetness. Turn him on in the room. Feel the place warm. Remember me. Oh, yes. I'll be there!'

So it was.

He always sat in the same chair, and thought of Mr Raybould, and played Haydn. It was always the same.

Rest. No more worry. All thinking clear. Answers made with a chisel in granite. The delicate masculine way, that was strong, with nothing of the bully, but sweet, not womanly, only male.

Here, he lived, as himself, Prem Naran, the name given to him by Mr Raybould in baptism, that would never be taken from him, here he lived, and one day he wanted to come back and stay.

Among his own people.

Harijan. Untouchable, as Mr Raybould taught, had come dark from the ages, an offence to the human mind and spirit, and still desolating the living.

Never sit down under it, he heard the voice. I have taken you from slavery. You will take others. Remember, the release is in wealth. Others press upon you with wealth. Acquire. Save. Invest. Use their system. Destroy them, as Arjuna destroyed the Atvars. He came to victory by using the same weapon as his enemies, but with a better mind. Always have a better mind. Outthink them. Put them to rout. The main purpose of life is to live rightly, Mahatma Gandhi has said. For all men. Think rightly. Act rightly. The soul must languish when we give all our thought to the body. He was right. You can feel it, can't you? And don't you know I am here?

He always heard, always knew, always had comfort, even if he cried, if crying seemed a comfort of its own. Never mind crying, the voice said, sitting over there. Cry if you feel like it. Let the agony run. It's better than lying on some idiot's couch and spouting nonsense. Does he know more than you? Open your wells and trapdoors. Let it run. The more it runs, the clearer you are. Clear is what you *must* be. Or what do you hold of good?

He dried his eyes, feeling renewed, knowing in those moments what he must do.

The list he wrote on Mr Raybould's desk, a green-leather-topped Napoleonic partner's desk, where Mr Raybould had his side, and he had his, his side to plot and plan, Mr Raybould's for thought and decision.

He made a list of Ministers and Governors, and gave them all a code letter. There would never be need for a name. Minister A had a secretary, A-1, and possibly someone else, A-2 or 3. Governors would be G, or G-1 or 2 or 3. Nobody would know a name. Anybody else would be coded. No need for names. In the event of nonsense from any quarter, Inspector Ram and his sort, nothing would be known except a letter and a number. Now, a question of how it was going to be worked. Simple. There was never any question that names would be used in Office Number Eleven. The codes would be enough, as in the names of railway stations. For the same reason. There was work to be done, and only he would know which work, what work, and why, with a cash result.

He felt lightened, strengthened, and switched off the hi-fi music. It would play again, from that note, its own wonderful soul-restoring sounds. Medicine could also come through the ears.

He looked about the place and sniffed its fragrance.

He carried it with him, always, that promise of return to himself.

And who was he?

He was, exactly, Mr Raybould's adoptive son.

Nobody, except for that act of kindliness.

Harijan, with all that thought, and a duty to a kindly man, first, and then to his brothers and sisters, and their children. There was no return. There was only forward duty.

He lit the candle before the photograph, and knelt, and thought of the voice, and felt the touch of a hand on his head, and swallowed the tears, and prepared himself, and left the candle burning with his grief and thanks, knowing Halima would have the flame, and went in the lift and out, through the cupboard, to the old house, and kissed the air, and walked out, seeing the cobra's eyes, two jewel points, from the roof.

Gond waited outside, and rode him down to the banyan. Babuji had the books ready, and a pencil down the column assured, and the tot of the cash in the cartons was correct.

'Babuji, I will send the men to build the offices I want,' he said. 'You will find men of the village to help and watch. I do not want men not of our tree!'

'They shall not be,' Babuji said. 'What of the typewriter and calculator?'

'When the offices are ready, you will know,' he said. 'The men will be here tomorrow. You will pay them. Babuji, rest peacefully in a memory!'

Gond rode through the quiet lanes very gently. Cattle strolled from him, goats walked, children played, women carried washing on their heads with jelly-sweet of backside taking weight, and dimpling.

'Gond,' he said, through the clear sun, down the long avenue. 'Your sister. Where is she?'

'Premji, she waits for you,' Gond said, to the wind.

'Tell her we need her,' he said. 'She will take charge of accounts and the office at Seripur. She will earn twice she had in the last position. After, if I find she has the worth, three times. After that, will depend upon her. I wish to meet her before I go to Bombay tomorrow. Wegner's nine o'clock tonight?'

'No, sir!' Gond shouted back, from the wind in front. 'The Janpath, in the bar, where I shall take her. I shall be waiting. No question. Wegner's, very well. Not for Harijan, at that time!'

'Good,' he said, brought back to everyday importances in the minds of many. 'Janpath, the bar, nine o'clock?'

'She will be there, with me, and I shall be there to take her back,' Gond said. 'I will come back for you, sir!'

'You are too young to go in the bar!'

'When I am dressed, I am older, sir!'

He went back to the Ministry, and more salutes, and an escort to the door of Two-Two-One.

Shiva, in a black sari, opened, and he shut, and she gave him the list, and touched a chair to sit. He wished himself cross-legged at her feet, but he thought of the knees of his Gobind trouser, and sat instead.

He knew every station and the stationmaster and most of the staff, especially in the yards and freight, and he saw their code names, over them all, in big red letters. He ran down the list three times without any failure, and looked up to see Shiva smiling.

'You are ready?' she said. 'It comes too soon, really?'

'Try me,' he said. 'Any station, I will give you code. Any code, I will give station. A bet?'

'I would like, but I have no spare money. Why don't you bet *me*?'

'I will bet, but you will find conditions hard!'

'We will meet at seven-thirty tonight, remember?'

'What is tonight and what is now are two different. Yes?'

'What is the bet?'

He counted ten one-hundred rupee notes on the desk.

'If I fail in only one station or code, these are yours,' he said.

'And if I fail, what?'

'Everything off, here, now, and play as a child to provoke her husband, yes?'

'I have never done!'

He tapped the notes.

'My bet goes to you on any mistake. No excuse. It is yours!'

She looked at the notes sideways.

'It is nearly two months' pay,' she said. 'Can I afford? You are such a *naughty* man!'

'I worship. What is naughty?'

She took the list, and flipped it straight.

'Very well,' she said, in a long sigh. 'I take the bet. How often have you seen children provoke their husbands?'

'Often!'

'How?'

'Next time, I will invite you. My own wife did. Many others. Why not? Are we ourselves, or are we still under the Raj?'

'Let us begin. Bareilly?'

'Choma!'

'Lucknow?'

'Goonj!'

He closed his eyes. The words beat as rain. He replied.

She went twice through the list, and backwards, and chose at random, station or code words, but he was always sudden in answer, and never wrong.

She slapped the list on the desk.

'O, hell!' she said. 'Now look what I have got to do. Why am I such a fool?'

'No,' he said, and got up. 'It is wrong to think in such a manner. And I was far more wrong. This money is yours as examiner. I passed because of you. At seven-fifteen tonight there will be time and place for other privilege. You cannot forget I only worship?'

She turned her back, hands clasped between the flowers.

'Very well,' she said. 'Seven-fifteen, tonight. But this time you will have no fear. I will see to it. Vutthi will meet you and bring you to me. The thousand rupees are mine without a receipt?'

'Without!'

'All I promised, I will pay,' she said. 'I am waiting for you. Don't be late!'

He went out and Gond took him back to the office. There were many pieces of paper, two of them important, and he settled them on the telephone with promise of money, which, of course, gave him a hold for the future. Nothing happened without money, but when money passed, other matters came into view, and favours came back, as they must.

It was the only way to be.

At seven, the paper work was finished, and he called a taxi, giving Shiva's address. He stopped a few hundred yards away, and walked in darkness. Near the house, Vutthi's white braids shone, and she took his hand with a shake to tell him nothing was loose, and led through the garden to a gallery door, in, to the warm scent, and up the stairs of pink carpet, to the white door.

Shiva, in a white voile sari, opened, and shut, and leaned against the panels, and pushed herself off, and went to the brass table, and lifted the bottle.

'Whisky I got for you!' she whispered. 'Yes?'

'I don't drink,' he said. 'I will drink the beauty of you, nothing less. They can't bottle you!'

'You make one shamefully wrong!' she said, and sat on a large cushion. 'First, I want to ask a big favour. Can you do something for me?'

'I can do things for many people,' he said. 'What is for you?'

'I have a house. It was an aunt of mine. She died very old. The tenant held on to the lease. He pays the rent, yes, of thirty years ago. But I have found he employs women there!'

'A whoreshop?'

'Exactly. But my aunt was a sainted woman. She would not

like. I do not like. How should I get rid of him? I can get five times the rent if he goes away!'

'But why should he go away? Why not pay you minimum forty per cent of the gross? Cash? Every week? Not better?'

'But a dream!'

'You think so? Give me the address!'

She wrote, and looked so frowningly at him.

'I don't believe you!' she said. 'You are having me on!'

'On what? All you have to do is say nothing, and find out if I am right. In cash. Will you believe me in hard cash? Every week?'

'I will believe you!'

'Good. Off with everything and let me see what I worship!'

'But you are treating me like an idol!'

'Why not? Aren't you? You deny you are somebody apart? Different from the common? Why are you secretary to the Minister? Is everybody? If he goes away, you do his job. Don't you? If he writes letters, you correct his language, don't you? You think it isn't known? You are his brain and his mouth. Doesn't everybody know? Don't you? For what, in payment?'

She turned away.

'It is what a secretary is for,' she said.

'Good. And at the Mashoba? Extra money?'

'It is necessary!'

'To keep going here? You should put a nice big screw on the Minister!'

'Tell me how!'

'Very simple. When I come back from Bombay?'

'Vutthi will meet!'

'Good. Put a screw. Better than promise of a pension. Yes?'

'If only. How I *hate* him!'

'Simple. I will show you how to screw a Minister. He screws you? Now you screw him!'

Naked, true goddess, she paid her bet in wondrous unbound black love moss. He put hands to forehead, and Vutthi took him out to the gallery door, and Gond flashed three red lights to show where he was.

'Back to the office,' he said. 'I will take a cab to the Janpath.'

'Ah, Premji!' Gond sharply said. 'I shall take you there. My sister only waits five minutes away. How could we leave you to go anywhere without us? We are *you*! We try to be *in* you!'

'Very well. Leave me and bring her. Look. Do you know this address?'

He gave the address Shiva had written.

Sideways nod.

'When I go to Bombay, find out all you can. Who the man is, how many women are working, how much, how many men. Pay the people working there. Everything I want to know. But *everything*!'

He gave Gond the notes, and they stopped at the Janpath. He went in, to a table on the left, and ordered double whisky, small soda, because it is fitting in such a place.

Gond came in a dark suit, white shirt, black and white tie, polished shoes, really not to be seen as Gond, but a young spark, twenty-five at least, with a girl in a blue-and-red sari, to his shoulder, slim, of enormous dark eyes in kohl, and a sense of shrinking, of vibrating fear.

'Premji, my sister, Khusti,' Gond said.

'Please sit down, Miss Khusti, what would you like to drink?'

'O, a soda, please? Orange?'

A soft voice, shaking, never looking at him.

'Gond?'

'The same please, Premji!'

He gave the order to the waiter, and turned to her.

'I am told you wish to work for me,' he said. 'Very well. I accept because of your brother. You know accounts? You can keep a set of books? You can type? You can use a calculator? You are able to control an office?'

'Able,' she said, the small voice. 'All departments. I went to the business school here. I have a certificate. And seven years in insurance. And I wish to work for you. You have been so kind to Gond. It is my duty!'

'Whatever you earn now, you will earn double with me. Gond will take you to Seripur tomorrow. He will tell Babuji my wishes. You will make yourself as comfortable as possible until the men come to build the office. I shall be there on Friday. Gond, find out times of arrival, last flight from Bombay. Meet me. I shall come back here. I shall stay here tonight. Pick me up at six o'clock tomorrow morning. How did you buy that suit?'

'Khusti bought it for me. She also bought the driver's suit and boots and helmet. She is the best sister. I will pay back!'

'No need,' she said, the small, small voice. 'He needed. I had money. He got!'

Prem counted notes.

'You must accept this,' he said. 'You are both in my employ. I am responsible. You cannot deny?'

'But it was also my love,' she said. 'Can you repay?'

Prem picked up the notes.

'You are right,' he said. 'Gond, you will take this money, and buy with a brother's love whatever you think Khusti would most like. You understand? No denial. How is Khusti to get to Seripur? There is no bus service, is there? Where do you live?'

'In my father's place in the tyre market,' Gond said. 'Behind. We are wishing to go away. We would like to find a place. We save!'

'But my father is a hard man,' Khusti said. 'He takes everything. He tears my clothes!'

'Find a good place,' Prem said. 'I will pay the first three months. Gond, you pick the best of your friends. Without a mouth. He will take Khusti to Seripur in the morning, and back at night. If Babuji wants something, he will get it. I will pay. Pick twenty of the friends you trust. They shall each have a Ganesh. Only yours will be black. You will form a company. I will arrange the details. Khusti will control the books. You will deal only with Dal. If you find somebody buying gas or anything else in another place, he is finished. Understood?'

Sideways nod.

'Khusti,' he said. 'If you are like your brother, your life is sweetened by all you hope for. Gond will see to it. I shall guarantee. But we have no mouths!'

'None,' she said. 'I have ears and eyes, but no mouth!'

'Enough,' he said. 'Why does your father tear your clothes?'

'He wishes to make me a bed-girl. I will not. For this we save. We think of you. You are Krishna!'

'No, no, no!' he said. 'Please. I am ordinary. I hope never anything more. Gond, you will not take your sister back to the tyre market. Tomorrow, if you can't find a place, she will stay here until you do. I will pay. She will not go back to the tyre market. As a brother, you will see to it. I shall stay here. Come at six o'clock. Miss Khusti, until Friday.'

She and Gond gave him *namaste* in both palms to forehead.

'Good-night, Premji!' she whispered. 'We have flowers in our prayers!'

Chapter 7

Delhi airport was a ghost of sleepy ones, and porters hid.
When anybody needed a porter, they reappeared but they
had another price. Gond solved. Prem waited in the line, saw
a face, disbelieved, but she was there.

Miss Turlo.

He went to her, and asked.

'Yes,' she said, tall. 'The Minister instructed me to take
notes. So I am here. You object?'

'Never,' he said. 'I have first appointment thirty minutes
after we touch down. You come?'

'Of course. It is what I am sent to do!'

The tall one, in a beautiful blind of clean breath.

She had a seat apart, and he made no effort to be with her.
But he had a further idea about the Minister. If that one
could dare to think that a Miss Turlo might restrict his area
of activity, then she, and the Minister, would learn.

He slept until they touched down.

Das had a car for him. Miss Turlo was elsewhere.

'Go here,' he told the driver. 'Wait for me!'

They stopped at the dock gates. A havildar wanted to make
unwonted enquiries, but a note assured entrance. They
stopped outside Godown Number Fourteen, a large place, and
a watchman came, but he gave him a note, and the side door
was opened.

The place was full. Of everything. He looked into his mind.
Engines, Spares, Bodies, doors, every part of a car. Dials,
small things, anything anybody wanted, all here. And by the
thousand. Radios, every kind. In the tens of thousands. Spare

parts for radios, by the thousands and thousands. A warehouse, ready for quick sales, but one look and he decided no knock downs, but only full price.

He was in the third aisle, and Miss Turlo came in heel-click.

'I am only making a note,' she said, high, in that space. 'I don't wish to disturb.'

'Take notes,' he said. 'You don't disturb. You will help. I have an idea what is here. Do you?'

'I am only told to see and report,' she said. 'There is a great deal here. Yes?'

'A great deal,' he said. 'Of no value. I have wasted my time!'

'You can't say that!' she said. 'There is so much!'

'Unsaleable,' he said. 'Who will buy? At what price? I think I must withdraw. I do myself great harm. Nothing here is worth real money. Very few things will realise a price!'

'But the Minister believes there are crores of rupees here!' she said.

'Rupees of what? Who will buy? Advertise? What is here? Contraband? Extra from Customs? What is the value? Shall I tell you? Or do you, intelligent girl, do you *know*?'

She looked about the quiet place, full of packing cases and crates, and nodded.

'I think I do,' she said. 'Outdated?'

'Exactly. Who wants it? Tell me. How do we sell? To whom?'

'It is all worthless?'

'I appeal to you. What do you say of articles taken in contraband of ten, fifteen years ago?'

'Contraband?'

'Why are they here?'

She looked about, hands in pockets of the long blue overcoat.

'Possibly,' she said. 'Possibly. We have to think again?'

'Of course. What else?'

'I didn't know it was so dead!'

'What is more dead than manufactories of fifteen or more years ago?'

'I begin to see how you think.'

'How else *is* there to think? Who is going to buy this rubbish? Outside, in the villages? Very well. Why should I be asked to waste my time? I am very sickened!'

'I think the Minister is most anxious for it all to be taken off the Department's hands. It is causing very much worry, you see?'

'Telephone to him. Tell him what I say. It is mostly junkish stuff. I can sell it only in lots. If he *wants* me to sell. But I won't do it without his word directly to you. Or else I go back immediately to Delhi!'

'Wait, now, please, Mr Prem!' she said. 'I know this is a very important matter from the Minister's point of view. We *must* have it out of the way. It's why he sent me. I will phone the office from the gate. Please wait!'

He watched her almost running down the aisle. She had long legs, pale brown hair, Anglo-Indian skin, coffee and creamy, everything he liked. He saw a telephone on the table by the door, almost hidden under paper and old ledgers, higgle-piggle. The number Dal had given replied, and he asked for four trucks to be sent to Godown Fourteen on the east wharf, and the same trucks to go loaded to Dal's showroom in Delhi, and come back for more.

'How many trucks have you got?'

'You will have ten five-tonners? I have twelve more altogether.'

'Send them all, with ten porters. Special money I pay.'

'They will be there. One hour. How about the gate?'

'They will be passed. Ministry permit. Get more!'

'Ah!'

He tore off the covers of some of the items, finding toothbrushes, cosmetics, whisky by the hundred crates, brandy, gin, champagne, a lot of other stuff, and then a sofa, in soft leather, that folded down to make a double bed. There were twenty. Ten would come to him, and two more for Gond and Khusti. He put one down and it kept its promise. It was firm, but soft. Bedding filled other big boxes. Gas stoves, refrigerators, kitchenware, household stuff, it was all there. There was so much. All the labels were torn off, and stencils had been painted out. But he saw enough to guess it was an aid-shipment side-tracked, and he thought he knew why the Minister worried. Found, it could be laid at his door. The Opposition would create an uproar. He might have to resign. Then there was threat of criminal prosecution. All sorts of curious thinking developed. Miss Turlo might have a hand in it. A lot of implications were in the cases of drugs and medicaments. Her father was a physician, and her mother

73

was something to do with hospitals. He knew her facts from birth.

He heard her coming back, the heel click of boots that made her inches higher, and stilting.

'Yes!' she said, a bit excited. 'He says sell at any price. Simply liquidate everything. If you can save him a few cases of whisky and some cigars, it is very well done. And you will bring the cash to him, and he will give you twenty-five, not twenty per cent. If that is perfectly satisfactory?'

'Yes. It is satisfactory. But how shall I trust you?'

She frowned, and turned to him, full in the eyes.

'Trust?' she said. 'What do you mean, *trust*?'

'You could have called anybody, police or Customs. How do I know? I could never prove I was working for the Minister, or anybody else. It would be denied. What proof? I have a letter. A forgery? You are here to catch a fellow trying to take advantage. How do I know?'

'It's ridiculous!' she whispered, afraid. 'It is so *ridiculous*!'

'Not!' he said. 'Think of my position if police break in, now. What am I to say? Everything can be denied. What is my defence?'

'No,' she said, blank. 'It's impossible. Everything is properly structured. Sell for what you can. That is the final word. I am witness. Also, that you have twenty-five per cent. To be paid before I go back to Delhi!'

'And what will you get?'

'I might have a present,' she said. 'A sari length?'

'It's all?'

'He's not open-handed!'

'Supposing I said twenty-five thousand rupees, cash in the hand? To stay here and take a note that everything is taken away? Supposing?'

'Too much a dream!'

'No dream. *Notes.*'

She threw back the coat and lifted her head and neck.

'It is so hot!' she said. 'This morning terribly cold. Now, *hot*!'

'Take off,' he said, and tugged the sleeve, walking her down towards the bed in shadow. 'I want to see you in the middle of *that*.'

She looked at the shiny leather.

'O!' she said. 'What a beauty of a thing!'

'You would like one? It will be delivered to your place. Not a word said anywhere.'

She put an open palm on it, pressed.

'I can't believe it!' she said. 'It's wonderful leather. *Real!*'

'It will go to your place. Give me the address. But I want to see you in the middle of this one. Naked!'

'O, I couldn't!'

'Take off. Twenty-five thousand. In the hand!'

'Somebody will come in!'

'You will come!'

'No. I mean, somebody will come in!'

'Nobody. I have the key. Take off. The middle of the bed!'

'I have never been. I am truly virgin!'

'The sweet better. I have never known a virgin of twenty-seven. You were playing with yourself?'

'O, no!'

'But now you will take off all, and play, and I will watch!'

'Somebody will come!'

'No chance. Off. Middle of the bed. Naked!'

'You are cruel. I could walk out. Complain to the Minister!'

'Twenty-five thousand rupees!'

She let the overcoat drop from her arms. Slowly, she pulled down the zip of her dress. She never looked at him. The dress came off. She stood in bodice and little pants, like a swim suit.

'You want more?' she whispered. 'It is awful!'

'It is beautiful. I didn't know you held such a wonder. Off!'

She took off her bodice. Her teats were small, but full, and his finger squeezed, and the nipples were long, pink. She pushed hands flat into the pants' waist, and took them down to her ankles, and stepped out.

She fell on the bed, face down.

'Be soon,' she whispered. 'Be quick. Whatever you want, take. But not very long!'

He took not very long and she was not such a virgin, but very good, and enjoying, and pushing to him, and making nice little sounds, and becoming beautiful suddenly. She passed a hand, and raised the left knee, both as if to feel the leather.

'There is no bathroom here?' she asked.

'At the end, just past the table with the telephone.'

'Excuse me,' she said, and picked up her clothes, and ran,

tall, creamy-coffee, brown hair flopping, but she had a black nuptial, so there was dye work somewhere, pretty, business for somebody, and he wondered if there was profit in opening a place only to dye the nuptial.

He went down to the telephone and called Das.

'Ah, Prem? So happy to hear you!'

'Come to Godown Fourteen. How many five-tonners did you get?'

'I can get all you want. Up to thirty. Full maintenance!'

'Come here without loud show at two-thirty. I will meet at the gate!'

'How many five-tonners?'

'At least thirty, for several hours every day, into Bombay, and then to Delhi. You have the warehouses. Empty them. We need them. Is Bhoomijai still in business?'

'Bring him? He is bigger than the rest together. Listening?'

'Yes, both. It is a question of crores. Cash!'

'Your only worry will be finding boxes to carry. Cash is *there*!'

'Bring him. I like the idea of Bhoomijai!'

Dal's men thumped the door just after Miss Turlo came out, dressed, cool, knowing nothing, showing less, and started to clear the desk, trying to keep her shining head from the dust.

He took the man down the main aisle to the engine crates.

'A lot of work,' he said. 'You need at leasty twenty men to keep the line moving. I think you will get ten engines on each truck. You will take them to Dal, direct, to Delhi.'

'He sent a telegram to give special help. This load will take at least four, perhaps five journeys. I can get more trucks?'

'No. Trucks spaced at intervals will not be a convoy. A convoy can be stopped!'

'Your head is hard. The drivers will have money?'

'For themselves, and to give away!'

'Four times the normal rate?'

'Certainly. Take your own from that. Special present at the end. No slip-ups!'

The man waved his hands.

'Where there is money, no slips!' he said. 'Delhi and return less than two days, day and night drivers?'

'Dal will send trucks from Delhi today for the rest. Fly to Delhi, and fly back. I want to find out if I can trust you. I must leave on Thursday. Count this, and give me a receipt. There, at the desk. Good?'

'Very lovely,' the man said, counting the wad with wet fingers and a thumb that looked as if it had been squashed wide by a press. 'I shall be back before you go. You can be sure to depend. Dalji has always depended. Thirty years!'

'You know Gupta Das, here?'

'Import, export, shipping, transport, Customs agent, and God knows what? Of course. Who doesn't? I am always working with him or his managers. Ask them about Mehta Roy. I am first in my line!'

The man's good fire was in his eyes.

'Harijan?' Prem said, to the far corner.

Roy nodded downwards.

'Good, again,' Prem said, quietly. 'I am also. Also few know. We will work together? There should be mutual – I shall say once more – *mutual* benefit? We understand?'

Roy took the tears with his fingers.

'I have heard courage from a brother,' he said. 'Now I have more. I shall help!'

'Good. Load up!'

The men came in, and from the way they set about the stack they were no novices, and they were getting sixteen crates in the trucks, with higher sideboards, twenty When they left, at intervals of thirty minutes, there were one hundred engine crates left, and fifty crates of spares, and hundreds of tyres in sets, and he put hand to forehead to pray he would find whole bodies of cars and trucks in all the rest piled behind.

Miss Turlo made notes, head on one side, to the neck, it seemed, in the river.

'What were those boxes?' she asked.

'I think dolls from Japan,' he said. 'They will be junk on the Delhi market. A good price, do we care?'

'How much?'

'If the truck comes to us, perhaps half a lakh. Depends on the dealer. Ready sale to children? In the villages, of course.'

'I would like one!'

'Should I open a whole crate for one? One missing from a crate, what does the merchant think. Somebody is cheating? In other crates, how many more? No. A deal is a deal. Be satisfied with your bed. It will remind you?'

'I would like a doll to remind me!'

'You shall have. With the bed. And remember. I am in Office Number Eleven. And you are having twenty-five thousand rupees. It's not enough?'

'Believe when I see!'

'Where will you stay tonight?'

'The Western.'

'You should be staying only at the Taj Mahal. You are entitled. I say you will be at the Taj. I will tell the Minister. How *can* somebody acting so importantly for his Department, stay at a lodging house? Telephone the Taj, now. We want two doubles. I will give him personally the account!'

'He will think we slept?'

'I will deny!'

She laughed, and took off the telephone.

'Until when?' she asked.

'Thursday morning!'

'He will *know* we slept!'

'Very well!'

'He will phone my father. There will be hell!'

'With the cash, and his cigars and whisky, who will he phone? Take whisky and cigars for your father. What will be hell?'

She laughed again. He was liking her.

'It was what the Minister told me, that first time,' she said. 'That young fellow will go a long way. If he attends to his business. The moment he is outside, the vultures will eat him. He meant politics!'

'I will never be. Believe me, I have seen enough. I know them all. Except for a few, I spit. But the few will never be any good. Too many against!'

'My father says so. He says he doesn't know why he goes on saving people to live on in such a muckrake of a world. It is sickening to be civilised!'

'But your father wants the drugs and medicines in this consignment?'

'The Minister promised there would be a chance!'

'You are here only because of that?'

'Don't look at me in such a way, please? Well, yes, I suppose. It is possible?'

'If the proper price is paid? Drugs and medicines are very high today. True loyalty to the Minister. I must get competitive price. Telephone the Minister. Ask what I am to do. Telephone your father. Ask what he is prepared to pay. Cash.

Before delivery. Or I will get my price here, and the Minister will receive it!'

'It is worth what?'

He turned the wad of paper to her.

'I have been through with medical catalogue,' he said. 'The price of each is beside entry. The total is below. You see it?'

She pushed a fist in her cheek, and her eyes were broken eggs.

'But not so *much*!' she said.

'It is an entire base hospital. Beds, equipment, surgery, drugs, medicines, everything. How much?'

'But not all that!'

'Exactly. That's less than half price. I get it cash, or no sale, and I can sell it for more!'

'I can phone my father?'

'Phone him. Tell him to get his transport here. All expenses are his. But he will produce that sum, cash, or the entire consignment is on the market at three times the price. Call him!'

'He could never get so much!'

'To sell for three times? Four, five times? Call him. Call the Minister!'

He went out in the sun, and another truck went out for Delhi.

Down at the main gate, he spread the notes, and told them about Mr Das coming at two-thirty. Everybody made the sideways nod. All in order.

Back at the godown, all smiles.

'He will fly with the money,' she said. 'He says it is cheap. But he wants to be sure of the drugs?'

'There are no drugs,' he said. 'There are cases of medicaments, but no drugs. It is the American way. They lock everything up!'

'But it is why he is bringing all that money!' she squeaked.

'He still has a bargain. And you get twenty-five thousand. Plus a percentage of what he pays. Of course? Do you work for nothing?'

She put down the pencil, and clasped hands behind her neck.

'Ah, Prem!' she said, in the glad voice. 'Such a beautiful day. How much do you think?'

'Not less than another twenty-five thousand? And you will tell everybody?'

'Not a small word. Never. Will you always let me work with you? Yes? I will work. I can tell you many things. Fifty thousand rupees? How wonderful. Prem, you are a beautiful man!'

Chapter 8

Das brought Bhoomijai in the evening.

Fat, and frowning because of his money, Bhoomijai looked down the list, scratching inside his shirt, and slipping his eyes to Miss Turlo with almost a splash of saliva.

'How much you are asking, and let us be clear, I am paying only very below current market price,' he said. 'I know the reason for hurried sale!'

'Share with me,' Prem said. 'Miss Turlo, you have worked long enough. You may please go home!'

'She lives here?' Bhoomijai asked, looking at the shining brown-haired figure in blue, going in and out of overhead lights, away. 'I would employ her. Highest salary!'

'Not free. I am employer. What *is* reason?'

'M.I.S.A., of course,' Das said. 'They are already starting arrests. But not Bhoomijai. He is beyond them!'

'What is M.I.S.A.? Have I missed?'

'Maintenance of Internal Security Act,' Das said. 'It came into full effect last night. There are hundreds of arrests. Smugglers, hoarders, traders in foreign currency, all in danger. But not Bhoomijai. He knows great deal. Too much, eh, Bhoomijaiji?'

'Completely ridiculous, of course. I have more to say than any informer. About everybody. Nothing will come to me!'

The scratch of personal cheques, the whispered promise of counted notes and a small clink of gold coin all seemed in the air, noisier than the truck starting its engine.

'It's not the reason for this sale,' Prem said. 'These godowns are the Department's. They are needed for consignments of

6

American grain. These goods can be disposed. They are no longer required for the Department. I shall sell to highest buyer. All out, Wednesday night!'

'You asking what?'

Prem wrote the figure.

Bhoomijai looked, and pushed the paper off the table.

'A triumph of absurdity!' he said. 'Who could think of it? You are young in business!'

Prem picked up the paper.

'I have Mudji Chagan coming in the morning,' he said. 'Jhem Patel in the afternoon. Between the three of you, I shall have my price!'

'I shall telephone them,' Bhoomijai said, sitting back. 'We shall arrange a price, and you can take it or leave!'

'*This* price,' Prem said. '*Cash*. Not one paisa less. *Now* telephone!'

'You are putting up my back. An entirely inexperienced paperpusher speaking such a fashion to me? Das, put sense into this fellow!'

'Well, a diplomacy would be wiser, yes,' Das said, almost creeping. 'We don't want to upset Bhoomijaiji, do we? This is why I got him to come here, isn't it?'

'Listen, the last time I talk,' Prem said. 'The price is *that*. Telephone where you like. You know your competitors would go any lengths beating you in lucrative bargains. Over that price you could sell five times. Are you teaching me basis of business? I passed many years ago!'

'I am disliking your tone and manner!' Bhoomijai said, staring the mudsplashes into black points. 'I could put you behind bars!'

'*Put*. One more word, I don't do business with you. We are understanding what I say?'

'Wait a little!' Das said, hands out, seeing himself sadly losing fat commission. 'We are knowing you are Ministry man. Where is your authority?'

Prem slowly took the Minister's letter from his breast pocket, presenting with a slapped hand.

Bhoomijai read, and looked, pushing chin under ear at the side, a shiny stare.

Das read.

'Well, it seems you have firm ground,' he said. 'If the price – ?'

'The original price is on that paper,' Prem said. 'I have

82

prospectives. Don't worry. I shall sell for one crore more, easily. I report to the Minister, morning and night. He knows where enquiries come. He is in position to cause great trouble!'

Das looked along the aisle to the dark doorway, and his eyes went sideways down to Bhoomijai.

'It would be bad time for complications,' he said, almost to himself. 'Very bad. Police. Customs. Income Tax?'

Bhoomijai pushed from the chair, and hit the table with his thick stick, and again, savage, and turned, stick up, ready to hit.

'I could have people to inflict certain hurts on you!' he shouted. 'Who are you to talk in low fashion to me?'

'That remark costs you one crore more,' Prem said. 'That is two crores over the blanket price I offered. For madness and unseemly behaviour, there is always penalty!'

'If you were always in Bombay, I would destroy you piece by piece!' Bhoomijai said. 'But you are a Delhi *desi*. Beyond my reach!'

'*Desi?*' Prem said. 'People not speaking good English? Very well. I am *desi*. Even so, I am better than any Bombay *prick*!'

'Oh, now, now!' Das said, fists to his ears, shut-eyed at the roof. 'How did we come to this? Business, business. Nothing more. Who is worried with Delhi or Bombay?'

'I, for one, am not!' Prem said. 'I fly to Delhi on Thursday, and I report to the Minister, cash in the barrel. No argument or insults will prevent. This merchandise, you know what it is worth? The price you pay me can be swollen three or four times. If you don't, others will. Alacrity is the soul of business!'

Das picked up the list.

'Let us examine!' he said, softly. 'Nothing lost in verifying. Many richly fat entries. Nothing but profit in the market!'

Bhoomijai rested on the stick to get up.

'I would like a glass of milk and a thick piece of saffron cake,' he said, in a long groan. 'I am very hungry. It is always very abrasing to my temper, you see. Find somebody to go!'

'I will,' Prem said. 'Pursue your examination. Milk and cake!'

He went out to the gate, and asked the havildar, and one of the men said he would go. He gave a note, and the man ran.

He passed more notes for taking.

'If police, or any others coming in, let me know,' he said. 'I am here till Wednesday night, or early Thursday. Many trucks will come from Delhi. Others will come from Das, here, in Bombay. Work with me, you are always right side. Always something healthy to put in the pocket!'

He pointed to the telephone, and a smile of permission let him dial Taj Mahal, and a miracle, it answered. He asked for Miss Turlo, and the receiver clacked.

'Miss Turlo? It is Prem!'

'O, Mr Prem. I am so glad. My father is here, and wishing so much to see you!'

'I have got Bhoomijai and Gupta Das nosing the goods. I will be at least an hour. How did he find you?'

'I called him this morning after you told me Taj. We shall stay until you are here. The grill is always open!'

'I hope you are?'

'For you, yes. Come soon!'

He waited for the man to run in, breathless, with the package and bottle, and he gave another note.

He went back to the godown, and saw the two on the east side, prodding and poking, looking at the list, and ticking.

'Cake and milk!' he shouted. 'Come and get!'

Bhoomijai waddled like a big goose, flat foot, dab dab on the inside of the shoe as if every step hurt. The big belly shook side to side and he breathed little sniffs, and his eyes were cowpats, with black viper spots, shiny. He tore the package, and bit a double mouthful from the cake, and drank and drank the milk, and swallowed, and made an air noise.

'How much I owe?' he asked.

'Hospitality,' Prem said.

'My valuers will be here. Five o'clock, too early?'

'Earlier? I finish on Wednesday. Prospectives here to-morrow. Four o'clock?'

'Five o'clock. I shall know more the value.'

'You know now. It is the same price, plus two crores!'

'Please say little!' Das said, arms out, in address to some god. 'Everything is too good for imperceptibles. Are we so ludicrous to ignore what is in our noses? With two crores added, the price is a gold mine. How can there be competitors?'

'I shall go,' Bhoomijai said, in bubbles of air from the throat, and pushing up on the stick. 'My valuers will be here!'

'Cash, for total, in cartons,' Prem said. 'The Minister will be strict about this!'

'Sit yourself down, for God's sake!' Das said. 'Business is beyond you!'

'Have a flying jump at your mother!'

Das pointed a thumb at Bhoomijai dab-dabbing down the aisle, a white heap of wrinkles.

'Give a chance!' he whispered. 'You are next to quick sale. Will you spoil with ill-considered words?'

'O, bugger off!' Prem said. 'He is supposed to be king of smugglers? Very well. He will speak to me correctly, and pay what I ask. Or I will sell to others!'

Das raised his hands, waving impatiently, stamping, knees out.

'Not such implacability, please. You are doing harm to lovely bargains. What are you? Salesman or destructor? Friend or utterly unconscious foe? You have the money in your hand. Why do you kick it?'

'Let me see it!'

'Five o'clock?'

'I shall be here!'

'Good-night!'

'Very well. But either you are my friend, or his. Which?'

'*You* are my friend. He is business associate. It is different? Do I put something in the bank from friends?'

'From me, yes. Why did I call you? Only to bring that swine in here?'

'He will also bring the cartons. You will see. Five o'clock?'

'*We* shall see!'

He waited until Das had gone, almost running, and collected all the paper, especially the jottings of Miss Turlo. She had collected bits of talk during the day. He wondered why. He put out the lights, shut the door, and gave the keys to the havildar on the gate, wishing that Gond were there to meet. But a telephone brought a taxi, and he got in with a feeling of going home.

A message at the desk asked him to call 81, and Miss Turlo answered.

'O, yes, Prem!' she said, suddenly very sweet. 'Come up. My father is here!'

'Does he want to see me without a wash?'

'Wash here. Aren't you hungry?'

'Perhaps.'

85

'I will call for drinks. Then we will go on to the grill?'

'I am coming up!'

She opened the door, very beautiful in dark red dress, and hair in another way on top of the head. Her father, in a grey linen suit, grey hair to the collar, looked at him, narrow, sizing, but he nodded.

'Doctor Turlo? You brought the money?'

'I have to see what's there, of course!'

'If you brought the money, very well. Otherwise the consignment is sold from tomorrow. I have important merchants treading over each other. I would rather deal with a professional man of national reputation!'

'I don't know quite about that!'

'I have made enquiries. The Minister is satisfied. It is very important?'

'Very, but of course.'

'I will wash. But I have no wanting for the grill. I am at the godown at five. You have a room here?'

'I am sleeping here.'

'In this room?'

'Yes.'

'With your daughter?'

'Why not? It's a double. Why waste money?'

Miss Turlo smiled, but to herself.

'Very well,' he said. 'I will go to my room. Be kind to send my drink there. One hundred and thirty-eight. Miss Turlo, eleven o'clock will be early enough. Doctor Turlo, be sure you have the money. Cash, or certified cheque on any bank in Delhi. Otherwise, I have offers. Good-night, sir? Miss Turlo, good-night?'

'But we were looking forward to a chat!' she said. 'Such a rush?'

'I have paperwork for tomorrow,' Prem said. 'Five o'clock is only few hours away. Clear heads are always better. Good-night!'

He saw Miss Turlo's almost accusing and yet guiltyish smile, and went up the stairway to the next floor, and let himself in.

In one light from the bedside, a big girl sat in a chair.

'I am here with the compliments of Dasji, my father, to console you, so far from your home,' she said. 'I hope I am pleasing?'

'You are exceptionally,' he said. 'How would you like a drink?'

'O, yes,' she said. 'Champagne!'

'O,' he said. 'You are the famous champagne girls?'

'Dasji has only us!'

'Good. I am bathing. When the waiter comes, order, will you?'

'Give me money for the waiter!'

He gave her change, and went into the bathroom, and in the shower he heard the waiter come in, and go, and while he towelled, come in again with a bucket in rattles of ice.

He put his head out.

'All right!' he said. 'I will attend!'

The waiter nodded, and went.

'You don't trust me?' she said. 'He was very handsome!'

'Take off,' he said.

She went to the bathroom, turning all the lights out except at the bedside. He poured two glasses, and drank his, a sort of sweet soda water, and poured another. She came back, a woman-shadow, and got on the other side of the bed. He gave her the glass. She drank and drank. He drank. She passed her glass, and he poured, and poured for himself, and drank. He lay back and put his head in her shoulder.

The telephone bell came down the long road.

'Half past four, sir!' the girl's voice said. 'Your taxi has been called!'

He sat on the edge of the bed. The girl slept. He wanted to do nothing. He was flat. He went to the bathroom and showered, and the noise disturbed her.

'But you went to sleep!' she said, sleepy. 'I am such no good?'

'Be here tonight,' he said. 'I will be earlier. I will tell Dasji!'

He got the taxi, and reached the godown a good five minutes before Das, and the team of valuers.

'They are Bhoomijai's people,' Das said. 'Hold tight, now. He is buying, any price!'

'Good,' he said. 'Thank you for a beautiful girl. She will be there tonight?'

'Of course,' Das said. 'I told her. As long as you are welcome, go!'

'You pay her?'

'Why? She is my eldest daughter. What I do, what I offer, no matter. Can't find a husband!'

'Such a beautiful?'

'It is entirely dispiriting. A father these days has such burdens!'

'I subscribe sympathy. But if a daughter is known to be used, is she in the marriage market?'

'Why not? A healthy girl? Not one day's sickness? And a large sum coming with her? A real *catch*!'

'She is a champagne girl!'

'Of course. What use to be less?'

Das went off to supervise the valuers. Hammers and jemmies were being used to open. The place sounded and echoed with thuds. Prem strolled, watching, being certain that odd goods went in no pockets. He went to the gate, and told the havildar to make sure by search that nothing went out on the person. A note covered.

Hours of strolling, but a man came in with tea now and again, and time went well, because everything opened brought new joys, and Das telephoned Bhoomijai twice to say the list was correct and the contents intact and what time he could be expected with the money, because the trucks would be there at twelve sharp.

Miss Turlo came in late, and looking fussed, but he stopped apology.

'Tell your father not before five o'clock,' he said. 'It will take all that to empty this place. His consignment will stay here, but I want to see the cash. Telephone here at three. When you come, bring good sandwiches, please?'

'I will bring the best. Three o'clock, telephone? Poor boy, no sleep!'

'Poor girl, sleep with her father!'

'Not that, no. He still treats as a child.'

'How is a child treated?'

'Well. Cuddled?'

'Areas of doubt?'

She laughed, and turned away.

'Everything is nice!' she said. 'At three, telephone!'

Das made a final calculation, and put down the pencil.

'If he doesn't buy, I will,' he said.

'I would rather you made the money.'

'There is only this damned M.I.S.A. Such a big nuisance. More arrests in the news this morning. Big people. But not the really big. Bhoomijai is safe. I am not. I would be inside and lose everything. I would have to pay my nose. No. I will let Bhoomijai, and collect a per cent. It is safer. You *are* safe. A Ministry man. How lucky you are!'

'What is exactly this M.I.S.A.?'

An act of the Government. They can go in, the police and Customs and Income Tax, and turn everything upside down. What they find you must explain If tax paid, if dues paid, where got, how, when, show books, receipts the past several years. You see? A solid embarrass. No use to hide. They break walls. Dig. They have the warrant So off you go, to prison. Who will you see again? How much costing? How long you are kept? Who is doing the business? A solid loss. No. Let *him* do this. Bhoomijai is safe. Gupta Das who is he? Who has he paid? A few, and nobody. Of importance? *Nobody!'*

'Who's Bhoomijai paid?'

'O, *man*. The provincial government here, and others. Lok Sabha, more than half The party funds. Who not? He owns many newspapers. Who goes against him? I was in mass murder how you talked to him. But he likes You answered. You got him cake and milk. You will find him a good friend!'

'Why?'

'If you are so ready to serve a Minister to such a pitch, you could also serve him How often do you find a Prem Naran? Shit or bust? I tell you, you made a friend!'

The valuers were sitting to check totals, and Das went to telephone Bhoomijai. Trucks backed in to take the rest of the crates back to Delhi.

Mehta Roy ticked his list, and pasted labels.

'Dalji told me to get other trucks, and not go with them, but fly to Delhi,' he said, under the voice. 'Tomorrow when the first trucks arrive in Delhi, I will fly back here. Everything is in order, and he has a place to put everything Big trouble in Delhi. This M I.S.A. People getting arrested Houses searched. Warehouses sealed. Terrible happenings. But not Dalji. Too big. Too many friends the right place!'

Trucks backed in, forklifts hoisted crates, men pulled and sweated, empty space spread along the east wall the tea man came with paper cups and sweet cakes, and Bhoomijai dab-dabbed from behind a truck looking as though he had gone to bed in what he wore. Beyond him, a Mercedes came slowly with two men standing in the open doors.

'Well, my boy!' Bhoomijai said, with a big laugh. 'Still you are working? How fine!'

'We are almost finishing,' Prem said. 'If you have got the money, your trucks can load.'

'Your money is in this car. Mine, of course. You would like to count?'

Prem shook his head and put his hands behind his back.

'No, sir!' he said, loud over din. 'Who am I not to trust the word of a businessman so well known? Who am I to cast doubts at rectitude? The cartons will go sealed to the Minister. His accountancy department will do all necessary. My duty is finished, except for one lot. I wish we had met before I accepted offers. But they are not of interest to you. I hope one day to be of further service? I am always at the Ministry. Room Eleven. Completely at your orders!'

Bhoomijai stared the mudpats with shiny black lights, the cobra under the roof at Seripur.

'Good boy,' he said, smiling yellow teeth. 'Good boy. I am in Delhi next week. I shall call!'

Chapter 9

He felt sickened in deep shock to count the Turlo money short by three hundred thousand rupees.

In that moment he knew There was nothing to do He could never protest. He saw Miss Turlo's turn-away smile. Dr Turlo had come in. grey suit, black tie, glasses on a black silk cord. the most professional man. and the men with him opened certain cases and made sure of quantities, and the canvas bags of money were put on the desk, and the crates went on the trucks, and he was left alone, except for the tea man, staying to make better tea and more money

But in the count, on the desk, and in the hotel room, the money was short. Nearly four o'clock, he finished.

He knew only hurt, bruised, almost to show.

He rang the room, but the night man said Dr and Miss Turlo had checked out, and the head porter thought they had flown to Singapore.

He looked at his hands, not even clenched.

Das lifted the phone after plenty of rings He was easy to explain.

'O, don't tell me!' he said 'Bhoomijai told me to say he is slippery Perhaps a good doctor. But he is a stealer. His patients say so?'

'Why has he *any* patients?'

'O, you know patients?'

'Of course!'

'Ideas?' Das asked, thick with sleep.

'I have very good. I think Not you, but tell somebody send him a telegram, that the rest of his consignment is still in the godown, and send two trucks immediately. The two will be sent, here to there, day to day. Three, four, five times a day, send telegrams from both drivers, asking instructions. Every day send telegrams. When you know it has cost him at least half a million to keep the trucks on the road, send the drivers home. Yes? Remember, he is a greedy man!'

'Ah, Prem!'

'I leave it to you?'

'Leave!'

'I go tomorrow. You got your share from Bhoomijai?'

'Got. Very good!'

'You get also from me. The same. Write only the sum to Office One-One, Lok Sabha. I will send!'

'Prem, nobody, only nobody, except you. Remember, Das is here, ready!'

'Prem is also ready. Any time. Give your beautiful daughter a kiss for me. Next time!'

'She will be there, Premji. Good-night!'

On the flight back to Delhi he wrote several paragraphs of ideas, trying to find out how he would deal with Turlo. It was a matter of pride and conscience. No man should make a fool of another without punishment. He surprised himself by finding he had written, 'It is better to give than to receive.'

Always Mr Raybould was saying it. He frowned at the words, wondering how he thought of them at such a time. Never go in the mud. Let others wallow. Maintain an attitude of superiority at any cost. A proper pride is essentially part of a man of good sense.

He sat back to laugh at a foolish idea, but the more he thought and laughed, the better it seemed, and when they were in the aisles ready to get out, he knew the idea was right. It fitted everywhere.

Gond waited with Ganesh, brilliant in polish, and he, ultra-smart in the black driver's suit, polished black boots and the shiny helmet.

'Premji, two messages,' he said, giving *namaste*. 'The first from Zona. If you will go first to her I know where she is. The second from Miss Dowl. Vutthi will meet you tonight. Seven thirty!'

'Don't use that name again. You never heard it. She is A-Two!'

'A-Two!'

'Take these boxes to Babuji to be counted. Take my suit-case to Connaught Place office. Ask Babuji to count three hundred thousand in one of the bags. Bring also to the office. Separately, count this sum in cartons, and bring also to One-One. Take two scooterboys with you if no space. I will have a cab to One-One. Understood?'

A sideways nod, and he took the paper, and Ganesh bulled, roaring through the traffic.

It was good to be back in Delhi, and the sky was a lovely blue, but behind it, he knew the wine of the idea, making everything look wonderfully different and new but best of all, he knew that Mr Raybould would like what he was going to do.

All he saw seemed the same at Lok Sabha, except that everybody either stood or saluted, and it was a fine feeling. His box was full, but he rang Minister A, first, and heard he was out, and so was A-Two. He rang Minister B, but he, and B-Two were out. Dr Turlo was not at his hospital, or at his private nursing home, or at his house, and nobody knew when he would return.

He sat to taste how everything was marvellously turning out.

In the next hours he cleared the box, and when Gond came, he had a long list of what to do in coming days. All important, and all highly and unexpectedly profitable.

Mawri and another messenger carried the cartons of money, and the heavy canvas bag to his office, and he locked up, and went out.

'Dal's,' he told Gond, in royal manner. 'How is your sister at Seripur?'

'She is liking!' Gond shouted, in the wind. 'The men are working. But no furniture for her work. Boxes only!'

'Tomorrow. After Dal, Zona. After that A-Two. Now listen carefully. Find out where Dr Turlo got those trucks from. The ones he sent to Bombay. Ask the drivers where the loads were taken when they came here. Go and make sure they are still there. If they are, take your scooterboy team and do with them what you did with Rada's furniture. A good reward for all of them, and four times for you. No scooters near the place. No loud talking. They have eyes and ears. No mouth. Clear?'

Sideways nod, big smile.

'Very well. What about A-Two's house?'

'The man is called Bundi. He is young. His father has spinning mills and other business. More than a hundred women use the house. About twenty live there with board and food. They can use the kitchen. They earn a hundred every time, and more with percentage on drinks and laundry.'

'How, laundry?'

'Customers pay for new sheets and pillows!'

'I never heard of it!'

'I talked to a couple, and also to the dhobi man. He sells the used, and has no pay for the house laundry, but he pays Bundi a percentage of what he gets for selling bed linens.'

'Who is he selling to?'

'Hospitals, schools, hotels. Many buy. Only once used. Best quality!'

'We shall go there!'

Dal still worked in the plate glass office, and threw out his arms and almost ran.

'Ah, my Prem!' he shouted. 'Everything here, lock and key. Did we say two hundred each engine? The pretty Chryslers?'

'A slip of the tongue. *Five* is what we only discussed But they are new, not out of original factory grease To give us both a chance. I think we should split the difference and agree. Seven hundred and fifty each. You will make three to five times that. Is there argument?'

'I will pay flat three hundred!'

'Every time there is argument, price is up. It is now eight hundred!'

'Three-fifty I am meeting your confounded avarice!'

'*Eight*-fifty I can take them back and sell myself. Don't push. I can go backwards. *Out!*'

Dal stared the bad mood. His belly was blacker and fatter than Bhoomijai's.

'Half in rupees,' he said.

'*All* foreign currency. Dollars, sterling, Swiss francs, no matter. Market price. Eight-fifty dollars each, or equivalent. Taken?'

'You will be dollar millionaire!'

'You are many times over, not only in dollars. Why do you deny me? I am not your friend? You will turn over more than three times what I do? What have I done to you? Supplied you with new riches? You will punish me for it?

94

Very well. There are plenty more dealers – '

'No-a-a-ah!' Dal said, arms out, pretending to laugh as if he kicked his toe against the leg of the desk. 'Very well. Deal, yes. Eight-fifty. Two, three days, we settle? Cash? What else good?'

'I think probable, not exactly sure, a large tonnage of drugs and medicaments, and medical equipment. Complete X-ray. Cardiac. A complete hospital, with kitchen and store-rooms and carpets and uniforms, also, lighting and generator. Offer?'

'Where is proof?'

'Catalogue. I will send Gond. It will need many five-tonners, perhaps ten to shift It is all here in Delhi. Perhaps you know doctor wanting for modern, new inventions, hospital, or nursing home?'

'Price?'

'Make up your mind. Sell for two or three times. Or we split fifty-fifty. Foreign currency!'

'Let me see catalogue!'

'Tomorrow. One word. If the name of Dr Turlo crops, keep tight mouth. He is in the market for new nursing home. But the Minister has more than a grudge. There will never be permit. If you have siren's song from that quarter, you could be included in displeasure. Haven't you got buses order for public transport outstanding?'

Dal opened his eyes and mouth as if he saw a tiger crouch for the kill.

'Ah!' he said 'I heard the name only with acrimony. It will never be heard again. Find lay of the land, there, Prem. When I might see a contract?'

'I will find But I need palm oil. You know that?'

Sideways nod.

'In reason, yes,' Dal said. 'But not fleecing!'

'Nobody will fleece my friends,' Prem said. 'It is my principle. If my friends pay, they have a guarantee of service. I am there, on the spot!'

'Ah, Premji, you are in right place. We shall do many nice business, no arguments, no ups in price. How soon for the contracts *and* the licences? What else is going on?'

'A good lot But I must buckle down for a couple of days. A lot is happening while I am away. See you tomorrow. What about the scootercabs?'

'End of the month. *Cash?*'

'*Cash!*'

Outside, he nodded to Gond, and they turned for Connaught Place.

Gond stopped at the corner, and pointed, and he went in, up the stairs, to a first floor office, a new building, all glass, and carpets, and white paint, but the windows were dirty. He went in, and a girl looked at him from an empty desk.

'My name is Prem Naran,' he said. 'I want to see Zona, please?'

'O, yes. She is expecting. Moment!'

She knocked at the inner door, and put her head in, and opened wide, and smiled around at him, nodding.

Zona sat at a small desk, and got up to put her arms about his neck.

'So much to say!' she said. 'Sit, and have a drink and a smoke, and let me talk. First, both the Disco and the Sludge are closed for alteration and painting. All our people were pushed out. Is it fair?'

'Of course not. We will open again. Tell them they have their usual money. Only find the new place!'

'I have got,' she said. 'On the other side. Big parking space. Better than this. You have a big enemy. Inspector Ram and his friends. They are hunting. Twice they are here. Looking what for? Alcohol, tobacco. I told Inspector we are no longer in the business. Sold to Dal, and Dal wants me to go up north and find new girls. Younger. He is paying good price.'

'Get some for us!'

'When shall we open?'

'End of next month, perhaps? I will keep you busy. I am going to move Mujid in here, and a finance man, and also a lawyer. We want five large desks and only leather chairs. Carpets. One office for each. Private. An impression of wealth. Security. Solidity. I am going in property. Purchase only. And transport. A lot of money in both.'

'You will need a lot!'

'I have got. You will tell Dal I will let you go for ten days only. Then you are bringing the girls back here, and we are taking the pick. I want ten cases of whisky and ten boxes of cigars at my office tomorrow. Bedwa will bring. Also, if instructions come from Seripur, it is from me. Always from me. And have those windows cleaned. We need a *chuprassi* and a khitmatgar. Ours, from the Disco. You will be earning twice your present wage packet, and you will have a car. You must think of a lot to do. Only for *me*!'

'I would never work for anybody, only you!' she said, and came close. 'But you have got only trousers on, and I hate buttons and zip. I won't touch. Please come in the dhoti. You know how I love to tickle?'

'Dhoti next time,' Prem said. 'Always be sure the windows are clean. Always a sign, dirty windows!'

He went down and found Gond, and they turned for Bundi's house, used by a hundred women, and lived in by twenty or more.

A big place, with an iron gate, and a garden, and two floors, not in good repair, and Gond turned in and stopped at the side door, open. An old woman came out, smiling.

'I want to see Bundi,' he said.

'I can take the money?'

'No money. Talk, only!'

'No girls?'

'No. Bundi!'

She nodded him in.

The place had the rotten sweet of a whore's bath and talc. But why was a whore's bath different from any other girl's? It was what they put in it to keep health.

The talc covered sores?

She knocked on a door, and opened, and turned her head. Bundi sat on the divan, reading.

'You are paying rent to Miss Dowl?' Prem asked, loudly.

'Rent? Rent I am not paying!' the man said, closing the book. 'Ask Mr Ramahar!'

'Who is he?'

'Lawyer for Miss Dowl. What's this nonsense?'

He got up, tall, a Gujarat, wearing a blue pagri wrapped around the top of his head, with a blue feather sticking out over his left ear, white shirt, blue trousers and sandals.

'It is far from nonsense,' Prem said. 'You are in danger. You know it?'

'You are in danger!'

'From?'

'*Me*. Get out!'

'Very well. On your own head!'

'I will throw you on yours!'

'I shall bounce. Good-night!'

'Go to hell, you very little incongruous bum!'

'Remember me!'

He went out, hearing music inside, and got in Ganesh.

'Take me to A-Two, and then find Bedwa, and tell him to bring the lathis here. Get your scooterboys and the trucks. When the lathis have beaten everybody, go in and remove everything. Do not destroy anything. Tell Bedwa to find this Bundi, and put him in the Jumna. Clear? Four times usual gift. Enough?'

Sideways nod, big smile over shoulder.

'Meet me at A-Two, and we shall come back to make sure!'

He got out a couple of hundred yards away, and found Vutthi waiting in her white plaits and put notes in the soft hand, and followed her up the pink stair, to the door, and in, to white lamps, and Shiva, lying on the big white divan, naked, smiling, holding out a hand.

'Ah, Prem! What about my house?'

'It will be empty tomorrow. Everything in place. Now. Proposition. Who is this Ramahar?'

'My lawyer, of course?'

'Your *cheater*. I will deal with him. Not to his liking. Listen to me. Tonight, the house is empty. I will put my own people in. I will have a hundred and more new girls. Sikh, and Gujarat, and Bengalis, all sorts of others there. Fresh. I will have doctor and nurse. It will be the best in India. Minimum two hundred rupees. Special services extra. Flowing champagne. All facilities. All profits, sixty per cent to you for locality, forty to me for running, both to share equally expenses. It could be half million a day. No tax!'

She turned on her back. Love moss climbed her belly beautifully.

'Ah, Prem! How I have wanted to be free of that office!'

'You are free. But wait. You know what the Minister is doing? The grains, and working bullocks-in-yoke with the other Ministers, selling licences, and all the foreign loans, and what else?'

'*Everything* else. Nothing they are not doing for money!'

'Tell *me*!'

'How?'

'Tell me. I can turn every move into profit. For both. Of course?'

'You would share with me?'

'How else am I in good place? How do I know? Your

98

knowledge, my brain, it's not a good partnership? You will always feel sweet in the bank. Because of *me*. Because I worship Shiva!'

'But isn't Shiva a man?'

'Man or woman. Where does Hinduism make a difference?'

Shiva raised her arms, and they fell on the bed, and she raised a knee.

'Hinduism!' she said. 'Such a term. What does it mean?'

'I don't know. I don't think anybody does. They pretend to. So do I. We are all equal. So? That is Hinduism. But what is the story behind this son-in-law of Ministerji over the road? What is between his Ministry, and *that* Ministry, and industry?'

'The son is socialist, or something. My Minister hates him. He will destroy that Minister!'

'How?'

'The land belongs to the Government. The industry was built on foreign loans.'

'And so? Where is the cheating?'

'The Minister builds without permits. He shares all profits. They all share. Share to you, share to me. Where is responsibility?'

'But for national good? Who has no benefit?'

'The people. They *pay*!'

'You don't like?'

'I *hate*. I work, and I work. And I *hate* the Minister. I wish I knew what to do. I roll in bed with him. I wish I didn't. If I didn't, he would throw me away. I wouldn't work. I know it. I go to bed. It's easier. When will you tell me how to *screw* him?'

'You will meet at the Mashoba again?'

'Next week. Thursday. Four o'clock. I am there three-thirty!'

'Look for me, between three-thirty and four-thirty. You will be late. You understand?'

'I am at the Mashoba not before four o'clock?'

'It is correct time!'

'What will you do?'

'You will see. But you will not stay. You will go. You understand?'

'Go?'

'Go like hell. I will have taxi waiting. Understand?'

'Perfect. Prem, you are not coming near?'

'I worship. You are so beautiful. Now, until Thursday. Lotus petals in a beautiful pale shower on black love moss. Again, only worship!'

He went out to darkness and Vutthi's hand, surety down dark stairs and out. Gond flashed red lights, and he found, and got it.

'Well?'

'Everything done. Bundi gone. House empty. But servants all Harijan!'

'Keep them. They have no ears, no eyes, no mouths. Take me to the New Place. Go back to the house of Bundi. Tell our people they are safe. Give them this money. Here is money for the lathis. I will pay Bedwa. Here is yours. To-morrow, New Place, six o'clock. You found where Dr Turlo put everything?'

'Everything was taken. It is all in place for you!'

'Nothing left out?'

'It is empty sand!'

'You will have much more. How did the girls go?'

'With lathis. A sweet slap!'

'They made a noise? No police?'

'Screams, yes. But they ran. They are fat behind. The lathis chose the fattest part. There are many drugs in that house. Much whisky. All is in safe place. We serve only Premji!'

'It's good. Tomorrow, before midday, you come to One-One. We have others waiting. Put your boys to watch Zona. Nothing is quite right. And Inspector Ram?'

'Tomorrow I tell. When I know. It is also not quite right. She works with Inspector Ram. They have the same apart-ment. Tomorrow?'

Chapter 10

Even though Zona might be living with Inspector Ram, and that was shock enough, still that girl in the front office worried him all through the next couple of days. He knew he must have seen her somewhere, and wherever it had been, there seemed a threat of some sort. He hardly knew how to think about it. He scratched his brains in all areas, without result, and he felt nervous, but not so much that the job suffered.

Too much to do was almost a description, but working at night from the early morning brought everything in grasp. Messages came from A and B. They were coming back from a meeting in Calcutta. From Miss Turlo, no word. Ministers G and P wanted him for interviews. Eight bankers and eleven industrialists booked a meeting with various departments for many reasons, and all of them had their several charges, and they all had to be arranged, with payments in full, of course, in advance. They all went right, simply, and he had notes from Ministers that they were pleasantly surprised at his, as one put it, radical efficiency. He always got a signature for money paid from the secretary, with the initials of the Minister, or whoever had charge of the section, and he time-and-date clocked them downstairs in the Records Office, and his files were in splendid order, and not a doubt in the world.

Except that face in the front office of Connaught Place. He *had* seen her. But where?

Zona had gone north to find girls, and Gond told him Inspector Ram had not been at the house since she left, but his uniforms were there, and books, not reading books but writing, not English.

'Try to get for me. I can copy and send back. Can you do it?'

Sideways nod.

He was called to Minister B's office at five o'clock, and Miss Turlo – no! B-Two – let him in, with a string of messengers carrying cartons, cases of whisky and cigars. They stacked them, and he counted, ticked them off, one by one, knowing that B-Two watched him every moment.

He gave her no glance.

'The total is correct,' he said, back to her. 'I want the Minister to have them checked. I will not go till it is done!'

'But we are closing in twenty minutes!'

'I will not go till everything is checked!'

'The Minister will be very angry!'

'Show him cigars and whisky. Tell him this sum in cartons. I want it checked. I will not go until it is!'

'You are so difficult!'

'Talk to Minister. Here is the memo!'

She tapped, and went in.

The Minister came out, and looked over wide horn-rimmed glasses, and smiled.

'Ah, my boy, you have done so well!' he said, and rubbed his hands. 'Good. Good. Never mind to count. Leave it all here!'

'Ministerji, I will take it to the safe. It will be counted. You will sign!'

'You will do as *I say*!'

'Ministerji, there is this sum in those cartons. If that sum is not there tomorrow, you have got a thief!'

'You suspect?'

'From experience, yes!'

The Minister looked at the paper with the sum, and smiled, taking off the spectacles.

'You have done so much more than I hoped!' he said. 'Did you take out your ten per cent?'

'Ministerji, it's twenty-five!'

'It was never more than ten! How is this? Am I unconscious of what I say? Open a carton, and take ten per cent of this figure. It is enough!'

'As you wish, Ministerji!'

He opened the pocket knife and split a carton. Notes were in bank-counted one thousand packets. He took out ten per cent of the total figure, and put them stacked square on the desk, and went to the door, calling Mawri, and carefully piling the heap in his arms.

'My desk in One-One,' he said, giving him the keys. 'Stay until I come down. Nobody in or out!'

'You are now giving orders?' the Minister said, hands behind, strict.

'In my own small place, yes. It is quite necessary to protect cash!'

'Agreed. But don't go beyond your place!'

'Ministerji, if I have no place, how can I go beyond? I do as I am told. You will not check what is yours?'

'Too long it takes. Never mind. Tell them to put boxes in my private car. You did surprisingly. No doubts in Bombay? No enquiries? Nothing hanging? Doctor Turlo? Everything in order?'

'My assurance, Ministerji. Everything in order. No names. Only mine. Who am I?'

The Minister put out a hand to touch his shoulder.

'So good boy!' he said, folding the large horn-rimmed glasses. 'I have much more to do. Come here tomorrow, four o'clock. Bijou, be very kind to him. *Very* kind. He has done remarkably. Very well, Prem!'

He went back to the office, and the glass door slammed.

'Come down to One-One,' he said. 'If you think only I work, you are wrong. I have a present for you!'

'For me?' she said, turning in surprise. 'Why, for me?'

'Don't we work together? A percentage for me? No percentage for you? But how is that fair? If you work, and I work, then proper pay, the same work. No?'

'Well. I suppose?'

'No suppose. Come down to One-One. Have your share. In everything else, your proper share!'

'I will come. Half an hour?'

He went over to One-One, and Mawri was still there, and he gave him a pack of notes.

'There will be more,' he said. 'You have no mouth. Don't show!'

Mawri raised a right hand in salute, and pushed the pack in his shirt, and went. The head sweeper squatted beyond the curve, and came at a sign, and he gave him a handful.

'More to come,' he said. 'Eyes, ears, but no mouth!'

Sideways nod, and a kiss for the giving hand.

He totalled paper and separated the done from the waiting, and phoned a few numbers, and a call came through, and while he waited, he knew suddenly, a shock, where he had seen the girl, a couple of years before, or more, and it was like a terrible voltage ripping hot over his body.

She was a daughter of a retired Raj soldier. He had a cook-shop for many years. His wife was the cook and they had many daughters to help. Every night, seven o'clock, he sat out on the grass in front of the place, with a strong electric light shining white on the Indian flag and the Raj's flag, with his daughters in white saris behind, and he in white shirt and trousers, not one move, as if they were carved in white clay, and people went in, and came out, because the food was good, and not much to spend, but he was still there, and so were his daughters, and sometimes his wife came out to put a hand on his shoulder, and stand still behind him, the beautiful strength.

A white group, against black sky, two flags above, cooking smells blowing, a man living his time not in his own country, with a woman not of his kind, with children half of his race, loving them, knowing his people had only contempt for them, but sitting, firm, clean, his own self, under two flags, chosen in bravery, and proving himself, in that chair, night after night. Yeoman, strong, English, of the ageless and wonderful, and inspiration for Harijan because Anglo-Indians were same level or worse.

That girl, in the front office, was one of those daughters, and all except two had gone into the police. Not exactly, but they had become agents, informers, snakes. He knew it from Tuko, the insurance manager, when he sized the premium for the Disco.

'If you are going to have complete insurance, for God's sake have a somebody here to tell you what to expect!' he said. 'Everybody can set a fire. It is too simple. You have a big kitchen? Very well. A little methylated spirit? Paraffin? Gas cylinders? Is it *so* much trouble? How do you think *we* feel? Insurance? We are paying criminals. Do I want to pay you for disaster? *No.* Then how do we defend? Put some-body in, and pay weekly!'

She had been one of the weekly defenders, watching others, gathering information about the staff, and people coming in. He remembered seeing her only once or twice, a little thing, and somebody else took her place. But why was she in that office? How did Zona find her?

With the help of Inspector Ram, of course.

He began to think somebody was trying to break him.

Perhaps he knew too much, or somebody could have laid information, and Inspector Ram wanted more evidence. Zona could give plenty. Her, living in the same apartment, that was a true shock. He would have to confront with a long talk, and a clean breast, or else the Jumna. He had no liking for the thought of that little hand, slyly in his dhoti, going in the river. But if she was a crack in the wall, plaster was the only answer, and no doubt, and he intended.

He looked outside, and nodded to the head sweeper, and told him to take the two cartons, which should have gone to Minister B, out to Bedwa, and come back for the 10 per cent in the block he was packing. That would make a total of not 25 per cent, as the Minister had promised, but just over 40, which, all things equal, was justice. A man should keep his word, or suffer. And after all, who did the work? The engines with Dal, of course, would be extra, and so would the many crates of spares he said nothing about, though at the right time they would be only gold.

Gond tapped a rap of knuckles, and held out notebooks, police official issue, and three thicker books, Urdu in all of them, that he had only a word of here and there.

'We will go over to Finance,' he said. 'Mr Sen. Then back here, and wait for me!'

Sen put down the pencil, and smiled, gentle as ever in the dusty dark.

'Well, welcome back,' he said, and reached for a thick envelope. 'Mukherjee and I went through these. In law, there is really no case. None. But there are large doubts about the other side. They would have serious questions to answer, and they would have to part with enormous sums in litigation. Mukherjee thinks he could pose the questions. To the tune of crores!'

'Listen to me. I know how much you earn. I know Mukherjee's. I will pay, starting tomorrow, three times what you are drawing now. To work for me. I will put five years' salary for each of you to draw weekly. Pension you will also have. A deal?'

'You can't do it!'

'If I show bank receipt tomorrow for both, you believe?'

'Only that!'

'Tell Mukherjee. Meantime, look at these books. I know

you are also Urdu scholar. See if I am mentioned, and who else. No mouth!'

'Cave-like silence!'

Gond took him back to the office, and he had almost finished the day's diary, and a messenger announced Miss Turlo, and she came in quietly, and he pointed to the chair, but before she could sit, he put a one-thousand rupee package of notes on the desk.

'Take off,' he said, still writing. 'That is yours, and another five thousand as well. Work with me is profit. Take everything off. Naked, sit in the chair!'

'Somebody will come in!'

'Nobody. The door locks inside. Off!'

Slowly, she stood, and undressed slowly, and he went on writing, and then he knew she was naked, and he put the pen down, and got up unbuttoning, and took her hand, and put her sitting over his lap, and felt it go in.

'Now we enjoy,' he said, hands pressing creamy coffee jelly. 'When you want, come down. When I think Bijou, I phone, you come. Everytime, money. But I want to know about the Minister. What he does. His friends. What he is doing!'

She moved, with her arms around his neck, and shutting her lips against little sounds, and he flooded, and sun shone, and he thought of the Guru's eyes, and she cried sweet in his shoulder, and moved again, and drew breath in an open mouth, and her muscles softened, and she was sitting on him, and he was soft, and fell out.

Slowly he stood, and pressed her to him.

'You are more beautiful every time,' he whispered. 'Come often. Tell me about the Minister. Everything is cash. I will help you. What use to cuddle your father? You also have two brothers. They also cuddle you? For what price? You give yourself away for nothing? Turn your mind. Be with me!'

'I *am* with you,' she said, and reached for clothes. 'The Minister is worried about newspapers. He is afraid what they will say. You sold that stuff? It is only part!'

'And your father?'

'He has a share in something. It is chiefly drugs, and antibiotics. You won't say I said?'

She was soft to his squeezing arms.

'Get me all the details,' he said. 'Everything has its price to you. Why should you work for nothing? Only to cuddle? How much? What silliness!'

'You are right,' she said, pushing a foot in a shoe. 'You are completely right. Very well. Tomorrow, shall I ring, or come down?'

'Come down, and we will find out what is worth. Do you hear the name, Inspector Ram?'

'Police? Certainly!'

'Explain to me why. Where he is interested. Who is behind. It could be danger to the Minister. And to you. I should speak to the Minister. Ram is too close for benefit. He could tip the apple carts. In all directions. An untrustworthy nonsense. We must throw him to the hyaenas. A howl from them, it's enough?'

He still worked at past eight o'clock, and Mawri came to say that Mr Sen from Finance wished to see him urgently.

'In!'

Sen looked distressed, waiting till the door was closed.

'Those damn books, man!' he almost whispered. 'Police records. Will you have me arrested? I dare not bring them here in case I was stopped. You are several times mentioned. A suspect. Many crimes. Too long to remember. There are many pages about ministers, what they are doing for money. Ex-ministers, also. Many others in the high-up. And his own bank accounts in many banks, and detailed lists of people giving, and dates. I wash my hands. I could be prosecuted. Finish!'

'Go back to your place. Wait for a scootercab to come. Give him the other half of this, and the books. See you tomorrow!'

He scribbled red pencil lines, and tore the paper in halves, and gave one to Sen.

'Give books to him only. Fifteen minutes!'

'I'm not in danger?'

'None. Be calm!'

He left Sen at the steps, and gave the other half of the paper to Gond, waiting in the darkness, and told him to go to Finance, show the paper only to Mr Sen, and take the other half, and a package, and bring them back.

A little past nine, and Mawri opened the door, and it was unpleasant to see Inspector Ram, but without the smile.

'Ah, Inspector!' he said, pushing the chair away from the desk. 'Unexpected pleasure. Mawri, when the messenger returns, keep the two papers, and hold the package in the Archivist's Office. Now, Inspector. Take a seat!'

'You employed a woman known as Zona?' Inspector Ram said, standing.

'Until a few weeks ago, yes?'

'You found her trustworthy?'

'Completely. Four years, no trouble. She handled cash, stocks, tickets, paid wages, made pay-ins at the bank. She was a wonderful manageress!'

'You don't know where she is?'

'Only she could tell. North, is all. Bareilly? Chandigarh? Even to Calcutta.'

'No special addresses?'

'No small idea. Why is this enquiry?'

'Certain articles are missing. From my apartment.'

'Of any value?'

'Nothing much.'

He was twisting the stick, fidgeting, and his eyes were down, and up, and down, and dangerous.

'How did she come to be there?'

'We were living,' the Inspector said, looking at him.

'I didn't know. I knew nothing about her private life. Business only!'

'How did you buy Disco and the place behind?'

'My foster-father left me the money. I invested. It was success!'

'Why did you sell to Dal?'

'I have a big job here. No time for other things. So I sold to Dal. He bought. Is it something to do with this matter?'

'Possibly. Is why I am here!'

'I shall call our Security Officer, Superintendent Murthi Singh. I am not having cross-examinations!'

Inspector Ram got up, and stood the stick upright on the desk, and leaned.

'Superintendent Murthi should not be disturbed,' he said, with a scrape in his voice. 'I will deal with you!'

'How deal with me? What have I done?'

Knocks, and Mawri put a head around the door.

'The messenger has delivered two papers and a package from Finance, Premji!' he said. 'You would like tea?'

'Tea, yes,' he said. 'Perhaps the Inspector would like?'

'Nothing!'

'One tea, Mawri!'

'One tea, Premji!'

'Show out the Inspector!'

'This way, please!'

'I will deal with you, I have warned. Remember!'

A savage stutter, and he was pushing past Mawri.

'Is the fellow mad?' Mawri shouted, and heard well down the corridor. 'He isn't allowed in here without permit. I let him in only for you. But next time, no!'

'Good. You go home. I will have tea, and work a little more. Send the package here!'

The books stolen from the Inspector's apartment had been marked with pink slips, with rough note translations in Sen's handwriting.

The Inspector knew a great deal more. Too much more. There were informers at Seripur, that was plain. He knew about the stores kept there. He knew about the cigarettes, cigars and alcohol purchases, and the names of the Customs people, and the cloth, perfume and cameras, and God knows what. He knew where to look. But he also knew about ministers, and others, and many State Governors, and more.

He also made plenty of money, in bribes. The names and dates were all there. Shrewd, but not intelligent, to write full notes in Urdu, a language not well known to most, and then leave where others might look, or steal. The police had their own way of gathering information, but he was deeply worried to think that others in the department might share all or some of the items in those books.

Himself, he knew he could be crushed beneath the level of earth, no effort, and barely a mark on paper. Reading the scraps of translation, he seemed to have the notion he was an easy mark. He could be blamed for a great deal. The Ministers could deny. They were safe. But Prem Naran was not. He had nowhere to appeal. At this moment, if the police raided, Seripur could be robbed of everything in the stores, and they would never again be seen, and neither would he, or Babuji, or anybody else Inspector Ram thought necessary.

They would all go.

He unpinned Sen's pink slips, and put in green where Minister A was mentioned, yellow for Minister Q, blue for Minister D, white for Minister P, red for Minister S, and sand for Minister M. There were others, but not so much, and he left the rest of the pinks.

He locked all the books, except one, in the safe with all the other papers, and went out to find Gond.

'Go to Seripur, find Babuji, and have everything moved from the sheds. Put anywhere. Empty sheds tomorrow. Workmen sleeping there? Send away. Somebody has a mouth. The police know. Tell your sister. Tell Babuji. Somebody is saying. Who? New Place, tomorrow, six o'clock?'

Sideways nod, fright in staring eyes, and the boy had gone, and Ganesh howled full-throat.

He called a scootercab, and went to Minister A's house. There was light, and Western music, and women on the vedanda. He found the *chowkidar*, and told him to see the *khitmatgar* and tell the Minister there was important business outside.

Minutes he waited, and the Minister was big, black in the doorway.

'How are you here?' he said, high voice, angry.

He gave the book, picking at the slips.

'I managed to find, Ministerji!' he said. 'I think there is no time. Is why I am heré!'

The Minister looked at him, nastily.

'I don't like to be pulled here and there!' he said, taking the book under the light. 'What is this?'

'Look the green, Ministerji!'

'After hours, totally prohibited!'

'Serious information, Ministerji?'

'I will see!' the Minister said, flipping pages to the green tabs.

But then he was silent, looking out to the dark garden, and again at the page, and out, to the dark.

He turned, slapped the book shut.

'Prem, you did wisely and well!' he said. 'I must take care of this fellow. My office, tomorrow, ten-thirty. Thank you. You are worth your weight!'

Chapter 11

Light just touched the banyan tree in tall silver drench when he reached Seripur, and Babuji sat at his desk, and people wanting loans waiting, squatting, almost round the circle of stones.

'Everything has gone,' Babuji said, and smiled purple betel teeth in greenish light of the gaslamp. 'Now, Prem. Who is the mouth? Only some miscreant in this Seripur of ours. I called all borrowers together last night. I told them no more loans until we find this dastardly gossip upsetting our pattern of decent economy. Who? I am regretting I must say your woman at the house. Halima. From telephone girl. She said she heard twice. To number in Delhi. Police number!'

'You have spoken?'

'I spoke. She is no longer in your house. I have found another!'

'Where is Halima?'

'Where her ashes have been taken by the night wind. Everything in the sheds, safe. Nobody will find. Well done?'

'Very well. But how is it Halima, so many years faithfully serving?'

'She had visitor many times. A mechanic, we heard. But not. A known police fellow. We found. Too late? But next time he comes with flowers and foreign sweetmeats, he joins her. You agree?'

'Agree. With gift, doubled, for those doing work. You, also. What guarantee no repeat?'

Babuji looked at rose light blessing with rising sun under the blue banyan shadow:

'Guarantee, no,' he said. 'How many fools are always blinded with love or promises? Always there are some. But if they are found, they know their ashes will join hers. That is the only *real* guarantee. Besides, now we are watching. Please go to the house and assure if the woman is agreeable. If not, another of your choice!'

'Very well,' he said, and gave him the Ram books. 'Babuji, your family language is Urdu? Please read, and tell me what this fellow has written. He would kill us!'

'I will deal only with these,' he said, nodding at the squatters. 'You will have back tonight, accomplished.'

'Careful you do not have a raid. If the books are found, you will *never* be!'

Babuji stood, stamped for blood, and waved a hand.

'No more!' he said. 'Tomorrow, come. Today, no!'

He went through the garden, knowing what heavy heart means, heavy to know Halima could stab him in the back, and still look after the house of Mr Raybould. Had she taken the informer down below? Did that pest Ram know of the building under the swimming pool? Had she told him of the safe behind the rock wall? The gold blocks? Everything? All the years, for nothing? Except to give riches to Ram. He would keep everything except a percentage for evidence.

His heart was heavy enough to beat terribly out of his ribs.

He felt a net closing, wire mesh cutting in the skin.

He went in, closing the door quietly as a thief. No sound, everything in place, only birds chatting outside. In the kitchen, only white cleanliness. In Mr Raybould's study, all shining. In the bedroom, blankets humped. Someboy slept, long breaths, safe, sweet. He went over, raised the blanket, a child's face, no lines, only peace.

Khusti, Gond's sister, the very pick of all picks.

Then, he knew, the office must be built on the house, part of it.

He went, not to make noise, and found Babuji locking the desk.

'Everything out of the house,' he said, giving the keys. 'They could come any day. Today, even. If they find nothing, they could burn. From temper. We can build walls and roof. Books, no. Other respected articles touched by loved hands, no. Everything out, and fourfold gift!'

Babuji put hands to forehead in perfect *namaste*, older, more of grace, and took the little silver bell, and the voice echoed down the street, and as a trick, doors opened, and men and women ran, folding dhotis and saris, and children ran behind.

'I leave,' Prem said, and nodded to Gond. 'He will be here tonight for your translation. We will put this hyaena in his own company!'

On the ride back, he thought of the threatened Ministers, and how he could prove he was more competent to deal with threats from the Police side, or from newspapers, or anywhere or anyone else. He saw many long avenues opening up. Zona could be useful. Living with Inspector Ram, she might give a few tips on next moves. B-Two might help in many ways.

But suddenly, he was sure that the secretary of Minister M, Miss Tata, would be the one, no doubt, only true and of trust, complete, nothing to complain, or lack.

At the office he looked at the papers in the box, small problems, nothing, to be finished in a couple of hours, and went out, found Gond, and howled over to Ministry M, and M-Two, Miss Tata.

She brought him up immediately, and again salutes, and he knew she had given the word, and he put the best of his mind with hers.

'A couple of problems?' she asked, head on one side, so nice.

'More,' he said. 'Your Minister is in serious trouble. You know it?'

'It is worse,' she said, very quietly. 'I know it. So does he!'

'If he goes, you will also go?'

She raised her hand.

'The civil service version of *suttee*!' she said. 'Very well. I will go!'

'No need. Follow what I say. Yes?'

She looked at him, Brahmin, high-born, educated everywhere, and he, she knew so well, a complete nobody, and yet she smiled, and immediately he loved her.

'Yes!' she said. 'I shall trust you. Completely!'

He loved her, at her feet.

What is so silly as love? But a concrete is an immediate mixture of cement and water. Who knows which is water, or cement, when the concrete is under the hammer? Who can tell?

It was a real love, but only for what she was, not for her,

as a woman, or for her body, or her sex, but only for herself, the Brahmin, not only the B.A. but the M.A. behind her name, both far beyond him, and her honesty, jewels in her eyes, and for what she thought of him and the trust she was giving him, and what he knew he could do to earn it, make it more consolidate.

While he thought, he put the papers on the table, flattened the pages, turned to the tabbed questions.

'First, this matter didn't come from this office?' he said. 'You never typed any of this? These are not your initials?'

'They are not. They are not from this office. See Mr Bhatt!'

'We are over the first jump!'

'Why?'

'It has to be proved that these instructions came from this office. That you knew these sums and quantities in foreign aid and currencies were being exported to other places. You did?'

'I did not!'

'But you have dealt with these matters?'

'When I realised that oddities were being practised as official business, I refused. I referred them to Mr Bhatt's Minister!'

'Who dealt?'

'That Minister's own private law office, I believe? I have never touched since that moment. You think something can be saved?'

'*You* will be saved. Nothing will be allowed to touch. What is the address of that Minister's private law office? And his son-in-law's?'

She wrote, and he took the page.

'What is of danger in this is the interferences of Customs and Income Tax officials,' he said. 'They will need a lot of money!'

She turned her back.

'I don't wish to hear about it!' she said.

'You will tell to the Minister that I need money? Not in cheque. For example, this address for the son-in-law is not the same as the telephone book. It is a cover-up? I cannot be in cover-up. You will mention?'

'Very well. I shall mention. That's all!'

'It's enough. Please let me know in Room Eleven I have help, and cash backing. By this afternoon, five o'clock?'

'Very well. But no correspondence!'

'Unnecessary. Miss Tata, M.A., I am Prem Naran. Your servant!'

She smiled him beautifully out of the door, and he took the memory of pale-blue-and-white flowered sari, and white sandals, and red toenails.

He knew time was short. With the Maintenance of Internal Security Act in force, the police, or Customs, or Income Tax, or all of them, could raid at any time, and take away any books or files they wished, or cash or jewellery, and it was certain most would never be seen again.

'Go to these two places,' he told Gond, giving him Miss Tata's paper. 'Bring in the scooterboys. Back and front door watch for the next few days. Who goes in, who comes out. Find out from any of our people working there, what is the type of work. Tell them to save all the paper. Who is working there, and where they live. Who is on the telephone switchboard. Banks used. Any detail we need. These people work first against *us*!'

Sideways nod.

'Your sister looks after my house. It may be raided today. She must not be there. When you leave me, go to Seripur. But not on Ganesh. You will be known. Take any other scooter. Come back to One-One. Be sure Khusti is very safe. I will go to the Minister's private office. I will see what there is!'

Sideways nod.

The Minister's private office showed a brass plate, as solicitor, broker, and bullion merchant, in a big building on the ground floor. Fifteen people worked in the outer office, with typewriters and all sorts of other machines. Prem walked about to see what he could, and came back, pleased to find the boys would have no trouble getting in.

'Bedwa can pick up waste paper as usual at six,' he said, back at One-One, and gave Gond the second paper. 'Names and addresses of everybody, here, chief clerks, names, addresses. Go in for all the files. These go to B-Two. She will give you more information for me. She said if it is the newspaper complaint, she knows. She has every fact ready!'

'She is of us? Miss Turlo?'

'Anglo-Indian!'

'The same?'

'The same. Take her a nice present, next time. Flowers. Chocolates. Every week, a present. Become known!'

115

Sideways nod, more howl from Ganesh.

The son-in-law of Minister P had a big office behind shru[b]
Many cars were in the drive. No brass plates said. He went
to a cool hall, and a woman writing behind a desk. Her h[air]
reminded of Miss Tata's, dark, shining, drawn back in thi[n]
plaits curled on the neck.

'Mr Arun is not available,' she said, not looking up fro[m]
his note.

'Please say I am from the Ministry,' he said, putting dow[n]
the other paper. 'I am in Room Eleven, Lok Sabha. The[re]
will be no further opportunity!'

She got up, and went in the small lift, and he took [the]
Indian Express, and sat on the corner of the desk, and re[ad]
about the hockey, and cricket, and it was so peaceful.

Gond came in the doorway, and nodded, arms out, tak[ing]
in the building.

'Everything!' he whispered. 'Nothing missed!'

He saw the lift light coming down, and signed to Gond [to]
go.

The glass door opened, and she held, smiled.

'Mr Arun will see you!' she said. 'He is so busy!'

They went up to the second floor, and carpets, and a l[ong]
room of desks, and two men among a dozen girls, all b[usy]
with paper, to a door, and she tapped, and held open.

Mr Arun sat at a desk in a room like so many films,
glass, and chrome, and leather, and books. He was a [soft]
fellow, about thirty-something, dressed in the height, w[ith]
silk shirt and striped tie, and shiny oiled hair, and s[oft]
glasses.

'Well?' he said, in a voice strained with cauliflo[wer]
through hair sieve. 'What I do for you?'

'I have this, this, and this,' he said, and put down a p[aper]
with each. 'There is no time. Arrests are imminent. Sea[rch]
warrants have been issued. Only you must decide!'

Arun read and flipped aside the sheets, and lay back in [the]
big chair, eyes up, staring.

'Not true!' he whispered. 'O, not *true*!'

'The search squads will find out. It may be today. I am
here for nothing. I have transport ready. Only say!'

'How do I know you are not police informer?'

'Come to my office at Lok Sabha. Come with me to [the]
Minister. How am I informer?'

'No guarantee. The Minister is also in danger!'

116

'Known. Why I am here? Tonight, you can be behind bars!'

'So will he!'

'So sure? He is Minister. Who are you? How long it will take you to get out of prison? How much it will cost you?'

Arun put hands on the chair arms, leaning forward, closed eyes.

'Very well,' he said, dead. 'I will say where everything is. Take it. Go to hell with it. But if I am in trouble, I will tell. I have the proof!'

'Only a fool wants trouble. I am here to stop it all sides. Give me only addresses. I have my own transport. But *now*. No hesitation!'

Arun sat forward, and took sheets, and wrote.

'If you leave out only one address, you are asking for twenty years or more!' Prem said. 'These people mean business. They have warrants. It means magistrates, prisons!'

'My father-in-law will help!'

'Never. Why am I here? Give me the places. Everything out!'

'How do I know I will get anything?'

'If you are raided, you will get nothing, except twenty years, and a large fine. Give me those addresses, and at least you will have a proper percentage, and you can go home at night. Where is point of conflict? Give, holding nothing. Banks will be open!'

Arun wrote, and put his head on the desk.

'I am finished!' he said. 'I am so finished!'

'You are only starting!' Prem said. 'You made one big mistake. You were tied to a Minister, and ministers like what *they* want. So? A disaster!'

'True, yes. What then, after this?'

'Let us see what will come. Perhaps *we* could work? Quietly. You are too well known. But you know where everything is!'

'And you?'

'I know where everything should *go*, and what price. You don't!'

Arun put a hand on his thigh, and looked out of the window, nodding.

'It is true,' he said. 'I have everything, and nothing is any use!'

'Give me a cheque for this amount for your father-in-law

117

only to sweeten the air,' Prem said. 'Without it, you kn
you can be in arrest this afternoon!'

'He, too!'

'No. Have great care. He is Minister. A lot of pull. Y
None!'

'I won't do it!'

'Good. So tonight, you sit on a hard board, and everyth
is in the hands of Customs and Income Tax. When will
be out?'

Arun swivelled in the chair, looking at the wall behind

'I *hate* him!' he said. 'My wife *hates* him. His daughter

'Hate will not release you from prison. Once you are th
you stay!'

'But this is so much *money*!'

'You can well afford. Better than years in prison. You
guaranteed safety.'

'Guaranteed?'

Prem looked at him, and raised flat hands.

'Why am I here?' he said, almost secret whisper. 'To s
you. Does the Minister want his family in terrible publi
and trouble? Money in plenty must pay the press to
these stories!'

'What stories?'

'They will be in tomorrow's editions. Unless I spread
wanted gifts. Why do you think I am here? The cheque.
beginning. Then we shall fight as the battle develops!'

'I shall be bled white!'

'Why? Once I have proved that money was paid, who
dare bleed? Against you, or the Minister? Remember, he
paid an enormous whack. You must also do your share.
is very safe. Why not you? For a cheque?'

Arun sat still a moment, and reached to press a butto

A girl came in, and he gave her the paper.

'A cheque for this amount,' he said. 'Bank of India. (
firmed!'

'Very well,' Prem said. 'Now we talk a little more. For
aid, and other loans, and the hardware. It is too easy to tr
Your enemies have always the advantage. If you k
where everything is, tell me. I can take it away. Who kn
me?'

Arun looked at him in a strange way, sideways, hating
yet imploring.

'I *don't* know you,' he said. 'How do I know I can tru

'Until we have worked, how *can* you know? You are a sensible man. You can only judge by results. There are so many items on these sheets. Where are they? Tell me. Let me get them out. I have my own transport. They will never be seen. But you will have your percentage. Forty per cent!'

'Forty? That is horrible robbery!'

'How much for the hands doing the job? How much the police, everybody else? Transport? Petrol? Storage? How much? Who speaks, if he is paid?'

'It is blackmail!'

'Speak other language. Money is the oil of this economy!'

'What is economy?'

'The way to live. Give me this information. Everything will be out tonight, and out of sight tomorrow. You have forty per cent, safe, at home, everything quiet, in order. Or else, tonight you are behind the bars, and who knows where you are? Who will tell?'

'I could split on my father-in-law!'

'Split what? Who listens? Prison people? How long till you *see* a lawyer? Which lawyer? One sent by your father-in-law? A prison staff paid by him? Open your eyes. Forty per cent is plenty against the nothing of prison. Nice girls, and drinks, and dinner, and plenty of hay, of course. Now, simple to do. In prison? A dream. For how many years?'

Arun wiped sweat, and his eyes were too staring, frightened.

He reached for the sheets, and wrote on the back, one after another, and threw them across.

'There!' he said. 'Take!'

'Very well. Tomorrow, gone. But if there is more you are holding back, remember you are still in the same danger?'

'So is my filthy father-in-law!'

'More chance of protection. You have none. Remember? When this is all out of the way, I will see you again. I will pay you some, and you will pay me some. We are agreed?'

'We will see when time comes. But if the police come here?'

'Go somewhere. Anywhere. You are on a business trip. Go tonight. If there is no evidence to be found, what is to be said? Who is to say it? But destroy the paper. I will have a truck at the back at six-thirty It's dark. Transfer every scrap of paper. Every small note. It will be taken to be burnt. No further worry. Come back in ten days, you are sublimely yourself. What more do you want? No worry!'

He got up, and Arun smiled as a small boy.

'I think you are right,' he said. 'I have been a nightm.
too long. I will have the files cleared. I know they are e
dence. Silly to keep. Everything will be at the back door
six-thirty. I think I must say I am thankful to you. Y
name is?'

'For the sake of the anonymous, let us say I am Off
One-One, Lok Sabha. It is where you will always find
In trouble, or out, One-One!'

The girl came in with the cheque, and Arun signed, bl
ted, and held it up.

'We are agreed?' he said, uncertain.

'Completely!' Prem said, reaching over to take. 'Eve
thing is in line. No further extremity. I shall be here in t
weeks with progress report. For the rest, everything ba
theek hai!'

He went out to find Gond.

'To the Ministry M,' he said 'Tell Bedwa to be at
back here, at six-thirty. Load the truck with all the pa
Have the scooterboys here in case there is overflow. T
everything to Seripur. Hide it. Find out what happened the
nothing or something, and when you are sure, come back
me!'

Sideways nod, and Ganesh trumpeted.

He went up to the Minister's suite, and the orderly tap
the door, and saluted, and Miss Tata stopped typing
another girl let him in, to the lamplight, so beautiful.

He put hands to forehead, and Miss Tata nodded, and
girl went out.

The cheque came from his pocket with great flourish
Miss Tata looked, and looked up at him, complete surpr
cool.

'How on earth did you do it?' she said. 'For such a su
'Your Minister will be paid at least his small part,'
said. 'At most we shall know where everything is. Then
can put where it belongs at proper price. Which banks
involved? How many ministers? Who made the deals?
the money stay in Switzerland, or London, or Paris, or di
come here? Who knows if it did? A lot of the material
for Vietnam and Cambodia. Was it routed, and side-track
Who cares if it was? Who? That is the whole question. V
is making money besides that Minister and his son-in-l

Arun? We don't mention anybody in other ministries. Here, your own, for example!'

'Shameful!' Miss Tata said, and turned. 'I don't want to hear!'

'But you must, because there is more,' he said, and picked up the cheque. 'There is much more to come. I know where a great deal is. Should I go to the Police? What shall I say? On information from this office, I came across this value? He is son-in-law of this Minister? They own two steel plants, plus what? All put up with loans? Machinery? This and that? Shall I say it? It could save your Minister!'

She shook her head, knuckles in mouth.

'Better to say nothing,' she said. 'It would only be a hideous mess. Come over tomorrow. Ten o'clock. I think you have done magnificently. At any rate, now, there's hope.'

But he felt empty. She was not what he had thought.

She should have torn the cheque.

Chapter 12

Bhoomijai stood in the doorway of One-One, in a burst
brown Nehru, a pink rose in the buttonhole, and be
jodhpurs, arms out, big laugh of yellow teeth, and the cob
eyes behind green spectacles.

'O, my dear boy, Prem, what a pleasure!' he shout
'How difficult to come into the royal presence!'

'Nobody told me, Bhoomijaiji,' he said, and stood to p
the chair. 'Please be entirely comfortable.'

'But you are so well known!'

'A matter of work, concentration and interconnect
only!'

'You have a name. I have been talking to several minist
They all said to see you with my problems. They are
many. Where shall I begin?'

'Give me the paper only. Let me read and study. Quick

'But what is on paper is evidence!'

'First get, and then prove!'

'Everything is safe here?'

'Why do the ministers use this office?'

Bhoomijai nodded, and the rose nodded also. He ope
the briefcase, and took out files.

'You will see my fight with the bureaucracy and the po
and the rest,' he said. 'I have imports of paper and ot
raw materials. Foodstuffs, Volatile spirits. Also armame
only for export. What can you do? Licences? Letters fr
ministries? Without identity? Payments?'

'Most important. *Cash!*'

Bhoomijai nodded.

'At all times, of course. Expected!'

'How shall we be in touch? You in Bombay, me here?'

'My office here. They will give what you want. The address is there. There is name of manager, Patel, and he is in always contact. Ten per cent to you? You will take per cent from everybody else?'

'It is because I take no per cent from anybody. Except the principal. If I take from minors, what authority have I got? They get their payment. They do what they promise. Why should I be a death maggot? Eating into what is theirs?'

'You take one payment inclusive?'

'One only!'

'You are missing many rich opportunities!'

'But I am doing right job for ministries. Twenty-five per cent only!'

'Highway, incontestable burglary. What do you mean, twenty-five?'

'We must remember, in these delicate talks, with so many before I am at the top, with everybody below to be prepared, a lot of cash will disappear. Who will pay?'

Bhoomijai nodded at the inkstand. Virtuous truths have their own shape. Sinners know them. Prem breathed less, waiting.

'Gupta Ramnath Das is working with me in Bombay,' he said. 'He is unfairly small. But he keeps everything he is saying. He could be link. Everywhere the same, he has no mouth. Useful?'

'Possible. But I do not want partner!'

'This would be only smallest nonsense. I would never think. No. As link, only. Telephone. Telegraph. Supplier of transport. No name. No receipt. Only take, deliver, go. If I am direct to him, where are you mentioned?'

'I must find if I can trust *you*!'

'And the last business? You were mentioned? The Minis-terji was not having his honest payment?'

Bhoomijai nodded, and the rose nodded crinkled petals of Shiva's beauty.

'So far, we shall agree,' he said. 'But there are bigger sums in future. You know?'

'I have already twenty times more, currently. By the end of the months, more than two hundred. Ask the Ministers!'

Bhoomijai got up, and put fat hands on the desk.

'Very well,' he said. 'I leave the papers with you. Remember, I shall deny!'

'I, also!'

'You will name me?'

'I have no mouth!'

Bhoomijai looked the cobra eyes, but they were under roof at Seripur, no harm. While king cobra is in his nes our royal guest, we shall never have rats, Mr Raybould s It was true. Leave the cobra. He has only his own busin Hamadryad is not only a snake. He is the son of a god. destroys what is worthless.

'I believe,' Bhoomijai said. 'I will be in Bombay toni Das will talk?'

'Safer. Das knows his way. And his place. Put wei If you find weak, tell me. Enough? I promise?'

Bhoomijai put a hand on his shoulder, and in a mom Prem was sorry, feeling the weight of a man without a

He had only himself. Everybody was his enemy. Even Ministers would throw him to the dogs. He had to be succ ful. He had to show profit. He had to pay. Getting in be night, so tired, he knew another day was coming, more p lems, money, money, and where to get? Could he pay, who, and *could* he trust? When would he step in the tr

He put his hand on Bhoomijai's arm.

'Be sure!' he said. 'I am One-One. I am *here*. What want, tell me!'

'You asked not for one paisa!'

'I have done nothing. Why should I?'

Bhoomijai felt in the briefcase and threw packets on desk.

'I am not less generous!' he said. 'No receipt. No si ture. Nothing!'

'Everything is flat, in order. You have any quarrel wi Minister?'

'That blue file!'

'Leave. Be calmed. Everything in order!'

Bhoomijai put an arm about him, and bent a warm h and he exploded the hunger of a man for a son he c trust.

'Prem. Till later!'

'Go, Bhoomijaiji. Remember, every small word wil smaller. Every small sound will not be heard. Everythi behind you. Hyaenas howl only outside!'

'Ah, Prem. My dear fellow. How we shall work!'

'You are correct, sir. Catch me in failure and then upbraid. But you will never!'

But the files were a whole string of land mines ready to flame sky-high and take everybody to smithereens. The blue file looked most promising and most dangerous, because people were starving and even dying, especially children, and all those tens of thousands of tons of grains were held in railway wagons or in warehouses from Bombay to Calcutta, waiting for top price and big profit. There was the danger M.I.S.A. could find out, and nothing would save Bhoomijai and the others in the deal. Already the newspapers were shouting for rolling heads.

The other files could wait, but not for many days. They were fused longer, but just as dangerous to blow up.

He took Gond over to Ministry M, and went up to Miss Tata's office. She wore a deep red sari, the same smile, but one look at the file and the smile went, and she turned away.

'I won't deal with it,' she said. 'I'll tell the Minister you are here. That's all!'

She came back, and left the door open, turning a hand towards it.

The Minister sat back, hands clasped, eyes shut.

'Well?' he said. 'Close the door!'

Prem shut the door, and put the file on the blotting pad.

The Minister put on spectacles, and flipped pages, nodding, and shaking his head.

'They stew up great schemes, and find themselves in trouble, and apply to me!' he said. 'Is my name mentioned in any of this?'

'Not one time!'

'Let it continue!'

He wrote a note, addressed an envelope, and licked shut.

'Take it across,' he said. 'Never come here again in this matter. You understand?'

Prem made *namaste*, and shut the door quietly, and Miss Tata smiled.

'At last,' she said. 'Passing the hot one. If you need advice at any time, come and see me. I don't want to see you ruined for a lot of pi-dogs!'

'But I am only trying to retrieve Ministerial reputations!'

She laughed quietly, all the beautiful teeth and the pink throat.

'Retrieve?' she said. 'What a dog does with a bone?
talk nonsense. They have *no* reputation. With anybo
What are they doing? *Nothing!'*

'What *could* they do?'

She shook her head, only a tremor.

'Their duty?' she said. 'Who expects it? What amoun
money will buy it?'

'You have no respect?'

'For the dust on my feet? I wash!'

'For me, the same?'

'You have your work to do? *Do* it!'

She seemed a piece of whispering stone, and he kissed
sari, and went across to A, and Shiva, and she took the le
and the blue file into the office, and came out, nodding
in.

'Well, now!' the Minister said, reading, almost happ
'This is at the right time. It culminates. What is the c
name for Muttra?'

'Kala!'

'And what is Pirit?'

'Agra!'

'Good. Tomorrow you will go to the first station, Gha
You will see these grain brokers and millers. You will g
the instructions you find in this proforma. No more, no
The additional items in this file will take part, conjoint.
have transport ready?'

'Ready, Ministerji!'

'Your rail and air tickets are ready, with a sum in ca
An account will be rendered to this office. In the final p
graph, you will find clauses about finance. They will
adhered to. All sums in cash Not under whatever circu
stances, any cheques. No writing of any description.
notes. No names. No place names. No dates. Understand

'Understand. I can take complete control?'

'Complete. Don't apply to this office in the event
accident!'

He went back to Shiva's office, and a pink-nailed h
touching the forehead, and another following paragra
with a pencil point, and she looked up.

'You know you have to be careful?' she said.

He nodded.

'Remember, several Ministers would like to know th
moves are being taken. To put cereals on the market to

is dangerous. It will be necessary to find out where they came from. Ministers in opposition could make political profit by denouncing. Hay while sun is shining? The safest road in politics? Don't be caught!'

'They could rub me clean with the wax?'

'Of course. Never to be seen!'

'But why? What reason?'

'What do you know?'

'No mouth!'

'I don't want you to go to Police Headquarters for passes. There is already a great deal there. I think the best is to go to these places and find out what is to be moved. I don't think it can be done any other way. From the point of view of *this* office!'

'I am on my own?'

She put a hand on his arm.

'To a certain extent, and very unfairly!' she said. 'If you have any difficulty ring this number. I will do all I may. See me tonight!'

He reached to kiss the hem of her sari, and she made no move, and he almost sang going down to Gond.

'I shall be away for some days!' he shouted in the wind, and the laughter of Ganesh. 'Always be careful of Seripur. Take care of the Zona office. Watch the other offices Have your boys always on alert. Keep an eye on Ghal behind the tyre market. And the house of Bundi. Others may try to go in without my permission. Also keep good eye on M-Two. Talk to Vutthi. Also at Lok Sabha. Find out who interferes. Talk to Mawri, and the head sweeper. Always gather the paper there, and at offices of Bhoomijai. But if Babuji has trouble at Seripur, if there is danger to Khusti, take out scooterboys *and* lathis!'

Sideways nod.

'Wait for me at the office. We shall go to Ministry Q!'

But M.Q. was new and different, and not even the same in furniture. He went in to present credentials, and nobody had heard of Room One-One.

'Well, then, find out!' he said. 'Ring the telephone!'

'Why?' the pensioner havildar said. 'Does it mean something?'

He telephoned Shiva, and she told him to hang on, and came back to say hopeless till a day next week.

'Time is the essence!' he said. 'There will be a pre
for him!'

Again she went away and came back.

'Tomorrow, five o'clock, he will fit you in.'

'I will be there.'

'You see me tonight?'

'Nothing will stop worship!'

He loved her laugh.

It meant he had almost two days more of work in D
He took Gond to Seripur and made sure that all was in o
The sheds were empty, and Khusti stayed safe in the ho
with more than a dozen women near, and Babuji said if
police came, the village would run to attack.

He left three packets to be shared by the village, and v
back to Delhi and the house of Shiva, which had been
by Bundi, now in the steady hands of Riba, in a white
and piled grey hair, with her own women, and everywe
so quiet and clean, and even shining.

'Many fathers have been to sell their daughters,' she
'All from ten years!'

'No!'

'Others have come to offer women?'

'Only grown women able to say yes or no, without mo
We shall not sell our own flesh. That's all!'

He went to Connaught Place, and the office, and fc
Zona was in Wenger's having coffee with Dal.

The girl in the front office looked at him from sly, sm
eyes. She was good-looking in advertising language, a l
make-up, blue dress close-fit, plenty of teat, and pt
fingernails.

'You like it here,' he asked. 'Everything good? Com
able?'

'Everything is very good!' she said, happily. 'I like it
much. It is a cut above!'

'Above what?'

'Well, ordinary offices. I am not having to run and j
everytime somebody is saying something. I can tell pe
they can see Miss Zona, or not. I use my own judgeme

'What sort of people?'

'All sorts!' she said, in a flip of the hands. 'Insur
people. Salesmen. Police!'

'Police have been here?'

'Many times. To talk to her. Twice this morning. I sa

Well, she come back from the north only this afternoon.'

'Is it Inspector Ram?'

'The tall one? Yes!'

'What does he want?'

'He never tells. Who can talk to a policeman?'

Sly smile, sly girl.

He went along to Wenger's, and found Zona in the corner with Dal, and they both stood to put arms about and welcome but he knew from their voices they had been talking about him.

'We were just saying about supplies of spirits and cigarettes for the Clonk and the Hammam,' Dal said. 'That's the new names for the Disco and the other. We must be certain of supplies!'

'No trouble,' he said. 'Everything as usual!'

'That's what I've been saying,' Zona said. 'No trouble at all. And girls, I have got the best. Dal will open Hammam tonight, eleven o'clock, and we shall see!'

'Good?' Dal said. 'I shall go. I expect to see wonders. Till then!'

'You have no idea what beauties I have found!' Zona said, when Dal had paid and gone. 'The starvation is everywhere. Girls throw themselves. Any promises of enough to eat. I have the top cream. But I am broke. Try paying food and fares for a hundred and forty-two hungry ones, and new saris and shoes tonight, and lodgings. Imagine? I am completely bust, and I borrowed from Dal to cover outstandings. I couldn't find you!'

'I will pay Dal now,' he said. 'Here is something to carry on. Who is that girl in the front office?'

'Maudie Tyndale. She is good Anglo-Indian family. She knows a lot of people!'

'Among them, Inspector Ram?'

She held hands white-knuckled between her breasts.

'Perhaps!' she said.

'You live with him?'

'Yes. I had to!'

'Why?'

'He would have arrested you and closed everything weeks ago. I begged not. So he said come and live. So I did. The easiest way? What could I possibly do? No work? You in prison?'

'You never thought of telling me?'

'Of course. But you had your job. You could be ruin
Why should I? Only lie in bed? Nothing any difficu
Everything goes on. What harm?'

'He knows everything. How?'

Zona frowned, shook her head.

'From me, not a detail!'

'Then how did he know what was banked each da
Where cigarettes came from? Alcohol? What was paid o
to who, and the dates? Who put that Maudie Tyndale
the front office?'

'I had to tell him something. He was always on to
I told him little things. To keep him quiet. Maudie?
knows nothing!'

'A police officer went with you north?'

She looked away.

He felt sorry. A police threat terrifies a woman.

'Cancel the Hammam business tonight,' he said. 'Mak
for ten days from now. Take the girls to this address. S
there yourself. You will be watched. Go back to the o
now. Tell the girl Maudie she is no longer needed. I will
a girl in her place. Do not attempt to be in touch w
Inspector Ram. Fully understood?'

She nodded.

'Go to that address now, check in the girls, and wait
me to come back. Try nothing!'

He paid, and went out to find Gond.

'I will wait here,' he said. 'Put a couple of boys on Zo
What she does. There is a girl in that office. I want her
Khusti will take her place. Go!'

While he waited in the noise, he knew that Zona was
She was frightened of Inspector Ram. She could go
prison for twenty years on trump charges. She had
defence. Only her body saved her. A hate for Inspector F
and his kind swole, and swole, until he could hardly see
little boy pulling his cuff. The infant eyes, the bones,
windy belly were common, in horror. Giving them too
money was less than enough, but too much was st
because it would go on nothing at all. He took the boy
the cookshop and bought six good sandwiches, a pile,
chupattis.

'Run home to your mother!' he said. 'Don't sell the

But from the way the boy ran, shouting, he knew
would sell bites.

Selling bites.

The common business of India, he told Gond, on the way back.

Sideways nod.

'But, Gond, what do you think? What do people say?'

'I think we have not enough. A bite is better than empty? Nothing in my mouth? Of course. Where else to get the rest?'

'And what do people say?'

'They wish the Raj was back. In those days, nobody starved!'

'It's true?'

'The old ones say so. They *know*!'

'Come for me at seven-fifteen. The house of Shiva. Then to Bedwa's wife. Then we go to tyre market. Afterwards to Dal. You have a watch on Zona?'

Sideways nod.

'Poor girl. I am not sure she will last. Khusti will work in that office from tomorrow. She will always have two scooterboys near. Understood?'

Chapter 13

He telephoned Das in Bombay to meet him halfway [to] Jaipur, the next evening, and wait in the airport, and to [find] all the trucks he could find to make long journeys and [big] loads, with three times pay for drivers, but only men [he] knew to trust.

Back at One-One he cleared the desk, and locked a[way] the files. He knew them by heart. Most of the tangles w[ere] free, but still there were knots that only plenty of cash wo[uld] untie, and the biggest were a nice mixture of Police, Cust[oms] and Income Tax. The problem was which to approach [first]. One step on the wrong toe could lead to a mountai[nous] sacred cow's mess.

He called Legal, and found Mukherjee still working, [and] made an appointment at Wenger's for nine o'clock.

At exactly seven-thirty he went up the pink stairwa[y to] Shiva's house almost with a sense of homecome, sniffing [the] fragrance, elated to think that once again he would see [his] goddess. But when Vutthi opened the door, he felt his n[erve] had been cut.

She wore a blue sari, and she laughed to see him stock[still] in the doorway.

'I'm so sorry!' she said. 'Only an hour ago I became [less] than a goddess. Only a girl. Such a nuisance!'

'It's to put up with. I am glad men have not that. I[s] it hurt?'

'Only uncomfortable. Sometimes crampy. Now, abou[t to-]morrow. That secretary, Bhatt, is almost as big a brute a[s his] viciously rapacious minister. You must be extremely car[eful]'

132

He is completely a thuggee. Don't make the mistake of saying too much. Take a briefcase. Show what the cash is. Say only what you want. Let him say yes or no. If he says yes, empty the money on the desk. If no, don't wait. Go before he can call the Police. Have a good excuse for why you are carrying such a sum, and where you got it. Be sure you can answer the question honestly!'

'I can answer. But if Bhatt says no?'

'If the money is enough, it will be yes!'

'If it is still no, what then?'

'Be careful to have somebody you can give the briefcase to. He might have police ready. If they arrest you, that money is lost. Bhatt will pay off the police, and keep the rest. It has happened!'

He looked at her, so beautiful, so entrapped in her womanliness, wonderfully risen in her godliness, breathing light and only godly advice.

'Why do you help me?' he asked her, hands out. 'Why do you descend from your place to help me? I am Harijan!'

'Very well, and what am I, and where are we different?' she said, smiling the Shiva smile. 'I am Anglo-Indian. Is there difference between us? Both, untouchable? But we have certain attributes of intelligence, haven't we? Me, educational. You, of the blood, and experience. Together we can do many things. But the first is to help each other. I will help you. I hope you will always help me. I need a *true* friend!'

He went to his knees, and held the small, warm foot, and kissed, and the foot was in his hand, and no move.

'Not only me,' he said. 'You have a people. Only call. Nobody shall harm you!'

'And my house?'

'Tomorrow is ready. Girls, plenty!'

She turned away.

'It's a horrible idea!' she said.

'Why horrible? Should they starve? What else could they do? As comfortably, and well? They are making money. It will be invested. In a couple of years, they are free of everybody. Could they do it in their own villages? Or anywhere else? Even you, to earn money?'

'It is true. What of tomorrow? My appointment with the Minister at the Mashoba?'

'But not as you are?'

'You don't know the Minister. It is further sweet sauce!'

'Very well. But the Minister will know *me*. At a little
tance!'

She put a hand on his shoulder.

'Don't run risks!' she said. 'Remember who he is. He
call down the war chariots of Arjuna!'

'Not on me. We shall see? Tomorrow. Remember, ince
in all thought of you. I worship!'

He took her touch on his shoulder downstairs almost a
trophy won in battle, and told Gond to go to Riba's hou
that had been Bundi's. The place was dark except at the de
Riba sat, with three other women.

'The girls are ready,' she said, and got up to shut,
lock, and bar the door.

In the big room at the back, all the girls were in
lines, and Zona was right. The cream. He chose those
wanted, thirty-two, and the rest Riba told to pack and
ready to move. Gond came at a whistle from the wind
and ran off to telephone enough scooterboys to take them
to the lodgings found for them by Dal.

One girl he told Riba to save for him, later that nigh
Tibetan or Mongol, but beautiful in a strange way, of
spread face, and lotus mouth, and eyes looking through
luscious almonds of time, and shy, never looking up.

He went to Wenger's with Gond, and Mukherjee ca
in carrying a briefcase, almost meeting on the stair
down. The place was full, but dull lights made everyb
nobody.

They ordered at a small corner table, and he set out
entire problem, without names or figures, and Mukhe
had no doubt.

'It is very simple,' he said, almost sleepy. 'I can su
vise and arrange. I will give you the names and offices. I
call them in the morning. This secretary, Bhatt, you
worried about? A straw figure!'

'Why is everybody so afraid of him?'

'He pretends. Throw away his pretension!'

'How?'

'Undermine. Let the lesser bite his ankles!'

'How shall I do this?'

'Let me. Is your offer of double amount of salary for
years still valid?'

'It is done. Here is your bank receipt. Are you wor
for me?'

He put the receipt on the table and closed the case.

Mukherjee looked at the paper by the lighter, and smiled, sitting back, a big sigh.

'How much I have to thank you for, Premji!' he said, so quietly. 'I can pay now the debts of many years. I can raise my head. My daughter shall have good marriage. My wife will no longer be a slave. Yes. I will serve you. There are many of us!'

'All will be paid. Give names. Now, tell me how I bite the ankles of this straw fellow.'

Mukherjee pencilled a plan, name to name, on the note-pad, and showed, suddenly, a break to police and Customs, and certainly to Income Tax. They were all linked, and each name and position was like a greasehole. Put in the grease, and everything moved smoothly. Grease, it was tacitly understood, was cash.

'Get me the names after you have rung them,' Prem said. 'I will send a messenger. Cash. They will let the secretary know?'

'He will know, and he will comply,' Mukherjee said. 'He knows where his bread is far from butter. Without his colleagues underneath, how can he function? And his Minis-ter, at best, is besieged. He can resign at any moment. And the secretary? Submerged!'

'So there is no need for a *lot* of cash for him?'

'By the time his ankles have been sufficiently nibbled, no. Generous donations to his biters, yes. For him, a token pay-ment will suffice!'

'How much?'

Mukherjee wrote a surprisingly low figure.

'More than enough,' he said. 'Remember, his Minister can resign at any moment. His letters of instructions to you would be of no use. But the links you have made below are only strengthened for the future. And I am working, and they know me. And they are all *us*!'

Prem took packs from the briefcase.

'These are for you,' he said. 'Tell them all they have the same amount. The messenger will only say "Blue File" and they will know it is from you, for services rendered. Enough?'

'Eminently satisfactory, Premji. I shall not resign for the moment. I can be of further use where I am. I shall burrow into my friendly contacts with Income Tax. *There* is the

135

danger. *There* is most cash to be spread. Police? I shall see!'

'There is an Inspector Ram. You know him?'

'Everybody does. A busybody fellow. But he can be chopped at the knees. He has taken so much from everybody. In the Legal Department, we know what he does. If there is a charge, he goes along and collects, and the charge is dropped. You should have made a friend of him!'

'I doubt. But in roundabout ways, perhaps, you can let him know? There is far more to eat at the table, than out on the maidan. That's where the cattle and the others starve!'

'The Inspector has never starved. He will soon be a Superintendent. He will know more, and make more. He has to get caught in the machinery!'

'How?'

Mukherjee folded the bank receipt.

'Let me see what I can do in coming days,' he said. 'There are certain red herrings which attract the unobservantly greedy. There are legal pitfalls. That type, because of his uniform and undoubted power, had tremendous pull on us ordinary, in the street. But the biggest rat can be caught. If he is a nuisance to you, he is a threat to me. Shall we see what can be done?'

'Payment commensurate!'

'Sen will be with me in this. In Finance, he knows control from the top. No power, but knowing is the same?'

'Same payment!'

'Then, Premji, I shall go home most happily. My wife has a beautiful face. I want to see, when I tell her what has come to us. Have no fear. Rest your weight and many times more. Sen, the same!'

'You are both from tomorrow working for me?'

'From yesterday!'

They went out together to the warmth of Connaught Place, and Mukherjee went to catch a bus. Gond flashed lights.

'Miss Zona is at the office, Premji!'

'Let us go there!'

Gond made a circular tour at the traffic junction, round the back, and stopped.

'Wait here, and we shall go to Riba's. Is anybody with Zona?'

'Only the front office girl!'

136

He went up the stairs, and rang the bell.

The door opened in darkness.

'Who is it?' Zona said, with fear.

'Me, Prem!'

'Ah, I was so afraid!' she said, shutting and locking. 'The Inspector was here with police. They searched everything!'

'If he lives with you, why should you let him?'

'I live with him because *he* says. I am only his kept. What can I do?'

'You don't want to live with him?'

'With such beast? Why?'

He looked at her young, and so old, face and the frowning pain in her eyes.

'Why didn't you tell me about this in the start?'

She turned her back, so white, shadowy shoulders, shining hair, dark, and leaned, looking at the ceiling, throwing out arms, spread fingers, helpless.

'What should I do? I wanted to save you. The business. It's all I had. Without it, without you, who am I? Where am I? With you I have my position. It's the only real one I ever had. Why should I lose it? By not letting a Punjabi *desgostoso* come in with me? Worth it? I let him!'

'Not from now. Go back to Riba's house. Take charge there. It will be built up. This girl, Tyndale? Out!'

'The Inspector put her here. Careful. *Cuidado!*'

'Out. From *now*!'

She came in short steps, almost a dance, hands to forehead, eyes dark in appeal.

'Listen, listen, *listen* to me?' she whispered. 'Let her come with me to the house? Employ her here. I leave the Inspector? Of course. Is the Inspector less interested because I leave? Because the girl *he* put here goes with me? More or less?'

'Well?'

She smiled, hands on hips, swinging side to side.

'He will ask for a share? Of course. We will have the girls as witness. Each one will pay him. We will have a lawyer to witness payment. Photographs. We had no chance before. At the Disco, how? But there, yes? We will show him taking money. We are all witnesses!'

'You use a brain. Very well. Take the girl, Maudie. Both of you start at the house tomorrow. Riba will run the cleaning. You run the social. Take the barmen from Disco. Supplies the same. Be open. Tell the Inspector. Ask how much he wants. But he can't stay there. He can't have a girl. We put him in place!'

She scratched fingers through her hair, looking down at shoes.

'Prem,' she said, questioning. 'But what about me, tonight? Where shall I go?'

'To the house, and Gond will call a scooterboy. Take a top room. I will be there later. The top rooms are apart. Choose the best. Give the girl another. Let her be your servant. Don't let her have an importance. If the Inspector goes there, don't see him. Hide. I will deal!'

She raised her face, hair away, seeming new in a strange way.

'Ah, Prem!' she whispered. 'I was sure. I knew!'

'Knew what?'

'If you knew about me, you would help. I was right!'

He put a hand on her arm.

'Take charge. Where is this girl, Tyndale, now?'

'At the back.'

'Take her with you. It's enough? You take charge, from this time. Take the money, keep accounts, food, servants. Here is cash for next days. Make a register of the girls. All details. Call the doctor. Weekly check. Cards in envelopes to our known clients. Bank every day. I shall be away perhaps a few days. I know what you can do. I trust you!'

She put hands to forehead, and he went, knowing that he could never trust her. Something in the air was wrong, either because of the Inspector, or for some other reason.

'Gond, keep special eye on Zona, and this office, and that girl while I am away. Yes?'

Sideways nod.

'Keep special eye on Riba's house. Something is wrong. I want to find out!'

Sideways nod.

'Tomorrow, six o'clock, Seripur. We bring Khusti to that office in Connaught Place. She is in charge. Perhaps she will need help. Give it!'

Gond left him at Riba's house to go back and bring Zona and the girl.

Riba opened the door, and took him up four flights to the room of Kamata.

138

'She speaks no word I understand,' Riba said. 'But she will earn much money She is special beauty!'

Kamata sat on a corner of the white bed, in a white room, with red Afghani carpets on the walls, and on a shining grey marble floor of a house once of the Raj, now too big, too rich, no more built.

Riba went out in a snapping door lock.

He sat beside Kamata, and took a cool hand, and she half turned away

He tried his rusty Hindi, and the few words of Urdu, and Pushtu.

Always she shook her head, and tears were on her face shining in the light, and she breathed deep.

'I would like to talk to you. he said, aloud, in English. 'What can I do? I don't like to see a girl unhappy!'

'I speak. she said, in the small voice 'I was four years in the English School in Calcutta The Chinese went in Tibet. My father disappeared The school closed. I am here!'

'But the Chinese went in years ago?'

'I was a child I stayed Then the headmaster, Doctor Ricotas, died Many of us lost a father. I tried But I am here!'

He looked at the candle shining on the side-table of drinks. greening bottles, making gold in others, bringing shining tears. like Kamata's, out of the ice bucket.

He looked at the candle shining on the side-table of drinks, months of grief and tears.

'I am a man. and you are a girl, but I also had a father not mine I think I know how you feel You don't want this life, because it's always against how you were taught By *him*. It is wicked?'

She put hands on knees and rested her forehead, and cried

He put a hand on the shaking back, feeling the warmth.

'Very well You shall not You will help Riba with the house She speaks English I will find a good place for you outside Very soon Say nothing that you speak English Riba only will know you understand Now be happily in peace Your other father knows you are safe My other father would say I am acting in correct and proper manner It was his way I pay a little of my debt. You also, in your tears. Be calm. You are safe!'

He went down to find Riba.

139

'She understands English,' he said. 'Nobody is to know. You, only. She will help you with the house. She must have a room apart from the rest where you can take care of her. Zona and Maudie are coming here. Listen to Zona. Make up your mind. Watch both. They have inside with Police. Take care, and tell me every detail!'

Sideways nod.

'When Gond brings those two, tell him I am in usual place down the road, waiting. I shall be back here in four days. If trouble, call lathis. Gond will always be here!'

He gave her a package of notes, and she held them to her forehead in *namaste*, and he walked into the darkness. He worried about Zona. She knew most of everything. Where cigarettes and alcohol came from, which Customs posts, and the names. She knew the banking accounts, and the double records. She knew everything except Seripur, and the large amount he had always kept for himself.

He knew then, looking into the darkness, seeing in red, no doubt, she must go, and the informer with her, Maudie. If she came into Court, she could be devastating witness, not to be argued. She knew, no denial possible, and defence worthless. She could prove. Paper perhaps she had. Then? No denial. He had been careless, trusting.

A fool.

Ganesh came down the slope quietly, sound of a friend.

'They are in the house?' he asked. 'With baggage?'

'No baggage, Premji. They didn't want to stay. Riba and the other women had to pull them in. They were screaming!'

'Why did they come?'

'To have a look. That's what they said. They didn't know I speak English. I never told. The younger one speaks Hindi. We spoke only that. Miss Zona said you will be in prison tomorrow, and the house will be closed, everybody arrested. And then she will have the place in her charge, and the other one will be assistant. Inspector Ram will control. I don't think?'

'I don't. Get the lathis. Take me to One-One. Tell lathis to put hands on those two. Finish!'

He went back to One-One, climbed the stair, touched finger to forehead at the havildar's salute, and walked around the half-lit curve, seeing the flashing colours of the wall paintings from the end of his eyes, to the door, and he opened, and stood.

The office had been ransacked without thought. Everything was everywhere. He walked slowly, as a cold death, to the safe. He chose the key with ageless care, and opened the door.

Empty. Files, receipts, IOUs, slips of paper, gone.

He stood in the corridor and shouted for the havildar, and waited till the run stopped in eyes looking at the floor.

'The office is robbed,' he said 'Who was here?'

'Premji, I think a detail from the police?'

'Since when have the police had right of entry without warrant?'

'They pushed everybody aside!'

'Inspector Ram?'

Sideways nod.

'And so, now, we have to find out why?'

Eyes down, fidget.

'Did you report to Security?'

Shake of the head.

'Why not?'

'Orders!'

'From Inspector Ram Who is he?'

'He is Chief Inspector, Premji. I have a pension. He could take it!'

He went slowly around the curve, towards the steps The files and the paper could finish him in One-One. He no longer was ministerially of any use He could go easily to Court and to many years prison Ministers could deny He could not.

Gond came from the dark, an omen.

'I believe Inspector Ram is either at his police post at Chanaka, or his own place, he said. 'Call out the lathis stronger than before Also thirty scooterboys Go in to Chanaka It is a small place. Find a pile of files One is blue Another red. Yellow Green When you see them, you will know With other papers Bring them all to New Place. Ten times pay for everybody For you, this!'

He threw a packet, and Gond caught.

'If the files and papers are not there, go to the office in Connaught Place Go anywhere Go everywhere I shall stay here. When you have them, bring to New Place. Ten times for everybody More for you. Understood?'

'And Ram?'

'The Jumna. Remember? You now have three to deal with!'

Chapter 14

Gond came to New Place in raps at the door at after three in the morning, bringing armfuls of paper, and others behind him brought more armfuls, and among them were the files, and papers, airline tickets, IOUs, everything. Inspector Ram's notes were in the margins of the blue file, and in the green file, but blood was still not dry in the yellow.

Gond made a downward punch of his fist, and held out his palms flat, and then touched hands together in a diving motion, and a swimmer's, and sagged, eyes up, lax, acting death.

From the notes he saw that Inspector Ram had been not far from his heels, and very near many of the Ministers'. Others too.

He went out to Seripur with all the paper. It was almost noon, after hours of reading, that he was certain the other papers had nothing to say. He told Babuji to hide them, and Gond took him back to One-One.

The newspapers told of big smugglers arrested all over the country. The disappearance of the Inspector had a three-line paragraph, and nothing about a raid on a Police station.

Mukherjee made a long call, with a list of names and Departments for bribes and Sen came over with a longer list in other Departments, and when he added up the sum beside each name, he was glad to see the total not even a decent fraction of what he had thought. In those few hours, Sen and Mukherjee had almost half-paid for themselves over five years.

He went to Riba's before going to the airport, and found

the house in work, most rooms active, and for a first day, a generous take. He asked about Zona and Maudie, but Riba opened her eyes wide, and pouted, raising her shoulders, and he asked no more. Kamata, out in the kitchen, smiled at him, and it seemed enough. The garden had filled with cars, and more were turning in.

Dal was not at the showroom. But down the wide street, at the office, Khusti sat at her big desk, very much a queen of all, childlike perhaps, but she had an air, not of presumption, but certainly of authority, strange in such a small girl. Nobody had called, and she had no worries.

Out at the airport, he told Gond to keep eyes everywhere, and meet him on the night flight from Bombay in four days, and Gond nodded and made old-fashioned *namaste*, slowly, no hurry.

In flight he lay back to sleep. He needed rest. But a hostess came with cold drinks. He was alone in a row of three. She let down the tray from the back rest, and put a plastic cup in front of him.

'Don't get off at Jaipur!' she whispered, close. 'Das will meet you at Bombay. Don't go into a trap. *Blue file!*'

He saw the smile of Das, and drank, and pressed a button to put the seat back, and slept.

She came to waken him at Bombay, and he gave her a note. He walked across to the building, but no Das, in the place or outside.

A small boy picked his jacket, infant's eyes, surprise, a smile, a nod, backwards, quite sure.

He followed.

Das sat in an old grey truck and opened the door to bring him in, taking the boy on his knee.

'Jaipur would have been unlucky for me,' he said 'I got the girl to let you know. You don't mind?'

'It makes everything more difficult, but why should I mind? If you got into *real* trouble, things would be worse. You have the trucks?'

'Every single one in this area, and inspected!'

'Good. Send a message. Everybody ready to take the road tonight!'

Das nodded, reached under the dashboard pulled out a radio mouthpiece, pressed the red button, and spoke several groups of figures.

The voice replied in figures.

'You have a good system!' Prem said, and lifted the boy on his knee.

'I must, to be even one pace in front. Ten o'clock, everybody ready. What orders?'

'Go to your office. How can we discuss here?'

They turned and twisted into a place like the tyre market, of people living in dust, and torn canvas, bony bodies, heaps of black rubber, and noise of talk, and radio, and people playing sitar somewhere, and smell of tired fat.

Das stopped outside an old house almost hidden by two marquees, both ragged, one inside another, and full of iron scrap. The boy ran on, finding a way by touch to the side door. Two women got up, old, but healthy, clean dressed, and made *namaste*. Das waved, and went upstairs, and opened the door to an office of great size, made by knocking the walls out of three rooms. The furniture was teak, with leather and chrome, and a lot of glass.

'You are at home!' Das said, in a wave. 'I live in my century!'

Prem stretched the map flat, and gave Das the list of railway stations, and the code numbers, pointing to them on the map. Das copied, and wrote instructions for his drivers. The foreman driver was to go to the listed grain broker in the town, leaving the fleet behind, and get a release on the password. He would then take the trucks to the railyards, and load all grains to the number of sacks on the pass, and when he was loaded, he would take the trucks to the mill, that name, and that address, and first ask for the code word to tell that cash had passed, and he could unload in safety. That done, he would go on to the next railyard, next miller, same drill, password that money had been paid, railyard, load grains, take the tonnage to the next mill. When he was finished, wherever he was, he could load his convoy with anything he liked, passengers or freight, back to Bombay, and keep the proceeds, except for petrol, and any repair that had to be paid for.

'And for me?' Das said, looking at the map.

'Whatever the transport costs, it is double. The second, return half, is entirely yours!'

'But we are shifting thousands of tons of grains? This is purest gold!'

'Not for me. Or for you. How do you think I got this?

Ministerially. Interfere, they will comb you. Have you seen the fine comb working?'

'It is why I did not go to Jaipur!'

'Very well. You have your own sins. I have mine. Why should we compound? Let us take what there is. We should be grateful!'

'Ah, Prem. Such a nice bucket of cold water. Very well. I shall do my best!'

'You know you will have a present at the end?'

'It is why I say I give my best!'

'Who gives as much? I want a truck to go in front. Three drivers. One in charge. Two relief. I want to be in Pritigarh in the morning!'

Das went to the door, and called to the women for food, and put his head from the window to shout for Vash. Food came on trays, with tea, all good. Prem took off the Gobind suit, and wrapped a dhoti, got into a Nehru, put a plastic bag over suit and shirt, and when the truck came, he was ready, except for the blankets and a pillow the oldest woman gave him. She got a note, and kissed his hand.

He woke in the town, and washed, drank tea with the drivers, and went down to the station, full of people, and hundreds lying flat, with cloth pulled over their heads to guard from mosquitoes, looking like corpses ready for the ghat.

The nightmen at the station seemed tired and said the stationmaster would come on in an hour or so. The grain wagons were all about half a mile down the line and everybody on the staff would be glad to see them go. The newspapers started getting full of vinegar because nobody knew where all the goods wagons were, and the local people had become a threat. They could break the wagons any moment, and the Police would turn only their backs.

'People are dying in the streets,' he said. 'They die? Who cares? Should *they*? They die anyway? So starvation death, or bullet, or bayonet, or lathi death, does it matter? They die. All they want is one good meal? Or only a taste of food? It's enough!'

'So much hugger-mugger?'

'It is worse. They are dying everywhere. If there is still food to sell, who has the money? They know the grain is in those trucks. They are every day getting nearer. One man on guard was enough until a month ago. Now? There's a com-.

pany of police. But if the crowd goes wild dog, they will march away. Who wants to be hurt by thousands of crazy?'

'Let us have a small bargain. Bring the wagons nearer where my truck can unload. We will open a wagon at the far end, and give everybody one measure of grain. In that time, my trucks will take on the load. No need for police. It will become known it was wish of kind-hearted stationmaster!'

The eyes became two eggs poached in smile of surprise.

'Such a good idea!' the nightman said. 'While they are pressing and shouting, doubtless the work is going on, and the string of trucks will leave the yards tonight? Ah, what brains you have got. You should be the Minister. Perhaps you would pass a law for me? More money!'

Prem folded notes, and slid them under the desk pad, and patted flat the list of stations.

'If you will telephone down the line to all these, or tap out on telegraphy key, you will have twice. Tell them all to expect my trucks, and clear them, same reward. I shall have the same sum for your stationmaster, so that he won't have grumbles. Here's the list!'

The nightman spread his hands, and reached for the telephone, and not more than twenty minutes later, all the stations had been called, everybody agreeing it was only for the trucks to go there, and load, cash under the deskpad for stationmaster and nightman, and a little sweetener for others, also the police, if any.

Prem slid notes.

'For extra service,' he said. 'Now, where is this company?'

He showed the name.

'Turn right at the door, you'll see across the road. If there is a bigger crook in the country, he can take the cake!'

'Known to be?'

Sideways nod.

'If cash is in question? Yes!'

He went over, and into a quiet front office with a dozen or so clerks in white, and an older man at the ledger desk took him into a larger office, and shut the door.

The fat bloater behind the desk reminded of Dal without the humour. He had the slittish eyes of a robber, and his hands seemed to crawl over the papers as if he feared they would fly off.

'Well?' he said, nasty as hate.

Prem put the letter on the desk, and watched the long

fingernail cut the flap. There was faint smell of joss. A niche held the Lord Krishna, smiling his aid to courage.

The fat fingers wrote, and the paper held out.

'Unload and take to that mill,' he said. 'A man will be there to count!'

'Cash first!'

'When it is delivered!'

'Cash first. Minister's strict instructions!'

'How much?'

Prem showed the total.

'Cash only!' he said. 'No cheques!'

Slittish eyes slitted more.

'So much I haven't got liquid!' he said, supposing shock. 'Half cash and a cheque forward dated?'

'Total cash!'

'You are exceeding your place!'

'Only cash. Minister's own face-to-face no-nonsense instructions. *Very* strict. Or the trucks will move to next buyer. I have long list, ministerially compiled!'

Fat finger pressing button, and old fellow coming in, catching keys thrown.

'That amount put in bags!' fat one said.

'I will put!' Prem said. 'I will count, first!'

'You doubt honesty?'

'I don't doubt honesty, or any*body* or any*thing*. I am only sure when I am sure!'

Nods, and old fellow going out, almost running.

A loud *click!* brought half the wall swinging out with Lord Krishna's smile.

The old fellow came back, and put a key in a safe door. The money packed high on a wide tray, and he lifted to slide on the side table.

Prem took the long canvas bag by the neck. The notes were bank counted and sealed. He filled the sack with three lines of packs, but the fourth had been sealed in another way with blue bands without a stamp. He put them aside, with the next, and the next, and went on filling the sack with bank-sealed packets, until the last two rows, and he put them aside.

'What is the desire?' fat one said. 'Why not all in bag?'

Prem tapped the blue packets.

'I will count each and every one,' he said. 'The Minister would be unforgiving if so much as one paisa was short!'

He counted, and found the first short, and noted the shortage, and on to the next, and fat one made impatient noises, and moved here and there to express bad temper, but the total went up.

'You are wasting my morning!' fat one said. 'Come. Hurry. Quickly!'

Prem went on counting, and totalling, and the old man came to look over his shoulder and psst! with his tongue as the sum went up, and fat one slapped the wall or the desk to show pleasure, and the clock ticked on, and the Lord Krishna smiled.

But the total was a staggerer.

'All counted, and this is the figure,' Prem told the air. 'More than one-third of total. Add, please!'

'Added, correct!' the old man said.

'Speak when spoken!' fat one shouted. 'Am I here or not? That accountant is a fool. Trying to cheat *me*? I will not tolerate debasement in front of strangers. Make a cheque for that amount!'

'Cash only!' Prem said, running a scraper under the thumb nail.

Fat one puffed with a deep breath

'I am sick of your impert*i*nence!' he shouted. 'I will make serious complaint. Effrontery to your superiors!'

'But only cash!'

Fat one pointed to the old man.

'You!' he said, choking with spit. 'Count, and bring. Let this low fellow disappear. He insults my presence. Relieve my premises!'

Prem followed the old man out, to a smaller safe at the end of the office, and waited until two younger men threw sealed and stamped bank packages in the sack, and the old man counted the extra notes into his hand.

'You were right to say your mind!' he whispered. 'But you lost a nice gift!'

'I am having gift from Minister!' he said, loud. 'Do you think I am here for health only?'

'Cut by thirty per cent, and ten per cent is yours!' the old man whispered. 'Everybody a price? Fair?'

'Fair,' Prem said, lifting the sack. 'He will get his share from many trucks of grains. I will have mine in Delhi!'

'I get nothing?' the old man wearily said. 'You Delhi fellows have the luck!'

'Not luck,' Prem said, going out. 'Only counted money!'

Outside the door, he nodded to Vash, the foreman driver, and on his wave, a long line of trucks came out of the side street and turned into the railway yard.

The goods wagons were coming in on three tracks, so many of them. People went closer, and shouting from the front, and suddenly louder, and the Police were strolling away, hands behind backs, no interest.

Prem put the sack of money in the steel box under the driver's seat, and locked.

'Stay,' he told Vash. 'Give me your keys!'

Vash gave.

'It will take hours to empty wagons,' Prem said, showing the list. 'As the trucks load, take the first to this mill. Others follow. Be careful of the count of grain sacks. I will open the last wagon to share with the crowd. Therefore the sacks at the mill will be less than correct number. Tell the fellow he made a mistake. Don't wait for recount. Tell all drivers to line behind your truck, and go to the next place. Understood?'

Sideways nod.

The stationmaster sat in white behind his desk, and very obliging, and in no time, two porters ran with a big brass measure, and the crowd parted to let them through, and a key opened the wagon doors, and the two got up, and one shouted to the crowd to get in line, and the other cut the sacks at the top ready to dole.

A crowd all went in a long line, not a policeman to be seen.

The wagons began unloading at the other end.

Prem went back to the trucks, and gave the keys to the first relief driver.

'Vash will follow us,' he said. 'The next place isn't far. Go there, and we shall wait for him!'

But there were dead people in the road, and many children among them, and the living held out hands to appeal, and they were polished bony, and the few babies had the swollen bellies of hunger.

'What is to happen here?' he asked the driver, a big Mahratta. 'We are making a stick for your backs!'

'The stick will break,' the Mahratta said. 'No strength, and too far away!'

'You are speaking very good English?'

'I am learning six years in school. Why not good? Where is job or money without it?'

'True!'

Drought dust blew across the road, hiding trees, making villages seem wrapped in moving dirty curtains, and people tried to run towards the truck, mouths open, voices unheard, hands asking food, and some fell in dust puffs, and lay. Cattle stood in the road, bony racks, treading only when the fender nudged them, but only just.

'I don't want bad luck to kick death to cattle,' the Mahratta said. 'Trouble for life. I knew one driver. He was colliding at night, and no chance to brake, and cattle crushed. You would not believe what happened. His both wives and most children dying, one now, two then. Cholera, fevers, everything. Many accidents to him, but completely clean before. Nobody wanting to work with him. So he had to go. I don't know where. But loud breaths from us!'

'He should have seen a Guru!'

'Unbelieving, no use. A socialist?'

'I never liked them. Ideas or personally, they are all anti. Thieves and rapscallions. They are doing terrible harm everywhere. Nobody can do his best. Look at all this starvation. Who can do anything?'

'I thought it was drought, two years, three years, nothing growing?'

'Socialist influence. Food can be brought to everybody. You have seen this morning?'

'I think you are good man to open wagon. They were thanking heart felt. You heard them?'

'I am business man. Socialist take, give nothing. Business man, no. I give. What is left is profit. Without profit, you are making a fool!'

'It is true,' the Mahratta said. 'I have never thought before. You are right. Business is giving. Socialists never. I am like new man thinking. But what is the proof?'

'Proof?' Prem said, as if he was not believing. 'Proof you are wanting? The wagons this morning, not full of proof?'

'Food grains. What is proof?'

'Where are food grains coming from? Printed on each and every sack?'

'America?'

'Of course. And every fool in the world knows that America has terrible abomination for socialists. What is America? *Business. Only* pure business. And they give. You saw it. You were there. Not so?'

The Mahratta hit the wheel.

'You are *perfectly* right, Premji!'

'Did Socialists give you this truck to drive and earn money for your family? Is Dasji socialist? He is business only, you know it. I am business only, thinking only business. I shall give you a good present when we finish. Would a socialist?'

'Ah, Premji. You are making wonderful teaching!'

'Don't let fools tell you America is enemy. They are only business, and they *give. Final* word. *Give!*'

All the towns seemed the same, starting with mud houses, and then a shop, and more shops, a tyre market, and a line of bigger shops both sides, and the streets full of people, most beggars, and almost everybody looking fear, as though they thought the air would catch fire, and burn them.

The stationmaster at Ghanj was an old friend, and all the wagons were in the right place, and generous palm oil made sure no mistakes. The broker in the side street made no fuss, and the money was correct. The meal they had in the cook-shop opened eyes.

A fine chupatti, with vegetable curry, rich and sweet, and hot enough to make them sweat under the eyes, made the Mahratta ask why such good food, and starving outside.

'I have my own garden on the river,' the owner said. 'I have wheat from a year ago. But you are strangers. Ordinary people don't get. And you are in private room. Nobody sees. Who else can pay price? Here, only merchants, or they have private table in their office!'

'If the crowd is mad and everything stolen?' Prem asked.

The owner shook his head.

'Police and Army near,' he whispered, bending low. 'It has been twice tried. Many killed and seriously hurt. If again, well, more killed. It is known in their robber heads. So far, I am safely in business. My brother is Inspector of Police!'

'But no stealing from garden?' the Mahratta asked.

'Police pensioners guard!' the owner whispered, as if it was proper answer. 'Who else has guns?'

Chapter 15

Gond took him to One-One that morning, and while he got out of the cab, a tall, old, white man in starched white suit and white topee came from the corner of the steps.

'Mr Naran?' he asked, touching the topee with two fingers in salute. 'My name's Tyndale. I believe my daughter's working for you?'

'Not for me, certainly. For a woman, perhaps? She used to manage the Disco. Mr Dal, the motor showroom bought it, and she went with him. Is there question?'

'How about Maudie? She told us and a lot of her friends she had a good job with you. Round the back there, in Connaught Place?'

'Possibly the woman took her there? But not for me. I never once paid her!'

'Y'know there's something about this I don't like!' Tyndale said, and his pale eyes were like moonstones with catch of light in the middle. 'She hasn't been home for a week. I'm going to the police. I don't think I can trust any of you!'

'The wisest. You will never do better. Where there is doubt, go to police. They only know!'

'If I find there's been any dirty business from you or anybody else here, I'll deal with the lot of you!'

He marched off quickly, and took a bicycle, too small, and wobbled into the traffic, holding on the topee.

Prem went into One-One and found the desk piled with paper In a couple of hours he sorted urgent, important, and not so, into three piles, and there were messages from Shiva and Miss Turlo, and from many other secretaries. But he went to find Gond, and told him to go to Riba's house.

It was not midday but the garden had plenty of cars.

Riba was glad to see him, and proudly showed the accounts, and the bank statements, all agreeably of profit, and Kamata slowly smiled in the kitchen, very nice to look.

'You don't allow her in the house or the bar,' Prem said. 'Completely not one step. Kamata is on one side, helping only you. Promise?'

'She is my daughter,' Riba said. 'Helping very much in the kitchen. Not else!'

'Good. Now. Where did the two women go? Zona and the other?'

Riba looked away.

'I think the ghats?' she said. 'I don't know. The lathis took. It is wrong?'

'Never mind. Go there. Find the exact place. Look for any scraps. Clothes. Shoes, Handbags. Ask each and every one of the lathis if any small thing was kept. I will pay well for each thing. If clothes were given to their wives, I will pay twice value. Find everything. Police are enquiring. Nobody saw them here. Warn all the girls. Nothing is known. Or else. Police. And business is off. We close down. I am also wanting two of your most beautiful, lively girls. Ready three o'clock. Best clients. Gond will bring!'

'I will do everything, Premji. Tomorrow. I shall know. When is my husband allowed here?'

'The old blue truck is too known. When I get him one new, very well. But no reason not taking a scootercab. Come when he likes. I will see him. Till tomorrow?'

'I will have good party. We will close nine o'clock. Early night!'

At One-One, two big parcels from Das, via Air-India – Bombay, were in the office, and while he worked on the files to give priorities, four more, larger, came in, and he told Gond to take them over to the office in Connaught Place, and ask Mr Sen to count and give totals.

He called Miss Turlo, and she said she would be down when the Minister left.

Shiva said, 'O, I am so happy to hear you are back. You haven't forgotten my appointment this afternoon?'

And he said, 'No, of course not. You will be one half-hour late?'

'Half-hour, very well. Tonight you bring lotus? Seven-thirty?'

'I am there to worship!'

He called Hari Chand, working at a camera shop, and told him to be at the Mashoba Hotel, rear entrance, at three o'clock, no excuse for lateness, and camerawork well-paid for interior shooting, with flash.

Miss Turlo, in pale blue dress, pretty and smiling, came in, and the usual happened, very good, even better, and she was hugging, and flooding one after another, and then like a helpless doll, arms down, head in his neck.

'You are becoming more cuddly!' she whispered. 'I am dreaming of you. Is it good?'

'Of course. Why not? Some juice in life? Is it wrong? What are we living for? Not to enjoy?'

'I agree, yes,' she said, putting foot in panties. 'But I used to think very wicked!'

'What is wicked about bodies? They are *us*. Natural. *Never* wicked. Only churches talking, and years ago. Putting their rules on us? An older civilisation? What have they to say? They are a thousand years old? Or two thousand? We are *ten* thousand. We are now independent. What have they to *say*?'

'You are completely right. *What*? Nothing so wonderful could be wrong, could it? I am so glad we have a lovely experience. So secretly!'

'You can help me,' Prem said, buttoning. 'You've got a file over there about the Police?'

'Serious!'

'I would like to read. Possible?'

She nodded, and turned to be zipped.

'Tomorrow lunch, I will leave it. Only for one hour!'

'It is enough. Am I mentioned?'

'Three or four times. Not *so* much. Not for indictable offences. Only suspicions. The Minister said he had the right man. Undoubtedly you were a scoundrel. But you cover your tracks. Everybody in the same boat. Tell me, Prem. Do you crook very much? Truly, tell me?'

He took her by the arms, and bent to kiss both teats.

'Only with official sanction,' he said. 'Outside, nothing!'

'Promise?'

'Utterly, completely promise!'

154

She went, shyly lovely, blew a small kiss, and shut the door.

Gond came back with a message from Sen. Only the Bombay money was short, and giving the amount. He looked down the code names. In the Bombay area, one code number had that sum.

He called Das.

'That fellow refused to pay cash!' Das bellowed on a bad line. 'I tried everything. Only cheque for half, and forward date IOU!'

'Where is the grain?'

'At the station. I had a bargain with stationmaster not to move. Was I right?'

'Right. How far is this fellow from you?'

'One hour, more or less. Bad road!'

'You have transport?'

'Ready!'

'Go back. Take the lathis. See this fellow. He is ignoring ministerial instruction? Who *is* he? Putting in contempt everybody? Sending our own elected Government to hell? What is this?'

'Premji, always you are right. What orders?'

'Go there, see this fellow. Let him see lathis. If *no*, still, or disobedience, break a leg. Beat First, get money. If not burn the house. Burn the office. But get the money. Exact amount. Then go to stationmaster, pay good handful to him and inferiors, load trucks and take back to Bombay. Sell for best price. Half to you, half to me. Well?'

'Premji, you are Lord Krishna by himself, so smart businesslike. Will do. All out?'

'Out. But I shall be here all night. Call me six o'clock tomorrow morning. I am waiting!'

He had a chupatti in the office for lunch, and called all the secretaries to make appointments for next day, from morning on.

Miss Tata laughed to hear his voice.

'I am so glad you are here!' she said 'Could you make it convenient to come here at five o'clock!'

'At five o'clock, or soon after. I am distributing ministerial papers. Is there something to do for you?'

'Prem, this is so nonsensical, really. But I would love a slice of Wenger's chocolate cake. We have no messenger with sense to know. You couldn't, could you?'

'It is done. Half an hour, perhaps?'

'Prem, truly you have a magic touch. I shall wait!'

Gond went away to Wenger's, and Miss Tata called when he was ready to go to the Mashoba.

'I have six whole chocolate cakes!' she said, laughing. 'Prem, you are wholesale!'

'For you, anything!'

'I shall not forget. I shall give an office party. You will come?'

'First!'

'Tomorrow I shall tell you. Prem, more than thanks!'

'Only your smile. It's enough!'

Three o'clock he went upstairs from the rear entrance of the Mashoba Hotel, and found the assistant housekeeper in the linen room. She knew him smilingly, and put the gift notes in her pocket, and told him to stay there, and went down the corridor to unlock the door of the ministerial suite. He went downstairs, and found Gond and the two girls, very good, and a credit to Riba, and took them up to the suite, and the door opened only by handle. He pointed to Hari Chand to hide in the small wardrobe, camera ready, and told the girls to undress naked, and put clothes in wardrobe and hang saris over the door.

'Listen to me,' he said. 'When the man comes in, you will be on the bed. You will say you are a surprise gift from a good friend. If he makes fuss, or threatens, Hari Chand will photograph. But if you know some pretty business, you will have him in bed between you and playing very good games. Hari Chand will photograph and everything is well done. When the other woman comes in, there will be big shouting. You know nothing. Dress, and go. Hari Chand, go. Bring photographs to me very quick. Gond will wait to take you. Understood?'

Hari Chand nodded.

'There is danger?' the taller girl said, frowning. 'I am not liking!'

'Only danger, chatting mouth,' Prem said. 'Special presents for both. Gond will wait for you. Are we happy in calm and peace?'

All three nodded, and Hari Chand went in the smaller wardrobe, and the girls took off saris and hung over the door. They were both young, and worth in the looking, but there were other matters. The three men in the corridor took notes, and he held fingers flat to his mouth, and they nodded. The assistant housekeeper had more notes, and another pat on backside jelly, very accommodating, and smile away, and promise to keep far, not seen, never mind if shouting, and no, absolutely and finally, no knowledge of outside activity of person or persons, strangers, in any manner. All in order.

Gond took him back to One-One, and went again to the Mashoba to wait for the girls.

Prem called a couple of newspapers and said there would be hell loose at the Mashoba in fifteen minutes, and send reporters for a juicy story to eighth floor, turn right at the lift, go down the corridor, fifth door on the left.

'Who is that?' somebody said. 'What is your name?'

'Go there for ripe mango!' he said. 'Shall I peel it for you?'

He had the priorities in order, and most of the important matters were almost dealt with, and all the not so important were disposed, and the head sweeper came in on his special knock, and brought in Gond.

'Premji,' he said. 'The girls are back, and safe. There was great noise at hotel. Many shouting. Hari Chand had camera smashed in pieces. But others took photographs. I saw. But Minister's secretary is coming, and laughing, and going away. I got her taxi of Kulwant Singh. It was correct?'

'Very correct. Wait for me. We are at her house at seven-twenty. Buy for me two dozen lotus. What has Dal to say of other scootercabs on order? When?'

'The end of this week, Premji!'

'You have your drivers chosen?'

'The best of full of ability!'

'No mouth?'

'Eyes, ears, only!'

Prem went over the ministerial business. In one, the foreign-aid goods linked to Bhoomijai had been disposed of, all calm. The next, the Minister and his son-in-law, was almost in control. The third, grain held in warehouses and many a rail siding in thousands of wagons was bought, and settled.

He went out to find Gond to go to Shiva.

Vutthi's silver braids shone in lamplight, and she came, hands out, to meet him.

'The Minister is here!' she whispered. 'His car is round there. Driver and one other in kitchen. He is screaming. The doctor is here. Come tomorrow, same time?'

'No harm to her?'

The braids shook.

'Laughing, only!' she said. 'He screams? She laughs!'

He put notes in soft hands, and took the lotus back to Gond, and told him to go to One-One.

A look at the desk and he was glad he came back.

Two urgent telephone messages, from Q-Two, and from Miss Tata.

He chose Q-Two as perhaps the more dangerous, and had her first call, a new voice.

'Ah, yes. You are the man in Eleven? The Minister wishes you here immediately. Shall I tell him?'

'Immediately I am there!'

Gond took him over to Block Q, and up in the lift to the Minister's suite, and his secretary.

Tall, young, very plain of best people, faraway in voice and look, she tapped, and went in, and came out, holding open the door.

The Minister, skinny, white-haired, big glasses very thick, looked over.

'I hear you've been useful to some of us, in a lot of ways,' he said, nicely. 'Look here. There is a movement in this area, and others, called Sons of the Soil. They want to confine all jobs to people of the state they were born in. No outsiders. Let us say, in Gujarat, nobody should have a job of any kind if they come from Maharashtra. This is against the spirit of the Constitution. We take savage advantage of our liberty. We are all brothers, do you see? Shall we soon have passports to go from state to state? This is what I want you to do. Only as a basic enquiry. Very restricted in scope. I want you to find out, in the quietest possible way, if this Sons of the Soil movement has any motion here. If there is any hold on the people. Where, who, why, and names if possible. It is not an enquiry for the police. It is private, without publicity of any kind. You will need certain expenses. My secretary will supervise disbursement. You think yourself capable?'

'Capable, Ministerji!'

'As soon as possible. Very well. Good luck!'

The secretary gave him a large envelope, thick, and pointed to a receipt. He opened the envelope, and counted, surprised by the total, and signed for the amount. He held up notes, but she turned her tall back.

'You may go,' she said. 'Never come here, unless the Minister requires you!'

'How do you say such thing?' he said, low voice. 'I am only here to serve Minister!'

'There are other opinions. Please go!'

He felt himself with a nose pushed into bazaar basket, a bin, a rubbish. Other opinions? Whose? Who had such opinion? How could a minister ask help in one breath, and the next, tall secretary, thin back, saying other opinions? Which other opinions? Who? To the ankles, he felt sick. He could try, he could do, but still people not knowing what he had done, or what had been done for them, only them, had noses in the air? Backs turned, pretending contempt, superior? For what? He did what they could not? What they never wanted to do, he did?

A sweeper?'

Untouchable?

Harijan?

They knew? It was known? They accepted?

Why turn their back? Why turn? Why not face to face? What other opinions?

Empty as a skinned and boned chicken he went downstairs, feeling faint, squeezed, nothing left except skin. He felt so angry, but, thinking, what is anger?

He called Miss Tata, and her voice was a mother's.

'Come over, Prem. I have something to say. How soon?'

'Only flash the space between us. Fifteen minutes?'

He had a careful look about the office. Anything dangerous he gave to the head sweeper to hide. The safe could always be opened. The extra money he heaped on Gond. It was so nothing. But it had effect, and Gond kneeled to kiss his feet.

'Now, no numbers. Only Miss Tata. You know? Never say. Go there!'

Ganesh screamed, and the havildar took him in the lift, and along the corridor to Miss Tata, and her smile, and a black dress, and a bigger smile for the lotus, that she sniffed and put on the desk.

'Prem, sit down and let me tell you,' she said. 'The Minister has just gone home. You have something for him? I asked you to come here to say I don't want any sums in this office. I will not accept. You understand? Take whatever you have to the Minister's house. He knows I will not accept it here. I want to know nothing about it. You understand?'

'Understand!'

'You have the address? Good. Now, I want to talk to you. It is very serious. For you!'

He looked at her, older, not pretty as Miss Turlo, or beautiful as Shiva, but having her own face to talk, and a prettiness in the air, and what is pretty?

'Prem, listen carefully,' she said. 'A lot of people know what you are doing. Everybody here gossips. They talk about everybody else. They are the worst. They are disgusting. But it happens. They live on gossip. It's a livelihood. You must live with me. Prem, you are in greatest danger!'

'Me?'

'For doing wrong things. This latest, for example. For Miss Dowl's Minister? This grain scandal? We all know. Who will have the blame? Who went to stations and unloaded trucks? Who took grain to the mills? With his own transport? How many drivers are witness? Who was in charge? Who gave orders? Who took money? Who brought money to the Minister? Prove it? It can be denied. The money can be accepted. It can never be proved. The Minister can deny. You can deny nothing. It can be denied there was ever any money accepted. Any names given. Any places named. You see?'

Prem stood nearer, not believing.

'I am feeling sickish, Miss Tata, you know?' he whispered. 'I was given orders by the Minister. Code names for stations. A list of brokers and bankers. All the money is counted correct. It is here. How shall it be denied?'

'Very simply. Point-blank denial. Minister's authority, you see?'

She was very calm, hands clasped in lap, smiling, but warning all about, biting.

'What shall I do?' he said, on his knees.

'Take whatever it is to that Minister's house. Take witnesses. Try to get a signature. Then, for some time, stay in your office. Don't move for *any*body. If you have trouble, see me!'

He took her hand to kiss, and she let, pressing to his mouth.

'I pay for my chocolate cake!' she said. 'Come to drinks next Friday, six-thirty!'

Going down in the lift he knew he was seriously advised by somebody in special place to know. Something, somewhere, had gone wrong.

He told Gond to find Hari Chand, the photographer, and take him to the office in Connaught Place, and tell Sen and Mukherjee to stay, and to come back with three more scootercabs to load the parcels of money.

He went direct to One-One, and sat at a polished, empty desk, and thought of the last days, and tried to see what and where something could go wrong, and who it could be, but he saw nothing, and he knew he must go to the Guru.

In blue light, he was in charge, but he needed help.

Gond took him to Connaught Place. Sen and Mukherjee sat drinking tea with Khusti, and Hari Chand leaned against the desk, looking sulky.

'I lost my camera!' he said, standing up. 'Who is to pay?'

'You will be paid!' Prem said. 'Shut up. What happened?'

'The fellow came in and saw the girls. He started to tell them to get out, but they put their arms around him, and pushed to undress him, making soft noises, and got him on the bed, and many good things happening. But the doorbell buzzed. That moment I took photo, but flash takes five seconds to recharge. In that time he had me round the neck, and the door opened, and three newspaper men came in, and two instantly took photographs. The fellow was like somebody mad. He shouted. He attacked. He threw my camera at them. The two girls dressed, and in the struggle they ran out. I picked up the remains of my camera, and ran. They were still fighting!'

'You know the names of the men?'

'Of course!'

'Go now in a taxi. Find them, and bring here!'

'Money?'

'Of course, money. For you and them. Quick. Khusti, wait here till they come back. We shall not be long. Go down and tell Gond and the others to put these packages in scooter-cabs!'

He turned to Sen and Mukherjee. They looked fearful, Sen's bony face, Mukherjee's fat cheeks.

'Be calm,' he said. 'We will take this money to the Minister's house. You will witness delivery. And signature, if lucky. This business you heard is work of Minister's enemies. He is in poor political condition. This could kill him. I must help. I shall buy the photographs!'

Sen dropped hands, smiling.

'Always you are loyal, Prem!' he said. 'I am happy to work for you!'

'If there are legal aspects, I shall cover!' Mukherjee said, also smiling. 'The room is paid for? They cannot intrude on privacy. Those photographs are criminal evidence of breaking and entering. Open and shut case!'

Gond and the boys came galloping, and in two journeys took the packages of cash in much noise of tramping feet, and Prem smiled at Khusti, and went down to Ganesh.

The Minister's house was all lights, and police were outside.

Prem tapped Gond's shoulder, and got out to walk, but at the gates an Inspector stopped him.

'You can't go in,' he said. 'Who are you?'

'I am Prem Naran, Room Eleven at Lok Sabha. I have several official packages for the Minister. Is something wrong?'

'An attempt on his life this afternoon. You didn't know?'

'I have been working till now. Please tell I have got important papers, Ministerial business only!'

'Stay here!'

Prem waved the boys ready with the parcels, and Sen and Mukherjee each carried one.

The tall Inspector stood on the step, and pointed the stick.

'Come!' he shouted.

Prem went in to the lobby, and to the next big room. The Minister's eyes were swollen and tears were still ready. In homespun dhoti and shirt he looked like Babuji's son, fat, but not so entitled to respect.

'Ministerji, the documents sent by Miss Dowl!' Prem said. 'Where I shall put, please?'

'Next room,' the Minister said, and opened the door. 'What total?'

'Your own, complete. Here is code list. Here, brokers, millers, and bankers. I have two cashiers to count. It will take not long. Most bank sealed and stamped. Others broken, but made up to full total. Count in front of you?'

'Count!'

He called to Sen and Mukherjee. They threw sealed packages one to another, making total, and flipped through the blue-banded packets, and gave totals, and added. Prem held up the paper with the Minister's paper, both the same figure.

The Minister looked happier.

'Send those men away,' he said. 'Pay them for their trouble. You trust them?'

'Would they be here?'

'Very well,' he said, when the door closed. 'You have taken your percentage?'

'All the money is here, Ministerji!'

'Take your percentage. There is a serious matter this afternoon. Newspapers!'

'Ministerji, everybody knows!'

The Minister shut his eyes, hitting a fist to his forehead.

'But *why* do I *do* it?' he whispered. '*Why?* Now, look here. Try to find the newspapers. Offer money for the photographs. No story. Understood?'

'Ministerji, it is done. When I heard tonight, I telephoned. I have also friends. I will clear this matter tonight. Tomorrow you will have photographs. No stories. But it will cost!'

The Minister kicked the smallest parcel.

'Take!' he said. 'Come to my office nine o'clock tomorrow morning. If you are successful, much bigger reward. I am almost ruined!'

'I shall prevent, Ministerji. You shall not be ruined if I can help!'

The Minister put a hand on his shoulder, and tears fell shining down his face, even splashing on the shirt.

'Prem!' he said, in gulp. 'You are a friend. Come tomorrow. With everything!'

Prem gave *namaste*, and took the parcel, and one larger for his percentage, and went out backward, and to the road, and gave notes to the scooterboys, and plenty to Sen and Mukherjee, and they took scooterboys to go home, and he sat back in Ganesh, so tired.

At the Connaught Place office, Gond carried the small package, and he took the larger.

'Get the lathis,' he said. 'Bring back soon!'

Four men sat waiting, with Khusti behind the desk, and Hari Chand feet up, on the couch. He stood.

'I am putting the case,' he said. 'Ten thousand rupees, total!'

'Just a moment,' Prem said. 'Remember we are dealing with law. You committed crime. You all knew you were entering private property?'

'You took me in!' Hari Chand said very surprised.

'To stand in wardrobe? You agreed? Why? Tell to the judge!'

'*You* tell!'

'With pleasure. I deny!'

'Deny?'

'Of course. You have witness *I* invited? How? At all times I was at Lok Sabha. *Many* witnesses. You are making foolish claims. Where are the photographs?'

'Money first!' one of the men, fattish, said, chewing betel.

'Photographs *and* story!'

'No story,' another said. 'We didn't get the names. The security people were on us too fast. We were lucky to get out. We've got eight photographs between us, if you want them? At a price?'

'Let me see!'

Hari Chand took a large book from the floor, and showed eight photographs of the naked Minister and the girls, very clear, to the last, with the Minister coming at the camera, clawing.

'Let me see the negatives,' he said. 'I want to check the numbers!'

But there was great fumbling, and looks between them, and no negatives, and Gond put his head in the door, and at a down sign of Prem's hand, the lathis came in, tall, in dusty khaki, sandals slapping, carrying six-foot flat bamboo rods with iron supports, not one with a smile, only a pensioner's hungry frown, and they stood, staring only death.

'These are searchers for negatives,' Prem said. 'Either they get, or you go home another way. Give the negatives!'

Three of them took spools from their pockets.

'The photographs of these?' Prem said.

Hari Chand took other photographs from the book.

They were worse for the Minister.

'I promised you five thousand,' Prem said, taking out a packet, and throwing. 'Here it is. Share it among yourselves. If I find you have kept anything, photographs, story, anything, you will have quiet visit from lathis. Now they know you. Each face known. Understood?'

Hari Chand nodded, and others nodded.

'All right,' Prem said. 'Remember what I am saying. Thank you for help. Good-night!'

Chapter 16

'Now, Premji,' Sen said, opening a thick folder, and taking account sheets from the rack. 'All these days I have been to the Stock Exchange and the banks, and having access to our Finance Department's files. Both of these fellows, the Minister, and his son-in-law, are criminals, according to the law. For them, there is no law. They don't break law. They ignore completely. Both are guilty so many times. To prosecute one, you must also prosecute the other. They are mirror reflections!'

'What is possible to do?'

'Mukherjee has the legal answers. Go for the son-in-law. The father is a Minister. He can put pressure. Everywhere. Police, income tax people, stock market, and of course, suppliers of raw materials. It is an enormous industrial complex. It uses everything. Most imported, so subject to financial restriction from Government. The son-in-law has gone to every length to deal outside. Of course, with help of father-in-law!'

'The figures?'

'So complicated, where to start? Original capital, small sum, ridiculous. Foreign loan, the first, enormous. First share issue, tremendous rush to buy. Second year, one thousand per cent profit on original investment. Split shares, tremendous profit, again, but no provision made for repayment of foreign loan. A desire to increase industrial complex for fertiliser, another foreign loan. More profit. No provision for loans in yearly accounts. Foreign diplomatic moves for repayment blocked by the Minister and friends. You see?'

'No,' Prem said. 'Business, yes, I know. But stocks and shares, and foreign loans, no. Where do I put the word? How shall I frighten the son-in-law to pay back? A token sum, only?'

Sen tapped the account sheets.

'More here than token sums!' he said. 'The smallest enquiry would break him. Only hint of word to M.I.S.A.?'

'I have already mentioned,' Prem said. 'I must do more. Has Mukherjee got the legal side?'

Sen gave him a couple of sheets.

'Keep pressure on the son-in-law. He is the one completely vulnerable. Shady dealing. Completely lawless conduct!'

'How can such a fellow keep his place?'

'Easily, Premji? It is known he is son-in-law of the Minister. So? Ministers have friends. So? Leave him alone. You might be bitten by a wild dog from any direction!'

Prem went back to One-One with Gond, and looked through the paper and telephone messages, dealt with them, and telephoned Bhatt, the Minister's secretary.

But the fellow put the receiver down.

In that sound, Prem heard the same as a thin back turned, a tone of voice, a lift of nose.

He called the Minister on the main switchboard.

'Yes?'

'Ministerji? This is Room One-One. I have news of first importance!'

'Come immediately!'

'Your secretary, Bhatt, will not let?'

'Not? Come over to me *now*. Direct!'

Gond took him over, and the secretary came at him almost to smash.

'Why are you putting me in disfavour?' he whispered, not quite laying hands. 'I can do you much more!'

'I am not in interest,' Prem said. 'I have an appointment with Minister!'

'Appointments made through me only!'

'I make my own. I pay you!'

He threw notes on the desk.

Bhatt looked at them, and went to the door, and waved him in.

The Minister took off his glasses.

'Good!' he said. 'What, and shortly!'

Prem set folder and account sheets to be read.

'Only once I have seen your son-in-law,' he said. 'I had cheque for you. This is different question!'

The Minister flipped pages, turned over account sheets, and took off the glasses, looking at the photograph of Gandhi.

'I don't know how you have done this,' he said. 'Is so much known?'

'Ready for publication!'

'I will prevent!'

Prem shook his head and folded the accounts.

'No prevention, Ministerji. The facts and figures are known. Too many have to be paid!'

'How, then?'

'Cash!'

The Minister opened the middle drawer and slapped a large cheque book on the blotting pad.

'How much?' he said, in a little voice.

Prem wrote the sum.

The Minister shut fat eyelids, and sat back.

'Not possible!' he whispered. 'Completely!'

'I shall ask your son-in-law for many times this total. It is back in your bank in ten days. Twenty-five per cent for me?'

Nod, closed eyes.

'And twenty-five per cent of the other?'

Nod.

Prem shut the folder and doubled the sheets.

'I shall be here in three days, Ministerji. Your secretary is no good!'

'You think?'

'I know. I paid him to come in here!'

The Minister took off his spectacles.

'I will deal with him!' he said. 'Three days, come here, open door!'

Prem went out, low, and Bhatt turned to take him by the arm, but he pulled away, and went for the door, and out, and Bhatt ran after him.

'What did you say, you little nothing?' he whispered, with teeth and big eyes.

'I told him I paid you!'

'Told?'

'Of course. Am I a nothing if I pay you? *You* are the nothing. A servant. Beneath my feet. I spit on you. Do you think you could buy *me*?'

167

Bhatt let go.

Prem went down to Gond, and over to One-One.

A message, urgent, from Archives sent him on the run.

One look at Mr Vishnai's cold face cut all pleasantry.

'Prem, I am very disturbed by reports about you!' he said. 'I am told by reliable sources that you indulge in hanky-panky for various ministers. Those names are on point of resigning or being replaced. The Prime Minister is cracking down. You heard that?'

Prem nodded.

'If anything is proved against you, then you lose your position here. More than that, prison for some years is staring you in the face. Why were you away so many days recently?'

'I was sent to Bombay for ministerial business. But, sir, you permitted!'

'Did you have dealings with Doctor Turlo, a respected physician?'

'Dealings, no, sir. He offered a sum for a consignment of hospital stuff. The agent dealt with him.'

'Money passed?'

'I expect so. Not much. The price was small. I didn't touch.'

'It went to the Minister?'

'To his Department. Direct!'

'If it is proved you had a hand, it could mean fifteen to twenty years rigorous imprisonment. That consignment was stolen here in Delhi.'

'His own transport brought it from Bombay. I had nothing to do with it. How could I steal consignment? Where to put? Mr Vishnai, next I am asked by a Minister to do something, I shall ask you, first!'

Mr Vishnai smiled.

'I always thought you a capable fellow,' he said. 'Let us make that bargain. Always tell me. What do you know of Miss Dowl?'

Prem thought hard.

'Very capable and efficient, and always very considerate to people in low places!'

'Nothing to her detriment?'

'Nothing. Nothing at all!'

'Be very careful in that Department. Warning?'

'I am taking warning with utmost seriousness!'

'Good. That's all!'

There seemed a warning in Baljit's smile, outside.

'Don't take it to heart,' she whispered. 'It is only a lot of rotten gossip!'

'What perfume would you like?'

'Joy!'

'You shall have. Will you keep me posted?'

'Of course. How should I not?'

He sent Gond for the largest Joy he could find, and Bedwa waited.

'Riba is sorry you forget the party,' he said. 'Everybody very sad!'

'Too busy. In a week, yes. You have the new truck? Keep it out of sight one month. The clothes of the two women?'

'Everything burnt. Nothing spared!'

'Are the lathis talking?'

'Not one has mouth!'

'Put somebody with ears. Five hundred rupees for information. Good? Truck out of sight. Remember? How is the paper business?'

'Very good and going up!'

'You are born in Kathgodam. You came here with the Raj. Forty years you and Riba are here. What do you know about Sons of the Soil?'

'Very dangerous. I can be sent away if not working for you!'

'Why?'

'I am taking job from others born here!'

'Who is the leader?'

'I am not knowing. Only local men cursing me!'

'Find out. Bring names. All addresses. Very quick!'

Gond brought the Joy, and he went to the secretary's office, and tapped.

Baljit took the parcel with open mouth and staring smile, and blew a kiss, and he shut the door, certain he would have information before anyone else.

The day's paper had almost been filed, and there were knocks.

Bhoomijai smiled, arms open.

'Ah, Bhoomijaiji!' Prem said. 'Come in. Please be seated. Why may I do?'

Bhoomijai opened the too old fat briefcase, and brought out a folder, putting it quietly on the desk.

'I have agreement with this Minister for import licences,' he said, far smile in cobra eyes. 'I have paid one third cash. Two thirds on delivery. It is now six months. He refuses to see me. *Refuses!*'

'You want your money back?'

'I want the licences. I can use politics, or friends in this House. Or the press. But I want those licences. Original bargain!'

Those licences were all in the province of Bhatt's Minister.

'Bhoomijaiji, that Minister is in very political muddy water. He can go any moment!'

'I want what I paid for one third. I have two thirds in brief!'

'I will go to the Minister. Now!'

'You are my wonderful boy!'

Prem went over to the department, wondering if he should see Mr Vishnai first, and thought not. It was a matter of a question, and yes or no.

He went up to the office, and walked in, no look for Bhatt, and knocked on the Minister's door and went straight to the desk.

'A certain Mr Bhoomijai, Ministerji. Bombay person, trading in all branches. He requires import licences. He has two thirds payment, cash. He paid one third. When to expect?'

'Two thirds? Cash?'

'With him. In brief!'

The Minister looked towards the door, and wrote, and blotted, and took notes from his pocket, not many.

'My address,' he said, in a low voice. 'Tell him to be there nine o'clock. He will have licences. I have kept them back to watch the market. Now is the time. This, for your trouble. No word?'

'No mouth, Ministerji. I may go?'

A nod, and Prem went to the door light-footed, and almost caught Bhatt at the keyhole.

He looked back at the Minister.

'This fellow was listening!' he said.

The Minister nodded, no surprise.

Prem went out, thinking two thieves of a feather.

He went to Bhoomijai, and gave him the address.

'Nine o'clock tonight,' he said. 'If you want advice?'

'Whose?'

'Mine. Don't take any money. First see licences!'

The cobra came out of the roof, head swollen, ready.

'Prem, you are first-class fellow, I think? Where I get licences if ready?'

'His office, where you pay money, and he signs licences to give!'

Bhoomijai nodded, still the cobra.

'He will,' he said, more cobra. 'Or I will raise down solid upheaval everywhere!'

'First thing, see licences. Second, pay tomorrow in his office. I will take you!'

Bhoomijai put heavy hand on his shoulder, and bent the cobra head.

'Always such good advice!' he whispered. 'Prem, you will not be unrewarded. You know?'

'Always your command!' Prem said. 'Questions are asked about the Bombay consignment. All safe?'

Bhoomijai passed a hand. No words required.

'Many are still being arrested in Bombay area,' Prem said. 'You are safe?'

The cobra smiled.

'Many,' he said. 'Not me!'

They went out, and found Gond.

'Take Bhoomijaiji to Mashoba,' Prem said. 'Quarter to nine, tell Kulwant Singh, take him to this address. You follow respectable distance. If something happens to Bhoomijai, it is disgrace to us!'

'You shall come in my business!' Bhoomijai said, laughing very good. You are having a brain!'

'A few lathis!' Prem whispered, over the voice of Ganesh. Sideways nod, and off.

But in the corridor he went straight into tall, thin, white, old Tyndale, drunk.

'I can't find my daughter!' he said, a man asleep. 'Tell me everything you know!'

'But what do I know? What *can* I know?'

'Where's the woman you said she's working with?'

'I haven't seen for weeks. What is she to me?'

'Man to man, I want to find my daughter. You understand that, don't you? Are you a father?'

'Many times!'

'So you know how I feel. When it comes to daughters,

we're all one colour. Not this or that. Just loving a girl who's your daughter. Can't you help me?'

'But how? Where shall we look? They can be anywhere. Somewhere. Where?'

Tyndale put a cigarette in his mouth.

But the cigarette wetted with tears, and the drunk smell was on the breath.

'I can't keep her mother quiet,' he said. 'She can't sleep. Even the police know nothing. They can't help. You're the last one saw her. Where is she?'

'I *didn't* see her. I told you. Follow the other woman. *That's* where she is!'

Tyndale grabbed him by the shoulders. Drunk or not, the old man was strong.

'I find you been in this, I tell you what I do with you!' he whispered in whisky, and the havildar came from behind and pulled off. 'I know she had something to do with you. I'll find out. You won't get off. I'll do for the bloody lot of you!'

He scraped, dragged with heels on the ground, and they took him outside the main gate, and slammed him against the pillar, and the poor man was still crying, and the havildar was trying to talk in kindly way to him.

Prem went back, hands behind, sorry for the girl. A sly one, but still a man's daughter. His own daughters, three of them, were all dead in childbirth. He was not sure how to feel.

The desk piled high, and he went on making stacks of important, not so, and urgent, and found a message from Shiva, and went over.

'The Minister isn't here,' she said, so suddenly sad. 'We can talk. I don't think he can last long. The grain scandal is in the papers. There is bound to be inquiry. You will be named. How will you reply?'

'I was ordered. I did!'

'You knew it was wrong?'

'What is wrong if I am ordered by higher authority?'

'A judge can answer it?'

'No judge can make *me* responsible for Minister's decision?'

'You knew it was wrong!'

'How is it wrong? I was told. Given papers. Written instructions. Ministerial level? If I disobey?'

She turned away, straight in the chair.

'It's so unfair!' she said, so quietly. 'The lower ones are always taking principal blame. The Minister can always slip free. Influence. Friendship. Political deals. We are helpless!'

Prem knelt, caught the small foot. It stayed in his hand.

'You are saying you are also in danger?' he said.

She nodded.

'I typed many letters. All of them impossible to misconstrue!'

'What is misconstrue?'

'Not to know what you are dealing with. To know very well that you are in complete criminality. And not reporting!'

'Why not?'

'I had to hang on to the job. I wanted my *job*!'

Prem sniffed in her air, so beautiful, so woman, herself, and alone.

He lifted the foot to kiss, and it stayed against his mouth.

'Where are the files?' he said. 'Where are those letters?'

'Down in the Archives section. No chance to have them out!'

'You know the reference code? Give it!'

She looked at a book, and wrote, and gave him the paper.

'You can do nothing!' she said, almost with a smile. 'We are finished. I shall be thrown from the Civil Service. You will probably lose your job, and face prosecution. For the grain business. You have seen the papers?'

'No. I don't read papers. But I read files. I will bring every file in this code to you!'

She smiled in her temple, and bells clashed.

'I shall not say I don't believe,' she said. 'I shall say I believe when I see!'

He kissed the foot, the ankle, and the knee, no move to withdraw, and ran down to Gond, and to the Archives, and Baljit with her coat on to go home. He gave her the paper, saying nothing, and she went away for minutes, and came back with box files in both arms.

'Bring back,' she said. 'It's an arm and a leg!'

'Tomorrow morning, seven o'clock, else in an hour. Wait?'

She smiled, and he bent to kiss her shoulder, and ran, out to Gond, and back, in darkening light, with pink clouds making the buildings look built in soft cake.

Shiva went through the files, looking at him each time she

lifted the metal holder to take out letters, and when she came to the end, cold, and frozen, she went again through the letters, and shut the last file, and sat back, staring, ice.

'I don't pretend to know how you did it,' she said, quietly. 'But I think from this, you've saved me. About you, I don't know. I shall do everything to safeguard you. Come tonight?'

'Seven-thirty? Yes!'

Back with Gond with the files under his jacket, and in, to Archives, and Baljit waited, and ran to put the files away, and came back in a big breath, and stopped on a toe of a shoe.

He gave her a thick packet, and she opened her eyes.

'If we work, we are paid,' he said. 'You work with me, I pay. When you have anything for me, come to One-One?'

She nodded, putting the package in her handbag.

'There is a man called Bhoomijai,' she said. 'He is barred from entry from today after four o'clock. Minister's order!'

'Which Minister?'

She held up the paper, clocked at four thirty-five.

Miss Thin Back's Minister.

He saw only the high nose, heard the distant voice, and honesty.

Chapter 17

'Now, Naran, I want you to tell Chief Superintendent Murthi Singh exactly what happened on the afternoon of the disappearance of this man Bhoomijai,' the Minister said, quietly. 'I think you have to be very careful!'

'Ministerji, I am not careful,' Prem said. 'I only tell what I know. Bhoomijai left here for the Mashoba Hotel. He told me he was staying there. Kulwant Singh, the taxi-driver, was going to call for him to be at Minister's house, nine o'clock punctual, at Minister's order. He did. We know he did. But nobody came out all night!'

'How do you know?'

'Kulwant Singh himself told me. He came to me. He wanted his fare!'

The Minister rested on his elbows. Chief Superintendent Murthi Singh looked at the pen rack.

'Did you know what was between those two?' the Minister asked.

'Bhoomijai wanted export and import licences. He already paid one third!'

'One *third*? One third of what?'

'One third of value. Of export and import licences. It was all sorts of things. I saw machinery, all kinds on the list. I remember television sets, radios, electronics, typewriters, Whisky. Cigarettes.'

The Minister looked at the Superintendent.

'I think that's about it?' he said. 'The man went to the house. There are witnesses. Where did he go? We don't know. Do we wish to? Is inquiry necessary? Who requires it?'

The Chief Superintendent moved sideways in the chair. He seemed large as half the desk, starched khaki uniform, medal ribbons, polished leather, Sikh head-dress, black whiskers, large, hard eyes, hard, because when they turned, it was like being hit with rock.

'How did you know he was going to the Minister's house?' he asked, in a soft voice, a mile away. 'Did you make the appointment?'

'The Minister made. I have his chit. Address and time!'

'Why at his house? Why not here?'

'Minister, only, is knowing!'

'Did he have any money with him?' the Minister asked.

'I saw none, Ministerji. He only said he would pay two thirds more on original bargain.'

'Naran, think carefully,' the Minister said. 'Actually, what was your part in all this?'

'Ministerji, he came to my office. He said he had licences to collect from the Minister. I tried to telephone. Telephone not working. I went to Department. Bhatt, his secretary, showed me in. I told the Minister Bhoomijai was waiting for licences. He gave me chit with address and time. I told Kulwant Singh, the taxi-driver, to pick up Bhoomijai at eight forty-five, and take to the address. That is all. From there, I never saw!'

'Where is this chit?' the Superintendent asked.

Prem opened the folder, and took out the page, and the Minister looked, and passed to the Superintendent.

'Why did he come to your office?' the Superintendent asked, again softly. 'Why not the Minister's?'

'He said he had waited six months, and the Minister refused to see him!'

'Why should you interfere?'

'He said he had friends among the ministers, and the Press, and Members of the House, and he would cause upheaval. For that, and no telephone, I went!'

'This man, Bhatt,' the Minister said. 'You knew him? The secretary?'

'Only to open door, Ministerji!'

'Did he know of this nine o'clock appointment?' the Superintendent asked.

'I am not sure. Nothing was said while I was there!'

There was stiff silence, a buzzing quietness of people thinking. Small sounds, creaks of polished leather in the Superintendent's sword belt, seemed ten times louder.

'You have a great deal of property, it seems?' the Minister said, looking at a paper. 'How did you amass so much?'

'I was left money and land by my adoptive father, Ministerji. He lent money for many years to the villagers at small interest. He rented lands. He fed everybody in time of drought. I followed. Nobody has died or starved. I do as he would wish!'

'It is true,' the Superintendent said. 'Our enquiries prove. You had no other link to Bhoomijai?'

'None, sir!'

'You never bought or sold for him?' the Minister asked. Prem held out his hands.

'Ministerji, how could I?' he said. 'Twenty-two years, I am here, from messenger, only, till now. Not one day of holiday. Not one hour of free time. When can I buy and sell? I am here, every hour, full time. Bhoomijai's business was only with the Minister. Never with me!'

'Very well,' the Superintendent said. 'Did you ever employ a girl called Maude Tyndale?'

'Never, sir. She worked for the manageress of the Slop Disco, Zona, apart from me, and somewhere else. The Disco was a dance place. It was my adoptive father's, but a partner ran it. He died two years ago, and I kept Zona as manageress. Then I was promoted, and I had too much to do. I sold to Dal of the auto showroom a little time ago. I have nothing further of interest. I think I saw Miss Tyndale only once. With the woman Zona. That must be well over six weeks ago. Her father has worried me about her. What do I know?'

'Did you have anything to do with Chief Inspector Ram?' the Superintendent asked, not looking. 'Officially, of course!'

'Officially, yes, only!'

'What about?'

'Sometimes clients parking wrong place. Inspection of licences. Search of premises for drugs. Never found, happy to say!'

The Superintendent took a book from a side pocket, opened it, and flipped pages.

'You knew a chemical manufacturer called Malwan Khan,' he said. 'That was not his true name. You were a partner?'

'He was my father's partner. I left in the money, and took only shared profit. He made vitamins and face creams, lipsticks. Cleaning fluids, soaps and dish and floor washing stuff. Aphrodisiac powders from rhinoceros horn. Cattle foods, and many other profitable lines. Soft drinks, sweets!'

The Minister laughed.

'Hope he didn't get things mixed?' he said. 'Extraordinary what people do. Did you make any money?'

'Enough to make investment just, only just paying, Ministerji!'

The Superintendent turned, shutting the book.

'Have you a house of prostitution on the other side of Nizamuddin?' he asked. 'Or a partnership?'

'No interest, sir, and no partnership!'

'You seem to be involved?'

'Not involved, sir. The old woman looking after it was a servant of my father's. I help her, only!'

'The former owner was a man called Bundi Binode. Now is the strange thing. All these people you have met, or known, have disappeared!'

Prem raised his hands, and looked up.

Moments.

'I don't know, sir. I meet many thousands every year. How many do I meet again? How many disappear? To go home, or somewhere else? As far as I am concerned, they disappear. Am I to blame?'

'Naran, you are a slippery customer!' the Superintendent said, putting the book in his pocket. 'Remember always you can make a mistake!'

'I have done nothing wrong!'

'It remains to be seen!'

'You can only say it because I am Harijan. I cannot prove my parentage. But I am defying you!'

'All right, Naran,' the Minister said. 'I shall see no advantage is taken of you. Superintendent, I think you exceed your duty. You may not threaten in my presence. Naran, you may go!'

Prem went out, almost dazed. In the outer office, he leaned against the wall, feeling the wonder of cold stone at the back of his head. He heard a movement in front, and a hand rested on his shoulder, not heavily.

'Poor fellow!' Miss Thin Back whispered. 'I am sorry. That was a horrid roasting!'

'It is all right!' he said. 'Thank you. Thank you very much!'

'Miss Tata wishes to see you. Will you go?'

'*Now*. What perfume do you like?'

'Perfume?'

'Which kind do you like? *French* perfume?'

'But I couldn't permit you to give me perfume!'

'Is my perfume worse than anybody's?'

'I could not permit *any* gift!'

Her hands were clasped, bent to the left, and her eyes were over them, frowning. She was taller. High heels?

'It is not a gift. Do we put flowers in prayers for gift? It is part of thought. I think of you with perfume. What is your favourite?'

'You couldn't get it!'

'What is it?'

'Mitsouko!'

'Write it, and I will get!'

She went back to the desk, and wrote, and gave him the paper.

'You won't get it,' she said. 'It's off the market!'

'Nothing is off *my* market. A few days?'

'I don't believe it. I'll bet you?'

'What?'

'Well. Ten rupees? But remember this. I insist on paying for it!'

He nodded, took her hand, kissed a dry palm, and went out, just in time to go in front of the Superintendent.

He knew he had to ride a careful bicycle in the next days.

Miss Tata in a deep red dress was a beautiful patch of peace.

'Prem, I called you to say the police are enquiring about you!' she said.

'I have just spoken to Chief Superintendent Murthi Singh. Suspicions, only. Why? Because I have worked for ministers!'

She nodded.

'*They* should be investigated, first,' she said. 'But you see, they'll get at them through people like you. And me!'

'If you have trouble, you tell me? I don't think they have the right!'

'What do Ministers care about right? They want power. Position. Anything to make money!'

'Why are you here?'

She looked over the lawns and gardens, and breathed deep, one time, and sat back.

'I love my Sindhi!' she said, almost to herself. 'It is what we should be called. *Not* India. It is a stupid catchword of the people we threw out. We are *not* Indians. It is an English word. We are Sindhu. But who *really* gives a damn? Everybody takes her, sells her, smashes her, makes her a criminal, a beggar. Bring your bowl for free food. Foreign aid. How do I stay in my *skin*?'

'But, Miss Tata. How *should* it be?'

'Well.'

She sat back, picked up a pencil, ran it through her fingers, put it down.

'We have a wonderful Prime Minister. I love her. We all do. She is the Sindhu mother. Of us all. But she is at the mercy of traitors. They are men without respect for women. They will use, and pay. Why should they respect other methods outside?'

'Go to the Police?'

She lifted a shoulder.

'For what? Who would listen? I would be held for questioning. Raped. Of course? What is a woman in this country?'

'But what do you want to do?'

'I want to bring more women in to Government. I don't think it possible. For the next ten, twenty years? But the men will ruin the country. They are full of greed. Money, or women. Nothing else!'

'But if the women let?'

'It is the way we are brought up. Miseducated. We are only playthings. Never mind we have techniques beyond the fools we work for. Shorthand. Typewriting. Computers. What does it mean? One set of genitalia is superior to another. Why? Because it cannot penetrate!'

'What is geni – whatever it is?'

Miss Tata turned her eyes to him, direct, clear, wide, beautiful.

'You have a cock,' she said, quietly. 'A woman has not. She cannot penetrate. And so? We must complain outside. We have nothing to say. Less to do. We are in truth the ones who must take it. Or leave it. We can scream and shout. Argue. What does it matter? It makes no difference. We cannot. But a man can. It is the natural law. Isn't it?'

'But you can say yes or no?'

'Yes or no, what?'

'Come in, or keep out?'

She turned, impatiently.

'O, Prem. How does a woman think in such a way? Only *you* think so!'

'I am a fool?'

'No. You are a man. You think as one!'

'I should think as a woman?'

'Impossible, of course. Of what use?'

'If I am sitting in your place, Miss Tata, what should I think?'

'Shame. Only shame!'

'Why?'

'I am part of criminality. I pretend not. I protect my pride. At the expense of my country?'

'Go to Police?'

'They are worse. They are paid!'

'All?'

'All!'

He listened to the soft steam of the kettle.

'Miss Tata,' he said. 'Why am I here? What did you want me to do?'

She looked at him, one turn of the neck.

'You helped a friend of mine,' she said. 'Miss Dowl? You got files from the Archives. Could you get them for me?'

The cry of a little girl.

'Give index number. I am here in thirty minutes. Less!'

'O, Prem!'

He took the paper and ran down to Gond, and half ran to Baljit's office.

She smiled, almost laughing, and stopped typing.

'Marvellous perfume!' she said, softly whispering, looking towards Mr Vishnai's door. 'It is so beautiful. More wonderful than I expected. It made me so happy!'

'I'm very glad. I am happy for you. May I ask another favour?'

She held out the small hands with red nails very pretty.

'Anything!'

He gave her the paper.

She looked, and the smile was a small frown.

She got up, and turned, and folded the paper.

'If I were caught I would be crushed by elephants!' she said. 'So would you. These are highly confidential ministerial subject matter. The other, *and* this!'

'You have saved one girl's job. If not her life. You can save another. Whatever you wish, you shall have!'

'Promise to bring them back immediately!'

'Inside one hour. *Promise!*'

She pulled open the steel door, and pushed the grille just enough to pass sideways, and he saw she was a small girl, and instantly he pitied her, not for smallness, but for the risk. She came back with two big red files, with rings. He took off his jacket, and put two fingers through the rings and draped the jacket over to hide, and nodded, and went out to Gond, and over to Miss Tata.

She almost snatched them, and sat, going through, taking out pages, and then, as Shiva, going through again, but slowly, taking out others, and shut the files, looking in front, not moving.

'You've saved me!' she said. 'I hadn't realised how awful it really was!'

'But if others have the originals?'

She gave him the files.

'They're forgeries, because copies are not in here!' she said. 'I've cleared our own files of anything I typed. Now I can breathe. O, Prem, I am so grateful!'

'Nothing!'

He went back and walked into Mr Vishnai, coming out.

'Ah, Prem!' he said, laughing three front teeth. 'I heard from the Minister. He was very pleased at the way you stood up for yourself. Good work. Keep going!'

'Thank you, Vishnaiji. I have example!'

Vishnai laughed in the air, and shook his umbrella as a sword, and walked on.

Prem puffed a breath and went on, almost slow, not to draw looks.

He knocked on Baljit's door, and she opened, and turned up her eyes, and took the files almost as babies, and ran for the steel door, and in.

He went back to One-One wet through, and so little life, that the new pile on the desk meant nothing. He sat back, shirt open, letting the fan dry sweat.

Mawri's knock brought him in, holding an official paper, and he held it up.

'Five of them we are losing!' he said. 'Ministers. Resignation. All crooks!'

Three of them were Shiva's, Miss Tata's, and Miss Turlo's.

The other two he knew, and their secretaries, but nothing to compare in power.

'Finally,' he said. 'But five more crooks go in. What is the difference?'

'They would be hurt to hear what you are saying!' Mawri said. 'They would sue for damages!'

'No wonder we have troubles. One crook makes way for another? Everything is the same? They should elect *me* there. I could teach them!'

'In crookery?' Mawri said, and laughed the high note, a vulture with red meat. 'Then we would *see* some crookery!'

'None!' Prem said, sitting up. 'There would be none. I would uproot and *kill*!'

Mawri looked at him, straight face.

'Why can't you be elected?' he asked.

'No votes. Who knows *me*? If Congress people are against me, how much money have I got to go against them? How long shall I be here? I would be replaced in minutes. What could I do after that? What?'

Mawri nodded.

'True,' he said. 'We are only completely hopeless. We are *us*. Nobody else like. And so helpless. Without hope. So, nothing. Why?'

He watched Mawri's thumbs turning. They were bent back.

'Lower rungs,' he said. 'Nothing higher. Where shall we *go*? Who *are* we? Nothing!'

'But there are many of us!'

'Shock a few. Who remains?'

'How shock?'

'Put in prison. Threaten. Bring to Police. Who speaks?'

'True!'

'Outside your job, what have you got?'

'Little. Not enough to live!'

'So. Behave. *Their* way!'

Mawri nodded, looked as if he would cry, and went out, quiet door.

The pile of paper had nothing, except a small chit from Miss Turlo, to see her urgently.

He went over. She was in deep tears.

'The man's going, and the incoming doesn't want me!' she wept. 'What shall I do?'

'The Civil Service will take care!'

'And send me to where? I want to stay here!'

'Wait until you find out. If nothing suits, I will find good place. Be certain. When is he going?'

'He's gone. Not a word to me!'

'He is in trouble. You are not. Why cry?'

'I feel I am nothing. Furniture, only. I am in terrible horror. How can I defend? I helped him? To keep my job? What can I say? Of course, I knew. I am guilty as accomplice? Of course. I have a law degree. I *knew*. But I wanted to keep my place. What should I do? Call the police?'

'They are as bad. Or worse. Be calm. Stay here. Tell me what happens. I will be here to help. I have helped, so far. Why not more?'

'Ah, Prem. You give such hope. I shall rely on you!'

'It is all. I shall take care!'

Chapter 18

He knew, when Baljit came in with the pink leave-of-absence slip, that Mr Vishnai was letting him go from One-One, and his heart thudded so hard he could only breathe in grunts, with sweat.

'Twenty-two days, one day for every year of service, by the Minister's order!' she said. 'You are at liberty from to-morrow, and you will report to Mr Vishnai only on the twenty-ninth, seven o'clock in the morning, full pay, all emoluments. Isn't that lovely?'

'I shall be replaced!'

She shook her head, smiling.

'You don't know how the Minister thinks of you,' she said, a small goddess. 'The Minister ordered this. He thinks you have been badly treated. Or carelessly. On the twenty-ninth, at ten, in the morning, he wants to see you. Prem, will you do something for me?'

'For you, *anything*!'

She looked down, and he got up to push the chair nearer, but she moved in a blunder, and knocked him into the seat and she fell in his lap.

He put an arm around her waist. She made no move, still looking down.

'My father and both his brothers are in serious trouble,' she said, very quiet. 'They have a business with this Minister. You can help?'

She showed the paper, and he nodded, and she folded the page and put it in her handbag.

Miss Tata's Minister.

'He is replaced?'

She nodded.

'It is why they are in danger,' she said, still down at the floor.

'Criminal activity?'

'I suppose it could be called so. But they were more sinned against, I think?'

'How?'

She moved in his lap, and her warmth came into all down there.

'There was a bullion deal, and foreign currency transfer. They signed and put up the collateral. The Minister used the foreign currency to finance imports. He made great profits. My father and his brothers will have the blame and no profit and no return of capital!'

'I don't understand that?'

'Nobody understands. How should I? But I don't want my father in prison. He acted in best faith!'

'Dealing with that Minister, he must have!'

She moved again, not to be misunderstood.

'An association of crooks!' he said. 'What should I do with them?'

She wriggled deeper.

'But I must try to save them!' she said. '*Anything* I can do!'

'Wait!' he said. 'You sacrifice yourself for your father and his brothers?'

She shut her eyes, looking up.

'It will cause such trouble to our families. And beyond. How shall we survive?'

'Your own survival? How about the starving? Others are starving and dying. Thousands of people outside your family?'

'We could also be starving!'

'Why?'

'People would know. They would burn us!'

He felt her warmth. She was not moving.

'All right,' he said. 'You stay here. I shall go over and see what I can do. I hope I can do something?'

'O, Prem, please do everything?'

He squeezed her, and she put a gentle hand against his face.

'I know you can,' she said. 'I will stay here!'

He went out to find Gond, and over to Miss Tata's office.

'A favour?' he said, and she wore a pale blue dress under the office black smock.

'Of course!' she said, clasping hands, turning fully towards him.

He gave her the paper with the names.

'Ah, Prem!' she whispered. 'The Minister is being replaced. He isn't here. All the files have gone!'

'Where?'

She shook the dark hair.

'His own people? The police? The political party headquarters?'

'You can't find out? I am working for somebody as helpless as you. Can't you do something? Give this poor girl the same chance?'

'A girl?'

'How do you think I got the files?'

She looked, and stared at him.

'You have something with her?' she whispered.

He raised a hand.

'Nothing!' he said. 'As with you. Nothing!'

She looked away.

'I think they went to Warehouse Eight. They will still be there. Until the new Minister takes office. I shall hope for you. And her. But how will you enter the warehouse?'

He went on his knees, and held the soft hand close to his face.

'I shall find!' he said. 'As I found for you, I shall find for her!'

He felt the hand press.

'I shall hope for you,' she said. 'I would like to invite you for tea sometime. Not here!'

'*Anywhere*. Any*time*!'

She wrote, and gave him the page.

'It will be only us!' she said, almost sharp, loud. 'I am having leave of absence. Until the next Minister takes office. Wednesday, at four? That address?'

'Four, next Wednesday,' he said, and got up, and rested the back of her hand where he was risen, hard. 'I shall dream. And I am hoping to help this girl!'

'Try Bay Number Three in Warehouse Eight,' she said, writing. 'I think that's where they are. But you will never find them. Or get near!'

He crushed her hand against him.

'Four, next Wednesday,' he said, and walked out, down to Gond, and gave him the paper.

'Take the boys, and go in. What paper and files you are finding, take to New Place. I shall be there tonight. Come for me at ten o'clock. I shall go to Seripur. All well with Khusti?'

'Very well, Premji. Almost finished, the office. Furniture?'

'All ordered. When roof is on, tell me. Electric typewriter? Calculator?'

'They are there, Premji. Babuji is spitting!'

'Even he must learn!'

He went back to One-One with a head full of mystery. Mr Raybould had always said there were times when you must sit down, and take note, count the animals, find out what the harvest will be, and go clearly into time, never blindly, always ready to change course, as a good navigator must, when he finds the map wrong.

He was finding the map wrong. Ministers were being replaced.

It was the time when Room Eleven should be most important in Ministerial exchanges. But it was shut down for twenty-two days. He was given leave by the only Minister of honesty. Everybody knew he was honest, even his secretary. But there was no guarantee, and little hope, that Prem Naran would go back to One-One.

He went through the safe, the file racks, the desk, and outside, in the clerk's collection, but after those many hours, he found nothing to pin him to any matter.

He was safe, so far as he saw.

But that was a dangerous place.

Anything could come up.

What?

What, possibly, could take One-One from his hands?

He knew he must go to the Guru.

He was careful to see everybody, and leave notes, and he took Mawri for a soft drink, but the only talk was about a move by everybody for a strike. The monthly wage was not enough. They had to have more. Starvation was on the doorstep. Everybody was living from the fat, except them.

Ministers and the rest, down to the top grades, were rich.

The clerks and messengers, the lowly, had little. But they did the work.

Without them, what could happen? If they stopped work?
If they came out on strike?

The place would come to a standstill, of course.

'Don't be a fool,' Prem said. 'Tell the others. Ten thousand
are waiting for every place, to earn, and have a pension, and
medical benefit, and the other things. Ten thousand, a hundred thousand. They would pay great price only for your
place. You know it? Why do you talk? You will be known.
First thing, no Mawri. You could be dismissed!'

Mawri nodded.

'But it is getting worse,' he said. 'We have starvation, not
wages. People outside are dying. Us, not yet. But near. Why
can't you speak up as you did before?'

'Isn't the time. Where is the meeting? No use, outside full
meeting. Ministers present and radio people, and everything
ready, knife-edge, to cut throats. Now? No hope!'

'Why not?'

'People not ready. We are the lucky. Every week we have
earned stated sum in packet. Who else does? Every week we
can buy so much. How many can? If we are in sickly condition, we can go to good doctor. No charge. Or hospital.
No charge. Many things. Bones we have to pick, but at least
they have a little meat. Others don't have even bones. Are
you being a red?'

'Ah, Premji, no!'

'Be careful. If the Prime Minister decides, right, everybody
under Grade Two, out, finished, what do you do?'

'She couldn't!'

'Of course she could. She has power. Have you?'

Mawri shook his head.

'Be sensible,' Prem said. 'Tell others to use their heads. Not
against a brick wall. Remember. The power is not with us.
We must be thankful, for scraps. And enjoy them. And say
nothing. We have no *say. Any*where. Our time is coming. In
my lifetime or not, do I care? It will come!'

'But it is hard to wait. Premji. Children are hungry, don't
you know?'

'Don't take away the bone from them. Don't talk. Don't
grumble. Don't listen to other people talking. Walk off. Show
you disagree. Eyes and ears are everywhere. Are you a fool
to be caught?'

'Ah, Premji. You are so high. Hob-nob with Ministers. So
clever. Everybody says, o, that Prem!'

'I am nobody. I am Harijan. If anything crops, send somebody to New Place. Do me a favour, I will have many favours
for you. Spend this on the children!'

Mawri took the notes and kissed them.

'You are leaving very safe. Any inquiry, I am sending
scooterboy. Especially if police!'

'Why? Police?'

'They have been to everybody. Asking questions. Nobody
knew anything. You are quite safe!'

Prem almost felt the threat. Instantly the air became
heavy. He seemed to hold the weight of space. Sweat came
on his head, and tickled down his neck and back, a touch of
insects almost making him afraid.

He had to sit down and count the animals, find out what
the harvest would be, and go clearly into time. But always
ready to change course if the map was wrong.

One-One seemed a small temple in blue light.

He sat at the desk, moving hands over the polish. It
needed a statue of the Lord Krishna, so that he might keep a
joss burning over flower petals sprinkled about, and special
small offerings of rice and sacred food in brass dishes, always
polished.

There were four ways to think of the Bhoomijai business.

First, the Minister might have got a few people to spirit
him off, either to stop his mouth, or to take the money or
both.

Second, Bhatt, the secretary, might have had the same idea,
with or without the Minister's knowledge.

Third, Bhoomijai might have finished his business with the
Minister, and either gone back to the hotel, or somewhere
else. Yet, nobody had seen him go. Kulwant Singh waited all
night Bhoomijai might have gone from the back way. In the
Minister's car? Leaving a taxi-driver, fare not paid? He was
mean enough. But it seemed unsound and unnecessary. The
taxi-driver waited. He was an important witness.

Fourth, Bhoomijai had money in the brief. Had he taken it
to the Minister's house? Against advice?

He telephoned the Mashoba, and asked if Bhoomijai still
had a room.

'Mr Bhoomijai has the Curzon suite!'

'Connect, please!'

Little animals seemed to run along the line, with a bee-
buzz, and nothing.

'No answer. Sorry!'

He went out to find Gond, and howled through traffic to the Mashoba back entrance, and up, to find Dilva, the assistant housekeeper.

'No!' she said, hands up. 'It is not my floor!'

He brought out the notes.

'This is for you,' he said. 'The same for her on the other floor. Go and see!'

She took, and went out, and he picked up a days' old copy of the *Times of India*, and read through the sports, but before he could read the hockey results, she was back, holding out a hand, with another girl, so quietly.

'This is Ruki,' Dilva said, and led to the lift. 'That office has been calling so much. But all callers kept out. Except you!'

'Why me?'

She looked smiles.

'A nice present from you? Anytime!'

'Nobody else though?'

'How many think we are important? *We* think we are. Who else?'

Ruki unlocked the door of the Curzon suite, and he walked in, to a room turned over, stripped, flung about.

Ruki threw out her hands.

'I must call the Manager!' she said. 'It is a robbery!'

'Don't call!' Prem said. 'How did you find out? Why did you come in? The DON'T DISTURB light is on. Why must you get yourself in trouble?'

He went about the room, kicking away sheets thrown over the floor, pillows, towels, and found Bhoomijai's clothes, heaped, though without the brown Nehru or beige jodhpurs. But he was dealing with a cobra, and cobras have their own ways.

He gave both girls more notes, and went down to the Manager's office.

American.

Forties, perhaps, dark, well shaved, dressed in blue, a bow tie, shining fingernails, a smile, but commercial, not good.

'We've had a lot of enquiries, but we don't permit search without warrants,' he said. 'A guest's room is his. While he pays!'

'Is Mr Bhoomijai paid?'

'His office here is in touch. Who are you?'

'I am a friend. Did he use a private strongbox?'

'Let me see your credentials, first. Too many people have been asking questions. Without the proper authority, I can't move!'

Dilva whispered outside that she knew Bhoomijai had a private strongbox, because her sister was in Reception, and she had the register.

He saw the jewel eyes under the roof at Seripur.

Gond took him to Bhoomijai's office, and he went in, asking for the manager, but he was out for a coffee. He found the secretary, an elderly woman, and she said Bhoomijai was not in his Bombay office, and they were worried about him.

'Generally he is here all day from six in the morning,' she said. 'Three days he is missing. And carrying a large sum. He should have taken guards. The city is not what it was. We have all become thieves and criminals. For what reason? Once we were honest. Now, no!'

'Why?'

'Money, Only money!'

The manager came in, hurried, short, tubbish, in a blue silk suit, white shirt and tie, horn-rim sunglasses, and breathing asthma, a real slaver.

'What do you want?' he said, a breathy voice, too loud.

'I am here to see Bhoomijai,' Prem said.

'In what matters?'

'He took taxi to Minister's house and told the taxi to wait. He waited all night. Because I booked him, he came to me for his fare!'

'See the Minister!'

'Minister has gone. Not coming back!'

'Nothing to do here!'

The warning voice said look at the map, count the harvest, find where, say nothing, and go clearly into time.

He looked at the sorrowed eyes of the secretary, and went out, to Gond, and back to Lok Sabha, and the office of Mr Vishnai.

He showed Kulwant Singh's chit.

'Minister's petty cash will pay,' Mr Vishnai said. 'Go in Baljit's office. I will call!'

He went out to Baljit, and she got up, and gave him a cold soda, and a squeeze of the arm.

Mr Vishnai opened the door.

'Go immediately to Chief Superintendent Murthi Singh,' he

said. 'Tell him all you know. Hold nothing. A lot is cooking. Who knows what is in the pots?'

Prem went upstairs, miserably, and Superintendent Murthi Singh waited for him, and almost threw him into the office.

'Tell me your facts!' he said. 'Hold nothing. Or suffer!'

Prem thought of the Guru, and closed his mind, speaking only the words given.

'That is all?' the Superintendent's voice said.

'All!'

'Why did you go to the Bhoomijai office today?'

'To get taxi fare owing to Kulwant Singh. I was sent away!'

The Superintendent put his fist under the beard, to prop.

'Bhoomijai went to the Minister's house?' he said. 'He has not been seen again? The Minister was giving him licences?'

'I know nothing!'

The Superintendent got up, and walked about, and again resting a hand on Prem's neck, and shaking.

A knock, and a havildar stood aside for Kulwant Singh, the taxi-driver, the head hall porter at the Mashoba, and Bhatt, all of them looking not comfortable.

Prem was touched on the shoulder, and the havildar nodded towards the door.

He went out, and sat on the form, looking at pale-green walls, trying to see the clear way, knowing he must talk to the Guru, and then live the days of liberty at Seripur, for peace, and the speech and thought of his own people, so far simpler and so less hurtful than the sharp ones of the city, where a threat could come from any door, or from round any corner, or out of any mouth.

The Superintendent came in a slam of the door, and stood in front of him.

'You can go,' he said. 'One question. Did this one, Bhatt, know anything of the dealings between the Minister and Bhoomijai?'

'He only could. He was the secretary. He must know everything!'

'You were friends?'

'As the tiger and the goat? I am Harijan!'

'Go!'

Prem went downstairs in hate for Bhatt and all those like him. He wished he could tear the world, destroy the Bhatts, make new, under a great banyan, and put Babuji as keeper of the book, at small interest, and everybody living in peace, with full bellies, as in Seripur, where children grew to proper size, and mothers smiled.

Thinking clearly of the way ahead, he tried to puzzle what the Minister, already in disgrace, and finished in Government, could gain by killing Bhoomijai, and then threw the thought aside, because Bhoomijai was far more useful alive than dead. Then, had Bhoomijai gone willingly? Where? The Minister was in disgrace, but he was still powerful, both in the Party and in industry. Out of office, the ex-minister and Bhoomijai still made a strong partnership. Heads together, those two could still be a powerful couple, with all their friends, inside and outside politics.

Where would Bhoomijai go. or allow himself to be taken? To have a conference? To plan a new campaign? There was no need for him to tell his offices, whether in Bombay, Delhi or Calcutta, anything. They went on just the same.

He told Gond to go to Miss Tata, and he went along with the escorting havildar to her offce.

She looked at him, the cool eyes, while he told her, and the dark shining head shook.

'They are probably in his place in the hills outside Rani-khet,' she said. 'I have the diary of ministerial private air-craft. It fits the time. I think you would be making a mistake to interfere. Mistake? You could be crushed!'

'But I am sorry for Bhoomijai!' he said.

She laughed, shut-eyed.

'Ah, Prem!' she said. 'It's why we love you. You are so sorry for the wrong people. Don't forget my tea next Wednesday. And be calm. Retire. Rest. Do nothing. Say less!'

Chapter 19

Seripur, in flowers, and the children laughing, well fed, and the mothers working, and lines of washing so much colour, and most of the men out in the fields chanting, and buffalo standing in water pumped from the river with machinery bought by Mr Raybould, and added over the years until the water system was best anywhere, and Seripur was top village in India, watered, well fed, far from danger, and all his, even the smiles.

He sat with Babuji in the early morning, listening to people coming for loans, glad when the cold morning winds warmed in the rising sun, and deep-blue shadow under the banyan became slowly pink, and all the time tin shapes in the branches flashed in welcome, and the coloured flags flew out, each a prayer, and the children ran to school, shouting in small dust of the street, swinging a fat bag of books, but under the left arm carrying the homework of the night before, so precious.

Mr Raybould insisted from the start that English must be first in importance, figures second, all others following, according to time available. A nation of more than five hundred million, with almost four hundred distinct languages, required one language only, as a mental and linguistic cement. Provided all people spoke the language they wished at home, they could also speak one language understood outside, and that could only be English. India could clearly make itself known, outside, in a language easily translatable. There might be argument about the translation of Hindi, Urdu, Gujarat, Pushtu, and all the rest.

There could be no argument about English. It said exactly what it said.

Prem employed only the most qualified teachers, and they had good prize-winners. He had big prizes for the best students, more for the girls than for the boys, because the girls had much more to do. The boys worked in the fields for many hours, and finished when the sun went to sleep. But the girls worked on until the evening food was cooked, and pots washed, and children put to bed. Then they studied. They did so much more. They deserved that much more.

Gond brought in Khusti to work the tabulator, and the electric typewriter, and in so few days he had his position settled, in order, and he sat in the big room under the swimming pool, watching the shadows of swimmers, looking at paper ribbons holding figures he dared hardly believe.

He was richer than he knew.

The money was all hidden in Seripur, not even a half on loan to borrowers. The rest should have been in a bank to earn interest. But which bank? How many banks would accept even one-tenth of the total without inquiry? How could a Lok Sabha messenger – or little more – even with private property giving profit, year by year present so much for banking? What could he say? Where did all that money come from? How could he answer? There were Income Tax inquiries over many years. How could he answer? What defence? Mr Raybould had never paid tax of any kind. That was in time of the Raj. After the time of Independence, the place was still poor, and he had only his teacher's salary, and so, no tax. But all these years later, so much difference.

What to do with the 'extra' money? Sales of crops, harvests of cereals, milk, mangoes, and everything else, added to a large sum, year by year. But the total was nothing compared with the cash in hand, not in books, but in notes, to be counted in packets.

What would the Customs, the Income Tax, the police do here?

He was shuddering.

Thinking was only shuddering.

Seripur was beautiful under a wintry sun, warm in the beam, cool in shade, but always a charcoal fire somewhere, to heat the legs and dhoti, and the palms held towards the coals. He heard Ganesh a long way off, coming in, singing, but horribly, and he heard trouble.

Gond got off in dust and took off the helmet.

'Premji,' he said, with dust making shapes about him. 'The Minister and so many others are dead. With a bomb. Mr Vishnai wishes you are back, please!'

Prem clasped his forearms, and looked hard at the map, and tried to see the harvest, straightening, shutting his eyes, nodding, and went to the house to dress in the Gobind suit, and put on shoes, ready.

The banyan was gold in sun when they went away, and the boys and girls waved, and Ganesh screamed, and the road was a grey song.

'Ah, Prem!' Mr Vishnai said, so glad, when he got to Archives. 'I knew I could count. Please take care of this multifarious nonsense. We are completely submerged!'

Prem put his hand under the files, lifted them, and took more papers from Baljit, and went around to One-One.

Light was still blue and more polish was so evident, and the air blessed him clean.

A long, paper-by-paper search through the files gave nothing not known. The odd paper, not filed, gave more. Bhoomijai had been with the ministerial party. Six had died, others were in hospital.

He went back to Archives, and nodded to Baljit that he wanted the main office.

'Vishnaiji,' he said 'There is much here. A lot might be laid on us. Why didn't we know? Constant play of paper between one Ministry and another? Seven ministers altogether? Are we all left out? Or not knowing? This man, Bhoomijai, had dealings with everybody. Didn't we know his influence? Or what he did? Or represented? Are we of the foolish?'

'We are not fools,' Vishnai said, quietly. 'We have only to do what we are told to do. What is your question?'

'Bhoomijai had an apartment in the Mashoba. It is paid by his office. We should search and find if anything is against us, or the ministers still in office. We cannot afford to be in mistake. We only will be blamed!'

Vishnai held his forehead, and looked, and nodded.

'You are right,' he said. 'How shall we deal?'

'Give me a permit to search the rooms and subsidiaries, if any. I bring anything of real evidence back here? He is in hospital. We can help him?'

Vishnai nodded to Baljit.

'Make out a permit,' he said. 'Let Prem go in. Let him bring back here all that Bhoomijai has at the Mashoba. It may prove useful. At least we will make sure. Take it to Superintendent Murthi Singh for police stamp. Everything properly in order!'

Prem went up to Security with flying squirrel bats winging mad in his guts. Murthi Singh could send policemen, instead. Nothing would come back to Archives. He was remembering the hotel's private safe. Anything there would go to Police Headquarters. It would never be seen again. How to prevent?

He remembered Dilva's sister in charge of the safe deposit register. But what could she do against that efficient fellow, the Manager? He would push a cold snout into everything to protect the hotel. And the interests of an important patron, of course.

The havildar took the paper into the office, and came out to nod him in.

Deputy Commissioner Aurora Singh, greyer, with more medal ribbons and a different colour of headband, sat with Superintendent Murthi Singh, and they were looking at the permit.

'What is your job, exactly?' the Deputy Commissioner asked. 'What do you do?'

'I am between Archives and ministries, and the members of both Houses, sir. Paperwork, only!'

'Why is this permit to search required? It should go to a Magistrate!'

'Sir, this man does much work with all ministries. Most of it is highly confidential. On level of Cabinet. Archives must protect sensitive matters in National interest!'

The Deputy Commissioner put the paper down.

'Sign!' he said. 'It's politics. We keep out. There's trouble enough!'

'We've been in there, anyway,' Superintendent Murthi Singh said. 'Nothing!'

He signed, and the havildar took it outside, nodding to follow.

Two stamps, one round, one oblong, and the havildar gave it.

Prem folded exactly, and put in the file, and passed the notes, and the havildar stuffed them in his pocket, and smiled.

'Anytime!' he said, smiling, different. 'Only ask!'

Gond took him to the Mashoba, and he walked to the Manager's office. The secretary went in, and held the door open.

Prem put the permit on the desk, and the Manager clasped his hands with shining nails to look down at it.

'Just what are you guys looking for?' he said, almost angry. 'The police have been here twice. Somebody else. His office checked him out this morning. He's in a hospital somewhere, isn't he?'

'I don't know. I want to look at the suite. Also, I want to see the safe deposit box. I believe he has items in charge?'

'I don't think so?'

'I will give you the number of the key?'

The Manager frowned, and shifted in the chair.

'I don't need it,' he said. 'We have a register. How do you know he had something in there?'

'He did business with Government. We know what is in there. The exact sum. Also the papers. We hope it is still there? Or the police will be here!'

'No question!' the Manager said, and pressed a button.

A secretary came in while he wrote.

'Take Mr Naran along to the key registry of the safe deposits, and open this box,' he said, and got up, giving her a chit. 'Mr Naran, anything wrong, come back and see me!'

'If anything *is* wrong, I will be back with the Commissioner of Police. Thank you, sir!'

He knew the Manager had made sign to the secretary. He felt it behind his back. She led him up the short stair, to the long curve of the first floor, and all the way round to the ground floor, and out to the reception. Round the corner, a man was just shutting a safe deposit door, and going away. The secretary went to Reception, and came back with a key. It was the same box the man had just shut. He kept an eye on it.

He used the key and opened the door.

The too-old brief bag was there, but thin. He reached in for the files and papers.

'Call the Manager,' he told the secretary. 'Everything is far from right. Don't leave. A telephone is there!'

She called as if she had expected.

He looked through the papers. They were letters, memoranda, notes to the Bhoomijai office, copies of bills, all of them deathly in the hands of the Opposition.

The Manager came, breathless.

'What's wrong?' he said.

'That bag is empty. Last seen, full. Where is it?'

'Where's what?'

'The money!'

The Manager breathed long.

'Look, his office was here this morning. Closing out the account. They wanted to empty this. I got the lawyer for the hotel. He said, take out the cash and put it in the hotel safe, make out a receipt, and put it in the bag. Did you look?'

Prem took the bag and opened it. The receipt was in the flap.

He gave the bag to the Manager and put the receipt in his pocket.

'Put that sum in here, and I will take it,' he said. 'Nobody had a right to take out the money. You will have to explain to higher authority. Did the office of Bhoomijai offer to give you a half?'

'No!'

'Why is it in the hotel safe?'

'The lawyer said it would be safer. People can search this box. Not the hotel safe!'

'Fill the bag, and I will count. I know how much was in. It must be exact. It was *more* than the receipt!'

The Manager half-turned, thought better and went on, and the secretary came back with the bag packed so tight he could barely open, but he saw bank-sealed packages, and closed, and gave the secretary notes, and he knew from her smile that he had a friend.

Vishnaiji held a middle finger to his forehead, going through files, and the papers, and making little horse-sounds – hnh-hnh! and vo-vo-vo-voh! and za-za-zaah! – and slammed a hand on them.

'You were right, Prem!' he said. 'More than right. Now we can defend this Department. Without this paper, no. Now, the money. What?'

'I have taken copy of receipt, clocked in, recorded,' Prem said. 'The bag is not opened. The sum is not counted. It should go in Archives in the heavy safe. Let Bhoomijai claim it in person. No representative!'

Vishnaiji nodded, and wrote.

'Baljit, register the bag, sealed, into the safe,' he said. 'Prem, take these papers to the Minister, only. Wait for his comments. Report to me!'

Gond took him over to Q, and Miss Thin Back's smile.

'Ah!' she said. 'The Minister is just leaving for the funerals. Let me see!'

She came back to hold open the door, and Prem went in to put the file on the desk.

'Ministerji, the Bhoomijai case,' he said. 'Director of Archive's compliments. He thought you should see!'

The Minister's eyes were cut-stone shining over the glasses, and he opened the file, and flick!-flick!-flicked! to the last page, nearly twenty minutes of no expression, and looked up, smiling.

'I shall take charge of this!' he said. 'It deserves to be seen. I think you've done extremely well. Even better than that. Was there any money in this?'

'It is in the heavy safe in Archives, Ministerji!'

'Well done. It will stay there!'

Prem made *namaste* and walked out to Miss Thin Back's smile, and down to Gond, and a singing return to Archives.

'I had a call from the Minister,' Vishnaiji said, so gladly. 'We are all so complimented. I can see you going up again!'

'I shall stay on, or go back to liberty?'

'Liberty, certainly. Now I know how soon I can find you. Have a splendid rest!'

Baljit took him by the arm on the way out.

'My father and his brothers?' she whispered.

'Safe. All paper burned. No evidence anywhere!'

She sighed, resting on one foot, head up, eyes shut.

'How shall I repay?' she said, not looking at him, and yet looking, smiling through her eyelids.

'I shall come in on Wednesday,' he said. 'After office hours, we shall meet at the Mashoba. I will send a taxi. Yes?'

She nodded, and he pinched lips tight, down in her sari, and she gave to him, and he fondled the curve of her jelly buttock, and went out.

Gond took him to New Place, and the hot stench of the ghats, and the healing wind blowing away, and going too far, and the stench of frying human fat coming in again, and the chants of funeral parties in dark evening. *Ram, Ram, Satha Hai!* – and the drums far over, and then nearer, and somebody singing in New Place, a man, changing to a woman, and then a man, and steps in jingle of bangles, and cooking smells, and crying babies, and still the funeral chants, one inside another, so many over each other, to put a dead one on the logs to fry, to cook, to make ash. Given time, the living were only ash, and the living went on making ash, only to be made into ash.

His wife was out, and he left money where she would find it. The rooms were clean. They always were. His linens were on the rack, ready for him. He pulled the petals from one blossom of marigold in the tall pot she had put them in, and sprinkled the statue of Kali, her favourite.

He went out, and Gond turned over the bumps of broken cement slabs and ordure, and screamed for the tyre market, and the chemical factory of Ghal.

But Ghal was a different man, no longer held in a yawn, but masterly, masterful.

'Listen to me carefully,' Prem said. 'I want to sell my share here. I don't want any more to do here. Can you find the capital?'

Ghal laughed, O, a brave, very confident fellow.

'When you please!' he almost trumpeted as an elephant. 'I have many interested. What is the figure?'

Prem wrote and gave him the paper.

Ghal shut his face.

'So much?' he said. 'Who will find it?'

'If not, I will find a team of graduate chemists to come in and take over to enlarge. I have the capital. Have you?'

'Perhaps I can get?'

'No perhaps. That figure, in three days, cash. I shall be here. All right?'

Gond took him to the office behind Connaught Place.

Sen and Mukherjee had gone, but Mujid still worked at his account sheets.

'I am finishing last days of Disco and Sludge,' he said. 'It was difficult because of sale of furniture and various items. I was not having help of Zona. I think Mr Dal's people are cheating very much. Electrical fixtures. Kitchen furniture. Bar inventories. They are not small items. They have to be reduced to figures. My responsibility. How to arrive at correct figure?'

'You arrive at your figure. That will be the correct one for me. I will then see Dal. Either he agrees, or the sale is off. Remember. You have a percentage of the figure you decide. Agreed?'

'Ah, Premji. I will be sure. It will be correct!'

He took Mujid's finished account sheets down to Dal. The showroom was still open, very light, and three people looked at cars, and salesmen chatted, but Dal left them, and came, arms out.

'Prem, my brother and sister!' he shouted, wrapping. 'So much I have missed!'

'I was on liberty. Look, Dal. Don't let your people make difficulties for Mujid. He is working for me. You took Disco and Sludge, closed doors, everything in, one piece. Now you are saying no?'

'Not true. You are making claims for two hundred per cent value. My accountants value at ten per cent. It's fair?'

'You agreed to overall price, one figure, cash down only. Why do you change?'

'It was not what my inspectors thought. Everything was not up to standard. At that price!'

'But you had contracted. Given assurance. One price. Where is it?'

'Now, Prem. When everything is brought to balance, price will be paid!'

'It will be paid *now*!'

Dal shook his head.

'I have had much expenditure,' he said. 'I will pay the balance, only!'

'Then no sale,' Prem said, quietly. 'I shall take over!'

'What about my expenditure?'

'Of small interest. Certainly, because of good food in the restaurant, and good bars, I am better known. I can open whenever I please. Where you never will. I can open to-morrow night!'

'You have no licence. The police will close!'

'Tomorrow I will have licences. If you do not want the girls, I will take them. You are having nothing except yes or no. You want the business or not? At that price, *cash*!'

Dal stamped on one foot, and another, and put up a hand to shield his eyes from the light, and tightened the dhoti, and rubbed down his backside, and all to hide he was thinking, but then he turned.

'I will pay,' he said. 'Contractual price, only. What is your barman, Barud, doing, telling my men they can have bottles only if he is paid?'

'Barud?'

'Why do you think I stuck my toes? A barman, telling me what I shall have, and what I shall not? Am I to be told by such?'

'You should have sent Gond with a message. I promise Barud will not annoy you again. I _know_ he will not!'

'Better for you. He is supplying other bars. With your stock? That should be mine? Closed doors? Everything inside, one price? And this low fellow, selling inside?'

'Nobody overseeing. It has stopped from this moment. I should have taken precaution. I shall find what stocks have been sold. I will credit you. What a shame. We cannot trust anybody!'

'It is so true. Even ourselves!'

They laughed. Dal's black belly jumped up and down.

Prem went outside to Gond.

'You know where Barud, the barman lives? Take a couple of lathis. Beat him. Tell him if he sells another bottle, he gets a broken leg. Come for me in the office, Connaught Place!'

Gond screamed off.

Prem strolled down the wide avenue of private houses, built for high officers of the Raj, lived in now by big business, and politicians. People slept as dogs, behind the tall hedges. Babies cried, silenced by the murmur and the teat, and men coughed, and spat, at distance. Dogs growled. The dead sprawled where death had taken them, almost to the kerb, or just beyond, as if they reached for the traffic to take them home. Shops selling tourist pieces were lit, but shut. A naked man lay in light, one eye catching glitter. Many naked men lay, holding a stick in one hand, and a brass pot in the other, their possessions, nothing else for a lifetime of nothing.

But no naked women. They died in hiding. Behind the hedges.

The big houses had gardens. In time of the Raj, houses put themselves against others for a prize for the best garden. A richness of flowers bloomed. Now, only dead women and bodies bloomed in the jungle. Nobody cared for flowers. Only marigolds to put round visiting necks and lotus to spread on statues of the gods, and in the love-moss of beauty.

He looked up at a big cinema poster, a man crawling over a girl, both very lovely and young. Everybody knew he was taking her any way he wanted, and she was letting. The film was called _The Essence of Love_. He wondered so many times about love, the English word, and the real meaning, never in words, but only in feeling. Words have no meaning except in the ear. Words go in the head. But the head is not where love is, and a heart is deaf because of its drumbeat. Truly where love is, he thought, could only be the lingam, the strong muscle, that arose with love, and went in for the pleasure of love, and came out soft, love gone. The word desire led to love, he saw that, and often he desired, but perhaps the time was not quite right, or something else to do.

Miss Turlo, and Baljit, and Miss Tata, and Miss Thin Back, and Dilva, and Ruki, and so many more, all were love. Shiva was love, but not to be touched, or if touched, then one with the others. Prahash was love. She had the dead children. He had to look after her. Why? Because? The way she looked at him. She had nobody else. She might have been one dying behind a hedge, or in the dust of a village. But because of his love, she was alive, with a kiss for his cheek, and clean linens, and good food always, at New Place.

What was love? The word in English, how to explain?

I love you. So often heard.

What meaning?

It seemed the English disease. The American, also. But they spent more money. English said it, and spent nothing. Indians of all states, anywhere, spent nothing because they did not believe. A woman was a woman. Her body and her intimacy were all.

Intimacy, Mr Raybould said, was something you feel with the fingertips of the mind.

But most people, men or women, have no fingertips, and so few have mind, and for them, love was a word, and it meant To Have, and no more.

Really not worth thinking about.

Chapter 20

In early mornings, under the banyan at Seripur, he sat with a hand on Babuji's feet, and heard the voices of borrowers wanting money to build a house, or buy fertiliser, or seed to plant fields, or dig a well, or make a fair marriage for a daughter, or send a son to college, or buy an air ticket to London for a mother to see her sons and grandchildren, and so many other reasons, and Babuji gave all they asked. He never never said no. Money lent at 2 per cent per annum, all loans to be repaid in five years, or interest went up to 10 per cent, and if not paid, then a visit from the lathis. A simple system that worked, and kept the village and the farms all round alive and healthy, to the disgust of many Brahmin landowners nearby, refusing to lend, unwilling to spend, willing only to take every paisa they could gouge, and living as a Maharaj, without a thought for others, and taking poor men's daughters for only part of rent.

They hated the Harijan. So many from Seripur had been beaten, or injured for hospital, or killed by the roadside. Police had nothing to do. Nobody gave evidence. Everybody was afraid. Anybody complaining might last a few weeks. But they would disappear. Nobody said anything. They dare not. Brahmin had power everywhere.

Harijan had only themselves, and nobody.

He sat, walked about the place, and later in the big room under the swimming pool, listening to Haydn, and thinking cryingly of Mr Raybould, and the blue light flashed, and the buzzer made noises. He turned off the power, and went carefully to the door, and opened, out, to the stairway, and closed quietly, and up, in the lift, to the reception room.

Khusti waited.

The small girl, only to his ribs, in a black sari, had the face of a porcelain statue, so calm, so beautiful, the mouth resting, eyes covered.

'Chand Gupta,' she said. 'Headman of Idrapur. Very serious happenings!'

He went out in the homespun dhoti, shirt, and leather sandals.

Chand Gupta, headman of Idrapur, in the district of Chaljaur, champion of Harijan, could be the most powerful man outside Lok Sabha.

He stood with several of his men, all smiling nicely, a good welcome.

'Well, Prem, my fine one!' Gupta said, and hugging. 'How famous you are becoming, and how proud we all are!'

'If I have helped us, it is only luck, Chandji,' he said, and leading back to the house. 'I am on liberty till twenty-ninth. Is there any service I can do?'

'Two more dead and five badly beaten last night. On the other side of Bilnaga. We are not safe going to market. On any road. What can we do? Outside our own village we can be killed or beaten and kicked. Men, women, and children!'

Khusti brought in the tray with chota pegs of Mr Raybould's whisky, and passed them round.

Prem raised a toast.

'Honoured guests!' he said. 'Very well. I can go now to Lok Sabha. I can see the Undersecretary for Interior, and ask his advice. Are there any suspects?'

Chand took papers, and gave, standing.

'They are all millionaires in crores of rupees, cash, and big estates,' he said. '*Our* land is much better. We have fertilised for the past six years. We have grown the new cereals. We have deep wells so we don't suffer so much from the drought. They want to frighten us away, and then they walk in. A gift, for nothing? They won't have it. We will fight. We will have dead, and broken bones. But move? *No!*'

'What they are doing is against the Constitution,' Prem said. 'We are fully protected. We are guaranteed peaceful life equal with everybody. Brahmin or Harijan the same before the Law!'

'We have champion!' Chand said, pointing up. 'A man of requisite education and knowledge, and a high place in

Government. Now, Prem. What would you say to being our elected member to Lok Sabha? We have never voted for a Brahmin. But we have more than enough votes to elect *you*!'

Prem felt breath leave him.

Room One-One, or a seat in Lok Sabha? Grade Two messenger or sitting Member? No question.

Prem Naran Raybould, seated in Lok Sabha, champion of his people, tireless in their cause, great matters to direct, federal business to decide, name always in papers?

He breathed deep, held, let go, felt sweat run.

'Yes!' he said.

Chand lifted arms and shouted, and the others shouted with him, and they made a ring, and crowded out of the house, and danced and clapped, and sang the victory song down to the banyan, and all the people shouted there, and many came with garlands, and he was bright and fat with marigolds, and Babuji came crying, and put the grey head on his shoulder and sobbed, dry.

No hope to talk in such a noise, but Chand took him to the truck. In the quiet of the cab, he held out a thick package of notes.

'You will have to start your campaign,' he said. 'There will be plenty more. We are all made-up minds. Me and my committee are going through the electoral area, not one house not visited. *Every* vote picked up. You will go in landslide. Only one matter?'

Chand's stare sobered.

'You have no little outside business? Nothing your opponents could find reprehensible? Newspaper stories? Scandals? All clean? Nothing below the board? No areas of vulnerability?'

'There will be none tomorrow, be certain!'

Chand nodded, satisfied.

'You are man of too much excellent accomplishment to jeopardise with ridiculous matters. Cut clean!'

'It will be done!'

Chand drove off with his men, and Prem walked back, with the crowd patting his shoulders, and kissing his hands, and he went to the statue of Krishna lying beneath the canopy of risen cobras, behind the banyan, and put the garlands around the warm bronze, and the people bowed low, and he knew he must go to the Guru.

He went back to the house to bath and put on the Gobind

clothes, and kiss the photograph of Mr Raybould, and Gond came at exact time.

'Lok Sabha,' he said, and gave a paper with Miss Tata's address. 'This address at four. Any reports?'

'All well, Premji. Nothing moving. Police very quiet. That fellow Tyndale was twice at Lok Sabha. He was sent off. Riba is quite happy. Much business. New Place, nothing. Ghal, the chemist, has money ready. Dal has all the scooter-cabs ready. I have the boys. When, for licences?'

'Fill out forms, and come for me tomorrow, ten o'clock. Connaught Place office?'

'Mr Mukherjee, Mr Sen, and Mr Mujid every day there. Only peaceful!'

Everybody at Lok Sabha was pleased to see him, and he went to the office in smiles and salutes.

The blue light, polished desk, reminded of the room at Seripur.

He felt sorry to be leaving.

He went around to Archives, and Baljit opened the door, and almost kissed, but the inner door was open, and Mr Vishnai called him in.

'The dedicated public servant!' he said. 'Can't keep from the job. As it happens, I have a small one. This fellow Bhoomijai is coming from the hospital. He is raising fire from the pit for lost money. Go to him, this address, and say the money is here. Make proper claim, he can collect it. Can you, today?'

'I will go now, Vishnaiji. Also, I have been asked to stand as candidate for Chaljaur at Lok Sabha!'

Vishnai threw up his hands.

'I always knew it!' he shouted. 'Ask anybody what I have *told* them. That man will be sitting Harijan member one of these days. So now you are going to be? How wonderfully excellent, our own man going up? You have backing?'

'Chand Gupta!'

'You are *in*!'

'I will see Bhoomijai, and report tonight, if time, or to-morrow without fail!'

He went out to a warm touch of Baljit's hand, but he was glad he had an excuse to hurry. Baljit, and Miss Tata in one afternoon were one too much, and he wanted to appear well in Miss Tata's eyes.

The hospital had the same smell of chemists' shops and

clean lavatories. A clerk sent him to the fourth floor, private apartment, and Bhoomijai sat in a big chair, thinner, head and one arm bandaged, and a leg on a stand.

'Ah, Prem, my good son, I am so happy to see you!' he said, a tired voice. 'What is this I hear, they robbed me of a great sum?'

'Bhoomijaiji, not robbed. Taken in safe custody. Only come with proof, and you shall take from the Lok Sabha safe. If it had stayed in safety deposit, and Police had found, how much would be left?'

Bhoomijai nodded.

'Very true,' he said. 'Reasonable. Wise decision. You will bring it?'

'Personal appearance only. Signing before magistrate and getting pass. Nothing else to do!'

'I am very weak and so painful, Prem. Couldn't you bring it here if I sign?'

'It is Government, Bhoomijaiji. Rules and regulations. Only in person, signing, money is given. It is safer for you. Many would take. You would never see!'

Bhoomijai nodded, very gloomy.

'You are always right, Prem!' he said. 'I am learning to trust your judgement. You are smart fellow. We shall speak after I am out of this hellish place, so much pain, costing so much. Are the police taking interest?'

'Also Income Tax, and Customs. Very strict!'

'You are saying nothing?'

'I have no mouth. But your office manager? You trust?'

The cobra eyes lit as jewels.

'You have suspicion?'

'Why was the money left in safe deposit at Mashoba? To be cut three ways, between your office manager, the police, and the hotel manager? Why did your office manager not claim as your property? He knew it was there. Why not claim?'

Bhoomijai nodded.

'True,' he said, weak. 'I must first of all have my health. Without my health I am so painful. How can I think? Prem, come and see me in Bombay soon. I regard you in a special way. If you hear anything, telephone me quickly. You know how I think of you?'

Prem bent his head to rest on Bhoomijai's, and the old one touched him with a father's kiss.

'Keep strong eye on my office,' he whispered. 'That manager, Patel, came to me from Civil Service. He is a fool. While I am away, who knows what he will do?'

'Tell him to report to you with daily figures, certified, every afternoon, five o'clock,' Prem said. 'Those documents are accountable in Court. Make him responsible!'

'Very, very good!' Bhoomijai said. 'I will immediately call the fellow. You are such a hope. I am completely refreshed. You will not suffer!'

Prem went out, and found three duty nurses, and gave them notes, and told them to take care of Bhoomijai.

'He won't last long,' one of them said. 'Bad heart, bad kidneys. Bad everything. And such a bloody nuisance for a patient. Isn't he out tonight? Or tomorrow? I'll be glad to smell him for the last time!'

'He is very old,' Prem said. 'Take care of him, and I will take care of you. All of you!'

He reached Miss Tata's house, off the road, in a large garden, at three minutes to four, and an old woman took him upstairs to a big room, white, with pictures, and European furniture.

Eight people, five men, three women, sat and looked.

Miss Tata, in white sari, gave her hand.

'Prem, these are all friends,' she said. 'I wanted to present you as one I know can be trusted. You are wasted where you are. We are members of the Two-Seven-One Club. Bankers, industrialists, politicians, diplomats, the top. We need liaison between all areas. You are ideal. Salary and allowances about three times what you earn now. Free uniforms, linen, and of course, many perquisites of office. You are interested?'

'Do you speak French?' an old man asked, pointing the stick.

'I had three years of French,' Prem said. 'I read and write better than I speak.'

'German?' another old one asked.

'Three years, also. I read better than I speak.'

'Well, then,' Miss Tata said, giving him a cup of tea. 'Shall we nominate you for the post of head hall porter? A most responsible position you would fill with distinction. I am sure, for all your professional life. Is anybody against?'

'I think a personal character is necessary!' another old one said. 'No use being sorry after, and taken for fools!'

'His personal file is on the table,' Miss Tata said, very

tired. 'Do you think I would ask him to come here without thorough investigation? Security, police, everybody, completely clean slate!'

Prem drank the tea in three gulps, and stood.

'Miss Tata, you are very kind to think of me,' he said. 'It is completely a matter of luck that this morning, I was asked to stand for Chaljaur as member of Lok Sabha. For that reason, only, I must decline your generous offer. Thank you very much!'

'Lok Sabha?' somebody said, aloud. 'It's possible? An upstart?'

'No, sir!' Prem said. 'Harijan. And I shall win!'

He went to the door, and Miss Tata followed him outside to the landing.

'How could you do such a thing to me?' she whispered. 'Such humiliation after so much careful planning to give you the best position in the country? Why not think it over? You could lose the election. Then you lose your present position, and any hope of this offer!'

'I shall be elected,' he said. 'I am grateful for your thought. When I am elected, call on me for any service. Also in bed!'

She stared at him, and started a right-hand smack, but he moved his head and the left hand, and he went under, and pinched fat lips down there, and pulled up, and out, and all the way down and under, and she stood with closed eyes, and in moments he felt her flood, and stood away.

'When you want me, only telephone One-One,' he said. 'I am always there!'

He went down the stairs, and she was still standing there, eyes closed, when the old woman opened the door to let him out.

'Riba's place!' he told Gond. 'While I am there, go to the house of Shiva. Say I will be there in thirty minutes. Are the licence forms ready?'

'Ready, Premji!'

'After Shiva, Dal!'

Riba's garden was full of cars.

She sat in the space beyond the front door with two other old women, as she always did, to welcome guests and take them up to their rooms.

She showed him the accounts and bank slips, all in order, and surprisingly good.

'Riba, I am going to sell,' he said. 'I don't want any more

to do. Another woman will come. Perhaps you will not be wanted. So? You will go back to Lok Sabha waste paper collection. I shall give it to you. With the truck. You understand?'

'I think so very good. I don't like this place. Quarrelling girls. Police coming. People drunk. Fighting. No. The paper is quiet. Good profit. Good life. Who wants more?'

He patted her hand.

'Where is Kamata?' he asked.

'I got her a good place in the Convent of the Immaculate Heart,' Riba said. 'She teaches needlework. Better?'

'Very well. I suppose, better!'

'I can get her for you any time?'

'Leave her. She has her life. Who am I?'

He went to find Gond, and over to Shiva. Vutthi waited white plaits in the garden. He went in to the stairs' pink carpet, and that smell of sweet woman, and Shiva opened the door in white stuff, thin, showing her through. Vutthi shut the door, and Shiva took off, in a whisper, and lay on the bed.

'What, so sudden?' she said, smiling, ruffling the love-moss.

'That house and garden, the entire property, plus the girls, a flourishing business,' he said. 'Here are bank slips last ten days. What will you take for clean slate, outright, only cash?'

He showed her the total of slips banked, and then the sale figure.

She opened her eyes, coming up on one elbow, only the prettiest teats.

'So *much*?' she said. 'It's possible?'

'Why not? Who else can show such profit? So quietly? No questions. Only open the door, and your business begins. But the Police are coming closer. Next, the Income Tax. They will want hulking payments. You cannot afford publicity. But this sum, properly invested will make you safe for life. You agree?'

'I think you are terribly kind to think so much of me,' she said, and lay back. 'I will say yes only on one condition!'

'What?'

She patted the bed.

'Take off your clothes, and come in with me!'

She turned on her face, throwing off the sheet, showing

white jelly hills open to him, but he leaned on the bed to kiss both, deep, pressing smacks of lips, and stood.

'I will come back later,' he said. 'First I shall sell. I shall be able to tell you when you will receive the money. Cash. No signatures. No names. Police, Income Tax, too close. And M.I.S.A.!'

'I have no Minister to defend me!'

'Better, you have *me*. The ex-Minister will face charges. Pity the bombers didn't kill *him*!'

'I hate the idea. Poor man. He is so lonely!'

'He deserves. After nine o'clock I am here. To kiss everywhere!'

He went out to Vutthi, and she took him to the gate, and kissed his hand for the notes, and Gond flashed a red light, and free-wheeled downhill.

'Police are watching the house,' he said, over the shoulder. 'Five of them!'

'We are not being followed, so far?'

'They watch who goes in and out. Vutthi told me many Government men go in to meet the Minister.'

'The ex-Minister!'

'They meet always at night Much money is passing. Bhoomijai is mentioned. I can find more?'

'Tomorrow. After Dal, we go to Seripur. You also can sleep there. You have a place?'

'I have a good place, Premji. What time tomorrow?'

'Six. Second thought. While I am with Dal, go back to this house. Find out what you can. Licences ready?'

'Licences, scootercabs, drivers, all ready, Premji!'

'Later tomorrow you have a desk at Connaught Place. Each scooter will have two-way radio. You will have master set. You will direct them. We shall buy more. Three months, you will control the city. You like?'

'I like. I will work. But who drives you?'

'Pick a boy you trust. He will be second to you. Very well?'

Nod.

Dal's showroom seemed all sunshine in light. Several people looked at cars.

Dal, for once in a business suit, strolled, listening to the salesmen, but he came over at once.

'The very man!' he said, holding arms out. 'My dear friend Bhoomijai was in here from the hospital, poor old fellow. He left a bag he wants you to take care of. He trusts only you. He's flying to Bombay this evening. Call him to-night. He has heavy news!'

'About?'

'M.I.S.A.!'

'What, to him?'

'Ministers perhaps will be charged. Him with them. The Prime Minister is a hard woman. A mother's love? A mother's heart? But if you upset her, she can give you a good drub. Everybody in this scandal will have a good drub. She will see to it. You didn't know she is a tigress?'

'I won't take the bag. It can stay here safely. I want you to look at a running business. Tell me what you think, and if you want to buy?'

He opened the folder, showing surveyor's plans of Shiva's land, the house, and details of water, sewage and electricity, and the valuer's certificate of the worth. He showed the list of girls, age, height and weight. Totals of expenses, food, laundry, and cosmetics, and servants for upkeep. Last, the banking receipts for only ten days.

Dal looked through, shut the folder, and rapped it with his knuckles.

'I know about it,' he said. 'How much you are asking?'

Prem showed the paper with the total.

'Less the cost of the scootercabs,' he said. 'Cash, of course?'

Dal looked away, so clearly doing sums.

'Very well,' he said, nodding. 'I will buy. When, full ownership?'

'Tomorrow, four o'clock. At two o'clock, cash!'

Dal nodded.

'A simple transfer,' he said. 'No documents?'

'None. Unnecessary!'

'Prem, I have never found you dishonest. At any rate, with me. This is entirely what you say? Cash, two o'clock, and I walk in at four? Owner? No question?'

'My heart is on it. If I cheated you, how long would I last?'

Dal nodded, and opened the bottom drawer in the desk, bringing out a bottle of whisky and two chota peg glasses.

'We shall have a little drink to the future,' he said. 'Those girls can help me at my new places. Fresh talent is always welcome. I shall open the Hammam next Thursday. You shall be my guest. Here is to us. To hell with M.I.S.A. They can't touch me!'

Salesmen came to interrupt with cheques, and he went out to Gond, down at the end of the concrete path.

'Shiva's house,' he said.

'Premji, the police are all round. Many cars there. Ministerial. I think they will arrest. They were going with handcuffs. I couldn't find Vutthi. Why would they go in?'

Prem thanked the Guru that he had made an excuse not to be in that bed, of such succulence.

'Ministerial crimes, perhaps?' he said, getting in the cab. 'I hope they catch. Let us go to Seripur. I think it is quieter there?'

Chapter 21

He walked about, those so many early mornings at Seripur, watching dew shine on spiders' webs, and children playing, waving to their mothers coming back from the big pond to hang out clothes, going out along the paths to find the men working in the fields, and the boys driving the bullocks round and round the wells to turn the tall bucket-wheels bringing up the water for the area, running out in pale blue canals here, and green lines there, among the broad fields of growing sugar. Further was corn, and beet, a new planting, and then wheat. Everybody wondered if the new strains would come up as the agro-office said. They had been wrong a few times. At others they had been right.

The earth seemed to decide. But fertilised, and watered, and so much spent in care, where was the error that caused that piece of land to give nothing more than sick shoots?

Baraswar, the old one, went with him along the top path asking questions, hands behind, looking down. He smelled clean from his clothes.

'You know, Premji,' he said. 'The look of that seed, for me, was enough. Five years before, we had that seed direct from United States. We had six times the usual crops. Last year, little. This year, the harvest went in a few bags. Our suppliers are cheating!'

'You are sure?'

'Why are seeds good one year, and not the next? I have kept back seed from other years They grow. The new seed, supposed the same? It dies. Why?'

'Not good seed?'

'Not good people!'

'Somebody is replacing best seeds with worthless?'

'Everybody knows!'

'Why not say it before?'

'What use? Let the seed first come up. If it is good, very well. If it is not, there it is, look at it, in the ground. Nothing? *Now* we have the right to say!'

'But we paid biggest price?'

'Of course. Everybody did. For six times crop cereal? It is more than worth!'

'Who supplies?'

'Babuji pays. He knows. He could tell?'

But the truth of shock was in the big ledger Babuji bent back, to show the quantity of seed, and the amount paid and receipted. A company in Delhi, with branches everywhere.

Bhoomijai was the owner.

He went over to the office. The roof was on, and the ceiling plastered, and the walls were almost dry. Two men worked on the tiles, and he sent them away, calling the Lok Sabha board, and getting a line to Bombay.

'Das Brothers, importers, customs agents, and transport –'

'This is Delhi. No names!'

'We are completely listening!'

'The company known as Transeeds, Incorporated, supplies to the entire country –'

'Very well known!'

'I want five hundred bags of Number One Green Omaha. Put it on trucks, bring it to Seripur. I pay for transport. I pay *you* the price of the seeds. We are completely?'

'Complete. Tomorrow, without fail, in the night or early morning. You pay Mehta Roy?'

'Present for him, and all drivers. No mouths!'

'Not one. You know Bhoomijai is in nursing home, here, very sick? Not likely?'

'I am sad. Get the seeds!'

He called Brij Lal, Gond's other boy, and went to Lok Sabha. Paper on the desk of One-One was not important. Baljit and Vishnaiji were not in. He went to the Connaught Place office. Mujid and Sen worked on the Seripur accounts.

'Mukherjee is at the Law Courts,' Sen said. 'There is a serious matter. The original Raybould lands are in question. Was he a citizen?'

'Nearly three quarters of his sixty years, he lived here. He

218

followed Gandhi. Was he a citizen? Did he ask? Did anybody?'

'Now it is serious. If you cannot prove title to land, you are finished. Title deeds you have not got? If you cannot prove, what have you got?'

'Find me the names of anybody complaining. Find addresses of legal offices. I will deal. These fools believe that Harijan must be kicked from the way? Very well. I will teach!'

'Ah, Premji, we all love you You don't know how much. Continually you climb. Continually we are behind you To support. Never doubt. One day, you will be Prime Minister. Why not? You have something to do? Who is a Brahmin? Of what use?'

'We shall find out. They pretend to be the blood glue of society. Holding things together? One day, we will withhold our work. Not a strike. Not anything. Only we shall not be there. Nobody to talk to. Let *them* work. Let them clean the pots. Let them drive the piss and turds to the sewer ditch. Let them take care of the house Let them do so much that we do. We shall then talk. It will be many years, I think. You think so?'

Sen nodded.

'Many years, many deaths,' he said. 'It is the other Independence. For us. But the British *wanted* to go. They were sick of us. They were right We were rotten. We are still rotten. We have no principles We have only us. We are our only defenders We can be bought. It isn't so? Everybody?'

'But,' Mujid said, piling paper. 'We *know* why we are bought. We take the money It is useful. But those who pay? Do *they* know?'

'Of course *not*,' Prem said. 'They want what *they* want. We give it? For money? It goes on? We can be bought? We are rotten? Very well. But those above are rottener The rot will come down. Soon, it will come down to us. Then we can tell them. No more. Finished *No more!*'

He went back to Lok Sabha, and among the new pile of paper on the desk, he found a message from Miss Turlo, one from Miss Tata, and a red *urgentest* from Das.

He thought for a moment. Why would Das call red?

He picked up the telephone, and called Bombay.

'Prem? O! Listen. Bhoomijai is dying. No doubt. He is calling for you. He wants *only* you. *Please* come here. He calls you his only son, his small brother. *Please* come. *Please!'*

'I will come on next flight –'

'I have you booked. Only go to airport. Your ticket is paid!'

'Who pays? I should be in charge to say where I go, where I do not!'

'Don't you understand? Bhoomijai is dying. He is one of *us.* He is *calling* you. Get here. Go to Air-India for ticket. A car will meet you. He has no time. Have you?'

'I will be there!'

Air-India, in a girl's voice, said that the next two flights were full. He could have a seat only on the twenty-two thirty.

He called Miss Tata, and a woman said she would have no news till six o'clock. Perhaps the new Minister would be coming in, and so Miss Tata would be late.

'Please say Prem Naran called from Lok Sabha, Room One-One!'

He called Miss Turlo, and she was bright, ready to come down!'

In moments she was there, pinkish cheeks and shining hair, and a black dress, tight to show her very good waist and other pretty points.

'What do you think!' she said. 'I am so excited. I am going to join the embassy at the U N. Isn't it too marvellous? On Monday I am flying. Wish me luck, Prem. I shall write and tell you the latest. I think I shall be married there. He's got plenty of money. If you need help, let me know!'

'It is very good and deserving,' he said. 'But you are not going to sit in the chair once more before you go?'

'I can't. I must show the new girl what to do. I am here only for minutes. To say how I have enjoyed. Prem, is there chance of more money?'

'Yes. Take off and sit down!'

She laughed, very lovely.

'I will first see the new girl has more or less idea. Then I will come down. By the way, the outgoing Minister is very anxious to see you!'

'Tell him to be not so impatient. Say that I move with extreme caution. I do not wish ill-advised moves to be cause of his arrest. And mine!'

'You are truly right. He has so many enemies. I am sorry for him. But he had done so much damage to others. Nobody has sympathy. They will kick him. If he gives enough to Party funds, he will be ambassador somewhere, and quite safe. But he wants to see you before he goes!'

'I am ready anytime.'

She blew a kiss, and went out, leaving a feeling that something important was wrong, a matter hidden, for the moment, that could suddenly burst and submerge in disaster.

He took the heap of files in the case of the ex-Minister out of the safe, and went through, page by page, trying to see error, or omission Mukherjee, on the legal side, and Mujid, accountancy, had done a pure job of hard work. The totals were enormous, in rupees and other currencies. Nothing seemed incorrect. So far, all solid.

The telephone rang, and Miss Tata spoke, 'Hullo, Room One-One? Could you be at my house, tonight? Nine o'clock?'

'I shall be there!'

'Please do. It is important. For you!'

Miss Turlo knocked, and came in with a tall girl, blacker, in a flush-pink sari, and smiling as if she held a secret.

'This is Miss Jhaban,' she said. 'She knows all about you!'

'I am pleased to meet,' Miss Jhaban said, giving a soft hand. 'I have so much to learn. I am even frightened!'

'Any trouble, come here!'

'It is only what I told you,' Miss Turlo said, taking her arm. 'All questions, go to One-One. They will be settled. In the chair!'

Miss Jhaban turned towards her shoulder, and her lower lip went down, and trickly little sounds came out, only perhaps smiles given shapes.

'The Minister will see you in ten minutes,' Miss Turlo said. 'I don't think he is pleased with what you have done. Too long, and not enough!'

'I shall be there. I will cram it down his neck. I would like to see you both naked!'

They laughed at each other, and held each other, and they were funny sounds, like chickens praising the morning, but Miss Jhaban's were fatter, with spit at the corners of her mouth, bubbling.

Knocks on the door, and Mawri put a hand round.

'Air-India, Premji,' he said 'You are confirming flight to Bombay?'

'Confirm Twenty-two thirty. I shall be back tomorrow.'

Miss Turlo and Miss Jhaban went out with him to Brij

Lal and Ganesh, and they went quick to the Ministry.

Everything was in packing, and men were carrying crates, and the office crisped with paper.

The ex-Minister stood alone, in white homespun, with a big glass, drinking, and his grey hair was all pulled up in little curly ends, not very pretty.

'You have been leaking to the Press!' he shouted. 'How they know these things?'

'I am not reading papers,' Prem said. 'Others have mouths. I, none!'

'Who else could tell them these libellous statements about sale of foreign aid?'

'Your own office staff. They could all earn money from newspapers. But nobody could pay me. I have not received one paisa from anybody. And you promised twenty-five per cent. Did I get it?'

'I? Twenty-five per cent? Are you insane? Broker's commission only. And you are not worth!'

"Very well. If I am not worth, why should I want? Please keep!'

'You are big for your boots!'

'No, sir. My boots have no place. I wish you only future best!'

'I don't wish your best. I believe you are inside man. Working for tax-inspectors. How do they know so much?'

'What could I tell them? Bank of India could tell more. Any bank clerk can give information. Use your brain!'

The Minister threw the glass at him, and splashed himself.

'So much you are saying to me, immaterial fellow?' he screamed. 'Put yourself in absence. Go!'

Prem went downstairs, among the removers, slowly thinking.

Some matter had alarmed the ex-Minister. Room One-One would have the blame. Everything would be put at that door, and nothing to defend.

Question was what to do, what, for the best. The ex-Minister could look after himself, with all his friends and newspaper power.

Room One-One could not. The door could be shut, locked, finish.

Half an hour to the appointment with Miss Tata.

Mawri followed at a sign. He took all the files for the head sweeper to hide, and the notes to grace the ready fist.

'Nothing will happen to you, Premji!' he said. 'We are barbed wire to protect!'

Brij Lal drove down to Miss Tata's house, and the old woman took him in to a younger servant and she took him upstairs to the same room, with only Miss Tata, in white sari.

'Well, Prem, one matter first,' she said. 'I hold nothing against you for anything that happened at our last meeting. It is over and done. No remembrance. You agree?'

'Agree. But very good!'

'Good or not, it is over. Now. There is a report that you are persistently undermining Ministers. Reports to the police, Income Tax, Customs, and to many Delhi reporters? Yes?'

'It is spotless lie!'

'I wish I could believe. You *are* doing things for Ministers quite unlawful!'

'Only what I am directly told by Ministers. On orders. I have proof!'

'Read this paper. It is this morning's. There are others. Or have you seen?'

He shook his head.

'Ministers accused of corrupt practices. Thousands of railway wagons used as warehouses for grains sold on black market at highest prices. Corruption in railway staff. U.S. aid deflected and hidden. Fully equipped hospitals find ready buyers. M.I.S.A. officials take vigorous action. Well?'

'I know nothing. Nobody has asked me. I did only what Ministers ordered. Could I say no?'

'You knew it was illegal?'

'If Minister gives order, can I say no, it is illegal, and have dismissal? You also knew. Did you report?'

'I refused to deal. I turned my back. Don't you know I did?'

'Is it excuse? Not to report?'

She stared at him in a different way, very ugly.

'Are you daring to judge me?' she whispered. 'You loathsome little monster. I can have you crushed!'

'Everything I have done is on paper at Lok Sabha, time-recorded and copied, and you are in, every time we spoke, and I said you wanted nothing to do with criminality, or the illegal. You refused. Isn't that right?'

'I could pray you were so honest!'

'Come to the office. I will show. When will you come?'

'I can't. Tomorrow I shall leave for London. We are all

223

being changed. With some of the Ministers. If you are asked questions, please remember I was always kind to you, will you? Promise?'

'Why should I be asked questions?'

'Everybody is being investigated. You, certainly. I wish I could advise you. But I shall not be here. Good-bye!'

The servant got up from where she sat and went towards the door.

But he felt so angry.

A loathsome little monster? But why? She could have him crushed? Again, why? Who would crush? The old man pointing his stick, and saying Upstart? Head hall porter of Two-Seven-One Club? What was it? Blame coming from the top, all the way down, to Harijan? Prem Naran?

Always there was a scratching post. Always somebody easy to blame.

'Wait,' he said, holding a hand open to the woman at the door. 'Miss Tata, take off. Or shall I tear off?'

'You will not dare, will you?' she whispered. 'Shall I call help?'

'Call. But take off. Everything!'

He pulled a chair towards him, and sat, unbuttoning.

She took off the sari, and opened the bodice, and slipped laced drawers down.

Pinkish, and too fat, and no hair. Clean-shaven every part, and not pretty.

He felt quickly sick, and itching to leave.

'You are not worth,' he said, buttoning. 'I shall go. You pretend. You? Brahmin. But you are *nothing*, Now, I say, Harijan, good-bye. But I shall keep my promise. Not a word against you. Understand?'

He walked out, and downstairs, and gave notes to the young woman and the older, and they were laughing together.

'How did you like her bare backside?' he asked the young woman. 'Who wants it?'

He left them, holding the notes, clutching each other in silent breathy screeches.

Brij Lal kicked the starter, and Ganesh turned in red warning lights.

'Go to the house of Shiva,' he said. 'After small time to the airport.'

But the house was dark, and only the chowkidar's lamp lit the veranda. Brij Lal went to ask.

'They have gone to the family summer house at Naini Tal,' he said, climbing in. 'Two or three weeks. They went this morning. Mother, daughter, servants, all gone. Where now, Premji?'

'The night is complete bungle. I will go to New Place. Then to Connaught Place. After to airport. I have time.'

New Place was always the same at night.

Lamps were in most windows without glass, and cooking fires made red light on ceilings. Many families cooked outside, and children ran, and small fires made everybody orange one side, black the other. Only women's saris touched extra colours, and white of eyes shone sometimes in flames.

Many drums were thumping in different places in the ghats, and the skies over there rolled purply pink and dull yellow, flaming scarlet when fresh human fat reached the burning logs, even, at times, white, and always the voices chanted *Ram, Ram, Satha Hai!* one over another, among dozens of funeral parties carrying a body. Night breeze brought smells of roast flesh and herbs, and several sorts of incense, and always the drums and voices made rough music, all night long, even to sunrise, but the smell came strong on the wind one moment, and faintly, the pure roast on another, and in between a sweet of rot, and then the ghat smell, strong, warning of flesh, fat, and burning logs, and he knew that one day, somebody standing where he was, now, would sniff the last of Prem Naran, and nothing to tell the difference between anybody, Harijan or Brahmin, man, woman or child, all of them the same to the night wind, that messenger from Krishna, of the warning hand.

He went in, to Prahash, the small, smiling one, with his clothes ready, and food made, only to be cooked.

'No,' he said. 'No time. Only to see and make sure. What has happened?'

'The Police have been twice. Searching everywhere. Finding nothing. Why do they come here?'

He put arms about her, pulling close.

'Because they think something is here. They find nothing? It will always be. Tell them I am Room One-One at Lok Sabha. Here is money. I shall be here in five days. You have nothing to worry!'

Brij Lal was a good boy, but Gond was better, and when

they got to Connaught Place, Khusti still worked at her big desk at the end, and in the mixed noise of many radio voices, Gond switched the receiver and sender, taking orders, and two telephones were always ringing from people wanting scootercabs.

'Find a small office for scootercab business,' he told Khusti. 'Brij Lal will work it. Gond will be with me. Everything else good?'

'The Police have been twice to search,' she said, in small voice. 'They found nothing. Mr Mukherjee has traced the original Raybould title documents. You are quite safe. The local registers were destroyed. He found them in National records. Mr Dal hopes you will go to opening of Hammam on Friday. He has many new girls!'

'I am flying to Bombay tonight,' he said, looking at Mujid, at the far desk, totting wide account sheets. 'I shall be back tomorrow. Keep an eye!'

She smiled, completely a mistress of her place and any happenings, a small but powerful goddess, and he ripped the petals of blossoms to shower upon her.

Gond drove Ganesh out to the airport, and he leaned back, and slept, and went through all the clerking and rubber stamping, and sat in the aircraft, and slept, and wakened with gentle touch at Bombay. He stood in the aisle with others sleepy, and went out to the heat, and more rubber stamps, and a man came to him, and held out a hand, and he followed, to a black Mercedes Benz.

'You don't know me, Premji?' he said. 'I am Mehta Roy!'

'Of course,' he said. 'I expected you in Delhi. With the seeds!'

'They have gone. But poor Bhoomijai is dead. On the ghats. We go now to his office. Das is waiting. Bhoomijai has left everything to you. You are complete owner. This is his car. Should I get for you cold drink?'

'I am very sad. Let us go there.'

They went all the way down, along the bay, and lights on the water in zig-zags of red, and green, and yellow, into the thick traffic of Bombay dockside, and they stopped at an office with many people. They were holding, and shaking, and a girl's breath shouting into his mouth, and he was unsure, but Mehta pulled him, and an old woman stood in front.

'Remember, Premji!' she screamed. 'I have worked twenty-five years here. Don't throw me away!'

He pulled back, stood in small space, and raised his arms. Instantly, a quiet, as edges of blades.

'Nobody, and I have told you, *nobody* will be put away, and I tell you as Harijan,' he said. 'Wherever you had work, you still have work, and you will always have work. I will guarantee. I am not Brahmin. I am Harijan. Also was Bhoomijai. He, on the ghats, and I, here, we shall be the same. Aways helping. One burning, one living, the same. Go home to sleep. Tomorrow, it will be always the same. Or perhaps better. It's enough?'

Chapter 22

Though trying not to think himself dreaming, all around him was a hard fact, and hardest of all, here, on his knees for the third time that day, among the piles of flowers in front of Bhoomijai's cooling ghat, without dreams or doubt he knew himself sole heir to the empire of corporations in many kinds of business, newspapers, paper mills, cereal and food companies, fertiliser, steel, coal, iron, so many, too many no time to know, dozens of people in charge also unknown, a conundrum, and he knew he must go immediately to the Guru, but first to Lok Sabha.

They went back to Bombay, a long line of cars, to the Bhoomijai building, and the small office without windows of Bhoomijai, no carpet on tile floor, and a table and hard chair, and papers in many cardboard boxes piled, and on the floor piled, and in a niche, Ganesh, always raising many trunks, a carving in gold.

Against all Bhoomijai top office people almost screaming, wanting him to stay, he flew back to Delhi that night, and Gond was outside, and he went to Lok Sabha, and wonderfully, to the blue light, and the peaceful desk of Room One-One.

He knew he was not there any more.

Finished.

But he wanted to keep.

Why?

Because it was hub of a wheel, and he liked to be hub.

Out of the rubbish of paper on the desk, only one was important, a directive to see the Commissioner of Police,

Security, immediately, timed almost an hour before.

He telephoned, and the operator said the Commissioner would see him.

He went to the night clerk at Archives, and signed for all copies of his dealings with all Ministers, and carried an armload up to Security, and in, to the Commissioner, very grey, with rows of medal ribbons, and Superintendent Murthi Singh, and many others.

He put the foot-high block of paper on the desk, and heard himself say, 'First read these. But don't call me. I will call you Not here. To my office. First floor. Bhoomijai building. I have finished at One-One!'

Nobody said even one word.

The lot, from top down, wordless. Medal ribbons, nothing to say.

But sadness was really in that moment, knowing he had given up One-One, the only place he had known himself, arbitrator, conciliator, counsellor, adviser, pilot in heavy currents, all among the wishes of the great men of his country, in the hot red gut of Sindhi itself. The top men.

And what were they?

Social. Hateful. Greedy. Stupid. Trying, Failing. Nice. Humble. Intelligent. Dull. Honest. Crooked. Capable. Inefficient. Quiet. Shouting. Kind Cruel. Supercilious. Humane. Contemptuous. Friendly. Dignified. Ridiculous. Thin. Fat. Clever. Idiots. Pretentious – a beautiful English word, which Mr Raybould had once explained as the difference between a house-cat's milk snarl, and a tiger's growl – it came back always to dishonest. Dishonourable. Not to be trusted. Except one? Miss Thin Back, and her Minister. Two to trust.

But he was the raw one.

Raw.

Without skin. Only nerves. Knowing nothing.

He felt fright.

Room One-One, yes, after all those years of experience, he knew what to do.

But the first floor of the Bhoomijai Delhi building, in control of many activities he knew nothing about, no. He was only a child, and lost. He could make an abject fool of himself, and Mr Raybould had said, be all, be anything, but never abject, especially not an abject fool.

He knew he must see the Guru.

He put the chair cushion on the floor, and took off his jacket, and lay flat to sleep.

The head sweeper came in at five o'clock, and saw him, and went out, and came back with scented water and a towel to wash, and good, hot sweet tea.

Gond was ready, and so was Ganesh, and they howled down the dark Mall, towards the place of the Guru, along the Jumna, on the other bank, under the banyan, in the small cave bedded with straw, and the two wild dogs, his pets, howling and whining at anybody else, but loving him, and letting him keep a fat rat, and three talking mynahs, and a monkey, and singing birds, and bees sometimes swarming on his head, and a king cobra in a basket.

The Guru opened his eyes only when Gond turned Ganesh, and stopped the engine.

'You are only now with the fourth personality,' he said, raising the hand on his knee, palm out, fat fingers. 'First, yourself, lowest, Harijan, sleeping in messenger's hut. Then, later, New Place. Not long. Your father watches you. You are given Seripur, Now you are in third personality. Business. Decide in favour of yourself. Fourth personality is greater, more difficult. But he is born. Take advantage. Let nobody make decisions for you. Be the fourth personality in strength and substance. You have many enemies. Confront them. Defeat. It is an order you must not defy. Only death can defeat you. Let your mouth say what your brain directs. You cannot be wrong. Remember. You work for a people. Are there so *many* of you? Bring to yourself men and women you trust. None of them to kiss your feet. Only to serve. As you will. Not for money. Never for money. Only for people. Raise them up. Raise them. *Raise*. It is your word. Remember!'

Prem put the packages of banknotes on the step, knowing that poor people would have food, and made *namaste*, and went out, low in head, down to the pathway. Birds sang chirrup song, so loud, and the mynahs were saying what the Guru had said, and he heard it again, many times, and the monkey stood on his head, and the rat sat on hindlegs, and the wild dogs ran down, and pretended to bite, but they were inviting a scratch behind the ears.

'Bhoomijai building,' Prem said 'Warn your sister to be ready to change. And no more scootercabs. You can drive a car?'

'Anything, Premji!'

'We will go later to Dal. I shall buy Cadillac. You will drive. You will earn twice present money. You have found a place to live?'

'No, Premji. They will give us only two rooms. But she must do housework everywhere, and I must be gardener. But have we time?'

'Not. I will find nice apartment today. Take Khusti to Bhoomijai building. My office, first floor. She will be principal secretary. Tell her to do there what she has done at Connaught Place. There may be more movement? Very well. Also for me. But she works for me. So do you!'

'We work, Premji. I shall also have another uniform? To drive important car?'

'Go to Gobind. He will give you proper uniforms, shirts, shoes. You shall be second to none. You are hearing?'

'Hearing, Premji.'

'To Dal!'

Air conditioners cooled the showroom, and a small banner blew over a group standing about a Ford, and while he wiped sweat, he knew he must buy silk summer suits and thinner shirts. Dal pushed through the group, and came, arms out, almost running.

'Prem!' he shouted. 'Only now I am reading. How does it feel to be original and *certified* multi-*bill*ionaire? The papers are full. Prem is magic on everybody's lips. Let us have a champagne. On me!'

'I want a Cadillac. New!'

'Cadillac I can get. But why buy from Dal? You have got your own showroom not two hundred yards!'

'Dal is my friend. I want Cadillac!'

'You shall have Monday next, without any fail. Cash?'

'Only cash. Also a small car each for Mukherjee, Sen, and Mujid, with driving lessons. Also cash. Any enquiries, Bhoomijai Building, first floor, Miss Khusti.'

Dal gave him a bubbling glass.

'To the most greatest health of my multi-*bill*ionaire friend, Prem Naran!' Dal said, over his glass. 'To the hope of much business, and much good profit, how can we miss? Even Cabinet Ministers will be on their knees before you!'

'When will you open Hammam?'

'Tomorrow night. You will be my guest of most honour, my table. Bring anybody. Everything is free. And best girls!'

231

'How is the house?'

'House is doing day and night business. So excellent. I think I robbed you!'

'Of nothing. I shall not drink more. Needing clear head. I go now to my showroom. In one month it will be better than Dal!'

'No doubt. You have pull, and finance. What more for complete success?'

The showroom down the street seemed modest, but inside was large, and several Mercedes Benz were on stands, with Alfa Romeo, and Volkswagen and Japanese cars, and two salesmen came towards him.

'I am Prem Naran,' he said. 'I own this business. I want *that* Mercedes Benz. My driver will be here in an hour. Present your account to my office, first floor, in the Bhoomijai building. Have you Cadillac?'

The first salesman bowed, raised his hands.

'No, sir. We do not have franchise. Dal, only. But we have better. Rolls-Royce and Mercedes Benz, and Daimler. We have Silver Phantom Rolls-Royce. And a two-seater Daimler. Beautiful. Unique in this country. I can interest?'

'Deliver one of each, the best, to my office. I will decide. What else do we sell?'

'In the next space we have trucks. All tonnage. With air pumps, water pumps, gas pumps, all types of generators. Many other articles. I may show you?'

'Send details to my office. My driver will be here in one hour. You will deliver to him?'

The salesman bowed low.

'I have read in papers, Premji,' he said. 'So much honour to meet!'

He went out to Gond.

'Go to Gobind for uniform and all other things, and come back here for two-seater Daimler. Bring to the office. I will take taxi to Bhoomijai Building. Five o'clock, come for me and we go to Seripur. Take also delivery best Mercedes Benz, best Rolls-Royce. Everything, the best is all. You have ears?'

'Have ears, Premji. Khusti is already in office. She has doubt she has not better dress. She should buy?'

'Wait for her. Take her to buy. Everything she is wanting. Best shops. You give my name. Only cash!'

He took a taxi to the Bhoomijai Building, near Connaught Place, and he felt fright at the size.

It was his? Very well.

Seripur was also his, and larger. But not so many questions without answer. And yet, in the same moment, he knew that Babuji had always done all the work at Seripur. No doubt. Premji had been only supervising visitor. Nobody. Nothing to decide. Everybody went his own way, his own life, and the sun, the moon, the earth, and the water did the rest. The decisions were made. Only if the seed was wrong, or if not enough water, then would be time to gather at the banyan, and talk about what was to be done. Then, Premji had nothing to say, nothing to decide. The experience of years would take charge, and all would fall in place, and everybody could go home singing, knowing that Premji would shoulder any cost and Babuji would write in his big book, and all would be well, with a sprinkling of blossom on the shrine of Krishna in shadow of the banyan, and hymns for the living, sung in the rising sun, and a chant of hope for those being born.

A crowd waited on the steps of the Bhoomijai Building, many with garlands, but he heard nothing in the loud noise of talk and shouts, as he walked up, taking garlands and thanking with a nod, and going on, into the big space, to the lifts, and the salute of the liftman, to the first floor, and across the marble space to his office. But there were several, and he walked through. Many secretaries tapped machines. A second door led to more secretaries, and a third to more, and then Khusti sat alone, and his office was beyond, large, bare, even smelling unused.

A bare table, and a hard chair.

Strip lighting.

Bhoomijai, of the office without windows, and cardboard boxes for files, and a goose-dab of feet, and a shape of white wrinkles, yes, he was here.

He had to be sent away with that breath of the ghats.

The night wind had taken him. But his memory would stay in the mind, only, not here in this office. Not in any office. Not anywhere.

'I am Patel,' a voice said, behind. 'I am in charge. I am General Manager, all Bhoomijai enterprise!'

'I want a large desk and a large leather chair,' Prem said, without turning. 'The best carpets on the floor. I want a bronze, or better, of Krishna. I want other modern style light. I shall be away for this week. See to it!'

'There are many to see you. Will you see them?'

'Ask Miss Khusti to make appointments when I return. Until then, I see nobody. Clear?'

'Sir, many things have to be considered. A hand has to be at the wheel. It is common sense?'

'Yes. I shall find out what sort of hand, and also what common sense. Also I wish this building renamed. It will be called Bhavan Naran Raybould. Understood?'

He felt the depth of the bow, and heard the door close.

Knocks, and Khusti came in, a plain dark-blue sari.

'Sir, Gond is waiting,' she said. 'You have orders for me?'

'Make appointments for me from Monday, seven o'clock, morning time. Make sure this office is furnished. Change lighting. No striplight. Flowers on desk. When Gond comes back, go with him to best shops. Buy dresses and shoes. Everything. But always wear sari here. Tell all secretaries, sari only. Give me list of their pay. Tell me their complaints. Everybody must be happy. And you, too!'

'I am only happiest,' she said, eyes down at small hands. 'Only I don't like where we live.'

'Find a nice apartment. Near here. Price, never mind. Your money is double from today. Tell the General Manager, Mr Patel, my order.'

'When we find apartment, you will come to see? You will eat, please? I shall cook!'

'I will be there. Take care of our girls. Brahmin, yes, will have place if necessary. But employ only Harijan where possible. Enquire at schools. Where Harijan girls are educated. If there is no school for Harijan, I will create. We agree?'

'We are most agreeable, sir,' Khusti said. 'I have tea. You would like?'

'Have an Italian espresso machine put in. Only coffee from Brazil and Colombia. Buy coffee cups. Only best china. Silver spoons. Find the best cook. I will have a kitchen here. We shall all eat well. Midday meal and all coffee, free. Get in touch with Mr Sen, Mr Mukherjee and Mr Mujid. Arrange offices here. Ask Mr Sen to call actuaries. We need a pension plan. Book me to Bombay on Monday. I go now to Seripur until Sunday. Arrange to have radio installed here to Seripur, Bombay and Calcutta. Later, all offices of business, everywhere. All understood?'

'It is understood, Premji. Please have perfect rest. Flowers are in prayers!'

He looked sideways at the dark, bent head, knowing she had nobody to take care of her, except her brother. And himself.

The small one, so confident, so assured.

'Why have you no fear?' he asked her.

'I have Premji,' she said 'It's not enough? He is greater than a god. A god has him in all care. Why should I fear in the light of a god?'

'Why do you think this?'

'Gond told me You have a Guru. He is more wonderful than the greatest other Why should I fear? I shall do everything you say. It will be correct, no doubt?'

'No doubt,' he said, seeing the Guru's eyes, and went through the outside offices, and all the girls standing up, though he waved them down, and out, to the lift, and down to the bare space, and out, to Gond, in dark-blue uniform, double-breast, with two rows of buttons, and black leggings and boots, high in polish, and a cockaded cap, one hand on the door of the dark-blue Daimler

'It is right, sir?' he said, in high salute. 'It is *pukka*, Premji?'

'No doubt Seripur, please!'

The car whispered without whispering, a lovely box of silence.

'It makes no noise,' he said.

'Only unimportant people make noise, Premji. Important people are quiet. They know themselves. Isn't it so?'

'It is possibly so. Leave me at Seripur. Go back to Delhi and help Khusti to find an apartment I will put down one year, cash You can repay month by month. How is the scootercab business?'

'Very good, Premji. I shall give accounts at week-end. We could use at least ten more.'

'Order twenty from Dal. Confound the competition. Always!'

Seripur shone in white morning light, only the smoke of chimneys going blue, straight, without nudge of breeze, and leaves of any tree in green or flashing gold, and Babuji in whitest homespun, under the banyan shadow, and all the people in many colours sitting on the stone surround, and the tin shapes shining in the branches, with all the coloured cloths and flags flying for the gods, all prayers to be heard, and the gentle smell of burning human and cattle dung to make the ground live, and give again green goodness for the sun to heat and bring ripe sweet to the eating bowl.

He went to sit with a hand on Babuji's feet.

'You have much more money,' he said. 'Let your loans be generous!'

'I have still to deal with the same people,' Babuji said. 'An amount of money? What is that? It is the person, not the amount. However much more money, will they pay back?'

'Why is it important?'

'But of course. The children learn that a debt must be repaid, in the time agreed to. If hard future comes, then I can see what should be done. Children also see. From the child to the man in a small compass. The child must be shown right ideas. Otherwise, what is to be the end of Harijan? We must be right. Or we are wrong. What would be the end? Harijan? Untouchable? Untrustworthy? No. They must all learn the right lessons. Borrow? Pay back. Give your word? Keep it. Make a promise? Let it be kept. On time. Or come here, and explain. You disagree?'

'I agree. But you need someone to train in your place. Someone you trust. Someone I also trust. Who?'

Babuji wrote another line in the big ledger.

'Send Khusti back here, and I will teach her,' he said, looking at the page. 'She is only completely honest. She could not be paid. She could never be bribed. I know many young men. Useless. They are poisoned by the modern method. Anything you do has a price? I say *no*. *No*. What you do is your duty. Do it, and go to your other life, clean. Clean as a child's eyes. Send me Khusti. I shall go to the ghat humbly, and happily, and knowing that all I have built is in beautiful hands. It's not right?'

'It is *right*. She shall come here. Where is Gond?'

Gond went in a smile and a whisper, and the village women brought in by Babuji found a small house to make ready for Khusti, and new furniture from Delhi, and the men came with tools and plants to dig a garden all round.

He went to Mr Raybould's house. He thought of letting Khusti use it, but then he knew it would be wrong. It was only his to use. Mr Raybould was always there. Only *he* understood Mr Raybould Khusti needed her own house, without other owners, or other gods.

But then, who was to be secretary in Delhi?

One, of course, only for Harijan. Another for anyone else. But who?

Miss Thin Back, yes, she would do. But for Harijan?

He felt restless.

He was away from everything.

He knew he must have a car at instant need, to go anywhere. He called scootercabs in Delhi, but a boy's voice said everything was out.

Luckily, Babuji told him a truck was going in to Delhi loaded with melons and cabbage. He sat beside the driver, swearing he would never again rely upon chance. Cabbage and melons were excuse enough, but not for Prem Naran. There had to be transport, and instantly.

He was Bhoomijai, and something else.

Harijan, plus a great deal more.

A great deal more *what*?

He tried to see what he meant.

It was one thing to think. It was quite another to do.

How was he to do whatever had to be done?

He was only himself, among cabbages and melons, and the sanction of the driver, a fine fellow knowing nothing about him, but only that he would be paid a little extra for taking a passenger into Delhi.

For the moment, he was only cabbage, or melons, or anything else.

He guided the driver to Lok Sabha, and gave him enough to surprise him, and went in, to the high salutes, and around the circle to One-One, and blue light, and a piled desk, and a deep feeling of being home.

But he was not.

His office, he knew, was in Bhavan Prem Naran Raybould. This little place was only a step along the way, that yesterday seemed the be-all and end-all. But it was not. It was only small clerk's dream. A minor nonsense. The office given by Bhoomijai, that dead one, was so much greater.

He had no right to be sitting there.

He had all right to be sitting in his office in Bhavan Prem Naran Raybould.

It was his.

He got up, looking through the paper on the desk, of no nothing. Nothing at all. But he had all responsibility for so many companies. What was this desk, what was this blue light, what was this office?

What was he?

He shut his eyes, and in a movement of the forearm brushed all the paper on the floor.

That was that, and finished.

He walked out, looked back once, and saw the desk, the blue light, that had seemed so much, and now was nothing, and spat, and slammed the door.

Slammed.

Enough.

No more.

Chapter 23

A few days at Seripur made him sure he could never live there except as an old man doing nothing except wait for the ghat.

With no louder noise than children playing, or a buffalo bawling, the quiet seemed like a white velvet curtain between him and the world he knew. He missed the traffic and all the people in the streets, and the buildings, and the smell of work. But most he missed his office.

A desk had always been a sign of power. He liked to try to see his desk in the Bhavan Prem Naran. He thought of it almost with regret, because he was here, wasting time, and not there in charge. But he made himself stay, because those days were the only holiday he had known since leaving school. Always he had been working, first to keep fingers on pulse, and then to stop all the outsiders waiting for his job.

But now were no outsiders waiting. He could afford to challenge by staying away, and letting Mujid, and Sen. and Mukherjee run wild through every company, all departments, and through the chartered accountants, where it was highly probable that Bhoomijai had falsified figures, making the system of companies, as a whole, open to Income Tax or other enquiry, and resting a defence on Parliamentary or political privilege bought with cash or other favours.

He decided not. Everything would be open. Proper tax would be paid. Nobody would be able to point a finger at Prem Naran, now, or ever. He wrote what he wanted on many sheets of paper in those hours downstairs in Mr Raybould's house, and on Mr Raybould's side of the desk, so that all should be in place. With Haydn's music always playing, it was the place only for honesty.

He felt clean inside. He knew he should see the Guru before he went to his desk as head of Prem Naran Industries, nobody else to say a word.

He needed strength.

Khusti called him every day after opening letters in the morning to tell him what had come in, and at six at night to say what had happened in office hours. A lot did. Mujid found falsifications, so many, Mukherjee had proof of embezzlement going back in the years, and Sen noted cases of conspiracy to defraud, too many to tell.

'Very well,' he said. 'Save them up for me. I will deal. I am restless here. I can't sleep out of Delhi. Send to me Gond. I will be at the Mashoba tonight. You have the suite for me?'

'Taken, Premji. Gobind has the suits and shirts ready. He should be there?'

'Yes. It will save time. The other thing opens tonight?'

'Hammam is in two nights, it was said today. Strong smell of paint, and complete failure of air condition. And no girls!'

'But why?'

'Dal wants to pay twenty-five. There are so many girls starving. But he charges two hundred. And more. For himself. The girls want more. They have to send money to their families. Isn't it correct?'

'It is correct. Talk to the top girl. Tell them I will support their strike. With cash. I will see Dal. Send Gond. I am very nervous!'

'O, Premji. Please not. We are so *with* you. I call the Mashoba tonight? Nine o'clock?'

'Very well. *Depend* on me!'

He knew they did, and it went out to others in full sentence, or whispers, all the way out, to the millions, and it was further strength. In the newspapers they would also know. He knew he must have weekly meeting of reporters, and only his own choice, Harijan, would write. He wondered if he was just. Very well, Harijan would have first say. Brahmin could also have say. But not complete. Why not? Brahmin might have great deal to say. They had more education. What was education? A way to think, and do? Harijan had to learn. But not from Brahmin. He had the argument in his head. Case for Brahmin, very well.

For the denied Harijan, more, no doubt, but there had to

be so much more reasoning to give right. Where was the reasoning? He had never seen any. It was a question of religious standing. For him, there was none. For Mujid, Sen, Mukherjee, Khusti, Gond, Prahash, Das, Dal, and how many more, and Miss Turlo? – Shiva? – even less. They lived. They feared nothing. Fearing or not, still they lived in a prison. Without doors or windows, with no air.

Untouchable.

But all that was against the Constitution.

Who gave a small damn about the Constitution?

Only some of the better politicians. Miss Thin Back's Minister. And who else?

He knew them all, and there were none.

She would make a fine secretary for the Brahmin side. He had to think how she would work with Khusti. In different offices, he saw no trouble.

A long way off he heard Ganesh, but he felt hurt.

Why should noisy Ganesh come, and not the quiet box of silence? He walked slowly down to the banyan, and Babuji worked with the long line waiting on the stone surround. Everything was so much as it had always been, even to the early day of Mr Raybould.

Nothing changed.

He was sure that nothing would ever change.

There was nothing to change anything.

Ganesh howled, and stopped, in stunning silence outside Seripur Trading Office, and Gond came running in black driver suit, carrying helmet.

'Why did you bring this?' Prem shouted. 'Where is car?'

'O, Premji!' Gond said, foot back, hand to mouth, bent head. 'I thought he deserved last journey. He has so much memory. He is so good boy. Please? Without him, who am I? I love him. Should I not say? He is Ganesh. My brother. He deserves last journey? *Please?*'

'Very well,' Prem said, putting a hand on the bent neck. 'You are right. Take me to New Place. After two hours to Mashoba. At seven o'clock, take me to Dal. At nine back to Mashoba. Tomorrow morning, six-thirty, to Bhavan Prem Naran. Understood?'

Sideways nod.

'Your sister had clothes? You have apartment?'

'Have, Premji. Everything very good. Khusti will speak

tonight. I shall bring only to New Place, Rolls-Royce Phantom. Even a woman is not as beautiful!'

New Place in day-time seemed a horror from photos of war. No windows upstairs, no curtains, some with planks nailed over, or rusty corrugated iron, and piles of human and cattle dung each with a black cap of flies, in a buzzing heard, above the voice of Ganesh, and when Gond made him silent, the sound came loud as a warning, screaming in the rise from every pile, going quieter in settling, bubbling as if cooking in a pan.

He looked at his watch.

'Go back now to Khusti,' he said. 'Tell her to get the manager of my construction company here first thing in the morning. Give me report on rebuilding the place. Soonest possible!'

'When it is ready, we can have rooms?' Gond asked. 'It will be better than we have got. Khusti does not like. The owner has many hands!'

'Give the lathis his address. Tell them to visit. Tomorrow, those lathis will come to my office. I need personal guard. They shall have proper uniforms from Gobind, and pay, weekly, with all meals paid. Fifteen of the best. Five on duty each eight hours, day and night. Settled?'

'Settled, Premji. Seven o'clock?'

He watched Ganesh go, and the flies came up as black and blue cones from the piles, and settling again, and picked his way, and Prahash stood at the open door to welcome, and his clothes were laid out, and the bath poured in the low voice, and a such good smell of cooking.

'Builders come tomorrow,' he said. 'I will make this the most beautiful of any living quarters. Even the best European. While they are building, you shall stay at Mashoba. The best suite. You would like?'

'What is Mashoba?' she said, in a whisper, hands under chin, eyes open, shining dark.

'It is hotel. Best hotel. Only the richest. World-wide international. You want?'

He tried to touch her shoulder, but she turned, turned, and turned, and stood flat against the wall, staring horribly.

'No!' she said, high, loud voice. 'My children are here. How can I leave them? I bath them. I cook for them. I send them to school. Our eldest boy is winning scholarship. My girls are all asked for. Good marriages. How can I leave them? They must have good meal. How can scholar come from no good food? How is a girl beautiful without oil? Who is to care for them if not mother? Father too busy. So many hours business? No. I will *not* leave. Builders always making mess. I will still take care. It is nothing. I will *not* leave. It is *my* house!'

He understood. So many things. Food bills so high. Cloth bought. Of course, to make the children clothes. Meals always ready.

For them, not him.

For the dead. Not the living.

He put strong arms about her.

She cried, but so hard, her bones could break.

He held.

'You will stay here with our children,' he whispered. 'Nothing will take you away. I am always here. This is always *your* house. Nobody shall take it. Why do you cry?'

'Not,' she said. 'It is silly. I will get your plates. What the English say, dinner. What silly to have several words for one thing. Why not one word everywhere?'

He knew she was mad, but only quietly, from the time her old aunt had brought her from Ahmedabad those years before, and the papers proved all details of child marriage.

He bathed, and dressed in the dhoti and shirt, and she was in pretty prattle about the neighbours, and the stench of the ghats blew in, and all the plates were better than any of Seripur, and certainly the food at the Mashoba. He wondered why the rich would eat such rubbish because it was printed on a card. He knew he must get a cook, and he thought of the Tibetan girl, but her name he had forgotten. Riba could tell him. Gond would find her.

Seven, exactly, a knock, and Gond in his uniform, and the Rolls-Royce, truly beautiful, in length and wonder, and a smell of new leather, and other things unknown, perhaps the scent of hands, Raj hands, that had made her, and the Raj minds that thought of her. In all of it, he tried to see the Harijan. How could any of them make such a glory? How would they begin? Who could teach? Who might be the Mr Raybould? Who could take his place?

He knew.

Himself, only, and he swore to strong memory, yes, he would.

Prem Naran Raybould, it must be. And it must also be the Bhavan Prem Naran Raybould.

Bhavan Prem Naran Raybould.

It would be only correct.

Dal's shone out in the street. Inside, many people looking at cars. Dal came from his office, in office clothes and many colours in tie, fat and polished, full of efficiency.

'Prem,' he shouted, as ever. 'Always I am thinking of you. So much to think. What your papers are thinking about me? They are going hogwire, man? Am I exploiter? Profiteer?'

'I have not seen. I have been resting, private estate. Let us talk of Hammam girls. You pay them twenty-five rupees every customer. You charge two hundred. You pocket one hundred and seventy-five. It is wrong. They are wearing out their bodies. They must be paid. Each girl does twenty or more times. At twenty-five a time, five hundred a day. How can she send proper money to her family, and save for old age? She has to keep herself well. Pay the doctor. Buy clothes. Have hairdress. How?'

'Prem, you are not businessman. Other places, they have ten only!'

'Pay them one hundred and twenty-five each time, and forty per cent of drinks and extras, or I will open in competition. I will break you!'

Dal threw out his arms.

'How can a friend so long talk like this?' he almost sobbed. 'So much profit I am losing?'

'Plenty you are having. There are more than one hundred girls. Twenty and more times a day. Seventy-five for you each time. Enough. More than enough. Agreed? Or tonight I pay them, and tomorrow I will open. You will have no girls!'

Dal's eyes squeezed tight, looking from the side.

'Because you are Prem Naran, you have no longer life than others,' he said. 'Be careful how you say. Here, you are very newcomer. Take advice. Many think so!'

Prem looked about, scratching the back of his head. Gond stood in shadow.

'You are asking a row,' he said, 'A *big* row. Be careful!'

'A row you are having. I am not being dictated. I, also, know what I will have. You are not in best odour. *I* will run *my* business. I am not dictated by jumped-up!'

'Very well,' Prem said, in long outward breath. 'It is so be it. We are in eternal competition. I promise. You will never have a girl. Even a rake from Muzarfanagar. Where they must starve, I will bring here and fatten. Find your own cigarettes and alcohol. Finished!'

Dal clapped hands over his head, bit his mouth in lower teeth, and turned, and Prem walked out.

'Prem!' Dal called, in small voice. 'Prem. My friend. Don't go. Don't leave me!'

Prem got in the car, and Gond backed down the apron.

'When the lathis have finished with your landlord, they come here,' Prem said. 'No lights. Smash all the cars. Smash everything, but not windows. Dal, anybody else, put in Jumna. Head girl at Hammam, my office, tomorrow, six o'clock. Ask where Tibetan girl is from Riba. My office, same time. Understood?'

Sideways nod.

'Premji, what is your right to throw men in Jumna? It is a cold river!'

'It is not so cold as what those men are doing all the time against their own people. A girl has no defence against many hands? A girl has no choice between a proper price and another, far less? Where shall they have justice? You can tell me to go to hell? Very well. I can tell *you* to go to hell? Very well. But can a girl tell anyone to go to hell? Without starving? She is a village girl. No school. Nothing except a body she lets for a certain price. Part of the price goes home to feed her family. What is her defence, if not me? Supposing Khusti was in such a way?'

'Ah, Premji, I would kill!'

'What am *I* doing?'

'Premji, you are right. I am only *with*!'

The foyer of the Mashoba made loud noise, with tourists going away for night plane, and piles of suitcases being thrown out for top of bus. The receptionist, so pretty in red-and-green sari, gave him key, and three messages. Miss Khusti waited in lounge. Miss Das, from Bombay, waited in lounge. Miss Ochilvie waited in lounge.

Who?

O-C-H-I-L-V-I-E spelled in letters.

He looked at receptionist's so smiling eyes.

'I would like to see all apart,' he said. 'Not in my place. Where?'

'Private room,' she said. 'I will arrange. Please follow porter. I will send, one, two, three. So simple?'

245

He liked the promise of her smile, and slid a note, watching it crumple in her hand, wondering who Miss Ochilvie might be. A strange name, never heard.

He went to the room, green carpet, good armchairs, big sofa, cushions, and wide ice box full of soda and tonic the porter opened, and a table lined with whisky and everything else.

A knock, and Khusti came in, so small, so darling, almost on knees.

'O, Premji, I can't stay at the place I found!' she whispered. 'The man is so horrible!'

'Go back there. He has gone. I shall be at the office six-thirty. Sleep quietly. Sleep well. You have nothing to worry!'

'The police, and Income Tax, and Customs have been. They are so terrible. So much shouting!'

'Quieter tomorrow. I shall be there six-thirty. Go home, and sleep!'

She gave *namaste*, and went out, so tiny, he wanted to hold, but not.

He was left in dusty silence. The sweepers had been busy with the long brush. Dust clung in the air. He felt stifled.

Knocks.

Miss Das, from Bombay, came in, dressed in silks, yes, the only word, cavorting, springing out hips, turning teats here to there, black eyes so large in kohl, earrings jingling, bangles rattling, all wealth in her step.

'Ah, Premji, my father said you would like to see me?' she softly, so softly, said. 'I would also!'

'Good,' he said, in the impatience of wanting to know who Miss Ochilvie was. 'But I have more business. Find yourself a room, and I will visit. This time, not to sleep!'

She smiled, and turned, and in the jingle and rattle, went out, and shut the door.

He waited.

Small raps, and the porter opened, and said something, and a tall girl came in.

Miss Thin Back.

Beautiful in white, a little gold chain bag in the right hand, white gloves, hair in a big bun, almost no paint on the face, staring, perhaps afraid?

'Well,' he said, not to frighten. 'Such pleasure. Please sit down. A glass of champagne?'

'Nothing, thank you,' she said, calm. 'Mr Naran, my

246

Minister will resign. He is not popular. When he goes, I also go. I believe you could save him. He is being blamed for the grain scandal. So many thousands of truckloads put into stations for weeks until prices for grains went up. You know where the blame lies. Couldn't you say? In your newspapers? Try to help him? It's why I am here!'

'Everything I know, all the facts, are with the Commissioner of Police. I personally delivered. What more shall I do?'

She sat back in the chair like a small girl, breathing in, out, a long let-going.

'You have newspapers,' she said. 'I can give you all facts.'

'Give me. I will publish. But can you tell me more than I know?'

'Inter-ministerially, perhaps?'

'Very good. I tell you, I will publish. Are you Anglo-Indian?'

She looked at the floor, moved her feet, pulled the gloves.

'For my sins, yes,' she said. 'Poor Daddy!'

'Why poor?'

'He was killed on the frontier. My mother had to fight so long for a pension. She was Indian. Brahmin. She married against advice. Her family deserted her. Her people did. I mean, her Country. Only the Minister I worked for made himself her champion. He knew my Daddy. He got her the pension of my father's rank. That's why I must help him. You see that?'

'Of course. You love him?'

'For what he did for my mother? Yes. In no other way!'

He looked at her.

'If you wish, I would like you to work for me, here,' he said. 'I know what you earned as secretary. I will pay twice. Also with pension. All food and coffee, only best. You will deal only with Brahmin and Anglo-Indian. I have also secretary for Harijan. No confusion. I am Harijan. I defend them, and Anglo-Indian. You wish to work? You have your own office. Yes, or no?'

She stood, holding the gold bag in front of the flowers, almost as shield.

'I shall think,' she said. 'I will telephone tomorrow?'

'Until midday,' he said, and got up. 'I have plenty of girls waiting. I would prefer you, because you have ministerial experience. You don't have to be taught. You know your

Minister is finished. Why don't you make up your mind?'

She turned towards the door.

He looked at Miss Thin Black. Herself. So beautiful.

'I feel I am a traitor,' she said. 'That kind man is thrown away. But he is *good*. Too good for politics. What will he *do*?'

'He is a man. Plenty of opportunity. What will *you* do?'

'I will telephone tomorrow, Mr Naran. I must think!'

'Very well. Could you also telephone your Minister, and tell him I would like to talk? There is important position here. To bring our people together. Harijan, Anglo-Indian, Brahmin, all Hindu castes, Muslims, Buddhists, Parsis, Zoro-astrians, all of us are separate. Unhappily. But I employ tens of thousands of all of them. It is my duty to help. Ask if he would join me. Take charge of the human side. Bring them together!'

She half-looked around at him, smiling, almost a pretty devil in her eyes.

'I don't think he would want to work for *you*!' she said. 'What would his friends say?'

'If they knew he was drawing twice Minister's salary?'

'It would not be enough for the come-down!' she said, walking away. 'Government Minister and working for petty industrialist, not the same thing. Good-night!'

He shut the door and went slowly along to the lift, and his suite.

Anger made him feel sick. Going in, he had a dose of whisky, and picked up the Delhi *Orb*, his morning news-paper, and read the front page, black letters, about Ministers caught in corruption, with photographs.

He telephoned the editor, Jandi Mowra, and he was on the line in jiffy.

'I am Prem Naran Raybould, and I want you to write good stories about the Minister, first photo on the left in this morning's paper. I have just seen. It is wrong. Write an apology to that Minister only. Everything good to say, say it. Understood?'

'How do I know you are Prem Naran Raybould?'

'Come now to Mashoba Hotel. Ask for me. Do not pro-crastinate!'

He was filled up with laughing and pleasure. Always he had wanted to use that word in right place. Only now he was able. So good. Especially showing editor élite knowledge in

English. A lasting lesson. Boss of the newspaper, evidently. But also boss of the language.

Door buzzer.

He opened, and Gond saluted.

'All done, Premji!' he said. 'That fellow, landlord, Khusti didn't like, Dal, two of his fellows, finished. Showroom completely finished. Head girl, Hammam, I have got downstairs. Bring her up?'

'Tell her to open place tomorrow night. Charge two hundred and fifty. Keep two hundred each girl. Forty per cent on drinks and extras. Any enquiry, apply to you. You will ask Khusti. She will ask me. I will have Riba and her women there. And put it about. I will sell the entirety. One lump sum. Why don't the girls go co-operative? Every girl fair share of profits? Find any Harijan pensioner for legal post. He will know the law. Why not? They will have their own business. I want nothing of it. Lump sum, and finish. You know somebody?'

'I think so, Premji. I will tell tomorrow. Six-thirty, Rolls-Royce?'

He nodded, and shut the door, and went to the telephone, and called the room of Miss Das.

He heard the loud breaths and the chatter of bangles.

'O! Premji. My father is arrested. M.I.S.A. I must go immediately Bombay!'

'There are no flights, girl!'

'I am taking car. I must get there. I must help. My mother is going mad!'

'Take early flight. You are sooner there. By hours. I shall book now?'

'Ah, Premji. Always you are right. I shall come down?'

'Come down. Everything will be right. I shall have him out!'

'O, I know. I knew. I shall be *immediately* down!'

Chapter 24

Khusti made the appointments from seven o'clock every morning, and until eight and nine o'clock at night, he saw the managers and their accountants, and compared their figures with Sen's and Mujid's, and always there was big difference, and the people went out with tails between.

'All crooks, born and bred,' Mujid told the account sheets. 'If money was not paid, how long they last?'

'How they last?' Prem asked.

'Amounts paid to crooks in Customs, and Income Tax. Bring out tax returns for last ten years. See how many crooks!'

He slammed the desk.

'Such good idea!' he shouted. 'Have returns for past ten years. See all payments. Take away whatever paid, from the total demanded. See the difference. Publish in newspapers. Give cheques to Government for all difference. Send all crooks to prison!'

'Premji!' Mukherjee said. 'You will also go. You are head of company!'

'Not then!'

'Very well. But if you admit one, you take responsibility for all!'

'Untrue. I am uncovering!'

'Taking responsibility!'

'To pay back!'

'Very unwise, legally. I shall advise strongly against. Precedents created. Let *them* make demands. If the Income Tax Commissioners, the Customs or the police come here, listen to them, and show the figures. Hear what they have to say. You know a little something, Premji? They will go in shameful silence. They are bastards. They know it. Let them join the company of dogs!'

'But our yearly accounts from the day I came in will be in order. Everything exact?'

Mukherjee made a movement of head and hands, as if pushing from ghats.

'You leave yourself so wide open!' he whispered. 'Who will protect so much paper? Any fool in power can grind you into the ground. If you pay so much, why not more? Any agent can make further claims. Will you ever be free? And can you *do* what you want? You have to think of licences. Import. Export. With an extra bureaucracy against you, *can* you? Are you able? You can guarantee? As we sit here, are you able to see the issue of such massive numbers of licences without bureaucratic interference? Or lengthy delays? If ever?'

'You make squalid picture!'

'Squalor is part of us, Premji. Wherever you look. Sullen, desperate squalor, Mmh? We explode a nuclear bomb? But our people are dying of starvation. Who is caring? We scream cheers we have joined the nuclear power? Another hockey match won? What is this? We are criminal children. No type of court will ever judge us. We never grew beyond being children. And our behaviour is always infantile and criminal. It's not so? What, really, do we care for laws? How many in Lok Sabha? We both know the process. We have worked in it. Do we *truly* have any respect?'

Mukherjee went out almost crying, and Khusti came in to put visiting cards on the blotter, not yet eight o'clock.

'Three from Customs, four from Income Tax, and two very high police,' she said. 'They wish immediate interview, or arrest!'

He gathered the cards in a small pack, and gave them to her across the desk.

'Tell them to put substance of their request for interview in a letter,' he said. 'I have nothing to say to any of them!'

Khusti took the pack of cards, and closed her smiling eyes, and looked at him, so beautiful.

. 'We know why we love you, Premji!' she said, and went out.

But in a moment, the door slammed open, and so many men were inside and shouting.

'You are no sort of god!' one of them, grey-haired, shouted. 'You will not absolve your responsibility!'

He pressed the bell for Khusti, and so quickly she was there.

'Call all Security Guards, and throw these in the street!' he said, very quietly. 'I recognise none of them!'

In moments, the guards came in and man-handled, except the two Police officers, and the voices went down the stairs, and quiet.

He saw the danger. All those men could make up their minds at their desks. If they were paid or not, or, properly said, if they were not bribed, then they would not work.

Where was business?

The signature, and the many rubber stamps were all, and more, to those presenting them, only proper.

Nothing else was important.

The signature, the stamp.

The letter, or the form, itself, nothing without the signature of some grunt.

Pay, or not?

Bribe or not?'

The business of Prem Naran Raybould Enterprises could come to a paper wall. Nothing to be done. Without the grunt, and the stamp, nothing.

He asked Khusti to call Mukherjee, and gave her the numbers of Shiva, Miss Turlo, and Miss Thin Back.

The telephone rang. No reply from Shiva. Line from Miss Turlo busy, call again.

'Miss Ochilvie, sir!'

'Hullo, Miss Ochilvie? I hear your Minister has gone?'

'Yes. He's going as a professor of economics. In an American University. I think it's in California. I didn't have the chance of talking to him, unfortunately. I was simply skated out, and offered a rotten little job in Madras. But how can I live *there*? Is the berth you offered me still open?'

'Of course. Come in any time this evening. We can talk!'

'Yes, sir. About six-thirty?'

'It will do.'

Mr Raybould had once tried to teach him the meaning of the verb, To tingle.

Only now he knew.

'Yes, sir!'

From Miss Thin Back?

He wondered if she would take off. All?

A thought ridiculous, he almost said aloud, and started on the stack of paper Khusti had brought in.

Everything he found simple to do, because of the years attached to Archives, where everything was filed. The pros and cons of supply, and measures decided, he always read them all, and if they meant so little then, he found far more meaning now, and he was remembering, with profit.

At eleven o'clock, Khusti called him to the conference room to talk to the editors and chief reporters of his newspapers. They all got up when he came in, and he smiled them down, and asked each, in turn, if there was anything worrying, and one after another they all said no, sir.

'A great deal worries me,' he told the water carafe. 'Many areas in our Country are very disturbed. Why aren't you?'

A big man in the front row stood up.

'I am the editor of the *Orb*, the best in the chain,' he said, in a deep voice. 'We would like to know where we are!'

'Where are you now?'

'In a wilderness. We are pulled this way and that. We have no policy. Before, we reported and printed. But sometimes the late owner sacked the editor and the reporters. Often all of them together. For stories against his friends. But we also have families. We have to live. Children can't eat principles. We would like to know our policy. As a group!'

The act of deliberate putting-down-hands-flat on the blotter seemed to be part of Mr Raybould, and the Guru.

'The policy is always to print what you know is correct,' he said. 'Nothing less can be correct. I have no friends. I am Harijan. When have we had friends except among ourselves? How many of you are Harijan?'

They all raised their hands.

'Bhoomijai chose well,' he said. 'But he put reins in your mouths. I take them out. What you know, you will put in print. I will be behind every one of you, one hundred per cent. I have no favourites except our own people. Enough?'

The *Orb* editor laughed and rubbed his hands, looking at other smiles.

'At last I think we have somebody thinking as we do!' he said. 'I am very happy. What is to be the policy about ministerial corruption?'

253

'Report, front page, all facts. Put gossip outside!'

The *Orb* nodded.

'And is there a general policy?' he asked, suddenly cautious.

'General policy is tell what is correct. For *us*!'

Khusti came in with a slip of paper.

Miss Thin Back's Minister waited.

'Gentlemen, I have an appointment,' he said, standing up. 'I shall look forward to a weekly meeting. I want to see you attack what is wrong. Always on *our* side. *We* must be our *own* champion. Who else will protect us?'

He heard the hand-clapping beyond the closed door.

The ex-Minister waited in the small office for interviews when the big office was in use. He leaned against the table in a white suit and blue tie and made no effort to shake hands.

Prem sat down.

'Mr Naran,' the ex-Minister said, without moving, and looking at the wall, altogether a large gesture of contempt. 'Thank you for your offer of employment. It's one area that needs concentration, I agree, but I'd already accepted a professorship. However, I came here to talk about my last secretary, Fionnuala Ochilvie. She's daughter of old friends of mine. If I were not married with a large family, and half my age, *I'd* marry her. She's a wonderful girl. One handicap. She's Anglo-Indian. Don't let it detract from her worth as a brain!'

'It does not. For that, she is here!'

The ex-Minister nodded, without shifting.

'I am worried she's coming here,' he said, looking down at shiny shoes. 'Your reputation is far from the best. The man you inherited from, Bhoomijai, was the worst sort of uncaught criminal. We all knew it. We couldn't do anything about it. He solved his problems with money. We are notoriously fallible. What do you intend she shall do?'

'It is my business, not yours,' Prem said, and pressed the button. 'Professorji, you will please leave!'

Professorji, ex-Ministerji still sat.

'I have the utmost contempt for you,' he said. 'A contemptible bloody little crook of a messenger!'

Khusti came in.

'The security guards,' Prem said. 'Put this man on the street. He is not to come here again!'

'You can be got rid of!' the ex-min-professorji said.

'So can you. Sooner!'

The security guards came in quickly and took him by the arms, and pulled, and he struggled, but nothing helped, and he was out, down the steps, in the street.

'Double the security guards,' he told Khusti. 'There will be further trouble with that fellow, and his friends. If I am not wrong!'

'Gond will attend to him,' she said.

'No. Gond has enough. Double security. Take on ten more lathis. Send them for uniforms. Inattention to detail is always prime error. Give me good espresso, please!'

He found his hands shaking.

It was a shock to know what was thought of him, even among the Ministers he had felt were more friendly than the rest. But a contemptible little crook of a messenger? It was too much. He should have had the fellow beaten in the street.

But he was warned.

Doubtless some people had an iron in the fire for him. He would have to be careful where he went. He would have to find bodyguards. At New Place, and Seripur, only, he was safe. In other places, no. The suite at the Mashoba satisfied his wants, his guards would join the servants outside the door. The hotel was full of friends, anyway, and he thought it silly to look for a house or anywhere else to live, because really he had no need.

The managers of the sales companies came in, one after another, with reports and figures, and Mukherjee sat opposite, listening, and Sen and Mujid sat each side, making notes, and Patel sat at the end of the table. At three o'clock, the industrial company managers came, until almost six o'clock, and he talked to Patel.

Khusti brought in a note.

Miss Ochilvie waited.

'Excuse me,' he said. 'Please go on, Mr Patel. Do you know I feel something is wrong?'

Patel nodded, looking over his glasses.

'It was happening before the death,' he said. 'Bhoomijai made so many enemies. Now it is becoming clear. Our licences are drying up. We are not getting service. We are losing our best salesmen to Japanese and Arabs, and many others. More money, higher commission. It is raw competition. We must fight back!'

'Very well,' he said, seeing small smile from Mukherjee, and knowing why. 'Please make report, and tell me what you

think should be done. These gentlemen will help. Decide
between you. This company is not to be destroyed. Are we
agreed?'

Nods, and he went out, to the big office, and Miss Ochilvie,
in dark blue, only beautiful, tall, half in shadow, and a teat
in light, and the bone of a hip, and light points in smiling
eyes.

Cobra?

'I hear you had a call from my late Minister?' she said. 'I
told him to mind his own business. I like the sound of this
position. Especially the salary. There's nothing else com-
parable. But how do I know how long I will last? How do I
know I'm paid that figure?'

'Twice your last? Very simply, I give the order to my
Accounts Department. They give the bank two years' salary.
Each month the bank pays you your cheque. Simple?'

'Yes, but who has the guarantee?'

'The bank is paid the total entire. They pay you from that
sum, weekly or monthly, as you wish. I will call Accounts.
Would you press that bell?'

She pressed, and Khusti came, and he finished writing, and
gave her the slip, and she went out.

'Is that your secretary?'

'One of them,' he said. 'She deals only with matters of
Harijan. You will deal with the rest. European or American.
I shall find an African for Africa. We have a lot of business
there.'

'But no Indians?'

'Of course. I am looking for somebody to deal only with
Brahmin, Jain, Parsi, so on.'

'Why all this dividing? Why not one chief secretary?'

'There will be one. When I find out what is necessary. I
have been here only a little time.'

'When do you wish me to start?'

'When the bank lets you know the size of your credit. It
will be tomorrow. Start the day after!'

'Start on a Saturday? We don't work on a Saturday!'

'We do. Also, where is necessary, Sunday. What difference?'

'The Minister was right. You are throwing yourself in the
maw of Bhoomijai's ghost. Don't do it. For your own sake!'

He went to the door, flung it open to slam against the wall,
and shouted for Khusti.

'Destroy that chit!' he said, to the small figure. 'Nothing. Finish!'

He went back, and shut the door, quietly, and took out his wallet, and counted five thousand rupees on the desk. He switched on the desk lamp.

She stared at him, wary, eyes wide, fists at shoulders.

'Five thousand rupees,' he said. 'They are yours. Take off your clothes!'

'O!' she said, up at the ceiling. 'How dare you!'

'Five thousand. Take off!'

'Certainly not, you swine!'

He counted five thousand more.

'Ten,' he said. 'It is worth to see you naked. Off, everything!'

She looked at him, the dark eyes, and at the notes.

Raps on the door, and Khusti came in.

'Gond is waiting, sir,' she said, the little voice. 'The others have gone into the general office to continue discussion. Is that all, sir?'

He took the ten thousand.

'Give this to Miss Ochilvie when she leaves,' he said. 'But only if you have three on the buzzer!'

Khusti shut the door.

'How do I know she'll give it to me?' Miss Ochilvie asked, very much more rough, not all the lady.

'She will do as I ask. So will you. Take off!'

Almost unbelieving, he saw her put the purse on the desk, and take off the gloves, pulling finger by finger, until they both lay, as claw paws, slowly sinking to hand shapes, and he heard the long whisper of the zip, and she put the dress over the chairback, and took off stockings, and put arms behind to take off bra, and throw, and shake her hair, and take down panties.

She was not Miss Turlo. Never, never Shiva. Better than Miss Tata, because she had hair. But short. Bristly, many times shaved or cut.

'Thank you,' he said. 'Enough!'

She frowned, fists at sides.

'What do you mean, enough?' she screamed, in a whisper.

'It is enough,' he said, and pressed the button three times. 'You are nothing what I thought. Get your money at the door. Good-night!'

He went out, to the main office, and sat in the cool air.

Khusti rapped, and came in, and put an envelope on the desk.

'It is nine thousand rupees,' she said. 'I thought one thousand more than enough for her. Not right?'

'Perfectly. Put the rest in your pocket. Small present!'

'No!' she said. 'Present for her is not for me. Gond is waiting. You will go?'

Mr Patel came to the door, fat briefcase dangling.

'Mr Prem, a word please?' he said quietly, and Khusti went out. 'I understand your feeling about money to Income Tax, or Excise, whatever it is wished to be called, and Customs, and police. Very well. But the entire business was built on it. Now, there is no money? The business will go to others. What should be ours is somebody else's private property. Nobody will help us. We are dead!'

'It is only money?'

'It is money, only!'

'Without money, no business?'

'None. As you will see!'

'Mr Patel, tomorrow make your enquiries. Wherever is necessity, find out who, how much. We need business. We cannot be behind. When you have your figures, come to me. Yes?'

Patel bowed the fat tum.

'Very well, sir. It is better. There is hope!'

'Mr Patel, how is the country's business climate to be preserved in such a way? Where are we going?'

'With a little help and time we shall go well enough. People in Civil Service don't earn well. No hope of getting raise. They look to private sector. If they were properly paid they would doubtless be very arrogant. We would never get anything, only in their time. So really it is better this way. We pay, we get, least delay. Tomorrow you will see how difficulties are swept. Good-night, sir!'

'Good-night and thank you.'

So it had to be back to the old way again. No hope for the honest. But, of course, if a man was not paid enough to take care of a family, then he had to do something to make it up. In effect, he was only having proper money from private sector, and at the same time doing good quick job. From that point of view, a small payment was right and proper. The machine has to turn. Obstinacy creates nothing.

258

He passed through the offices. All the girls had gone except Khusti, giving letters to the mailboy.

'You are late,' he said. 'I shall have a girl for mail only. You do too much!'

'I am quite happy,' she said, and opened a drawer, taking out a small cube of jade with a key on a chain. 'We moved to the new apartment. Very near Mashoba. Top floor. Small but exactly right. You promised to come, remember? Please do. We owe everything to you. A drink first, yes? Then later I will cook when I have bought enough pots. Tonight, tomorrow, any time. Please?'

'Of course,' he said, watching the night shift of the security guard lining up for inspection. They had lost all the bony threat of thin pensioners. They were tall, filled, smart in blue uniforms, buttons, blue turbans with a gold PNR badge in front. They were back in a life they understood, inspections, turnouts, duty. They thrived, and everybody was safer. Khusti smiled at them, at sharp orders, at him.

Gond drove to the Mashoba, and passing through the foyer, his name was called.

'Mr Das, in Bombay, sir!' the girl said, and he pointed upstairs, and went for the lift.

'Yes?' he said, at last, sitting at the desk, piled with paper.

'Prem? It's Das. Listen to me. I can be arrested. Things are also moving underground. Police have twice been. Searching. I'm not sure what for. But they were at Godown Fourteen. Questioning. I paid the gate staff very well. No trouble, there. This Doctor Turlo has been here with Chief Commissioner. He is after your body and guts. M.I.S.A. fellows have been in to Bhoomijai's places here and at the house on the beach. They can't touch anything because lawyers still working on estate. You have a boy, Gond?'

'Yes?'

'They are enquiring. Put him on a plane for London. Get him out. They could use a few tricks to make him talk. At least six months he is out. Following?'

'Follow. I shall be in Bombay on Wednesday. I will call. No more calls here. Send telegram!'

He started the day's work, going through the paper, but thinking also of areas of weakness. Many could talk. If they could be made into solid witnesses was another matter. But a little talk by one, a little by another, and it would not take long to build a case. All the while he initialled, he saw the people the police might threaten, the mouths that could damage. Miss Turlo was one.

He called her number, but no reply.

The telephone rang.

'O, Mr Naran. It is Vishnai. From Archives. You have completely forgotten?'

'Come *up*, sir. Please come up *so* immediately!'

Door chimes, and Vishnai, bare head, shining sweat, big gold rims, white shirt starched, raw silk dhoti, big smile, arms out, and a squeeze in a scent of frangipani.

'There are certain matters and not much time,' he said, sitting. 'First, I am proud you are here, owning Bhoomijai. I always said you would go up. Baljit knows. Anyway. You gave certain documents to Superintendent Murthi of Security. The Ministers involved are all terribly angry. You are a liar. A complete crook. You made a fortune, and with it, you bought Bhoomijai. So you are here!'

'Untrue. Ask his lawyers!'

Vishnai made a flattening motion with his hands.

'We all know it is not true. Is only why I am here. You must not throw yourself on the ghats. Ministers' secretaries said you pinched them, you squeezed teats, hands up clothes, take off everything, lie down. A real Krishna among the milking maids!'

'How long would I last with you?'

'Is what I said. Somebody, somewhere, had sword, very sharp. For you. It is put-up case. If a man wants to squeeze teat, pinch seat, put hands up, feel, take off everything, what is awful? Did the girl say yes? If she said no, then her Minister would complain to me. Not one did. But what terrible crime is in commission? Who is hurt? A girl shows what she has come by at birth? Who is naughty? She, for showing, or he for enjoying? A man looks. He loves. It's a crime? We are still in time of the puritans? Are we puritans? Puritans or Christians? Are we? I came here to warn you. Police, Income Tax and Customs are making a case with ministerial help. Most of them out of office. But still much influence. Careful!'

'Vishnai, why don't you join me? I need you. I need a real hand to control. Supervise the paper. Secretary in chief. Twice your present salary, twice pension, and emoluments. Everything, all sums, in the bank. Yes?'

'I must think,' Vishnai said, standing. 'So many years. I

260

could bring Baljit? She knows more. Double, also?'

'Double. All emoluments. Join me!'

He went down to the foyer and put him in a taxi, talking about people they knew. Nothing had changed, but Vishnai said he was worried that the Opposition would win next time. No doubt he could be put somewhere else, not so important. And so? A call to Prem? At least the head of Bhoomajai Industries had certain quality.

A man so high up was someone to run on. For help.

He walked out in the night air, almost cool, sweet with breath of blossom. Khusti's key made a bump in his pocket. A promise of a drink had been made. He went back to the porter for a taxi, and showed the address, only eight blocks, left and straight down. There, one light made a patch. He told the driver to wait, and went in. The board had no names. No bells. He remembered she had said third floor.

He went up, and stopped at a short passage, at the end, one door, but no bell. He rapped. Rapped again. Nothing. He put in the key, and it turned. The room was dark. A smell of joss. He could see the shiny edges of furniture, and went around, to another room, a kitchen, pale in enamel, and next, a bathroom, smelling soap.

The last door, open, dark, He went in. Light from the window showed two black bumps on the pillows. He felt the switch and pressed. In the leather bed he had given, Gond and Khusti slept.

They awoke, and Gond sat up. Khusti pulled up the sheet.

'Tomorrow, six o'clock come for me,' Prem said. 'After, to Mr Mukherjee. Fill in passport forms. You will go to London. Six months. Get another boy to drive in the day. One more at night. You go to Gobind. Get suits for England, and shoes. Have you always slept together?'

'Always,' Khusti said, the voice small. 'Why not? I am married. So is he. At five years. I have no husband. He has no wife. Then?'

There seemed no reply.

'Tomorrow at six,' Prem said, and went out, carefully shutting door, and down to the taxi.

In any case, why not? he was thinking, all the day out. Who was to say?

A boy and a girl, living and sleeping from the time they were small, in the smell of burning rubber, in torn canvas and dust, on the same charpoy, who was to say what?

After all, Miss Turlo, never in torn canvas or dust, or the smell of burning rubber, could cuddle her father and her brothers? Shiva could roll with a Minister to keep her job, and take money willingly from a whorehouse she pretended to despise?

Who could say what, and be believed?

And how many would spit and say, don't be silly? It happens.

We live and we die.

Is it your business?

Harijanjikijai.

No?

Of course.

Chapter 25

So small the time, he could hardly believe the difference in
New Place.

Marble left over from other jobs made a lovely pinkish-
smooth covering, and sewage tanks took everything away
from the surround, and the cattle were in stalls far enough
off, and private bathrooms inside, and privies outside took
care, and no smell of burning floated through the windows
in double-glaze, with air-condition.

Vishnai had a second-floor apartment, Baljit had a small
place on the third floor, and an empty three rooms on the
fourth floor was for Gond and Khusti, when they came back.

Prahash, on the first floor, always lifted her hands in eyes-
shut unbelief. Everything was wonderful. Hot water from
taps. Bathroom by itself, and a bath and shower, and a door
to shut. Gas cooker. Electric ice-box. Everything worked
where everything before had never been. She was in poetry.
Nothing more she wanted.

But the only time he slept there, on the roof, although flies
and mosquitoes were gone because of the pesticide unit, he
had no rest.

The drums, and the voices at the ghats kept him awake,
and the stench of the burning dead blew, and blew, and his
nose refused. He smelled his children, and Bhoomijai, and
himself, also his mother and father, and all the other
thousands chanting and drumming among bubbling fat, and
ash. He dragged up his sheets, and put them to his face, and
went downstairs, so tired.

At the office, Sen and Mukherjee showed lists of who and

what was to be paid to Customs officials, and Income Tax inspectors, and police, and he initialled, and passed to Accounts.

Patel came in, that morning, rubbing his hands.

'We are on the uprise, sir!' he said. 'At last there is hope. We shall not lose the contracts for Iran. Kuwait and Abu Dhabi. Safe. I am a little worried about Peking. In Singapore, perhaps problems. But they can be solved. We rely upon the resilient!'

'What do you mean, resilient?'

'It is not only on our side. It is also the others, in front of our sincere endeavours. Both must come to proper terms. *Cash!*'

'Very well.'

He knew he was being defeated by the everyday.

But business had to go on. It had its own rules. There was no other way. He had to follow, or go to the wall.

No licences, no business. No palm oil, no progress, in or out. Ministers, Governors, the same. Pay, or nothing. The principles of Room One-One were in splendid operation. And what?

Bhoomijai's cobra eyes smiled everywhere.

He had his nest in the roof. He would feed on rats. But always be certain, if you interfered, he would puff out his hood and try to kill you.

Prem knew he must talk to the Guru.

He heard the dogs at Seripur barking their wisdom at night.

Vishnai, in his new office, made himself into a rock.

He had his own way of dealing with paper, and decisions were quicker, easier.

Baljit, as principal secretary, got along with all the girls as Khusti never had, and she became in the first day a far better right hand.

But he missed the little one. Also he missed Gond. But the pair could never be separated. He remembered her quiet pull-breath tears when she gave him Gond's passport and air ticket, and the quick smile when he said she must go also, and get herself passport and ticket.

He saw them off on Air India, telling the hostess they must have VIP treatment, but no meat of any kind, only vegetables and fruit, and no alcohol. They put their arms round him, and more tears, and then they were turning to wave and gone, in jet blast, so final.

He missed them, the two little ones. From their letters, they missed him. But a warning had to be taken at value. The police did come, twice for Gond, but nobody knew him. Gond was not his real name. None of the scooterboys had ever heard of him.

Nobody had a mouth.

Baljit called Brij Lal, Gond's final choice for his place, a steady-eyed boy, taller, a fine mechanic and a good driver, and very Harijan, with a love for the Daimler, first, and then the Rolls-Royce, because, he said, the Daimler was smaller, and had to be treated more as a child, but the Rolls-Royce was a grown woman, needing all care but able to go about her work without talk from anyone. Besides, she was so beautiful. The Daimler also was beautiful, but as a child. The Mercedes also, but not the same, not a woman, not a child, but a good friend.

'How is the scooter business?' Prem asked, getting in the car. 'Who is running?'

'It is very good, Premji. We are having Nimmi on switchboard, now. She is very good. Was bank clerk next door. She changed to us. More money. Business is all time good. Everybody copying but we are best. Mujidji does our accounts. Big profit. Where to, sir?'

'The Guru.'

'I had letter from Gond. All good. Only homesick!'

He went direct, along the Jumna, but the car was not Ganesh, and he had to stop at the head of the path going down.

Prem went on foot, seeing all the bloom for the first time, the so many lovely blossoms of lotus, and the other flowers, in a hundred colours, so wonderful, and the small grey cave, and the bed of fresh straw, and a bale of new hay for any animals passing, and the rat sitting on hinds, and the monkey turning, standing on hands, and the mynahs talking, and saucy cobra looking over the top of a deep rush basket.

Guru sat erect in new daub of ash on arms and face, smears on chest and legs.

Prem bowed deep in *namaste*, and knelt, and sat cross legged.

'You have only now become fifth person,' the Guru said. 'It is correct. As a lonely one in high place you will know

265

enemies. Turn your head. Let them destroy themselves. You should protect only the weak. Those opposing, trample on, as the elephant. He has every thought steady for where he goes. If he is angry, fear him. He will destroy. If the weak are destroyed in passing, very well, they will live again. Think about only what you must think. Everything else has been thought about. Think about what you must do. Everything else is done. Either what you think and do falls right into right place, or you suffer. Think correctly in terms of the right for the right.'

'How do I know the right, Guruji?'

'As you know day from night. Are you a fool?'

'But, Guruji, I can be a fool. But how shall I know what is right?'

'As you know your way back, and your way here. You have no choice!'

'And if I am asked to represent Harijan in Lok Sabha, should I accept?'

'Krishna has said, "Being driven by vapour, clouds pour rain, and there is harvest, and people live." The vapour is the breath of people. The clouds are opinion. You are the rain. The harvest is the happy spirits it will bring. It is your duty. You can do nothing else. Or bring down all thunder on yourself. You have your duty. Your light is before you. Direct yourself!'

He put down the packets of notes, and the mynahs were saying every word again, and the rat hopped, and the monkey stood on his head, and the cobra waved in the basket, and he went away, low, seeing the ground, from the waist, and climbed the path to the car, and back to Bhavan Prem Naran Raybould, and peace at his desk, and paper.

Baljit came in with the correspondence tray, a heap.

'Mr Chand Gupta is here at six with the electoral committee, from Seripur and other places,' she said. 'I have small buffet and drinks ready. Miss Ochilvie is in the waiting room. Shall I call her?'

'What does she want?'

'A job as secretary? That lady stuck-up has no place here. The girls would murder!'

'Show her in. There is something wrong, perhaps?'

Miss Ochilvie came in, waiting until the door closed, white, plain, a pleated dress, pearls, hair in a long bun.

'I've thought about it ever since,' she said. 'You cheated me. I wasn't given what you promised!'

'It is true. I found out when you had gone. You need the money?'

'It's the only reason I'm here. My step-father had bad business with Doctor Turlo. They suffered a terrible loss. No insurance. Every penny gone. My sister must go to the University of Lucknow. I must find the money!'

'How much for your sister?'

'At least six thousand rupees. Fees, books, clothes, keep. My poor mother is going mad. They haven't got, and they can't get!'

He counted six thousand from his wallet.

'That is for your sister,' he said. 'Now for you, as I promised. If you strip. I was disappointed. You have no hair. But I like a woman's hair To see. To feel. It is not like outside hair. It is she, herself. Where she is only woman. It is not anything to do outside. Never seen. It is what I like. You agree?'

Her eyes seemed warm, and her mouth came to swell, and she began to undress, and he went back to signing letters, and then, palely, at side of eye, he knew she was naked. She was far more beautiful than he remembered, and not so bristly. In fact, goldish long.

He unbuttoned, and held out a hand, and she came a step at a time, almost as if she slept, and sat, slowly, and she was tight as a small girl, and flooded in a moment, and then he was clutched, and she bit his ear, and his cheeks, and his mouth, and he was bleeding from her teeth, and all the time she flooded, or seemed to, and then he saw the monkey standing on his head, and heard the mynahs, and the Guru's eyes were gold, and then, was no more.

She lay heavily upon him.

He had time to feel the long, thin, silken back, so white, so much.

'Everybody knew you had the biggest,' she whispered. 'Now I've found out. It's true!'

'Who said so?'

'Oh. The word goes round. How many girls have sat in your lap?'

'It is not for me to say!'

'Good. As long as I am not mentioned?'

'Never!'

267

'I would like to come here again?'

'Next time, to Mashoba. More time. Better?'

'Far better. But next time, no money!'

'Only present. Give me only call. No need for secretary!'

She went so tenderly, with a little squeeze, and a kiss both cheeks, and he was thinking about the biggest, and remembering the Minister's jealousy. Was that, really, what had made him so silly?

Baljit came in and held the door.

'Chand Guptaji is in the boardroom, sir,' she said, down at the floor. 'There is every beverage, foodstuff and sweetmeat. No alcohol!'

'You sound bad-tempered?'

'She was in here too long!'

'She? Miss Ochilvie? Who are you to say too long?'

'I work for you. What does *she* do?'

'Baljit, Baljit. Please. Let us talk later?'

He wanted to warn. She was top-class secretary and she could run an office. But she was not going to be talky or run *him*.

A word to Vishnai might fix.

He went down the corridor towards the boardroom, hearing loud voices, and the chuprassi opened both doors, and he went in to such shouting, he stood almost afraid, but Gupta came in a heavy run, and wrapped arms in strong scent of jasmine, and everybody saying happy things in loud voices, at least twenty, all older men in homespun.

'Prem, you have no idea how we have worked!' he said, taking him down to the head of the table, with a lot of papers spread. 'Every householder. Every place. Every man and woman. Oldest, youngest. These are the headmen. I will introduce!'

He went round the circle of smiling masks, all making *namaste*, covering for a moment, and then the lines of many years, the sun wrinkles, eyes that had seen so much, the sniff of the earth, the hard, shiny hands of the plough nearly slipping out of his lily pads, and the smiles, but really pleas for help, at last, from a son of their own, after generations of neglect.

'Up here, for a moment to sign the electoral applications,' Gupta said, going to the head of the table. 'The moment your name is on the line, you are elected. Three months, you are in Lok Sabha. Or I will throw myself in suicide. Please,

Premji, our brother, put, please, so honoured name. The children even now are singing for you?'

He signed paper, after paper, and more paper, and other papers.

Gupta lifted all of them, white, high above his wide, staring, shining eyes, and screamed, but he was nothing in the noise from everybody.

They were all dancing and shouting, and tears bright in their eyes, and silver down their cheeks, and scrubbing off with backs of hands.

'Wait!' Gupta shouted, arms up. 'Let Premji tell us what he will do!'

They were quiet in moments, and Prem stood.

'I remember my father,' he said. 'He was Christian. Same as us. Outside. Harijan. His first thought was school. If a man does not know letters and figures, he knows *nothing*. Therefore, I shall make laws for schools. For boys, and also girls. They never have chance. But they shall. Then hospitals. I lost six children. We had American foreign-aid doctor. She had nothing to work with. What is use? We shall have hospitals for women and children. Third, farm machinery, ploughs, and fertiliser, and best seed. All in central parks. Everybody taking turn. Then water pumps. Generators for light. It will be for first five years. If we are right in first five, or before, we go on to other things. Our own University. Harijan, only. The first!'

They were all shouting and dancing, and Gupta held him in strong arms, and made signs for silence.

'Premji!' he shouted. 'Only that programme. Nothing else. It is enough. We have all the money!'

'I need no money. I have enough. Everything I have said, I will do. Only elect me, and see!'

More shouting, and Baljit came in to put mouth against his ear, very soft.

'Khusti and her brother are outside!' she said. 'They had to come back. There was a fire in their hotel. They lost everything. London was cold, all rain. They came back. Where shall they go?'

'Seripur. Khusti will help Babuji. Exactly as before. Gond will help with the mechanics. He knows machines. See they have all they want. They are not hurt?'

'Only frightened. We must be careful of police?'

'Of course!'

'Money?'

'Naturally!'

Gupta went off with the papers and the headmen to the Mashoba, and a dinner they had not expected, that Baljit ordered, with musicians, and everything to make them remember Prem Naran.

He went back to the office and a pile of paper, and Vishnai waiting beside the door.

'Premji,' he said. 'I am in great excess of reluctant. But I must speak!'

'Speak!'

'This fellow, Turlo. A medical fellow. He is saying everything about you. I think you must take steps!'

'To what?'

'Make him quiet. He has many Ministers and police on his side. He says that you and Bhoomijai were responsible for downfall of many ex-Ministers. You are Communists. You plotted all the months. They wish for somebody to blame. Beyond themselves. You were at the heart. Bhoomijai was big power. Your newspapers are making great noise of corruption. Others are saying the most corrupt is *you*!'

'Who is paying me?'

Vishnai smiled.

'It is crack in the pot,' he said. 'Nobody can say. If they cannot say, they cannot prove. But this fellow Turlo is powerful over wide area. He must be silenced. You don't think?'

'No. Let me see what he does. There is always the law to deal with him!'

But from that moment he distrusted Vishnai, and with him, Baljit.

They both had a high salary, and rooms in New Place at little rent, but they were not beyond a bribe from outside.

Who? Very well. But why? Baljit's bad temper was a sign. Why would she dare be short with him?

It would be worthwhile to find out, and play Ganesh, and crush, as a troop of wild elephants.

She was easiest to attack.

He signed all the paper, happy to see the rise in figures, and when she came in to take the tray, he held her sari.

'Wait!' he said. 'What is this change I see? Don't you like your job here? Have you better?'

She pulled away. The worst sign.

'I think I was foolish to come here!' she said. 'I thought it was job for lifetime. How long will it last?'

'Explain!'

She breathed deep.

'Premji, you don't read papers? Even your own? Ministers in and out are accused of everything. Everybody knows behind all of them was Bhoomijai Today, *you* are Bhoomijai. What does it matter he is dead? You are doing same. With same money. *His* money. Now, *your* money. What is the difference? Police are every day here Kept from you. Income Tax men. Customs. How long before they have got you?'

'Who is behind the Police and the rest?'

'I think Vishnai knows. But he is ready to go. He has seen everything in the files. He says it is calamitous. It is horrible word. I don't like!'

'Feel quite safe. Send in Vishnai. Put in a call for Bombay. Gupta Ramnath Das. Exports.'

He called Lok Sabha for Mawri.

'Mawri? It is Prem. You want to work for me? It is double what you earn Pension?'

'So much, Premji. The head sweeper, Drava, also!'

'The same. Both come now?'

'We are there!'

Das came on from Bombay.

'Das, I want you to go into Bhoomijai's office in Bombay. I am sending special keys Air India this evening's flight Take transport. Go in tonight. Take all paper. All files. Load them. Burn them. Nothing left. Follow?'

'Perfect follow!'

'You send me expenses. It will be ten times back to you. But guarantee. Not one piece of paper not ash?'

'Trust Das. Only ash. When you like Neelya?'

'When she wants!'

'Mashoba? Tonight? She is there!'

Vishnai came in. His turban was a little disarranged as if he had scratched his head. He looked away.

'Very well, Vishnai. Tell me!'

'Premji, I know you are man of good heart,' he said, so gentle, without sitting down. 'But you follow a wicked man. A thoroughly dirty fellow. A tyrant robber. You are not doing what he did? I know it. But I have the evidence of what was done in the files. More in Bombay. More in Calcutta. I think the police will raid. If not police, Income Tax.

271

M.I.S.A. What is difference? You will be arrested. So will I!'

'Nobody can point finger. No evidence I had any part!'

'All evidence. You wrote, and presented to Security!'

'Every paper is a copy from Archives recorder. Dated, timed. Every page is from a Minister. Signed. It was instruction. I was employed. Should I refuse? I am Government servant. Shall I be kicked out for disobedience?'

Vishnai nodded, clasped hands, staring at left-hand corner.

Prem saw the Guru's eyes.

A warning?

Be a Ganesh, and crush?

'Very well,' he said. 'You have nothing more to tell me?'

'No, Premji, nothing!'

'About the files, nothing?'

'Nothing!'

'I shall see you tomorrow. Seven o'clock?'

Vishnai made *namaste*, and closed the door quietly.

He waited, watching the desk clock, and went out to the silence of the general office, to Baljit's desk.

It had been cleared. Her name tab had gone. The drawers were empty. Not even a paper clip.

The two, Vishnai and Baljit, could have come in, preplanned to the Bhoomijai–Prem Naran complex only to find information, and then go back to Lok Sabha, leaving anything else to M.I.S.A.

He went down to the havildar of security guards on duty.

'There will be a visit during the night,' he said.

'We know, Premji,' he said, at attention, very tall. 'Vishnai told to us. Let them in. It is on your orders!'

'Listen carefully. In three hours, Gond will be here with scooterboys. You know him? Very well. He will have trucks at the back. He will take only paper. Everything, paper and files, he will take. But if others come, M.I.S.A. or anybody else, you will not fight. Help them in every way. I shall be here at three o'clock. Call all men. Full strength. Every man, ten times pay. Understood. No mouth!'

Stare, and slow nod, and sudden turn, and shouting to the others, and many running to meet.

He called Brij Lal at Connaught Place.

'Go to Seripur, and bring in Gond to Bhavan Prem, and tell him to take away all paper, and after, come to Mashoba,' he said. 'He should be here in an hour. I shall wait. Call all scooterboys to Connaught Place. Hidden. No noise. Five trucks. No mouth!'

Mawri came breathless, many apologies, and Drava waited in dark shadow.

'Premji, something is happening, and I waited,' he said. 'Vishnai came back. Baljit is with him. They speak of you lost. Lost everything. No money, No property. Only prison. It is true?'

'Does it look true? I want you to fly to Calcutta tonight. Go immediately to Bhoomijai Building. Here are keys. Find a truck, this address. All files, any paper, take out. Put in pile, quiet place. Put a match. Every piece. Nothing left. Kick the ash. Burn without trace. Understood?'

'Understood, Premji. But the building has guards?'

'Here is packet for paying. Fly back tomorrow with report. But burn all paper. Yes?'

Mawri went, and he called Drava.

'Gather all paper here, at back door, every file, ready for Gond. Put in lines on the floor. Remember there is upstairs. Every piece of paper everywhere. Nothing left. Here!'

He gave the notes, and his hand was kissed, and he went down to the front door, and the duty man opened with high salute, and he went out in warm night. whistling a scooter-cab, for Mashoba.

Reception was crowded with tourists, but he saw his favourite girl, and went to the end of the desk.

'I shall dine in the suite,' he said. 'I expect a call from Bombay, and also a couple of visitors. You will put through?'

'No trouble, Premji. I would also like to visit!'

'Only let me know. You will?'

She smiled, and wrote, and he went to the lift, and up to the peace of his own place, full of flowers, so pretty, and a gold Krishna, and a gold Ganesh, and he broke the heads from blossoms, and sprinkled petals, thinking of the Guru, and the monkey standing on his head, and the mynahs, so many voices, and the cobra waving in the basket, all friends, all dear.

He bathed, and went through the day's paper initialling, and picked up copies of his newspapers for headlines, only nothing, and the man came with dinner trolleys, very good, and he lay down on sofa, thinking he would like a tiger cub, but it would be trouble, or a small girl, to watch her grow.

Telephone awoke.

'Premji? Gond!'

'O, Gond! How are you? And Khusti?'

'Happy, happy, happy, Premji. To be back, and serving. All papers done. Not one leaf. London was so cold. So much rain. We lost everything in fire. Khusti is at Seripur. She loves Babuji!'

'Bring her in tomorrow. Buy best clothes. Go to Gobind for everything. Bring Rolls-Royce here, eleven o'clock. New Place, all quiet?'

'Everything quiet, Premji. We have petals in our prayers!'

'One matter. New Place. Apartment D. Apartment H. A man Vishnai, a woman, Baljit. If he has wife or others, or if she has man, or others, leave alone. But go in tonight Put in Jumna. Or ghats, not far. But tomorrow, *not*. You know what I say?'

'Know, Premji. Kiss for feet. So happy to be here!'

Chapter 26

The Commissioner of Police put a long list in front on the desk, and stabbed each name with a pencil. It took time, like clock seconds, and the rubber bent under every stab.

'All these people have had personal dealings with you,' he said, grindingly, in Sikh rage. 'They have all gone. No trace? Two of them living in a building owned by you? You know nothing of them?'

'They are all free people. Why should I know?'

'You had nothing to do with disappearance?'

'How could I?'

Mr Davaj Motilal, the Bhoomijai lawyer, uncrossed his legs, and tapped the gold pen.

'You are getting very near the bone, Commissioner,' he said, quietly. 'I cannot permit my client to answer that sort of question. I am prepared to take my client in front of a magistrate, or if you will, a Judge in Chambers. But I cannot permit this type of unconscionable interrogation. It offends every aspect of the Law!'

The Commissioner of Police stood, pulling down his tunic, straightening the sword belt.

'Sometimes I could say damnation with the law,' he said. 'We are handcuffed. We cannot move. We know we have a case. But no proof!'

'How can there be a case without proof?' Mr Motilal asked the pen.

'Well,' the Commissioner said, so deep breath. 'We know. But no proof. We shall not stop. We will go on!'

He took the small leather stick, and walked out.

Mr Motilal pushed his papers in a pile, and his clerk gathered, and took away.

'You will have to be excessively careful!' he said. 'They have got half a case, perhaps. But why?'

'Bhoomijai,' Prem said. 'So many were in his debt. Many have been to me for loans. I have said always no. I am not Bhoomijai. Why should I pretend to be?'

Mr Motilal opened his mouth wide, and nodded slowly.

'Of course!' he said. 'Bad feeling among many in the higher echelons? It explains a great deal. But I'd advise closer liaison with the Commissioner. In the long run, it will pay!'

'Pay him?'

Mr Motilal frowned.

'Nothing quite so crude!' he said. 'A generous sum for police pension fund, perhaps, Or gymkhana? Or widows and orphans? Or the police band? Something innocuous of the sort. The little matters everybody else forgets. The Chinese water torture method. A drip now and again on the forehead. Even such a hard case as the Commissioner can be brought to see light. Money is not without its advantages. My advice? Pull in your horns!'

He went, and Prem sat to consider, but there was nothing much. He had no horns to pull in. Business went as usual, even better than before.

Rhada, in the central office, had worked with Vishnai and Baljit just long enough to learn their methods, and she was quicker, smarter, and he wanted to show she liked, and when she came in with the afternoon tray, he looked up at her.

'You are doing the jobs of three people,' he said. 'Your own, Vishnai's and Baljit's. Go to Mujid in Accounts. Say that I want you to earn three times present salary. Also say that if, in one month, you are still as good, four times. Pension up, same scale, and emoluments, the same. Agreed?'

He put an arm about her below the waist, feeling plenty of warm woman-jelly. She was not exactly pretty, but dark Harijan, plain-style girl, thirties, no airs. But sharpest brain.

He signed all, and she went, a little pink, smiling.

He sat back to close his eyes. He had two board meetings, one for steel, one fertiliser. He was only beginning to know how to deal. He knew that directors and managers could be bribed by others to sell areas of stockpile. But without proof, what could be done?

He had nothing to say. He signed minutes. But he waited, as cobra under the roof at Seripur.

Jewel eyes. *Bhoomijai!* Waiting? Smiling?

That cobra came out at night to find what he wanted to eat. But he was dangerous until he curled up with a rat, or anything better. A small baby? How many mothers did not want a baby?

He was sure, none at Seripur. But cobra was there, and also with the Guru.

Patel came in, worried, and stood, licking his lips.

'Mr Prem, something extraordinary is taking place. All our files have gone. As you know. Also, now, from Calcutta, *and* Bombay. Everywhere the same. Gone!'

'Gone?'

Patel flapped hands.

'Gone completely? Who could it be? In Bombay and Calcutta, they are going mad. Who can do business? Vishnai gone, Baljit gone. Now this!'

'Did you call Police?'

'What use, sir? They came in and looked about. They asked the value. What can I say? It is only paper. Business records. It would be of value only to competitors. And to M.I.S.A.!'

'Why?'

'A great deal of Bhoomijai's business dealings? With certain persons? Payments? Not always legal. Foreign currency. Ah, yes. Very guiltily involved. No doubt. But splendidly protected by friends. Remarkable man. Of no culture. Primitive education. But extraordinary eye for business!'

'Did you get along with Vishnai?'

Patel trod from one foot to another, shaking his head.

'I was prepared to work with him,' he said, pointing a finger at the floor. 'But in passing days, I found him pushing into areas not concerning. Asking so many questions. Wanting to go in vaults. I refused. Without your permission? But vaults are now empty of paper. Everything else, gold bullion, jewels, nothing touched. Who could do it?'

'Call the Bank of India. We shall use our vault over there. Get the security company. Call our own security guards. Everything in the vault, *out*. It will go to Bank of India. From today, we start new page in Bhavan Prem Naran. No foreign loans unless legal. No payments unless to promote local business. Put full pages in all newspapers. Because of

277

accident to computer, last two weeks' correspondence lost. Please send copies!'

'And foreign companies?'

'You have correspondence register? Send telegrams. Please send copies all correspondence past three weeks. In one month, we are completely ourself. What problems?'

'Mr Prem, how could this entire stealing, this completely removal robbery take place? Tons of documents? How, without great help of security guards? Are they blind? Or deaf? Tons of paper, and nobody knows? So much work? So much noise?'

'Mr Patel, this place has *been* run Bhoomijai style. What was yesterday was Bhoomijai. Today and tomorrow, it is *me*. I have no interest in records. I will make my own. I do not have use for past paper. I shall have enough concerning *me*. This is all I require. Find out how the paper was taken, and where, and report to me!'

Patel made many movements of arms and legs, a man without words.

'But, Premji!' he burst from the mouth. 'How it is possible? *Every*thing gone?'

'You had some interest?'

Instantly, Patel was quiet.

'We shall pick up where left off,' he said. 'No blame. No recrimination. It is reasonable?'

'I would like espresso. Please say as you leave!'

He knew Patel had something hidden. Something, everywhere, was not exactly. Shouting too much, and so late. Bhoomijai knew his people. Why would he put Patel in charge?'

He pressed the button, and Rhada came in.

'First, find for me Patel's file, in the personnel cabinet in his office. How he came here, and what he had done before,' he said. 'Call Seripur, and bring in Khusti and Gond. We do *not* call him Gond. The name is forbidden. The police are still looking. We call him Niz. Understood?'

She smiled, nodded, and went out.

The telephone, again.

'Shiva!' the voice was shaking, urgently.

'But no!'

'But yes!'

'But when?'

'Now, now, now, immediately!'

278

'Very well. But what kept? I was waiting. Starved to worship. You didn't care?'

'Ah, Prem. We have had such trouble. Everybody outside, on strike. No cars going down. None coming up. No petrol. What could we do? To keep warm, yes, we had wood. Lovely Naini pine. What else? A walk round the lake, and a cup of tea? It's enough? Not for me!'

'What time?' he asked, dry throat.

She laughed, so pretty sound, like small ducks somewhere. 'At nine? Vutthi will bring you. I will wait. Nothing on!'

It was nice to think, but he was worried about Patel. Why had he thrown so much time away without complaining? What was the reason? The day after the files were gone, no complaint. Two, three days, no sound. Four days, stamping legs? Why?

Rhada came in with many files.

'Mr Patel has double lock on door,' she said, in soft voice. 'He has many files of every kind in cabinets. Many about finance, and also currency exchange dealings. Shall I bring?'

'Take security guards,' he said, leaning back. 'Bring all files, every piece of paper in here. Call the Connaught Square office. Send five scootercabs here. Take all files to Seripur, to Babuji, and tell him to burn, with all paper. *All* of it!'

He was cat on hot pins until the cabs were packed and sent off, with sixth for overload.

He rang for another espresso, and Rhada told him the fertiliser committee was ready.

'Without Patel?'

'He has gone out, sir. I don't know where!'

He got up in rage, and almost ran down the corridor, and the *chuprassi* opened the doors.

Twenty representatives sat about the table. They all stopped talking, and stood.

'Gentlemen,' he said. 'Mr Patel has absented himself for some unknown reason. I see no use for proceeding. I am not sufficiently at my fingertips in these matters. Therefore I think we meet again at this time, tomorrow. The company will foot all expenses. Is there a question?'

An older man in homespun at the end of the table raised a finger.

'Sir, I am from Haldipur,' he said, in tremble voice. 'We are planting, almost. We need fertiliser. I was hoping to convince Mr Patel to send. He promised last year. We had nothing. We lost so much in the harvest. But also, we paid. Total. Wicked price. We had nothing. If we don't get this year, then we are dying. We are finished!'

Prem looked at all the faces of wood, listening to sudden silence of men closing mouths against anger, hearing small voice of appeal for help, even against hope.

'Is anybody else in this condition?' he asked the room.

They all raised a hand.

'You are all paid from last year?' he asked. 'You have proof? Receipts for cash?'

Sudden bendings, and clickings of briefcases, papers coming, abundantly, in spread.

'Wait!' he said, holding up hands. 'Rhada. Take all details. First, the representative from Haldipur. Find what quantity fertiliser. How many trucks. Order trucks loaded. The representative will lead the convoy in my car. Brij Lal will drive. Sir, will it satisfy?'

The old man came running behind the others, and he was crying, and he came arms out, and hugged.

'We all heard of Premji!' he whispered. 'Only now, yes, we know!'

They were all shouting in chatter, and he held up his arms.

'You will all take turn,' he said. 'You shall all have the trucks. The fertiliser will be there. Rhada, all names!'

He walked out to go away from them. Their hope, and their smiles were too thick. He could cry.

But many shadows were in the long, high corridor, and he saw the blue turbans of police.

Patel walked forward, smiling his fat face.

'Ah, Premji!' he said, all teeth. 'These are members of an M.I.S.A. commission. The Superintendent of Police has a warrant. You accept?'

'Of course. Everything is open. If you want anything, come to my office. From now, this moment, you are no longer working here. You understand?'

Patel laughed so much.

'Listen to who is talking!' he whispered, cut with laughing. 'Wait till I produce my bon-bons. This way, Superintendent!'

Prem walked on to his office, hearing one key turn, and another, before Rhada shut the door behind. He wanted to kick Patel in the fat. He had put up too long with disposable nonsense of low order. He listened to silence, and voices coming nearer, very loud.

The door swung open, and Patel almost ran in, and stopped, with the others behind.

'You have stolen!' he screamed. 'All paper. My office is *mine*. What right have you got to take what is mine? *Mine!*'

'What is yours?' Prem asked. 'You are no longer in this company. Put together what you own, and go. Tomorrow, do not come back. You have no place. Understood?'

The Superintendent pushed Patel out of his way, and came towards the desk, taking a long orange paper from his left pocket.

'This is the Magistrate's warrant for M.I.S.A. search,' he said. 'We shall severally inquire. I want keys to the vault. We shall examine all floors, basement to roof. Including this safe. You agree?'

'To everything,' Prem said, and gave all the keys in his pocket to Rhada. 'Please help them!'

He went out to the coffee bar, and nodded for a cup, picking up the paper to look at the sports page. All the teams he liked were playing in disaster. One page to another, only black unmitigated, disgusting.

Rhada came in.

'They have searched your office, and the safe and the vault, sir,' she said. 'They have gone upstairs. Mr Patel is kneeling in a corner. He is crying so much!'

'Take him a cup of coffee. Put his traps together, and out!'

Rhada laughed.

'I shall tell,' she said. 'Traps? It is funny!'

'Tell them to keep an eye. If he has a gun, he could make a holus-bolus!'

'I took the pistol from his desk,' Rhada said. 'I think it is why he is crying!'

'Poor man. Give him *two* cups of coffee. Where is the gun?'

'I gave to havildar of security. I may go, sir? My mother is not well. My work is done completely.'

'Please go. When finish, always go. See that Patel has gone. Good-night!'

He put a cushion on the floor, and took off his jacket to stretch flat, and shut his eyes, thinking of the Guru, seeing the

281

monkey standing on his head, and the rat on hinds, and the cobra slowly waving.

Taps, not Rhada's, woke him, and he heard the havildar say the door was shut to Patelji.

At last, and so long at last, he felt a sense of power without fear. Always there was a nag in head that Patel could make a fool of him, either by showing him not capable of reading accounts, or by proving him complete dunce in front of all the long table, so shining, of directors. Now he had business well in both hands, and many friends, and he breathed in head, and eyes, and ears, and in lungs and heart, and went in peaceful sleep.

He woke to telephone.

'It is Khusti, Premji. We disturb?'

'Come in, come in!'

'Bring good espresso?'

'Of course!'

He took jacket to bathroom for necessary wash, and he was ready to see Khusti and Niz carry in cups on tray, and put arms around, and listen to news of Seripur, almost without good hearing, because he knew he must go to the Guru.

He must ask about, and try to know the damage of Patel. He put matters together, counting the harvest.

Fertiliser had been hidden in time of Bhoomijai. Stocks kept back meant higher price. Promising early delivery, and keeping promise, possibly meant Patel would go short of his backsheesh. The same with steel stocks. Coal. Timber. Paper pulp. So many different matters, all tangled in Bhoomijai fashion. Seeds. Grains. On each and every one, backsheesh for Patel. Bhoomijai could never work alone. Only through a manager. Patel had chance to make crores annually, no Income Tax.

Except that death put all business in other hands.

Why would he want to go to M.I.S.A.? To cover his misdealings, of course. How would he excuse himself? By giving files a doctoring? Working with Vishnai? And when Vishnai went in thin air, where did he find himself? Did he know Vishnai was put there for express purpose of wrecking Bhoomijai Enterprises? Was there financial agreement between Patel and Vishnai and the Minister, or ministers interested? To strip stocks, and sell at peak prices?

So many questions.

Guesses.

No answers.

But, poor Patel cried. He saw the ruin of all he was living for. And so he went to M.I.S.A. probably to win the rewards? Or a percentage of what they could find of hidden stocks? Or to clear himself? Or a piece of all of them, and further, to revenge himself on a new owner?

It held together in crazy fashion. Bhoomijai style.

Always the jewel cobra eyes. Always the straw whispers in the roof. Quiet, but tread carefully. There are fangs, and a strong, hooded neck. And a few minutes to live. Only in hysteric pain of twisted nerves, and blindness.

Mujid, Sen, and Mukherjee, with a small staff, were in Connaught Place to prepare accounts of all since the Bhoomijai death, and there were so many, as well as the expensive electoral movement going on in the Chaljaur area.

So much to think, so many sheets of accounts, only a small day for doing. What burdens in the head, and yet Bhoomijai had carried most only between his eyes. The rest was for Patel, and the office staffs in Delhi, Bombay and Calcutta, and all the other places, a part to one, a part to another, so that nobody knew what the entirety was, or who was involved, or how the stocks were kept, or where the money went, or which banks clerked the accounts.

In that way, ministers pocketed, and Bhoomijai pocketed twice plus, and more, he had a nice ministerial hold for the next time, and Patel licked the dish polished of cream, and only others starved, or died, unknown.

He walked through the empty offices, and out, across the shining greyish marble floor, with Khusti on one side, and Gond, now Niz, on the other, almost a head of a family, and waved to the security guards saluting

The havildar unlocked the main door and held it open.

'There is a woman outside, Premji,' he said. 'I think she wants job for cleaner!'

'Tell her to see caretaker,' he said. 'Has it to do with me? Khusti, talk to her, please?'

Khusti went out to the street, and she was speaking to a bony, dark woman in plain white sari, grey hair pulled back, black ribbon hanging, old eyes, looking over, up, strange, and she was saying words, what? and hiding hands under both arms.

'Wait,' Khusti said, and tried to hold, as a daughter. 'I

am sure we can find you place. Why not come in day time?'

'I buried my husband,' the woman said, loud. 'I lost my daughter. I never found. My husband tried. He was so fine, beautiful man. It was heart attack!'

'Very well,' Khusti said, soft, as a mother. 'Please? Come tomorrow. I will see you have a job. It's enough? I am sure Mr Prem Naran will agree?'

'I agree,' Prem said. 'I will see to it!'

'You are Prem Naran?' the woman said, quiet, still looking over Khusti's shoulder, staring, wide, almost frightened. 'You knew my husband? Alfred Tyndale? He died yesterday. He made me promise to find you. You killed my daughter!'

'Wait,' he said. 'Let us be careful what we are saying!'

'I know what I say!' she screamed, so suddenly. 'My poor husband had heart attack. *Only* he was angry with *you*. You killed Maudie. I kill you!'

She pulled the blue barrel from under the left arm.

Khusti held her, and Gond jumped, and the security guards fell in a pile.

The gun went twice, and Khusti's sari burst blood, and she fell on her knees, and Gond rolled to the side, bleeding a stream, red, and the woman pushed the security havildar with bony arms, and he threw himself on her, and again the gun cracked, smothered, and the woman's eyes were up, in the eyebrows, and the white sari spread red.

Prem felt himself lifted where he had tripped and fallen, and carried inside, up the steps, across the grey marble silence, through the offices, to his own place, and gently settled in the chair.

'Everything is in order, Premji,' somebody said. 'We have sent to tyre market for father. Doctor will be here, and ambulance. Please rest!'

'The old woman is Christian,' he whispered, last strength. 'Get priest. Tell family. We must not be lacking. You hear?'

He slept, black.

Opening eyes, he saw the ceiling.

People talked.

'Aha!' somebody said, leaning over. 'Awake? Very good. You caught your head. Not much. How do you feel?'

'No damage,' he said, sitting up, touching bandage over forehead, cold. 'I would like coffee. What has happened?'

'Premji,' the havildar said. 'Gond and Khusti will go to

the ghats. The old woman has been taken by family. And police. The daughters of the old woman are screaming to kill you. The offices in Bombay and Calcutta and Jabalpur have been calling urgently. Also we are full of the Press!'

'Send them away,' he said. 'Clear the building. Is it ready at the ghats?'

'Tomorrow, early, Premji. The father has too much work tonight, he says. You agree?'

'No. Arrange procession now. They shall go together. Have carriage made. Beside each other, and hand in hand. As they lived. Have flowers. Many flowers. They shall not go without notice. Call my newspapers!'

He looked at the ceiling.

Nothing was there, only white.

But then a strong arm, and Rhada was holding.

'I heard on radio,' she whispered. 'Have no worry. I will do everything!'

He rolled his head into her breast, and slept, and then he woke, and felt her arm about his waist, and he put feet down, one after another, along the same dark path, the same smells, and shouts, and thumping, hollow drums, and knew himself at the ghats once again, and the men were climbing to lift Khusti and Gond to the logs down there, and he turned to her, and cried.

Fire went up, and everybody clapping hands, and shouting, and bowing heads.

But he felt his lungs in water, and he was crying, crying, only crying.

Mr Raybould was dead again.

Something, two of them wonderful, somebody, two of them, so good, taken from him.

Rhada's strong arm held tight.

That evening he must come to gather warm ash for a small vase to put in the monument he would have outside Bhavan Prem Naran. Both of them, Gond and Khusti, hand in hand, in bronze on a black marble block, gold letters, only best quality. He could see it, but Rhada had to find somebody to carve, also for Mr Raybould, only a head, in a nice place inside the hall, to smile shiny in the mornings.

Yet, under so warm thinking, other far-back cold frights came to pull faces that one day he would be here, and his meat and fat greasy in the night wind, and people smelling, and hearing the drums, and all the shoutings and screams, and quiet only when the East came pink over the ghatflame, and it was time for small sleep, and hot tea, and at sunrise, the rough music starting again, and the paths filling in one more day, and all the people wrinkled in sleep and grief, and drums loud in the ears and bursting the head. Noisy, only for health, and the muscle of their time, knowing that one day they also would be on the logs, and others would be screaming and drumming for all of them, only to rouse somebody – who? – Krishna? – that time was out, and only ash to tell of life, and open up, to let them see the truth with newest eyes.

Fly to Bombay for a long week-end seemed best, and taking Fionnuala to Bhoomijai's house on the beach, and perhaps Neelya Das would like to join in with plenty of champagne. A thin one, and one fattish, might be very good, if they liked each other. About girls, who could know?

Everything, really, was the same.

Nothing, anywhere, he could not do.

Now, he only wanted to go from the screams, and the drums, and the smell, and back to the Mashoba suite of golden gods and such lots of flowers he was well affording, no doubt, and a peace, the truthful peace, of Haydn.

Peace, only.

'Very well,' he said to Rhada. 'It's enough. We'll go back. Have breakfast with me?'

She smiled up, and nodded, and her arm was still tight, and he put his arm about her, and they walked.

NEL BESTSELLERS

T030 467	STARMAN JONES	Robert Heinlein	75p
T026 817	THE HEAVEN MAKERS	Frank Herbert	35p
T031 462	DUNE	Frank Herbert	£1.25
T022 854	DUNE MESSIAH	Frank Herbert	75p
T023 974	THE GREEN BRAIN	Frank Herbert	35p
T023 265	EMPIRE OF THE ATOM	A. E. Van Vogt	40p
T027 473	THE FAR OUT WORLD OF A. E. VAN VOGT	A. E. Van Vogt	50p

War

T027 066	COLDITZ: THE GERMAN STORY	Reinhold Eggers	50p
T020 827	COLDITZ RECAPTURED	Reinhold Eggers	50p
T012 999	PQ 17 – CONVOY TO HELL	Lund & Ludlam	30p
T026 299	TRAWLERS GO TO WAR	Lund & Ludlam	50p
T025 438	LILIPUT FLEET	A. Cecil Hampshire	50p

Western

T017 892	EDGE 12: THE BIGGEST BOUNTY	George Gilman	30p
T023 931	EDGE 13: A TOWN CALLED HATE	George Gilman	35p
T020 002	EDGE 14: THE BIG GOLD	George Gilman	30p
T020 754	EDGE 15: BLOOD RUN	George Gilman	35p
T022 706	EDGE 16: THE FINAL SHOT	George Gilman	35p
T024 881	EDGE 17: VENGEANCE VALLEY	George Gilman	40p
T026 604	EDGE 18: TEN TOMBSTONES TO TEXAS	George Gilman	40p
T028 135	EDGE 19: ASHES AND DUST	George Gilman	40p
T029 042	EDGE 20: SULLIVAN'S LAW	George Gilman	45p
T029 387	EDGE 21: RHAPSODY IN RED	George Gilman	50p
T030 350	EDGE 22: SLAUGHTER ROAD	George Gilman	50p

General

T034 666	BLACK ROOTS	Robert Tralins	95p
T020 592	SLAVE REBELLION	Norman Davids	35p
T033 155	SEX MANNERS FOR MEN	Robert Chartham	60p
T023 206	THE BOOK OF LOVE	Dr David Delvin	90p
T028 828	THE LONG BANANA SKIN	Michael Bentine	90p

Mad

N862 185	DAVE BERG LOOKS AT LIVING		70p
N861 812	MAD BOOK OF WORD POWER		70p
N766 895	MORE MAD ABOUT SPORTS		70p

NEL P.O. BOX 11, FALMOUTH TR10 9EN, CORNWALL:

For U.K.: Customers should include to cover postage, 19p for the first book plus 9p per copy for each additional book ordered up to a maximum charge of 73p.

For B.F.P.O. and Eire: Customers should include to cover postage, 19p for the first book plus 9p per copy for the next 6 and thereafter 3p per book.

For Overseas: Customers should include to cover postage, 20p for the first book plus 10p per copy for each additional book.

Name ....

Address..

....

Title ....
(MAY)

Whilst every effort is made to maintain prices, new editions or printings may carry an increased price and the actual price of the edition supplied will apply.